THE UNFINISHI

Andrew Branscombe has b
fashioned, priggish way. He doesn't realize that Hilda is still married
to her husband, separated but not divorced. So when Charles Patrell
returns and begins to interfere with his plans, Andrew accidentally
kills him in a fit of rage and fear. Panicked at first, his terror soon turns
to exhilaration as he realizes that he can get away with the deed. All he
has to do is keep everyone from the truth.

First there is his sister Eva, who is trusting enough to believe
everything he tells her. Then there is Hilda and her thirteen-year-old
daughter by Charles, Coralie. And Charles's old friend, Vincent
Colton, who mysteriously shows up without anyone knowing why.
The web expands with Charles's young live-in girlfriend, Blanche,
who must be dealt with. Finally there's Jerry, who stumbles on the
scene at exactly the wrong moment and helps Andrew get rid of the
body—and now won't go away. Fortunately for Andrew he is up to
the task—daring and clever fellow that he is—because a lesser man
would have surely been caught by now....

THE GIRL WHO HAD TO DIE

"I'm going to be murdered," she said in her muffled, sad little voice.
Jocelyn is only nineteen but is convinced that she is going to die. She
meets John Killian on a cruise ship heading back to New York. And
when later than night she falls over the rail and into the ocean, it looks
like her prediction has come true. Imagine Killian's surprise when the
rescued Jocelyn insists that he was the one who had pushed her.

She's poison, he thought. She can't help that, anymore than a rattlesnake
can help it. But I have to get away from her.... When they dock, Jocelyn
convinces Killian to accompany her to the Bells' for a visit. She claims
that she is in love with Killian, and will keep his secret no matter
what. Then a fellow passenger, Elly L'O, along with the ship's purser,
Chauverney, appear at the Bells', followed by Angelo, who had been
their ship's waiter. Each one seems to have a connection to Jocelyn—
even Mr. and Mrs. Bell—and it soon becomes clear to Killian that they
are bonds of hate. But Jocelyn claims innocence. Is Killian being
groomed to be her next victim—or her murderer?

ELISABETH SANXAY HOLDING BIBLIOGRAPY

Invincible Minnie (1920)

Rosaleen Among the Artists (1921)

Angelica (1921)

The Unlit Lamp (1922)

The Shoals of Honour (1926)

The Silk Purse (1928)

Miasma (1929)

Dark Power (1930)

The Death Wish (1934)

The Unfinished Crime (1935)

The Strange Crime in Bermuda (1937)

The Obstinate Murderer [aka No Harm Intended] (1938)

Who's Afraid [aka Trial by Murder] (1940)

The Girl Who Had to Die (1940)

Speak of the Devil [aka Hostess to Murder] (1941)

Killjoy [aka Murder is a Kill-Joy] (1941)

Lady Killer (1942)

The Old Battle-Ax (1943)

Net of Cobwebs (1945)

The Innocent Mrs. Duff (1946)

The Blank Wall (1947)

Miss Kelly (1947)

Too Many Bottles [aka The Party Was the Pay-Off] (1950)

The Virgin Huntress (1951)

Widow's Mite (1952)

THE UNFINISHED CRIME

♦ ♦ ♦

THE GIRL WHO HAD TO DIE

TWO COMPLETE
MYSTERY NOVELS BY
**ELISABETH
SANXAY
HOLDING**

STARK
HOUSE

Stark House Press • Eureka California

THE UNFINISHED CRIME / THE GIRL WHO HAD TO DIE

Published by Stark House Press
1315 H Street
Eureka, CA 95501, USA
griffinskye3@sbcglobal.net
www.starkhousepress.com

ISBN: 1-933586-41-9
13-ISBN: 978-1-933586-41-0

Cover design and layout by Mark Shepard, www.SHEPGRAPHICS.COM
Proofreading by Rick Ollerman

PUBLISHER'S NOTE

First Stark House Press Edition: January 2013

Reprint Edition

CONTENTS

ELISABETH SANXAY HOLDING

I'm writing about someone I hardly met – my grandmother. I grew up
with her daughters – my mother and my aunt – her darling girls. From them,
I learned some of her myth as a mother and of her strength and struggles as
a woman. She came from a dynasty of strong women who were independent
spirits in a world that had rigid ideas of a woman's role and place in the economic order. From the depths of the Depression, she took responsibility for
the economic survival of her family and harnessed her art, her craft, a quest-
ing mind and a social conscience to that goal. She was a free thinker; she loved
to swim, at ease in the open sea.

When going through some family papers, I found two large cardboard
boxes stacked high with lined foolscap sheets. Her small, close, uniform and
intense writing covers sheet after sheet, ink now fading. These are her man-
uscripts. Hundreds of thousands of words, crafted by hand, bring her strength
of will, her drive to produce into the room. What did it take to sustain that
determination over those furlongs of faded foolscap? I want to put on record
how hard won her achievements must have been.

She was a conscientious worker and craftswoman. She took her craft seriously, relying on deliberate thought, planning and hard work. She set herself
the discipline of sitting down to write every morning. In the first seven months
of 1928, she completely re-wrote a 90,000 word novel and wrote a 60,000 word
serial and eleven short stories. Her day was organized into a routine that she
strictly adhered to, not pausing for a cigarette or coffee until the appointed
hour. Her daughters knew not to disturb her when she was working.

This was no hobby – it was an all consuming effort. She could not find
peace without knowing she could provide for her mother, herself and her girls'
future. The family fortunes were unpredictable, plagued by insecurity and
lurching from the sale of one story to another. She experienced the misery of
her writing getting stuck, while being tormented by a sense of haste to get
working before she became penniless again. The Wall Street crash and the Depression left her penniless, unable to sell any work. Her family went without.
Her sense of honour meant she agonized over the inevitable debts that accrued.

It was a wearing way to live. Her health was not good. In 1923, at the age
of 34, she had pneumonia and was tormented by how she could continue to
provide for her two little girls. By the time she was 39, she was experiencing
extreme fatigue; her energy and confidence were low and she had trouble
sleeping. Fatigue and depression continued to plague her but she strove to
overcome all this by sheer force of will and strength of spirit driven by her
fierce loyalty to her daughters. In spite of her ill health, her last novel was pub-

lished in 1953, just two years before she died at the age of 65.

   She rarely had the luxury of working without these financial pressures, of experiencing a sense of satisfaction from what she produced, of standing back and working on the big canvas of her novels. In her lifetime, she never reaped the benefits of great rewards or the critical acclaim that her work eventually came to attract. But her spirit and strength of character lives on in our family – six grandchildren, eight great grandchildren and four great great grandchildren. There is something of her in all of us. We are proud to celebrate this internationally esteemed writer as our own. I would wish for her to know that her work is still valued and enjoyed well into the 21st century. It's still out there engaging people's minds and intelligence. I would want her to rest reassured that her labour still bears fruit in her legacy to us, her family, and to her readers.

JUDITH ROSE ARDRON
SHEFFIELD, ENGLAND
OCTOBER 2012

INTRODUCTION

We have the Depression to thank for Elisabeth Sanxay Holding's career as a mystery author. Until 1929, she had been writing serious, mainstream novels like *Rosaleen Among the Artists*, *Angelica*, *The Unlit Lamp* and *The Shoals of Honour*. She published six novels before the Depression, starting with *Invincible Minnie* in 1920, and ending with *The Silk Purse* in 1928. Early critics noted her expert characterization, and in the *New York Times* review of *The Silk Purse*, the reviewer said: "They are as real a collection of peoples as ever said yes when they wished to heaven they could say no."

So when the Depression hit in 1929 and she was no longer able to sell her leisurely character novels, Holding turned to writing mysteries. Or, more properly, suspense novels. Because, simply put, Elisabeth Sanxay Holding is the precursor to the entire women's psychological suspense genre, and authors like Patricia Highsmith and Ruth Rendell owe her a very large debt of gratitude.

Holding was one of the first to write mystery novels that didn't so much ask whodunit, but whydunit? In fact, we know whodunit because it's quite often the main character. It's the "why" that is always the most important part of her books. The psychological underpinnings of her novels form the basis of the mystery. Her characters always act from a very determined point of view. Whether from guilt, discontent, deception, misconception, or even pure altruism, they act out their dramas with very little consideration for other points of view. And therein lies the conflict. They have all got blinders on, seeing just what they want to see, each with their own misguided agenda. They lie when it will get them in the most trouble and tell the truth when it's in their own worst interest. In other words, her characters feel very real to us—we believe in them.

A rich, alcoholic husband grows tired of his well-meaning but lower-class wife. Everything she does irritates him. He decides he must get rid of her but his drinking is making him delusional and easily annoyed. Who can he trust? As he rushes from one hidden bottle, one seedy bar to another, the answer is clearly "no one." When his chauffeur comes to him with a plan to catch his wife with another man, he jumps at it. After all, sooner or later you've got to trust somebody.

This is the basic plot of *The Innocent Mrs. Duff*. What makes the book so compelling is the degree to which Holding gets under the skin of this self-deluded man. She wrote the story in a crisp, staccato style and makes the reader feel every bit of the scheming husband's mounting alcoholic mania. Though casual drinking was more a part of the daily lifestyle in Holding's day, she wasn't afraid to shed some light on its darker aspects. In fact, she had previously explored the theme of the alcoholic male in the The Obstinate Murderer—albeit more sympathetically—and clearly knew this personality well.

The Innocent Mrs. Duff and The Blank Wall (filmed twice, as The Reckless Moment in 1949 and The Deep End in 2001) are arguably two of her best works and the only two novels of Holding's that remain in print, thanks to Academy Chicago. Dell published several of her novels in paperback in the 50's, and Mercury published a few in digest form as well. And back in the 1960's, Ace Books published twelve of her books as Ace Doubles. But since then she has almost entirely gone out of print. A sad state of affairs for an author whom Raymond Chandler called "the top suspense writer of them all" in a letter to his British publisher.

All in all, Holding published eighteen suspense novels in her lifetime, beginning with Miasma in 1929, and ending with Widow's Mite in 1952. Many of these novels were also serialized in national magazines, and almost all were published in paperback and foreign editions, as well as by mystery book clubs. She also published quite a few short stories in magazines ranging from McCall's, American Magazine and Ladies' Home Journal to Alfred Hitchcock's Mystery Magazine, The Saint, Ellery Queen's Mystery Magazine and The Magazine of Fantasy and Science Fiction. She even wrote a children's novel, Miss Kelly, the story of a cat who could understand and speak human, and who comes to the aid of a terrified tiger.

Elisabeth Sanxay was born in Brooklyn in 1889, the descendant of an upper middle class family, and was educated in a series of private schools, specifically Whitcombe's School, The Packer Institute, Miss Botsford's School and the Staten Island Academy. She married a British diplomat named George E. Holding in 1913 and together they traveled widely in South America and the Caribbean, settling in Bermuda for awhile where her husband was a government officer. She also raised two daughters, Skeffington and Antonia, the latter of whom married Peter Schwed (until his recent death the executor of Holding's estate and a retired author and publisher with Simon and Schuster).

Holding was thirty-one when her first book was published. Right from the beginning she introduced the theme of discontent that she was to use so often in her mystery books. Invincible Minnie starts off slowly—telling at first when it should be showing—but evolves into a fairly lurid tale, the compelling story of a headstrong woman who uses sex to control men and get her way. There's no pat, happy ending either. Minnie runs roughshod over everyone, including her sister and children, and prevails through sheer determination. Holding's lean 40's style was only seen in glimpses in this first effort, but her characterizations were already taking shape in the relentless actions of Minnie and the various people she controlled.

With her second novel, Holding lets the story tell itself, vastly improving over the style of her first book. *Rosaleen Among the Artists*, a bit less melodramatic than *Invincible Minnie*, tells the story of a self-sacrificing young woman struggling to survive and find love in New York City. Though polished off with a sweeter ending, there is much travail as Rosaleen hits rock bottom before finally being united with her soul mate, Mr. Landry. In fact, the two are so matched in the stubbornness with which they hold onto their ideals—tenaciously sacrificing their own happiness at every turn—that they almost wear each other out by the end of the book. Ironically, it is their own principles that almost kill their only chance at love.

In 1929, when the Depression killed her mainstream career, Holding had to do something to help support her two daughters. She could have started writing nice, cozy romantic mysteries, but she just didn't have it in her. The characters she was creating were too contrary, too impulsive—too flawed—and not particularly romantic. They didn't act in their own best interests, holding onto ideals that invariably precipitated trouble. It's as if they felt compelled to do the very thing that caused the most havoc, even if for all the best reasons.

As a consequence, the mystery novels Holding began to write were dark affairs, having more in common with noir than standard detective fiction. It's easy to understand why she was such a favorite of Chandler's. Murder and mania are always lurking in the wings—and the menace doesn't always exist from the outside, but is quite often found from within. These are characters with something to hide. Sometimes there is a happy ending, sometimes not. Sometimes there is a detective, but he's usually as clueless as everyone else. You might say that Holding's characters are quite often lucky if they can make it to the last page with their health, if not their sanity, intact.

In *The Virgin Huntress* we follow young Monty on V-Day as he meets an older woman, Dona Luisa, and is brought into a world of class and culture he had always dreamed of. He is a charming if somewhat insecure young man, somewhat expedient—perhaps too expedient—in his past dealings with women. In fact, he is constantly nagged by secrets from his past, secrets that begin to fracture him as Dona Luisa's niece Rose begins to pry into his past life. By the end of the short novel, Monty has become completely unraveled, the victim of his own expediency. It's not a pretty portrait.

Another of Holding's favorite themes involves fractious family relationships and domestic disputes. *Dark Power* is a perfect example. In the first chapter we meet a young lady, Diana, who discovers that she is quite penniless and soon to be out on the street. Before this happens, however, she is suddenly rescued by an eccentric uncle she didn't know she had. He happily escorts her back to the family home, where she meets such a thoroughly dysfunctional collection of relatives that by the end of the book she barely makes it out alive.

Holding also loved to examine the way stress works on characters, particularly middle-aged men, and would combine this with her theme of domestic disharmony. *The Innocent Mrs. Duff* is an obvious example, but *The Death Wish* is another in which a man, Mr. Delancey, who had always thought himself happily married, comes to a moment of crisis in which he discovers that he actually hates his wife. She has slowly been emasculating him by controlling his purse strings, but when his best friend reveals a similar domestic situation and announces his plans to kill his own wife, Delancey is plunged into a world of self-doubt. At first he is shocked by his friend's confession, and when the wife is found drowned, he hopes that it is the accident that it seems to be. But a seed has been planted, and nothing in his formerly phlegmatic life will ever be the same.

Holding's deft hand at characterization makes all these situations ring true, giving them a psychological perspective that not only presents all her characters' foibles sympathetically, but creates the tension that propels her story along as well. Their actions are understandable, given the circumstances, and all the more frustrating because they are so identifiable. In *The Death Wish*, we watch Delancey try to convince himself at first that his wife is simply moody and a bit insecure. He wants to think the best of her. But the reader knows that his wife's insecure nagging is stifling him, her words little barbs that sink in and latch Delancey to her side, subtly but firmly controlling him. We feel his weakness and frustration, his mounting domestic horror, and nothing that proceeds from this realization seems anything less than inevitable. Not even murder.

This is Holding's true forte, that she can make the commonplace, the ordinary, so horrific and so suspenseful. But make no mistake, whether writing about dysfunctional families or failed marriages, her books are full of mystery. In *Lady Killer*, a young recently-wedded ex-model named Honey is on a cruise ship in the Caribbean with her older husband, who is turning out to be a fussy, fault-finding old crab. At the same time that she begins to realize that a life with this man will be completely intolerable, she also becomes aware that the man in the next cabin might possibly be trying to kill his wife. She begins to set about a campaign to protect this poor, plain and unfortunate woman, who doesn't really seem to want her help. In fact, no one on board seems to feel that Honey has any business stirring up trouble.

But the more Honey finds out, the more mysterious her fellow passengers begin to seem to her. Even her own husband begins to seem alien to her. And when she finds a body, even that isn't quite what it seems. But still the little mysteries pile up, and we are swept up in Honey's suspicions and doubts until even we begin to believe, like her, that *no one* is to be trusted.

Miasma presents us with another set of mysteries. A young doctor named Dennison has just about reached the end of his financial resources when he is contacted by a wealthy older doctor in town who wants him to take up residency in his house and assume the care of his patients. All well and good, except that the doctor's young nurse immediately warns Dennison to leave, mysterious patients come and go in the middle of the night, and his predecessor has gone missing. And then there is the weird drug that the older doctor prescribes to certain of his patients, one of whom is now dead from an apparent heart attack. Holding keeps the mysteries coming until both we and Dennison are wondering what the hell is going on here; daring us to put the book down no matter how late it is and how early we have to get up the next morning.

And then there is her rarest mystery, *Strange Crime in Bermuda*, a peculiar tale of a missing person on an enclosed island community. Young Hamish is asked to journey to Bermuda at the request of his old friend Malloy, but when he arrives, Malloy sets an appointment to meet him and then fails to show up for their meeting. It soon turns out that no one has seen the man that day, but everyone has a different idea of what of what has happened to him. A sense of confusion and dread sets in as we experience the unfolding events from Hamish's stubborn, narrow point of view. Hamish is continually misled by his various misguided allegiances, until he himself becomes the prime suspect. The resolution is both obvious and unexpected.

There is a reason that Dorothy B. Hughes said that "connoisseurs will continue their rush when each new Holding reaches publication." Her books are first and foremost very readable. Not only are they excellent examples of psychological suspense and first rate character studies, they move along at a nice, brisk pace. Holding was never one for overwriting. Her dialog always sounds just right, all the doubtful pauses and self-serving/self-deceptive lies in place. We may not always like these characters, but Holding makes us feel compelled to keep reading about them.

Elisabeth Sanxay Holding's mystery novels have been out of print far too long. Until her death in 1955, she was one of the best, and it is a pleasure to be able to bring her books back into print again, many of which have been unavailable in any edition for well over sixty years. It's time to rediscover Elisabeth Sanxay Holding. Her books may have gone out of print, but they have never gone out of fashion.

GREGORY SHEPARD
PUBLISHER, STARK HOUSE PRESS
SEPTEMBER, 2003

The Unfinished Crime

by Elisabeth Sanxay Holding

To
Elizabeth Sherman

CHAPTER I

Branscombe lit a cigarette and pushed back his coffee cup, with a look of annoyance on his haughty face.

"Isn't the coffee good, Andrew?" asked his sister, anxiously.

"Fair," he answered, and that worried her. It was quite possible that he was very much affronted by the coffee, or by something else on the table, and if it were so, he would keep quiet about it for a day or two and then bring up the subject when she least expected it.

It was not the breakfast that displeased him, though; it was some dissatisfaction so obscure that he could not have named it. His health was good, his financial position was sound, his love affair was progressing well. Mrs. Patrell liked him; he knew she liked him. He had seen no rivals, had never heard her talk of any other man; he felt almost certain that she would marry him if he asked her. Only, he could not make up his mind to ask her; he hated to ask anyone for anything.

He rose and walked over to the window, a tall young man of thirty, lean, correct, with an air of distinction about him; grey eyes and black hair, with the high-bridged Branscombe nose—a handsome man in an aloof and chilly fashion. His sister sat looking at him and she wanted to laugh.

It sometimes seemed to her that the laughter within her was like a living thing that fluttered. She wouldn't really have laughed at Andrew; she loved him and admired him. She knew how seriously he took the Mrs. Patrell affair. But it was difficult for her to be serious about anything. She was a slight, pretty, fair-haired girl of twenty-three. She was by nature careless and absent-minded and gay, and it was a strain to live up to Andrew's standards. She failed very often.

"Mrs. Patrell wouldn't," she thought. "She is really the perfect wife for Andrew.... Of course she must be a good deal older than he, but she doesn't look it. And it doesn't matter. Somehow, Andrew isn't young."

"Are you going to drive in to market, Eva?" he asked.

She understood the implications of that question because she knew Andrew so well. He wanted the car himself and at the same time he wanted Eva to go to market and be intelligent and economical about the housekeeping.

"Well, I think I'll walk," she said, for that was what he wanted her to say. He was silent for a moment.

"In that case," he said, "I think I'll take the car." And off he went.

Eva finished her coffee and lit a cigarette. She did not want to walk into town this hot morning. It was a mile and a half each way, along a flat, uninteresting road.

"I'll say I had a headache," she told herself.

Andrew never questioned headaches and that made her feel guilty, and a little mean. She had a clear enough vision of her brother's weaknesses, but they aroused no resentment in her gentle and tolerant heart. She was very fond of him and very sure of his affection for her. Only she wished she could get away from him sometimes, even for a week. She wished every day of her life that she had just a little money of her own.

Andrew always gave her money, when she needed it; the trouble was that she had to convince him that she did need it. He admitted the necessity for fairly expensive clothes. He scorned anything cheap, but he also hated waste and extravagance and she had long ago made up her mind that she did not.

"If I had money of my own," she thought, "I'd *like* to waste it. Now, let's see about these boring meals.... To-morrow's liver, isn't it?"

Twice a week Andrew wanted calf's liver for breakfast, and she had to eat it, too, as a precaution against anaemia. She rose with a sigh and went into the kitchen where the cook and the house-maid sat at breakfast. The sun was shining in; the table was covered with a clean white cloth, and set out with a cheerful assortment of china which did not match. There was a nice little bouquet of sweet peas in a glass, and a large enamel coffee pot. The two women rose as she entered, and she felt apologetic at disturbing them and faintly envious. The house-maid was young; she went to dances and the movies with her boy-friend; she had a good time.

"And I *never* do," she thought.

It might be her own fault; sometimes she thought it must be. She made friends with people, but Andrew always said they were unsuitable people; when they travelled he was severe about chance acquaintances, and she had grown a little nervous. When he had taken this house in Connecticut for the summer, he had told Eva it was a nice neighbourhood, and according to her temperament she had felt hopeful. But not after she had been here two days. It was a summer colony of sedate and comfortable houses with a casino and beach, and it was inhabited by young couples with small children and mid-dle-aged couples who played bridge. There was only one unattached young man, and Andrew didn't like him. And Eva did not quite know whether she herself liked Llewellyn Evans or not. He was good-looking, he was polite, but she found him faintly irritating with his impersonal courtesy.

"I've got the list all written down, Miss Eva," said the cook, "if you'll be wanting me to 'phone in for it."

She wanted to get rid of Eva, naturally, so that they could resume their breakfast, and Eva was glad enough to leave this uninteresting matter in the cook's competent hands. She wandered back to the dining-room and stood by the window, burdened with a familiar feeling of restlessness and vague guilt.

"I oughtn't to leave everything to the servants," she thought. "I ought to bustle around and superintend things."

Andrew was always occupied. He was making a study of the eighteenth century in England, he read a great deal, and he was writing a book. He told her often that she ought to keep up her French, ought to practice on the piano, or take more exercise. She felt sure that his advice was valuable; yet she never did these things. The days were so long....

Llewellyn Evans had come out of the house next door, where he was visiting his sister and her husband, and Eva watched him critically. He was carrying a book, and that meant he was coming here. He was always borrowing books from Andrew, and always returning them when Andrew was not at home. It couldn't be a coincidence, yet he never would say that he came to see Eva.

"Something secretive in the fellow," Andrew had said.

And as she watched him, Eva was inclined to agree with that. He walked lightly and swiftly; he was slim and neat and very dark; with his olive skin, his pointed dark brows, his sudden and rare smile, he had somehow a foreign look.

But he was not a foreigner, nor was he so interesting as he looked. He was a born New Yorker, an accountant spending a long summer holiday here. He had a serious interest in tennis, he was a masterly swimmer, but in the art of conversation he did not excel. He was extraordinarily quiet, not because he was embarrassed or constrained, but as if he did not choose to communicate his thoughts. He had never asked Eva to any of the dances at the Casino, never asked her to come out in his car.

This morning it was as usual. The bell rang; she heard the house-maid go along the hall to open the door.

"Mr. Branscombe in?"

"No, sir. He's gone out."

"Is Miss Branscombe at home, then?"

"I'll see, sir."

Miss Branscombe was at home, and Mr. Evans entered the cheerful little drawing-room.

"Good morning, Miss Branscombe," he said.

A sudden rebellion swept over her. She did not want to be Andrew's sister, Miss Branscombe. She did not want to sit here and chat aimlessly with young Evans for half an hour, and then be left to her empty day. She wanted to shock and startle him.

"Another of these darn books?" she said. And was horrified at herself.

But Evans apparently took the remark as a matter of course.

"It seems like a good excuse," he said, quite unruffled. "I never read 'em, you know."

It was as if with these two sentences they had established a curious intimacy.

"Then why do you bother with them?" she asked.

They were both still standing. He gave her a quick, narrow glance, and smiled.

"I'm afraid I've got to have an excuse," he said. "Your brother doesn't like me."

This frankness confused and troubled her.

"Andrew's very reserved," she said.

"No," said Evans, smiling again. "My people were Welsh, you know, and I've got second sight. I know he doesn't like me."

"If it's just one of those 'feelings' about people," she said, "I've had them lots of times, and they've always been wrong."

"No," he said again, but not smiling now. "You wouldn't know."

She looked at him, and found his narrow dark eyes regarding her steadily.

"You'd just be kind," he went on. "You could be with a person day after day, and not see...."

His unwavering glance, his words, disconcerted her.

"That doesn't sound very flattering..." she said. "Just stupidness?"

"You're not stupid," he said. "Only kind. Only so charitable that you couldn't see the ugly things."

"Do you?"

"I do," he said.

She wanted to take that lightly, wanted to laugh; and she could not. He was still smiling, but it was a smile that increased her uneasiness, for it did not touch his eyes.

"I don't like you to stand there reading my character," she said, almost petulantly.

"I wasn't. I came to ask you if you'd come to the Country Club for lunch. We're playing the semi-final doubles this morning...."

It was the first invitation he had ever given her and she was surprised at her great desire to accept it. But Andrew was very much opposed to the Country Club and its members. Too much drinking went on there, he said, *and worse*. She could imagine his chilly displeasure when she came home. He would be offended for days.

"Of course you're free to do as you please," he would say. "You're not in any way obliged to take my advice or to pay any attention to my wishes."

It wasn't worth it.

"I'm sorry," she said, "but I can't very well...."

"I wish you'd come. I want very much to talk to you."

"You can talk here."

"Not in this house."

"It's a rather nice little house," she said. "Are you having an attack of second sight about it, and seeing sinister things here?"

Then she wished she had not said that. She knew that he did not like this house, and she knew why. It was because it was Andrew's house, and he didn't like Andrew. An almost fierce loyalty came over her. She loved Andrew.

"Stop in on your way home and tell me how you came out in the semi-finals," she said, and held out her hand with an agreeable smile.

It was a very definite dismissal, and he accepted it, but with no appearance of disappointment or resentment.

"But you can't tell, with him," she thought. "You can't tell what he's really thinking.... I think Andrew was right about his being secretive."

Well, he was gone, and it was not likely that he would return.

"Who cares?" she asked herself.

But somehow she did care, somehow a miserable loneliness came over her. Andrew had no friends, and would never allow her to make any. It could not be that everyone they met everywhere was unsuitable. It must be that Andrew was too difficult to please.

Would it go on like this, she thought? She and Andrew isolated from the rest of the world.... She went out on the veranda, stood looking out over the neat lawn bordered by a privet hedge. Everything in her life was neat and orderly, and hedged in....

"I hope Andrew will marry his Mrs. Patrell!" she cried to herself. "I *wish* something would happen to him, to make him more human."

CHAPTER II

Branscombe, driving along the country roads at his usual moderate speed, was not pleased with himself. He was vaguely and uncomfortably aware that he was not sufficiently "human," and never had been. His father and his grandfather had been owners of a prosperous factory in a little town up the Hudson. The Branscombe house had been the largest and finest in the town. The Branscombes had been cultured and civilized people living among bar-barians; they had had a library, they travelled. Andrew had grown up with the idea that the Branscombes were superior to other people. He had taken that idea to boarding-school with him, and it had not made him popular.

He had never been popular anywhere, never easy, and never happy. He had always been stiff, formal, over-fastidious. While he was in college his father had died, leaving everything to his son, with the verbal request that he look after Eva. Andrew had sold the factory, which he knew he could not run. He had taken Eva to Europe to the correct places, he had seen that she went to one of the right schools. He had looked after Eva.

As far as he could see, he neglected no duty. It was not necessary for him to earn money, and he had devoted himself to scholarly pursuits and to his writing. He took that very seriously; he read, he wrote, he took sufficient ex-ercise. It was a good life; he could imagine no other that would suit him half so well, and if he married Hilda Patrell, he did not intend to change it. She would be in it—that was all.

She had been lunching with a middle-aged couple who lived near him, a cou-ple of whom he approved, and they had introduced him to her on the beach. He had been curiously interested in her, but he had mistrusted his emotion until Mrs. Carroll had talked to him later.

"We're so fond of Hilda," she had said. "She's so splendid. Her marriage was *most* unfortunate, but it hasn't embittered her.... She's come back here to live in the house where she was born.... One of the fine old families.... Everyone has the *greatest* respect for her."

Then he knew that his admiration for her was right; he had gone to call upon her, and she had been so cordial he had gone again and again, and never in his life had he enjoyed anything as he had these visits. She was a wonderful host-ess; she created an atmosphere that enchanted him. Once they were married that, of course, would be changed. He would no longer be a guest who would come and be happy for a time, and then return to his own house, his own room, his own ways. He would not care to live in Hilda's house. There were many complications. There was Hilda's daughter, and there was Eva. The old Branscombe house on the Hudson had been sold. Perhaps the best thing would be an apartment in town for the winter, and a good boarding-school for the child....

Perhaps that would not suit Hilda. She was unfailingly kind and friendly, yet she was, in her way, mysterious. He wished that he could talk to her about living arrangements before he asked her to marry him. He wished, indeed, that he need never ask her in so many words. There was something humiliating about it.

He was not going to ask her now, however. He had known her only two months. They could go on in this happy, tranquil way for weeks. Turning a corner he came in sight of her house, a square, old-fashioned wooden house in a well-kept garden surrounded by a picket fence. It was not really beautiful at all, or impressive, but it had its dignity, its serenity, it had so great a charm for him. Hilda herself was standing on the veranda speaking to the gardener, and his heart leaped to see her.

He knew that she must be older than he, for her daughter was thirteen, but she didn't look it. She was a woman of medium height, slender, but sturdily built, with broad shoulders and a straight back. Her skin was sunburned to a warm gold colour; her eyes were as blue as cornflowers; she had thick, fine, blonde hair, which she wore brushed back from her forehead and knotted at the nape of her neck. He admitted that she had no style, but he found her way of dressing singularly attractive. This morning she wore a sleeveless yellow linen frock, and he thought she was lovely. There was, he thought, something virginal about her, so that he could easily forget she had ever been married. Her child in no way detracted from this impression. Coralie was a curiously detached creature, free and elusive as a nymph. At heart, Branscombe was a little afraid of her, but she remained entirely in the background, and he could forget her, too.

Hilda Patrell looked up at the sound of his car.

"How nice to see you!" she said.

As he mounted the steps of the veranda, he felt again the warm, serene happiness he felt only with her. She always put him at his ease, banished his chilly constraint.

"I thought I'd stop by and see if there were any errands I could do for you in the village," he said.

He knew he had said this too often; she must long ago have seen through the flimsy pretext. But it was part of her charm that she would not be amused, or challenging, but would accept his words with polite seriousness.

"Thanks very much," she said, "but there's really nothing. Sit down for a while, won't you?"

It was wonderful here, it was perfect. The gardener was trimming the privet hedge; his shears made a crisp and pleasant sound in the quiet morning. The street before him, lined with old elms, was quiet; he knew that the house behind them was in exquisite order. They sat here together, this friendly, charming woman and himself; he did not need to make any effort; she would begin just the right sort of conversation.

But, unaccountably, she did not begin a conversation. She said nothing, and the silence became awkward. He glanced at her, and he saw a very strange look in her face; her blue eyes gazed past him; she was ignoring him. This disturbed him.

"Are you...? Were you busy, Mrs. Patrell?" he asked.

Then she looked at him, a long and steady glance, as if she was trying to read his face.

"I had a letter yesterday that upset me..." she said. "I don't know what to do."

"Money," he thought. "She's in some sort of financial difficulty."

She would want to borrow money. The idea caused a sort panic in him; so many people wanted his money: poor relations, collectors for charities, people with marvellous schemes, people who said they needed help.

"I can't..." he thought.

Then he looked at her grave and gentle face, and he was overwhelmed by tenderness. He was willing to lend her money. He would *give* her money. Rising, he went to her side, and laid his hand on her shoulder. He had meant it to be a gesture of honest friendliness, but it became something more. A delicate fragrance rose from her hair; he glanced down at her firm, slender neck, and his grasp tightened a little. She turned and looked up into his face, her blue eyes misty.

"I had a letter from my husband..." she said. "He says he intends to see Coralie often. He says he can easily find out where she goes, and that he'll meet her in the street, in shops...."

Branscombe listened, shocked.

"I'm sure something can be done," he said. "A lawyer—"

"I couldn't! I couldn't have Charles arrested or threatened, for speaking to his own child. I couldn't let such a thing be brought into court."

That was understandable.

"If you speak to Coralie," he said, "if you make her realize how much it would distress you for her—"

She shook her head, and he was dismayed to see tears well up in her eyes.

"You don't know Charles," she said. "Coralie's really devoted to me, but she's so young.... And Charles has very great personal charm...."

A dull resentment filled Branscombe. He did not wish to hear any more about this man who had been her husband. "It's in very poor taste..." he thought. "She might understand how I feel...."

"Ever since I got that letter," she went on, "I've been thinking and thinking. Only it hasn't been real thinking.... When it's a question of Coralie, I'm not logical.... She means so much to me—too much, perhaps...."

Branscombe stood beside her, sullen and miserable. He was nothing to Hilda

Patrell. She had this life of her own, made up of her love for her child, and Heaven knew what memories of her husband.

"I'm sorry," he said, stiffly.

"I can't think for myself about Coralie," she said, unsteadily, "that's why I've told you. Ever since I left Charles, ten years ago, I've lived so very much alone.... I was afraid to make friends... only when I met you... I knew I could trust you. I knew you were honourable and kind and understanding."

"Did you really feel like that?" he cried. He was delighted, but at the same time he was surprised, for that was not his own idea of himself. He had a mental image of an Andrew Branscombe who was austere and inflexible, certainly honourable and just, but too aloof to be described as "kind and understanding." When she said it, though, he believed it. He believed that she alone had read his heart.

"Hilda..." he said. "My dear girl...."

"Do you think," she asked, "that I ought to let Charles see Coralie, even if it should mean that... that she might turn away from me?"

"No!" he answered. "No, I don't.... Hilda.... There's only one solution. Marry me at once, and we'll take the child away with us until—"

"Marry you?" she said, staring at him.

He looked back at her, in growing consternation.

"You must have guessed," he said. "I've come here, almost every day—"

"But I'm married to Charles!"

"You're not divorced?"

"No. It's only a separation. I never even thought about a divorce."

She must have seen in his face what she was doing to him, for her glance grew soft.

"I'm so sorry... so very sorry, Andrew... I didn't realize... I was so happy to have you for my friend. I took it for granted that you knew I wasn't free."

"Do you love him?"

She was silent for a moment.

"No," she said, "not any more."

He was profoundly impressed by her integrity, her moral courage. He looked and looked at her downcast face, and he wanted to take her in his arms and kiss her.

"Hilda..." he said, "I'll do anything I can for you, dear."

She tried to smile. And suddenly it occurred to him that he was in love with a married woman. That was a thing he had always condemned without mercy, and he condemned it in himself. Yet it gave him a strange thrill of exultation.

CHAPTER III

He did not wish to suspect how he felt. He did not quite know himself how he felt. He was greatly agitated, but he was not sure whether this confused emotion was wholly distressing....

"I can't think it out," she said. "If I should have an open break with Charles, it might upset Coralie.... Girls at that age are so sensitive...."

It was her child she was speaking of, thinking of, not him. She had already put aside his love, his offer of marriage, as things of minor importance. He was sullenly angry at her for that, and yet he still wanted to kiss her.

"She's going to lunch with the Richman girl.... I don't see how I can tell her not to go. I can't keep her shut up.... But I don't want her to see Charles until I've thought it all out...."

"I'll drive her to the Richmans'."

"You will, Andrew?"

"Yes and bring her home," he said.

He did not want to talk to talk about this child any longer; he wished, indeed, that he could get away and be alone for a time to think over this thing that had happened to him. It was, of course, impossible. He had to remain, had to feign a serious interest in the problem.

"Will you come back to lunch with me, Andrew?" she asked. "If I can talk it over with you...."

He accepted somewhat formally, and he was not sorry that Coralie came out of the house just then. She was an extraordinarily handsome child, or girl, or whatever one should call her; she was tall and straight and slim with fair hair and steady brown eyes. She had an air of being completely independent, of living in some world of her own. She was polite enough, yet Branscombe felt that there was nothing respectful about her.

"May I drive a little way, Mr. Branscombe?" she asked, as they set off.

"This is a very powerful engine—"

"A boy I know has a car like this, and he lets me drive."

Branscombe wanted to refuse. He did not like anyone else to drive his car. But when they came to a long, straight stretch of road she asked him again, and he very reluctantly changed places with her.

"Only a little way," he said.

He watched her, her little sunburned hands steady on the wheel, her eyes intent on the road. She was handsome, but she was, he thought, entirely lacking in the soft, shy charm of a young girl. Was she like Patrell?... He refused to think of that.

At the next corner she stopped the car neatly.

"That's right," said Branscombe. "Rather a bad turn here. I'll take the wheel now, Coralie."

She jumped out, but instead of coming round to the other side of the car, as he expected, she stood still.

"Thanks ever so much, Mr. Branscombe, for bringing me this far. I think I'll take the short cut through the woods here."

"No!" he said, briefly. "I told your mother I'd take you to your friend's house."

"Mother doesn't mind my taking the short cut, Mr. Branscombe. I've done it hundreds of times."

"Well, not to-day," he said.

"I want to, thanks," she said. "I like it."

"Not to-day," he repeated, well aware that his tone of authority was not impressing her. "Get back into the car, please!"

"No, thanks," she answered, and turned away.

"Coralie!" he called. "Come back! I can't allow this!"

She looked at him with surprise, and a sort of compassion, as if his imperative manner was somehow pathetic.

"I'd *rather* go this way, thanks, Mr. Branscombe," she said, and started off, her hair bright in the sun.

Hilda trusted him not to let the child out of his sight, and no matter how ridiculous he might appear, no matter how much he resented the situation, he would keep faith with her. He drove the car on to the grass at the edge of the road and locked it. When he had done this, the child was out of sight.

He stepped into the little wood. There was a faint path there and he followed it, walking rapidly. He was in a towering rage. Not since he could remember had anyone so flouted him. He was accustomed to respect, from tradespeople, from servants. Eva sometimes argued with him, but she never disregarded his wishes with the cool impudence shown by this chit of a girl.

"I've got to control myself..." he thought.

He must not say anything to the child, must not let her see how angry he was. He would have to persuade her to return to the car, or, if that failed he would have to walk with her to her friend's house, and that would be almost unbearable.

"Damned brat!" he said to himself.

It was strange that he caught no glimpse of the child's white dress. She must have run, to get so far ahead of him. He *would not* call her, though. He quickened his pace, and in a few moments he could see the meadow that lay on the farther side of the wood. Except for three cows grazing there, it was empty.

It was not possible that she could have run fast enough to cover that wide meadow and be out of sight in this space of time. She must have taken some other path. He stopped irresolute; he went back a few steps. And then he heard her voice.

"But I don't care what other people say, dear!"

Her voice was clear and light. The voice that answered her was no more than a murmur, but unmistakably a man's.

"Patrell!" thought Branscombe.

He felt certain that Coralie had met her father, and that the meeting had been prearranged.

"The child's simply made a fool of me..." he thought.

It was certainly not his habit to act upon impulse; he was disposed to be over-deliberate. But this morning he was not his usual self. His talk with Hilda had profoundly upset him, and following that had come his anger against Coralie. He was not accustomed to emotional disturbances: for years his life had been orderly and quiet; even his love for Hilda been a tranquil enough thing. Now, however, he was so thoroughly disturbed that he went after Coralie without hesitation, and he went in a rage.

He had no trouble in finding her. She was in a little clearing, a few feet from the path, sitting on a fallen log, beside a man; a very handsome man, tall, slender, and easy, with a bold nose, black hair, dark blue eyes half-insolent and half-tender. And he was more than handsome; he had that bearing, that careless grace about him that Branscombe envied above all qualities. There had been boys in school with this nonchalance, and he, stiff, aloof, always suspicious of insult, had envied them. This was the kind of man women liked, and loved, and Branscombe hated him.

Hatred was a curious thing, that gave him energy, that warmed his heart. He stepped into the clearing and confronted Patrell.

"I'm in charge of this child, by her mother's authority," he said. "She's to come with me at once."

Patrell rose, and regarded him with surprise and amusement.

"I don't believe I've had the pleasure of meeting *you* before," he said. "Perhaps Coralie can introduce you."

The child had grown very pale, but she did not lose her remarkable, to Branscombe, her unhuman self-control.

"It's Mr. Branscombe, Daddy," she said.

"He's in charge of you?"

"No," she said. "Mother just said he'd drive me over to Lucy's. He hasn't any right to try to order me around."

"No," said Patrell. "I don't think he has, Coralie."

He put his arm about the child's shoulders; they smiled at each other. And Branscombe felt certain that Patrell would win the child away from her mother; he felt that Patrell was superior to himself in worldly wisdom, in boldness, in vigour, and in charm. But Patrell was bad and he was good. He saw it as simply as that. It was evil opposed to good. An idea came to him which was entirely opposed to his usual mode of thought.

"I deal with people frankly," he often said. "I don't pretend to be subtle."

Yet now, without the least effort, he had somehow analysed Patrell, and somehow knew the one way to approach him.

"I intended to write to you," he said, "about a certain financial arrangement...."

He was right. Patrell was immediately interested, although he tried not to show it.

"Sorry," he said, "but I'm not very enthusiastic about financial arrangements with strangers."

"I think this arrangement will appeal to you," said Branscombe.

"Well.... You might give me some idea...."

"Impossible—in the circumstances," said Branscombe. "Never mind. Perhaps it's just as well. I'd better think things over for a few weeks."

He could not have explained how he knew that the well-dressed, assured Patrell was always hard-up, always in a hurry for money, but he did know it.

"I may as well hear what you have to say," said Patrell, with amiable condescension. "I happen to have a few moments to spare. Coralie, sweetheart, run along, will you?"

"Shall I wait for you, Daddy, by the road?"

Patrell smiled at her. He knew his power over the child; he must see that she was troubled, worried, close to tears, but he did not bother to reassure her.

"No," he answered. "I'll see you again soon, sweetheart. Run along to your friend's now, and have a good time."

She waited a moment, looking into her father's face. But Patrell was not interested in her now.

"Run along, Coralie!" he said.

The two men were silent for a time after she had gone. Patrell stepped out on the path and looked after her. She was crossing the meadow, walking with a sort of proud unconcern, straight as an arrow, curiously touching in her slender immaturity.

"Well?" asked Patrell, turning to Branscombe.

"How much will you take to get out and stay out?" asked Branscombe.

He was surprised by his own words, his manner, and he was proud of them. He was proud of the hate and contempt he felt for this man. He discovered that hatred was a very different thing from the flustered irritability he had formerly called anger. Hatred fortified him wonderfully, made him fearless and resourceful.

Patrell lit a cigarette.

"That," he said, "would come pretty high. I don't think you could afford it, Branscombe. You've only got about twenty thousand a year."

"How do you know that?" cried Branscombe, in a panic.

There was nothing he disliked more than for anyone to know about his financial position. Even his sister knew nothing. Not that there was anything whatever to conceal; his affairs were in the most perfect order. But he didn't like anyone to know.

"Oh...!" said Patrell. "I thought I was justified in making some enquiries about you when I heard that you were making love to my wife."

For the first time in his life, Branscombe hit a man. He hit in a blind passion, and it was sheer luck that the blow caught Patrell on the chin, and sent him crashing to the ground. Branscombe stood looking down at him in a sort of ecstasy; the blood ran hot in his veins, he felt himself strong, triumphant.

"You swine!" he cried. "You swine!"

Patrell, lying flat, with his eyes closed, groaned and stirred. And Branscombe began to think. Patrell was only knocked out; when he came to, he would probably attack his assailant.

"Very well," thought Branscombe. "I can defend myself."

But he was not so sure of that. And he thought it very unlikely that he could ever knock Patrell down again, now that he would be on his guard.

Patrell struggled up on one elbow; his eyes were blank and dazed, his mouth was set in a vicious line.

"Damn you!" he said. "You wait...!"

He was on his knees now. A great terror seized Branscombe; he struck again, and Patrell fell back. But he was not unconscious. He was struggling up once more. There was a horrible look in his eyes.

"No...!" cried Branscombe.

Patrell stood up. Blood was trickling down his face; he shook his head, like a wounded animal; he was dangerous and horrible. Branscombe backed away from him. But he could not turn, leaving that menace behind him.

"You cursed fool!" cried Patrell, in a sort of furious amazement.

Branscombe hit him again. But he only swayed. A blow on the chest sent him down again. He lay on his back, panting; his face was a queer colour, his eyes were glazed.

Terror and rage overwhelmed Branscombe. He could not leave this horrible, bloody, panting thing.... It had to be finished, in desperate haste. There was not a stone, not a stick, not a weapon in sight. He pulled off his coat and threw it over Patrell's head, pulled it tight over his face. And Patrell struggled....

Branscombe hit him on the temple and then he was still. Branscombe rose to his feet, with a gasp like a sob.... The thing with its head covered was moving again. It was like a nightmare. Suppose it got up, like that....

He kicked it, in the ribs. And it moved no more.

CHAPTER IV

He was sick; he was shaking violently; he leaned against a tree, fighting against the waves of nausea that swept over him.

"I've got to control myself," he thought. "I've got to get away...." He tried to take a step, but his knees trembled; he leaned back against the tree.

"And I can't go without my coat," he thought.

He did not know how he could retrieve his coat. Take it off Patrell's face—see Patrell's face...?

"No..." he thought. "No... I'll drive to one of the towns near here, and buy another coat...."

But if he were to meet someone who knew him? The spectacle of Andrew Branscombe, so invariably correct, driving his handsome car, coatless, would be altogether too striking.

"And Eva would notice, if I had a new coat. She'd want to know what had happened to the old one."

He shivered, but he was growing a little more composed. He saw that he would have to get his coat and put it on.

"But if it's—stained...?" he thought, and shivered again. If the lining of the coat were stained with blood, he would do something about it later, after he had got away.

Go away, leaving Patrell here?

"Yes!" he cried to himself. "Certainly! Nobody can possibly know.... No one would ever think such a thing of me." It wasn't true, either. Somehow, what had happened was not his fault. Everyone would understand that. He was not the sort of man who did a thing like this.

"Nobody will connect me with it," he thought.

And suddenly he remembered Coralie.

She knew that he had been here with her father; she had left them alone together. If Patrell were found here, dead.... If? There was no "if" about it. He would inevitably be found. Someone might come *now*.

"O God!" cried Branscombe.

If someone were to come along the path now, and see Patrell lying there, and Branscombe standing by him.... Anyone seeing that would think Branscombe a murderer, would turn and run away, back to the road, would call the police.

The police. He would be arrested. They would say he had murdered Patrell.

"Self-defence!" he cried to himself. "The way he looked at me.... He'd have killed me...."

Yet, at the time, he had not been afraid of Patrell's killing him. It had been something else.... He remembered one snowy Christmas long ago, when he had been a boy. He had gone out in the woods with his new rifle, and had shot a rabbit. And it hadn't died; it had lain twitching and kicking on the ground, and the same feeling had come over him then, the same panic.... He had beaten in the creature's head with the rifle butt.... What was it, this atrocious passion to destroy a wounded and struggling thing...?

The silence in the little glade was strange. It was becoming dreadful. No bird twittered, nothing stirred. It was like a wax-work scene of a murder. And it was a murder.

He could never prove that Patrell had attacked him. The truth of the matter was that Patrell had not attacked him. He himself had struck the first blow—and all the other blows. He could not prove that he had killed Patrell in self-defence, for Patrell had done nothing to him. He did not know why he had killed him. No thought of such a thing, no impulse had come to him until he had seen Patrell at his feet.

"It was the way he looked at me. It was because I knew he was a thoroughly bad and dangerous man."

That would not do for a jury. A jury would consider only facts, and the facts were that Branscombe had been paying marked attention to Mrs. Patrell, and had killed her husband.

He must conceal Patrell's body at once, somewhere. Only, there wasn't anywhere. No place to dig a grave, and nothing with which to dig it. He could think of only one thing, and that was preposterous. If he could get Patrell into his car.... Of course, he could not. He could not carry the body that far. He might be able to drag it, but he would surely meet someone. Other people used this short cut.

"No," he thought. "I've got to get away, escape.... Go to South America—some place like that."

But he could not get at his money. Was he to flee, penniless, be hounded, live in terror, and, without money, certainly be caught? It filled him with rage.

"I *won't* lose everything!" he cried. "Never see Hilda again—or Eva.... Lose my money, my position in the world, everything—on account of that fellow. No, by Heaven! At least I'll make a fight for it."

He pulled the coat off Patrell's head.

"O God! O God!" he whispered, staring at what he had done.

This was not the insolent, smiling Patrell he had struck down. This man who lay with closed eyes had an awful dignity, his white face looked noble, immeasurably remote from the world. No one must ever see *this*.... Branscombe put on the coat, and taking Patrell by the feet began dragging him along the path. He got out of breath at once; sweat was dripping from him; he had to stop and rest; then he began again. Patrell's arms went back over his head and his limp fingers made tracks in the dust. His jacket rumpled under him, but his face was serene as ever.

Branscombe forgot all apprehension. He was utterly absorbed in this task he had undertaken. He pulled and dragged at the body; he had to take care to avoid stones and snags. One of Patrell's shoes came off.

"You dam' fool!" muttered Branscombe. He had to get the shoe on again, and Patrell's limpness was infuriating. It took so long.... Then he went on. He had been going on so long that now he couldn't stop. He was scarcely aware of what he did or why he did it. He had to walk backward, and stooping; when he stopped once more to rest, he was amazed to see the highway. He had actually dragged Patrell all the way through the wood, and no one had seen him.

His car stood where he had left it; otherwise, the road was empty in the summer sun. This was a frequented road, though. There was no time to waste. He unlocked his car, and as he did so, another car shot past.

So great a weakness came over him that he had to sit down on the running board. But when he thought it over, he realized that Patrell's body was still screened from the road by the trees, and that the occupants of that swiftly moving car could have seen nothing amiss. He must be quick, though, with this last part of the job.

"Don't let a car come for a few moments!" he prayed. "Just for a few moments...!"

This part was much harder than he had expected, harder than getting Patrell through the wood. Patrell wouldn't get into the sedan decently. He doubled up.... If another car came along now....

But no car came. He got Patrell on the back seat, lying down, his legs hanging over the edge. Branscombe covered him with a rug, and from outside there was nothing to be seen. He seated himself behind the wheel with a long, tremulous sigh of relief. But he could not think where to go.

"Got to get away from here, anyway," he told himself.

So he began to drive, at his usual moderate speed; his hands were steady enough; his vision, his hearing alert. Yet something was wrong with him. He no longer felt any fear; but a peculiar anxiety oppressed him, a sense of some extremely important thing forgotten.

"Did I leave anything there in the wood?" he asked himself. "A clue...? Have I done something insanely stupid, without realizing it...?"

Plenty of other cars passed him, but that caused him no alarm. Nobody would ever suspect what he had in the back of the car, and it was right and natural that nobody should suspect. He was not the kind of man to do such a thing; he could not quite believe that he had done it.

"The best thing might be," he thought, "to drive well out into the country and find some lake or pond...."

He knew of no such place, though, and certainly he could not ask anyone. "Some lonely road, then.... Leave him there...."

Coralie knew of their meeting. Coralie had left them alone together. If her father's body were found, she would tell what she knew. Patrell must not be found, ever.

"And how in hell can I manage *that?*" he thought, in a rage.

He hated Patrell more than ever, because he could not get rid of him. Here he was in the car....

There was a sudden wail that made him jump. He knew what it was, however, a factory whistle blowing for the noon lunch hour.

"I told Hilda I'd lunch with her.... But what can I *do* with this fellow? I'd like to throw him out in the road.... Serve him right. Only, of course, he'd be recognized."

It came to him then that what he really should do was to bury Patrell. For a few moments the idea comforted him. It was not only the safe thing to do, but it was decent. But when he contemplated the practical difficulties, they were enormous. To begin with, he would have to find a suitable place, and then when he had done that, there was the actual digging. He didn't know how long that might take; he had never done any digging. He had no spade, either, no implement, and he could not buy one. After twelve....

He would be late to lunch....

"Oh, damn it all!" he cried to himself, in angry despair.

He did not know where on the face of the earth he would go with his monstrous burden. He dared not stop the car, dared not leave it. In his wretched perplexity, he turned toward home, and knew he dared not go there.

"Mister!" called a voice.

Standing by the roadside was a boy in a dark suit and a cap.

"Gimme a lift to the station, mister?"

"No!" said Branscombe, and drove on.

Almost at once he had to stop at a cross-road for a red light. He turned his head to look back at that boy with the vague impression in his mind that he had had the appearance of a bad character. He looked, and the boy was not there.

That was peculiar. There was a high wall on the side of the road where the boy had stood, and on the other side was an empty field. He was not in the field; it was not likely that he had climbed the high wall. No other car had come along to give him lift. Where was he?

It was a minor problem, but, in the circumstances, almost anything had the power to disturb Branscombe now. He looked back along the road, so intently that he missed the change of the light, and had to wait again. Another car drew up beside him, driven by a severe, grey-haired woman in spectacles.

"There's a boy stealing a ride on the back of your car," she said. "They ought to be put in jail. They're a danger to themselves and everybody else."

The light turned green, and she drove on. But Branscombe stopped his car. If the boy had looked in through the rear window....

"I'll give you five dollars..." said Branscombe, reaching his pocket. "Here! I'm in a hurry."

CHAPTER V

The boy was standing in the road. He was not exactly a boy; it was his slight build and narrow shoulders that made him look so; he was a young fellow with a dark, oval face, black hair, half-closed eyes, and a broad grin that had in it no sort of cheerfulness. Branscombe did not like the grin.

"Keep off!" he said, briefly.

"Why?" asked the other, in a reasonable tone.

"Because I don`t want you climbing on my car. I won`t have it."

The other just stood there, grinning at him.

"Keep off!" cried Branscombe.

The boy went on grinning.

"Is he an idiot?" thought Branscombe. And hoped he was. "Now, clear out—" he began.

"Where are you going, mister?"

There was the quality of an evil dream in this dialogue; it was as if the boy existed in another dimension, and could not hear or could not understand what Branscombe said.

"Clear out!" he repeated, and the boy also repeated the last phrase he had himself used.

"Where you going, mister?"

"He is an idiot," thought Branscombe. "I needn`t worry." But what he felt was considerably worse than worry.

"If you climb on my car again," he said, "I'll call a policeman."

"A policeman!" said the other, with a hoot of laughter. "I can see you!"

"Oh, my God!" thought Branscombe. "Is he an idiot or.... Or did he see...?"

There they stood in the quiet, shady road. Other cars passed them. This wouldn`t do. This would look very strange.... He must get rid of this fellow.

"Here! Get along with you!" he said with a pretence at good-humour. "I'll give you a quarter, if you need it."

"I ought to get more than that, mister."

Branscombe understood that. Yet his instinct was to deny it, to evade the definite issue.

"Well," he said, "if you're in need, I'll give you a dollar."

The other only grinned.

"I'll give you five dollars..." said Branscombe, reaching at his pocket. "Here! I'm in a hurry."

The other took the five-dollar bill, but he did not move. "Why don`t you go?" cried Branscombe.

"Gimme a lift, mister?"

"No!" said Branscombe. He moved toward the front of the car, and the other came with him.

"Gimme a lift, mister!"

It was not a request now; it was a demand. In his fear and wretchedness, Branscombe wished the creature dead. "If I could run over him..." he thought.

"Jerry's my name, mister. I been out of work six months. you got any little job I could do for you...."

"Well, I haven't! And if you keep on annoying me, I'll notify the police."

"Listen, mister!" said Jerry, suddenly serious and confidential. "You wouldn't know how to handle a thing like this. You'll just get yourself in trouble. If you leave it to me, mister, I'll fix it up, and there won't nobody know one thing about it."

"Does he mean *that?*" thought Branscombe.

"For twenny-five dollars," said Jerry softly. "Isn't it worth that to you, mister?"

"Twenty-five dollars..." thought Branscombe. "But that's—preposterous!"

If the fellow meant that he would dispose of Patrell for that sum, it was preposterously little. He couldn't mean that.... Unless to him a thing like this was an ordinary, matter-of-fact occurrence. How strange to think that there were men to whom murder was commonplace; strange and horrible, yet somehow reassuring. It seemed to minimize the whole business.

But, of course, he must not admit anything to this creature.

"No," he said.

Jerry moved nearer to him.

"For twenny-five dollars, mister, I'll put that guy where there won't nobody find him. No worry for you, no trouble. *You* couldn't handle a situation like this—a man like *you.*"

He spoke with a sort of sympathy; he made everything seem normal. There was a little job to be done, which he would undertake for a small sum, that was all.

Yet Branscombe still hesitated. He needed more time to think. He wanted to foresee, as best he could, what the consequences might be of accepting this offer. What had he to lose? The fellow already knew that there was a dead body in the car. If he undertook to dispose of it, he would so involve himself that he would not dare to betray Branscombe. He would have made himself an accessory after the fact. He would have nothing to gain by informing the police, and moreover he wasn't, thought Branscombe, the sort who would be at all anxious to approach the police.

"If I refuse his offer...?" thought Branscombe. "I haven't been able even to imagine any way of doing the thing myself. I couldn't go driving around like this much longer. The most trifling accident would be fatal to me...." He glanced at Jerry, who was staring at the ground, his hands in his pockets. "No!" he thought. "It would be a mistake, a terrible mistake, to let *him* get into the affair."

Only, Jerry was already in it. He had seen Patrell.

"If I could induce him—bribe him to keep quiet until I've disposed of Patrell myself, then there'd be no evidence against me. Nothing but this creature's word that he'd seen something in the car. I could simply deny it."

He remembered Coralie, and despair seized upon him. She knew that Branscombe and her father had been together, and Jerry knew where Patrell had gone. Even if he did think of some way to get rid of Patrell, these two would know.

"I couldn't be worse off, if I let this creature do as he suggests," he thought, and again glanced at the creature.

Jerry had lit a cigarette; somehow that gave him a horrible jauntiness. His cap was pulled down, shadowing his hollow face; he was shabby and starved; twenty-five dollars might well be an important thing to him. And to Branscombe how small a sum for so inestimable a service!

"It—it was an automobile accident," he said. "This man was injured by my car.... It was his fault, but I don't choose to be involved...."

"Sure," said Jerry, soothingly.

"How do you propose to do it?"

"I'll take you to a place," said Jerry. "Only a mile, about. Then you leave me there with this guy, and you go home and forget it, mister. Nobody'll find *him.*"

"Very well," said Branscombe, curtly. "Get in front with me."

For he was in very great haste now to be done with this. "I can drive you, mister. I used to be a chauffeur."

"Very well!" said Branscombe, again.

Jerry drove remarkably well, but much faster than was Branscombe's habit. He did not object to speed now, though. He leaned back in a relaxation that was almost contentment. He was obliged to trust Jerry, and it was a relief. He had the feeling that a dreadful thing was ended, an intolerable burden lifted from his shoulders, and that he could rest now.

Jerry got off the main road and took to lanes and by-ways unknown to Branscombe, and almost deserted. He did not pay much attention to the route Jerry took; he didn't care. He was tired. The car stopped smoothly.

"You just get out, mister. Smoke a cigarette down the road a ways. And then you won't have no more worries."

Branscombe was able to do this with a singularly easy mind. The car stood before a weather-beaten old red barn at the end of a lane overgrown with weeds. There were open fields on either side, peaceful and empty under the hot sun. No human creature was in sight. He turned his back on the car and strolled off. He lit a cigarette and thought of nothing at all.

"O.K., mister," called Jerry.

He was standing beside the car, and Patrell was not there. From his wallet

Branscombe took out two ten-dollar bills and a five, and Jerry pocketed them.

"Thanks, mister!" he said, for all the world like a taxi driver pleased with a tip.

Branscombe backed the car and turned it and set off up the lane. At the turning he looked back, and Jerry was not in sight. He must have gone into the barn. Branscombe refused to think about what he might be doing in there. The thing was finished. It was regrettable, deplorable, but it was finished. He need not and must not think about it.

He was extremely tired and a little dazed. He lost his way on the unfamiliar roads, he drove slowly and unsteadily, and it was by sheer luck that he reached the main highway.

"I must let Eva know that I shan't be home to lunch," he thought. He had never neglected such matters; he thought it unpardonable.

"And I'll be glad to get a wash and brush—" he said to himself, and stopped, struck by a thought that appalled him. There might be, surely there must be, some trace in his appearance of what had happened.

"Blood?" he thought.

He had not touched Patrell except to take him by the feet.... Yet he was afraid to look at his own hands. He couldn't.... He must. He stopped the car and held up his hands. The knuckles of his right hand were red and caked with dried blood and dirt.

"How was it I didn't notice that before?" he thought.

If he hadn't noticed that, there might be other things too which he had not noticed. Blood on his clothes, in the car. He twisted the reflector, and stared at his image. His hair was a little ruffled, his tie not quite straight, but otherwise he was unchanged; he had his usual aloof and distinguished air.

He looked in the back of the car. The rug was gone, but he could see nothing else amiss, although he made a most careful examination. He smoothed his hair, straightened his tie, and drew on a pair of wash leather gloves. But he could not believe that he looked as usual; the nearer he drew to home, the more his dread increased. He thought that Eva would read something in his face.... He wondered if he would be able to speak in a natural voice....

His knees were trembling as he mounted the steps of the veranda. That wouldn't do. He must control that, and he did; when he entered the room he was walking steadily.

"I believe I'll take a little whisky," he thought.

An innovation, that was. He was inclined to be severe about drinking; he would not take even a cocktail before lunch.

"No alcohol in working hours," he always said.

To-day, however, was exceptional. If Eva saw him taking a drink, he would tell her he did not feel very well, and she would be kind.... The thought of her kindness was balm to him, he longed now to see her. He opened the door with his latch key and started along the hall, quietly, hoping to get his drink

from the dining-room before Eva saw him. The sound of voices from the drawing-room checked him; he stopped and looked in and saw Eva there with that
Evans fellow.

He moved away noiselessly, his heart beating with violence.

"Curse the fellow!" he thought.

He could not possibly face that fellow, that stranger, just now. He didn't
want Evans in his house; he didn't like him. It was wrong of Eva to let him
come; it was unkind of her, disloyal. He had needed Eva to be here, alone. He
went into the dining-room and unlocked the cupboard which contained his
supply of wines and liquors; he poured himself a small drink of whisky and
drank it quickly. He had a second drink; then, relocking the cupboard, he rang
for the house-maid.

"Tell Miss Branscombe, please, that I shan't be home to lunch," he said.

He went up to his room, washed, changed into another suit, and went out
of the house by the back door. He took the path that led past the drawing-room
so that he could look in at the window. Eva was leaning back in her chair, her
hands clasped behind her head; she was gazing seriously at nothing, and
Evans, sitting opposite, was looking at her.

Branscombe felt desolate, he felt hurt and angry.

"We don't know anything about the fellow," he thought. "Eva ought to
have more dignity...."

He could think of nothing but Eva and that fellow as he drove to Mrs. Patrell's. He had not expected this sort of thing from Eva.

"I wonder if she's seen much of the fellow, without my knowing it," he
thought. "I told her I didn't like him...."

Mrs. Patrell's sedate house-maid smiled as she admitted him, and at once the
atmosphere of this house enveloped him, the grace and tranquillity which
Hilda Patrell created. Eva did her best, but her housekeeping was artless, even
crude, compared with Hilda's. The way the flowers were arranged was a
work of art to be admired beyond words, the quiet loveliness of this room,
airy and fragrant, the shutters were closed against the hot sun, and in the dim-
ness the fine old furniture gleamed dully; there was a sense of permanence,
of seemliness.

And Hilda herself was like that. As she came into the room, he was startled to see how beautiful she was, beautiful without effort, straight and proud
and gentle. She had changed into a thin, dark dress that made her hair look
startlingly blonde. She smiled, her honest, lovely smile, and held out her hand.

He meant only to raise it to his lips. But at the touch of her slender fingers
a thrill ran through him, a sudden flame. He kissed her hand, he caught her
in his arms, and held her close.

"Hilda!... I love you...!"

"Andrew!... No!" she cried. "Andrew—you've forgotten Charles!"

CHAPTER VI

He released her at once, a little too quickly. For a moment she stood down-cast, pale, obviously much disturbed; then she raised her eyes to his face. She opened her lips to speak, but was silent, staring at him.

"Andrew..." she said. "Andrew, what's the matter?"

"Nothing," he said. "Nothing."

He was beginning to recover himself now, but as his thoughts grew clearer, it was worse for him. He wanted to turn away from her, to flee from this house. He was aghast at what he had done. He had taken her in his arms, told her he loved her, when only a few hours ago he had killed her husband.

"If she knew..." he thought.

If she knew, she would look at him with wild horror, she would scream if he came near her....

"You don't look at all well," she said, anxiously. "Will you take a little brandy?"

"Thanks," he answered.

He wanted that brandy badly. He poured himself out a drink that surprised her, and made her still more anxious.

"You're ill!" she said.

"I..." he began. He had meant to say something about having narrowly escaped being run into by another car, but this third drink seemed to warm and illumine his brain, so that he thought of something better.

"I didn't mean to behave like this," he said. "I hope you can forgive me.... But ever since you told me this morning... I'm not myself...."

A faint colour rose in her sunburned cheeks.

"I'm sorry," she said. "I—perhaps I ought to have seen...."

"I don't blame you, my dear.... And try not to blame me for losing my head for one moment.... Hilda, must I go away?"

For the first time he saw her at a loss. This obviously was a situation entirely new to her, and a little beyond her. She was without subtlety; she was candid and definite; and his attitude, being neither candid nor definite, confused her. "I value your friendship so much..." she said, with hesitancy. "But don't you think that perhaps...?"

"You mean you can't forgive me? Ever?"

She was silent for a long time, and he felt that he knew what she was thinking. Never had his mind been so lucid, so quick; he watched her, and felt sure that he would win, felt sure that he had said exactly the right words, in exactly the right tone.

"I'm afraid I'm rather strait-laced, Andrew," she said. "But—" Then suddenly she smiled, a valiant and touching smile. "We'll just forget this, shall we?"

They had lunched together before this, but to-day it was different. There had been, before to-day, a nebulous sort of friendship between them. They had been easy and happy together. Now she was constrained, ill at ease, and he pretended to be so.

In his heart, instead of shame, he had a strange, unholy pride. She thought his love for her an unpermissible thing, but it was so infinitely more guilty than she could possibly imagine.... She believed that she was a married woman.

"And how am I ever going to let her know...?" he thought.

He had not faced this before. She was free now, but she did not know it, and she must not know it. Nobody must know that Patrell was dead. But his disappearance would have to be explained in some way; he couldn't just vanish. That would be almost as bad as if his body were found. The man must have friends, relations somewhere who would become anxious at his absence. If a search were made for him, it would inevitably lead to his wife. Coralie would tell her mother that she had left Branscombe and her father together. Branscombe would be questioned....

"And," thought Branscombe, "if they question me, I'm lost."

In a few hours he would have to face Coralie. And if she asked him anything about Patrell....

"This is much more complicated than I realized..." thought Branscombe.

What he wanted was to be alone, to think this thing out. But he could not leave Hilda too abruptly; above all things there must be nothing strange in his behaviour which could be remembered and brought up against him later. They had coffee on the veranda, really good coffee, such as Eva never provided.

"I'm disappointed in Eva," he thought. She's...."

"Andrew...."

"Yes?" he answered, turning to Hilda.

"It wasn't right of me to trouble you with my affairs as I did this morning."

"I wish you wouldn't look at it that way," he said. "I wish you would feel that I'm unalterably your friend, Hilda. I wish you'd let me help you, in any way. It would make me happy."

Before this, she had been a woman of admirable dignity and poise, and now she showed an embarrassment that was almost awkward. It was curious and touching.

"Is it because she loves me?" he thought.

For a moment a great wonder filled him, something almost like awe. She was so honest, so valiant, so splendid; her love would be a thing to honour any man on earth. But then something else came, to drown his brief humility.

"There must be something about me..." he thought.

There must be something extraordinary about him for a woman like Hilda to love him. There must be an extraordinary strength and intelligence in him, that he could endure what he had endured this morning, and not be crushed.

"I've never understood my own character," he thought.

"Will you bring Coralie home at five, Andrew?" asked Hilda.

"Yes..." he answered. "Try not to worry, my poor girl."

"I can't..." she began, and stopped, looking at the street. A taxi had stopped before the gate, and a man was getting out, a square-shouldered man of medium height, stiff and straight, with a little sandy moustache. He paid the driver and opened the gate, came along the path, walking with a noticeable limp.

"But it looks like Vincent!" she said, frowning. I don't see...."

He took off his soft hat and smiled at her, a somewhat anxious smile; a good-looking man, thought Branscombe.

"Vincent!" she exclaimed, and what her tone implied Branscombe could not tell; could not tell by her face whether she were pleased, or distressed, or merely startled.

The man came up the steps.

"Mr. Branscombe—Captain Colton."

The two men bowed, and Colton looked at Branscombe with an odd in-tentness. The situation had altogether an awkward quality, which Hilda ought to have prevented. No one said anything for a long moment.

"It's—quite a surprise to see you, Vincent," she said, at last.

"I.... Yes..." he said. "I'm looking for a cottage in the neighbourhood, and naturally, I stopped in...."

"A cottage *here?*"

"Well, yes," he said, as if in apology.

There was something wrong here, something Branscombe could not grasp. Who was this fellow, and what was Hilda's feeling toward him...? She roused herself, with a visible effort, and began to talk.

"I wonder if you'll like it here, Vincent. Somehow it's hard to think of you in a summer colony.... Mr. Branscombe can tell you something about it. He and his sister have taken a house, out on the Point."

"Hm...!" said Colton. "Very nice."

There was another silence, which Branscombe ended. "We find it very agreeable," he said.

"You do?" said Colton, turning toward him politely.

"Quiet, of course," said Branscombe. "But we like that."

"I see!" said Colton, and then turned to Hilda. "Coralie..." he said, "she must have grown...."

"She's taller than I now. She's thirteen now."

"Thirteen, eh?"

It was, thought Branscombe, an idiotic conversation. And when he looked more closely at Colton, it occurred to him that the man's face was stupid.

"Coffee, Vincent?"

"Thank you, no.... Fact, I'll have to be getting along now, Hilda.... But if I may, I'll—er—call you up later—arrange to see you again...?"

"Of course!" she said, without heartiness.

He took his leave then, and went off down the path and along the shady street, very erect and soldierly in spite of his limp.

An extraordinarily brief and pointless visit, thought Branscombe.

"Colton is an old friend of Charles's," said Hilda.

Branscombe hoped that his slight start had not been apparent.

"I can't imagine what he's doing here," she went on. "I haven't seen or heard of him for years and years.... I wish he hadn't come."

"Why?" asked Branscombe. "Don't you like him?"

"I like him, in a way," she answered, frowning again. "He's one of the most honourable, generous men who ever lived. But he's a martinet. He was horribly upset when Charles and I separated. He did everything he could to bring us together again. That's why I wish he hadn't come. I'm afraid he might want to begin that again. I can't see what else would bring him here."

Nothing could have been more disturbing to Branscombe than the sudden and unaccountable appearance of an old friend of Patrell's—on this particular day.

"Could he and Patrell have come out here together?" he thought. "My God! Perhaps he has an engagement to meet Patrell this afternoon...!"

He told Hilda that he had an errand to do, and must leave at once. The abruptness of his departure might seem odd, but he felt that if he stayed here any longer, his behaviour would be still more odd. He could not talk. He had to get away and think.

He drove out into the country, drove at random. He marvelled at his own fortitude. He was not dazed or benumbed; he realized his position clearly. He had killed a man. Yet he had none of the conventional emotions about this act; no horror, no remorse. All that he felt was an overpowering dread and anxiety, and a determination to save himself.

He was menaced now on two sides. By Colton and by Coralie. Either one of them could, at any moment, bring about a crisis. He must be prepared to answer questions about Patrell.

"Coralie will say that we met. I can't deny that. She may be able to repeat some of our conversation. Well, suppose I say that I bought him off? Paid him to get out and leave the child alone. That would account for his disappearance. I could say that our bargain was for him to leave the country at once. That's the sort of thing he would do, too. Man without any decency...."

It seemed to him that this story was remarkably plausible and ingenious; it might well serve to keep people quiet for a time. Not for very long, though; he did not delude himself about that. But the great thing was to gain time.

Events were pressing too closely upon him, and he disliked being hurried.

Not until he turned back did he realize how extremely painful was the task immediately before him. He did not want to meet Patrell's child.

"She may refuse to come with me," he thought. "I hope to Heaven she will. Perhaps she's gone home already."

At this very moment she might be at home, telling Hilda of that meeting in the wood.

"Hilda may well think it's strange of me not to have mentioned it to her," he thought. "She'll wonder why I didn't tell her Patrell had gone and that she needn't worry any more."

He could explain that, though. He would appear reluctant and unhappy, as if it were intolerable to him to speak of her husband's baseness. He hoped ardently that the child would be gone.

But as soon as he stopped the car outside the house where she was visiting, the door opened and Coralie came running down the steps. She got in beside him without a word of greeting; he glanced at her once, saw an odd, hostile look on her face, and was silent. Patrell's child.... "Mr. Branscombe!" she said, presently, her voice curt and challenging.

"Yes?"

"I suppose you told Mother."

"Told her?"

"That I met Daddy. I *knew* you'd tell her. And it was *mean!* It was mean to worry her so. I didn't want her to know, because she couldn't possibly understand. She's wonderful about everything else, but she doesn't understand *him.* She's led a sort of sheltered life, and she simply couldn't understand a nature like his."

Patrell's words, these must be. The child was crying.

"I haven't told your mother," said Branscombe.

"But you will, of course. And it's mean! It's not because I'm one bit ashamed of meeting Daddy secretly. It's because I *hate* to hurt Mother. She wouldn't understand that I love both of them."

This was horrible, unbearable.

"I won't tell her, Coralie," he said. "Don't cry, dear."

"What?" she demanded incredulously.

"I shan't mention your meetings."

"But *you* couldn't understand!" she cried. "I mean, I could see you were against him. All the awfully respectable, people are against him, because he's adventurous. He doesn't care about money, and things like that."

"Don't cry, Coralie.... I'm very sorry."

She looked at him, her long lashes wet with tears—a look of silent, steady enquiry, a look hard for him to bear.... She knew...!

"You look sort of funny..." she said.

He would have to stop looking "funny."

"The thing worries me," he said. "Don't you think it would be better to trust your mother's judgment?"

"No," she answered. "I've thought it over a lot. The first time Daddy met me, I was awfully upset. He told me Mother wouldn't want me to see him. He told me how much he'd missed me ever since Mother took me away. But he left it entirely up to me whether we'd better go on seeing each other. I thought it out, and I made up my mind I'd go on. He's frightfully fond of Mother. He's really sorry for having been sort of wild. I thought that maybe later on I could get her to see things differently."

Branscombe said nothing.

"This thing is not finished," he said to himself. "It's only beginning. The thing that has happened was only the first step along a road—and I can't see the end."

CHAPTER VII

He left Coralie at her gate, and drove off, not even looking to see if Hilda were on the veranda. The idea of talking to anyone at all wearied and dismayed him; he wanted to go home and rest, lock himself in his room. But that he must not do; he must avoid anything unusual. He would have to dine with Eva and talk to her. He had to go on living, unaffected by what he had done.

It was necessary to find a definite attitude toward his act. He must know what to think about Andrew Branscombe. The just man, the aloof and distinguished scholar had gone; what had replaced him?

"I acted upon impulse," he thought. "I admit it was a mistaken impulse. But there was no premeditation. It was not a murder. Not a crime. You might honestly call it an accident. I killed him because at the time it seemed necessary."

He left the car in the garage, and walked toward the house. Eva was on the veranda, just sitting there in the late afternoon sun. He had seen her like this often enough, yet now it made a new impression upon him; now it seemed to him that she looked forlorn, a young, pretty creature, who should be active and gay. He remembered that she had protested a little against his plans for the summer.

"Andrew, couldn't we go to an hotel? Some place where it would be livelier?"

He had explained to her that the places she called "lively" were simply noisy, and filled with uncongenial people. But he had known that the people he called "uncongenial" were not so to her; he had known that she did not want a house like this, in which to continue their correct and unvaried routine.

"I've been a fool!" he thought, with a sudden fear. "I shouldn't have insisted on this sort of life for her.... I'll have to make some sort of change...."

If he did not, he might lose her, and that would be the supreme misfortune. She was the one human being who belonged to him, upon whom he could absolutely depend. He loved Hilda Patrell, but he did not need her as he needed Eva.

"Eva," he said, "would you like to drive over to Marlowe Beach after dinner? They say it's very lively...."

"But I'd love it, Andy!"

She seemed so very pleased and touched that he wished he had done more of this. His life would have to be different, livelier, so that she should be content, and not wish for anything more. They went to an hotel, sat on a terrace overlooking the sea, and the dance music from inside came to them, faint and gay.

(Patrell would hear no more music.)

Branscombe ordered a fruit lemonade for Eva, and whisky and soda for himself; he lit a cigar. The whisky was like nectar, the tobacco had an exquisite aroma, the sea wind blew soft against his face.

(Patrell would never smoke, never drink again. A man was a fool who did not relish what he had while he could.)

Eva talked to him in her cheerful, inconsequent way. He liked to hear her; she was young and pretty and careless. And he too was young. All the delights of the world were open to him; he had money and freedom. He was happy with an almost unearthly joy; it was as if he had by a miracle escaped some extreme danger. He was happy because he was alive.

He wanted to stay late on the terrace, for there was in his mind a dim dread of the night. He was afraid that he would not be able to sleep, and that, lying awake, his new happiness would turn to something very different. But Eva began to yawn and yawn; she admitted that she was sleepy, and he had to take her home.

He undressed and got into bed, and he thought he would read, read all night, if necessary. But he grew drowsy at once, and fell asleep; he slept his regular eight hours without even a dream to trouble him. When he opened his eyes, he saw a steady, gentle rain falling, and he was pleased. He always enjoyed a rainy day; he would sit in the library with his pipe and his books; he would get on with a little essay he had planned: "The Dog in the Renaissance."

Patrell....

"I'm not evading that," he said to himself. "I realize that psychologically it's very dangerous to evade anything of that sort. I'll face it squarely. I admit that I—that I did it. But it's irrevocable. I've got to turn my mind to other matters, and not brood."

What other matters? His writing, his reading suddenly appeared to him as sickeningly dull and futile. And that frightened him. How was he to exist without his scholarly pursuits?

"A more active life," he thought. "I believe that's what I need."

His love? He found in himself a strange disinclination to think about Hilda at all. That wouldn't do. That was dangerous. That was an inhibition. He *must* think about her.

The situation was profoundly disturbing. Hilda was a widow but she did not know it, and he could not tell her. He could not marry her; he could not mention marriage to her.

"God!" he thought. "What irony! I've committed a crime for her sake. And neither she nor I can profit by it."

"I wasn't aware of my motive in my conscious mind. But it was undoubtedly my love for Hilda that aroused that—that unusual anger in me.... It's not like me to lose all self-control. Only a very powerful emotion could do it...."

A strange peace filled him. He had committed a crime for the sake of the woman he loved, and she must never know.

"I can't see her again," he thought. "Not ever. She'll understand."

She wouldn't exactly understand, of course. She would think he did not come back because he had betrayed himself by the admission of a forbidden love. She would have to go on thinking it was a forbidden love.

"It's my punishment," he thought. He was quiet, calm, resigned. It was impossible to marry Hilda, and he renounced her.

"I'll leave here," he thought. "I'll take a trip with Eva."

The confusion and trouble of yesterday had left him. There would, of course, be details to arrange, but he could manage them, and there was no violent haste. Coralie was not going to tell her mother. If that Colton fellow had had an appointment with Patrell and was anxious about his absence, it would be some time before he would make any trouble. It was very disagreeable, though, to think about that fellow. If any trouble were coming, thought Branscombe, it was coming through him.

"As soon as I saw him, I felt uneasy.... Type of man I don't like. Secretive..." thought Branscombe.

But if Colton did in some way find out that Branscombe and Patrell had met, then Branscombe would tell his story of having bought Patrell off, and who could prove anything to the contrary?

He was sitting at breakfast with Eva when Hilda telephoned.

"Andrew...?" she said. "If you're not busy, may I see you this morning?"

He agreed at once, with a grave courtesy. But in his heart he was annoyed; he didn't want to see her.

"I suppose she's still worrying about her child," he thought. "She's almost too maternal. Obsessed with that child. I don't feel like discussing that thing interminably. And now that she knows how I feel, you'd think she'd have more tact...."

Still, when he saw Hilda, he forgave her, because she was so lovely, so desirable; and in her clear eyes he saw so candid a faith in him. She was still constrained, though, almost shy. She began to speak at once, as if what she had to say needed all her courage.

"Andrew.... There's something I've made up my mind to do, and I wanted to tell you first...."

"Yes...?" he said, and waited.

"I've been thinking things over..." she went on. "I... about yesterday...."

The colour rose in her cheeks; she was, he thought, singularly ingenuous for a married woman of her age. And it pleased him; it made him feel a man of the world. "I don't want anything to interfere with our friendship," she said, "unless, of course, you feel that you'd rather—we didn't see each other...."

"I want to see you," he said. "I want to be your friend. I want you to know that you can trust me never to take advantage of your kindness. My dear, as long as you want I'll be your friend, and nothing else."

He meant that, and it seemed to him that it was chivalrous of him to feel
so. She looked up at him with a smile, and for a moment they were both silent.

"I'm glad..." she said. And then, with a visible effort: "Vincent came to see
me last night. It's upset me."

"Did he say anything?"

"No! No, nothing at all. He only sat and smoked and talked about nothing.
That's really what bothered me. There must be some reason for his suddenly
appearing like this after all these years.... Yet he didn't say anything...."

Some reason... some reason for Patrell's friend appearing just on that espe-
cial day....

"I told you before how anxious he used to be to reconcile us. I don't know
whether he still has that idea.... Probably he has. Vincent's the most tenacious
person. He never gives up an idea. Once he starts a thing, he goes on and on...."

And once he had a suspicion, he would go on and on...? Saying nothing, until he was sure?

"I believe," she said, "that Charles sent him here. That makes an intolerable situation. I'm really fond of Vincent, but I can't—I won't discuss my affairs with him. Very likely he'd think that I ought to let Coralie see her father. But I won't! It's not vindictiveness. It's only that the child's forgotten
him, and I can't have her troubled and worried by a divided allegiance. You—
do you agree with me, Andrew?"

"Entirely!" he said.

"Then there's only one thing to do. I'm going to see Charles to-morrow."

"No!" cried Branscombe, off his guard for a moment. If she went to see Patrell, she would learn that he had disappeared....

"I've got to," she said; "it's the only way. I've got to see Charles and talk
to him. I'm going to ask him to let me divorce him. I never cared before. But
now—now I'll offer to settle something on him."

"So he's like that?" said Branscombe. "He'll accept money from you?"

His voice was unsteady with anger, but it was anger against her. Why
couldn't she let things alone? This thing she proposed meant extreme danger
to him....

"Yes," she said, with a slight quiver of the lips. "He'd do that. But in other
ways... he's not a bad man, Andrew, not cruel or evil. He's only reckless and
pleasure-loving. I'm sure that if I talk to him, he'll promise not to see Coralie."

Branscombe was silent. He could think of nothing plausible to say that would
deter her, no way to avert this danger. Go she would, and she would learn
that he wasn't where he lived, wasn't anywhere.

"Hilda," he said, "will you tell me where he lives?"

"But why?"

"It's so stupid of me..." he said. "But will you humour me...? If you're going there, I'd like to know where it is... in case...."

He spoke—haltingly; he had the tone, the look of a miserably unhappy lover.

And she accepted it. She gave him Patrell's address.

"Don't worry, Andrew," she said. "I'm sure that if I see Charles, he'll listen to reason."

"The hell he will!" thought Branscombe. Patrell would never again listen to reason or to anything else.

CHAPTER VIII

Blanche would have paid the room-rent if she could, and she felt that her landlady ought to appreciate her innate honesty.

"You treat me like I was a crook!" she cried.

"Well..." said Mrs. Hawkes.

"Well, what?" Blanche demanded.

She was very sensitive about her position, and never at any time very sure of herself. She was a charming girl, tall, somewhat too thin, with a pointed face and grey, dark-lashed eyes; she knew she was pretty, but that didn't help her much, because she knew that she had no style.

"When my husband gets back—" she said, haughtily.

"That 'husband' of yours..." said Mrs. Hawkes.

The implication was unmistakable, and Blanche was angry and ashamed.

"He'll be back I guess to-day," she said. "And when he comes he'll pay you, and we'll get right out of your dirty old room."

"It's dirty enough now," said Mrs. Hawkes. "How do you think it's ever going to be properly cleaned with you lying in bed half the day, and smoking your nasty cigarettes all over the place?"

In her heart Blanche was ashamed of that, too. She had been brought up to be neat and industrious; it was only recently that she had fallen into these lazy ways.

"Will you kindly tell me what business it is of *yours* if I smoke?" she asked, still haughtily.

"I'll be glad—" Mrs. Hawkes began, when the door-bell rang, and she went off to answer it. Blanche lay back on the bed, and defiantly lit another cigarette, and tried to think of cutting things to say to Mrs. Hawkes. There was a loud knock at the door, and Mrs. Hawkes re-entered.

"Here's somebody asking for that 'husband' of yours," she said. "Wants to know when he's expected back."

"Well, to-day, I guess."

"He says it's important. You'd better go out and tell him what you 'guess.' I've got work to do."

Blanche had a wedding ring, but it gave her little confidence. She realized that there was something indefinable about her which made Mrs. Hawkes and probably everybody else on earth immediately suspicious of her respectability. She didn't, she thought, look like a married woman, and if this visitor came on business, he would see through her at once. She got up, thin and supple in her silk pyjamas; she washed her face and powdered it, and applied a lip-stick. She brushed her soft dark hair, put on a dressing-gown and slippers, and went out into the hall.

A man stood waiting there, a tall man, stiff as a poker, with remarkably thick flaxen hair, and wearing eye-glasses. He had a look of severity that daunted her.

"You're Mrs. Patrell?" he asked. "I asked for Mr. Patrell."

It occurred to her that he was a detective, or a policeman, and that it might be a criminal offence to say she was Mrs. Patrell.

"What do you want?" she asked.

"I want to speak to you. It's urgent. Isn't there some room...?"

"No," she answered, and was glad there wasn't. This man made her uneasy.

"There's a certain amount of money coming to you..." he said, in a low tone. "I can't discuss it here."

He even knew she needed money. And she didn't any longer think that this was a detective. He spoke like an actor, she thought; he was impressive. She glanced at him and found him looking at her sternly through his glasses.

"Well, we could go in my room," she said. "If you'll excuse it being all up-set...."

"Very well!" he said, and followed her in there.

"I got up late this morning," she explained, with an apologetic smile. "I was sort of tired."

He did not smile, and he glanced about the room with an expression that dismayed her. He was obviously disgusted with its disorder, and disgusted with her, too. She was by nature a gentle creature, and for all her small vanities she was humble at heart. If this man were disgusted with her, she was ready to believe that she was disgusting, and felt miserable about it.

He closed the door.

"My name is Brown," he said. "Perhaps you've heard Patrell speak of me?"

"Well, I—maybe I have. I don't know.... I mean, my husband knows a lot of people...."

"I may as well tell you now, madam," said Mr. Brown, "that I know Patrell is not your husband."

"Well, he is!" she said, and began to cry.

"No," he said, "I understand the situation very well. Patrell told me himself. He asked me to come here to-day, to see if he had returned. If he hadn't, then I was to make a certain arrangement for you. You'll have to leave here at once."

"I can't."

"You'll have to," he said, with sudden vehemence. "If you don't, it will mean very serious trouble."

"For Charles? Oh! What's happened?"

"You must leave here at once."

"I can't. I owe the landlady."

"I'll attend to that. You must leave here, before anyone comes to question you."

"Question...? You mean—the police?"

"Patrell wants you to know as little as possible about the whole thing. For your own sake. He wants you to go at once to this other place, and wait there."

"Will I see him soon?"

"Not for a day or two. But I have some money for you.... Now, I want you to tell the landlady that I'm your brother, and that I'm taking you to Montreal, where your mother is seriously ill. Tell her Patrell is joining you there."

She was not analytical of herself or of others; she was much more trusting than was good for her. But suddenly, for no reason she could have explained, a strange, formless suspicion came over her, a distrust of this man that was almost fear.

"But why?" she demanded. "If there's anything wrong, why didn't Charles send me a note or something?"

"He didn't have time. And there's no time to waste now. You must start packing."

"No!" she said. "I don't want to just go away like this, and not even know where I'm going."

Mr. Brown came a step nearer, and she drew back; they stood facing each other in the close, untidy room.

"If you care anything at all for Patrell," he said, "you'll do as I say, now."

"No, I..." she said, frightened, uncertain, but obstinate.

"Good God!" he exclaimed. "The idea of the whole thing being ruined by a creature like *you!*"

That made her cry again. She had so little self-esteem to protect her from such hurts. And Mr. Brown had no compassion for her tears.

"I'll pay what you owe here," he said. "And I'll see that you're provided for elsewhere until Patrell comes back. If you come at once. Otherwise, I'll leave you—without a cent. And you'll be doing Patrell a great injury."

"But where is he? He said he'd only be gone for the afternoon, and he didn't come back all night."

"He'll have to explain that himself."

"But he must be in bad trouble if...."

"He is," said Mr. Brown, briefly. "And you'd better help him by doing what I say."

She stood before him, in the silk dressing-gown that had belonged to Patrell, her dark hair carelessly brushed, her face pale; she was penniless, she was unbefriended. She had every disadvantage, and still she opposed this man. Certainly not very effectually, but it was remarkable that she did so at all, for her nature was so pliant, so amiable, so credulous.

"But why didn't Charles send me any word? He could have rung up."

"See here!" said Brown, with contemptuous impatience. "This happens to be a very serious matter. Anyone but you would have read between the lines and understood that the police have got to be given a false scent to follow."

She grew very white. A few months ago she had been a respectable girl, very respectable, daughter of a small upstate farmer. She had been a waitress in a New York tea-room, and she had been proud of the job because it was a refined, high-class tea-room. She had been haughty toward men who had made advances, before she met Patrell. But she loved Patrell, and with him she had abandoned all her old habits of neatness and haughty virtue. Patrell had been lazy, and she had been lazy with him; he had thought it was a joke to owe money, and she had laughed with him; she had learned to smoke, she had learned to be extravagant. But her feeling about the police was ineradicable. To be in any way involved with the police was supremely disgraceful.

"Has Charles...?" she asked. "Did Charles...?"

"You'll have to ask him. I can't waste any more time. I came here to help you and Patrell, and you've been obstinate and suspicious. You behave as if I were trying to swindle you. Even for Patrell's sake I can't do any more. You'll have to make up your mind immediately whether you'll do as he wants or whether you'll add to his difficulties."

"I'll come," she said.

He gave her money for Mrs. Hawkes and told her he would return in an hour. When she went to Mrs. Hawkes she was crying, and the tears were genuine; she wept because Charles was in trouble, and because Mr. Brown had been contemptuous toward her, and had made her feel contemptible. She was never quite sure whether her life with Patrell was simply disgraceful or the gallant adventure he called it. She never quite realized what she was doing, and certainly she never had any idea where she was heading. In a way, it had astonished her that so superior a man as Patrell should fall in love with her, but after all, it was so much like a movie. He was her first lover; she could not imagine ever giving a thought to another man. Patrell was kind and good-humoured, generous to her when he had any money, and she loved him faithfully.

Although when he said that they would get married presently, after his affairs were in order, she didn't believe that. In the first place, she had come to the conclusion that he was a gambler, such as she had seen in the pictures, and she did not believe his affairs would ever be in order. And in the second place, she was quite unable to believe in a future. As things were now, so things would always be. Rather stupid, Blanche was: a girl with a dozen faults and weaknesses—and one or two virtues. She was loyal, she was kind, she was honest.

Her tears made her somewhat incoherent story seem plausible to Mrs. Hawkes.

"I hope your poor dear mother will get better," she said. "And I hope you and Mr. Patrell will be back here before long, dearie."

Blanche hoped so, too. This room in which they had lived for so long was dear to her; it was home. She cried again as she packed Charles's things with hers in two bags.

When Mr. Brown returned the bags were ready, and she was dressed in a thin dark frock and a wide-brimmed black straw hat. She was pretty, in spite of her tear-stained face, but she was countrified.

He had a taxi waiting, and he hurried her into it. She asked him questions about Charles, but his sharp answers disheartened her. She glanced at him, and suddenly it came to her mind that this spectacled man at her side hated her. She thought it was not mere impatience that he felt, not disgust, but hatred. And that frightened her. She wished she had not come with him, wished she had waited at Mrs. Hawkes's for Charles, even if Mrs. Hawkes had been very mean about the rent. Now she felt curiously and alarmingly cut off from her former life.

The place to which Mr. Brown took her surprised her. It was not a lodging-house; it was a small hotel in the West Seventies, with an air of quiet respectability.

"Register as Miss Brown—Miss—whatever your name is—Brown," he told her. "You're supposed to be my sister."

"But will Charles know to ask for me by that name?"

"Yes," he answered with a frown. "When Patrell comes, he'll make some other arrangement. But at present it would be extremely dangerous to use his name. Or even mention it to anyone."

She caught his arm.

"But—give me your address, will you?" she said. "I mean—so there'll be somebody I can—kind of keep in touch with...."

For she did not want to be Miss Brown, left here alone in this strange place where she must not mention Charles's name.

"No," said Brown. "I'll ring you up, tomorrow or the next day, to see if Patrell's come back."

"Will you *promise* to ring me up?"

He gave her a chilly, glittering stare.

"Yes. In the meantime, your room and meals are paid for a week in advance."

Her room was unexpectedly luxurious, a sunny, well-furnished room with a private bath. She smoked and looked out of the window, and at six o'clock she went down to the dining-room. She was still more impressed. She was shown to a little table with a lamp on it; she had a dinner which seemed to her remarkably good. When she had finished she wanted to smoke a cigarette in the lounge, but the sight of the queenly dowagers sitting there daunted her. She bought a magazine at the newsstand and took it up to her room. She undressed and got into bed, and for a time was interested in a love story.

And then something made her remember Charles, and she missed him. She cried and cried for him.

CHAPTER IX

She had made no mistake in thinking that Mr. Brown hated her. He went off filled with a furious scorn against her. Her room at Mrs. Hawkes's had been redolent of perfume, and it seemed to him that he could not get the scent out of his nostrils.

"A thoroughly bad woman," he said to himself, and thought of savage names for her.

Her dressing-gown had revealed a glimpse of pink silk; in her dishevelment she had looked odiously soft and pretty and submissive. He hated her.

"A woman like that deserves absolutely no consideration," he thought. Certainly he was not disposed to show her much. She was a complication he had not expected.

He walked to the place where his car was parked, and getting into it drove out of the city faster than was his habit. In Pelham he found a quiet side road where he stopped and took off the glasses and the blond wig, which he had worn, years ago, in a school play. He knew they did not constitute a disguise, but if Mrs. Hawkes or Blanche should ever be questioned, they would say that a blond man in eye-glasses had come enquiring for Patrell—and who would connect that man with Andrew Branscombe?

"I detest all this hole-and-corner business," he thought. "It's my nature to be frank and straightforward. I don't like all this intriguing."

But still less would he like enquiries to be made for Patrell. He hoped he had stopped Hilda for a time; she would go to Mrs. Hawkes's and she would learn that her husband had been living there with another woman whom he called his wife. She would learn that the girl had gone away with her brother. Perhaps that would be enough for her.

"But suppose she wants to go on with this divorce idea?" he thought. "That would mean a lawyer."

He could not have a lawyer involved in this. Only, how was he to stop it?

"I'm sick of the whole business!" he cried to himself.

It seemed a monstrous injustice. He was willing to admit that he had committed a wrong—an excusable one, considering the circumstances, but still a crime against the law of the land. He would, he thought, have regretted it, if only he could be *let alone*. He had already suffered so much....

"And now I'll have to go on and on," he thought, in a sort of despair. "I'll have to keep that girl quiet. I'll have to prevent Hilda from making any search for Patrell."

He had lived all his life more or less isolated from his fellows and protected by his modest fortune. There had been nothing that he wanted badly to get, to struggle for; he had never intrigued or plotted. But now that he had to, he discovered in himself a surprising facility.

He drove home, and shutting himself into the library, composed a letter.

DEAR MRS. PATRELL:
I hope you will forgive me the wrong I done you. My mother is dying and she has begged me to give up Charles and lead a good life. I only want him near me till this is over, and then he is coming back to ask your forgiveness like I do. I cannot sign my real name because of the disgrace I have brought on a respectable family, so I will sign it
                                         ONE WHO TRULY REPENTS.

He was well satisfied with this; it seemed to him in exactly the right tone; he believed it would keep Hilda quiet for a time. Her conscience would impel her to wait for Patrell to return before she started proceedings.

But he would also have to keep that girl quiet. Blanche, her name was; he had looked over her shoulder when she registered.

"I wish she was dead," he thought, and it did not seem to him an evil wish. "No future ahead for a hussy like that. Nothing but shame and misery. When Patrell doesn't come back, she'll look for another man."

Another man, he thought, would come and live with her in another untidy room filled with strange, disturbing perfume.... The girl was a disgusting slattern. But her skin was white as milk.... He got up and paced the library, very angry.

He intended to copy the letter on cheap paper, in a disguised hand, and post it in New York to-morrow. To-morrow Hilda would go to Mrs. Hawkes's and learn about Patrell's infidelity, and the next day she would get this letter. It seemed to him that he could do nothing more at the moment.

It was time to dress for dinner; he heard Eva run up the stairs, with a swift rush, like a child. And his heart melted toward her. He had always been very fond of Eva, but he had not realized how powerful was the bond which united him with this one human creature who depended entirely upon him. He was not certain of Hilda's feeling toward him, but no matter how much she might care for him, she did not need him. She was self-sufficing; she had her own money, her own life, her secure place in the world, her child. Eva had only himself.

As he left the library he almost collided with the housemaid hurrying down the hall.

"Excuse me, sir, but there's someone asking to see you."

"Who?"

"He didn't give any name, sir. He's waiting outside—"

"You know perfectly well that I won't see people like that. Send him away."

"Yes, sir. He said please to tell you, sir, that he did a little job for you yesterday, and could he speak to you about that."

Branscombe felt the blood drain from his face; he moved away, so that the girl should not notice.

"I'll—see him..." he said.

He knew who it was. There, standing on the path, was Jerry. Branscombe went down the veranda steps and approached him, and Jerry touched his cap.

"I thought maybe you'd give me a job, mister," he said, respectfully.

"No," said Branscombe. "I have no jobs to give anyone."

"I'm a good chauffeur, mister."

"No. I don't need a chauffeur."

"Listen, mister! That money you give me yesterday is all gone. I been out of work so long, I owed the whole of it, and more. I haven't had a meal to-day, mister."

When he looked at this scarecrow of a fellow, Branscombe felt a hatred so violent that it made him sick. He had never known hatred until he met Patrell; had never experienced any strong emotions; and now it seemed to him that he was being continually shaken by these internal storms. He hated this fellow, he hated Blanche, he still hated Patrell.

"I haven't got a cent, mister, and nothing to eat all day."

"That doesn't interest me," said Branscombe.

He wished the wretched creature would die of starvation. He could feel no fear of anyone so abject; he turned his back on him and was moving away.

"Here, now!" said Jerry, indignantly. "You can't treat me like this! Not after what I done for you."

Branscombe turned on him savagely.

"You were paid for that."

Jerry gave a hoot of laughter. Branscombe had forgotten that sound; it made him shiver.

"Now, see here!" he began, but without that heart-warming anger now; this was only bluster. "See here! I made a certain definite agreement with you, and I've fulfilled my part of it. I expect you to do likewise. I— How did you get here, anyhow?"

"I took the number of your car," said Jerry. "You must of expected *that*. You must of known you'd see me again, all right. Gimme a cigarette, mister?"

Branscombe marvelled at his own stupidity in having so easily taken it for granted that he was done with Jerry, that Jerry would be satisfied with twenty-five dollars. He marvelled that he had ever thought of Jerry as a sort of idiot, to be managed without any difficulty.

"Gimme a cigarette, mister?"

He took out his silver case and opened it. And he saw how Jerry looked at the case, and how Jerry looked at him. He understood very well what was going to happen to him. He was going to be blackmailed.

"Well..." he said, "if you've come to beg, I'll give you a few dollars."

A curious change came over Jerry. His lean body straightened, lost its scare-crow limpness; his hollow face had no longer that half-idiotic vagueness; he looked tense and alive, and horribly dangerous.

"O.K.!" he said. "If you want to hold out on me, I won't bother with you. There's someone else will pay, without no kick."

"The only way to deal with a blackmailer," thought Branscombe, "is to re-fuse from the very beginning. Never give him one penny. He won't dare to go to the police. He's too much implicated.... State's evidence...? Isn't there some arrangement by which a criminal can secure immunity by giving im-portant evidence...? He could say that at first he believed my story of an ac-cident.... But he won't want to do that. He'd have nothing to gain. The po-lice wouldn't pay him anything. This is—only bluff. If I stand firm—"

"*She'll pay*," said Jerry.

"Who?"

"Oh, his wife," said Jerry, casually.

"What—what do you mean?" cried Branscombe.

"Patrell's wife. She hasn't got so much, but she'd pay all she could. She'd figure you done it for her sake, see? And she wouldn't want you to burn for it. She'd pay, all right."

"God damn you! If you go near her—!"

"Jeese!" said Jerry. "Now you look like a killer, all right! First, I didn't see how you'd ever have the guts to kill a guy. But now I see it."

Branscombe turned away his head. A killer.... Was that fury he had felt ris-ing in him now the same thing that he had felt in the wood...?

"What's happening to me?" he thought, in wonder and fear. "I've always been quiet and self-controlled.... It's—it must be the circumstances.... I've got to keep my head."

No doubt about that. He would have to use subtlety in dealing with Jerry. And his mind instantly responded to his need; he saw the course he must fol-low. He must confirm Jerry's idea that he was a man to be feared.

"You'd better be thankful I'm not a 'killer,'" he said, with sort of con-temptuous good humour. "Or I'd have finished you off before this."

"I'd see you didn't get no chance."

"I had a chance," said Branscombe. "I had a gun with me yesterday. I could have put a bullet through you when you came out of that barn, and no one would ever have been the wiser."

Jerry glanced at him sidelong, and Branscombe's heart leaped, with a sense of triumph new to him. He felt that, in spite of his inexperience, he was ca-pable of dealing with this fellow.

"How did you find out the—the man's name?" he asked.

"I got ways of finding out things," said Jerry. "Never mind about that. Do I get a job, or don't I?"

"You don't. If you're in need I can spare you a little cash—"

"Not good enough."

"Yes. It's good enough," said Branscombe. "You've taken me by surprise. I haven't made up my mind yet how to deal with you. I'll give you a few dollars so that I can get rid of you for a time, while I think this over. And make up my mind what to do about you."

Again Jerry gave him that uneasy sidelong glance.

"Well... O.K..." he said. "I'll give you a chance to think it over. And you'll see that you got to help me out."

"I might—see something else," said Branscombe.

He took a ten-dollar bill from his pocket, and Jerry went off with it.

"I'll be seein' you," said Jerry. "To-morrow. And I got to have money to-morrow."

"I can manage him!" thought Branscombe. "I'm equal to this situation. And to any other...."

CHAPTER X

He decided that, for the moment, he would make no definite plan about Jerry.

"Or about Blanche," he thought. "They're both all right for the present. And I'm tired."

Hilda, too, need not worry him now.

"She'll be going to see her precious husband to-morrow," he thought. "Then she'll come home and brood over the thing, trying to decide what's right."

He felt an increasing resentment against Hilda.

"In a way, she's responsible," he thought. "Morally responsible for the whole thing. She's not a fool. When I came to see her, day after day, she must have known I was—to say the least—strongly attracted to her. Yet she kept on being so encouraging. Anyone could imagine the shock it was to find out that she was a married woman. Under the influence of an emotion like that—"

He had killed Patrell because of jealousy. He had killed Patrell to protect Hilda. He had killed Patrell in self-defence. He was ready to admit any motive, any passion, except that one which he refused to remember. He *would not* believe in the blind terror and fury which had made him go on battering the creature he had, by accident, struck down. So unbearable was the truth that he could never acknowledge it.

Jerry and Blanche and Hilda would all leave him alone for a few hours, and he would use the respite for the rest he so badly needed. He would do no thinking.

"I'll drive Eva to Marlowe Beach to-morrow," he told himself. "We'll spend the day there—a swim—lunch at the hotel."

The thought of a long day in the open air with his faithful companion made him sigh with relief. For that one day he would relax, and feel safe. After all, Eva was the one person who never worried him or irritated him.

He dressed, and went into the dining-room to shake up the mild cocktails he and Eva occasionally drank before dinner. She joined him there, and he looked with a new gentleness at her pretty face, her cheerful, absent-minded smile. His one friend....

"If the weather's favourable," he said, "I thought we might drive over to Marlowe Beach to-morrow morning."

She was always so very pleased to go anywhere with him, at any time. It was incredible to see that this time she was not. Her smile became anxious; the colour rose in her cheeks.

"Well.... Could we go in the afternoon, Andy?"

"Why?"

"I told Lew Evans I'd go canoeing with him in the morning." Her eyes were fixed on her brother's face. "Andy, I'd love to go to the beach with you, only—"

"Very well!" he said, and knew he must not reproach her.

He felt stricken. As they sat at dinner together, he kept glancing at her: he remembered his father's dying words to him: "Look after Eva...." He had looked after her. He remembered what an engaging little girl she had been, and how greatly she had admired her older brother.... Never yet had she rebelled against any of his edicts; sometimes she argued, but he had always been able to convince her that he was right. He was sure that, if he made a point of her coming with him to-morrow, she would do so, but he was afraid to try.

"Perhaps I'm mistaken," he thought. "Perhaps she's not really interested in that fellow at all. And if she is, it can't be serious. She's only seen him a few times; she doesn't know anything about him. She's always been very reasonable about giving up other—undesirable acquaintances...."

"Andy!" she said suddenly. "What's the matter?"

Their eyes met. The sky was still pale, a melancholy grey; the candles on the table wavered in the breeze; it seemed to him strangely sad here, and lonely. Only Eva and himself.... And did her face look white...?

"Andy! What's the matter?" she repeated, with insistence.

"The matter? Why? Why do you ask that?" he demanded uneasily.

"You looked so queer...."

"That's not very polite," he said, with a frown. "How do I look 'queer'?"

"I don't know. I guess you really didn't. It was just the light."

"I insist upon knowing how I looked 'queer.'"

She laughed, her sweet, careless laugh.

"Oh, Andy, I don't know! It was nothing. Some shadow, or something, on your face made you look—different for a moment."

"Different in what way?"

"I don't *know!*" she said, laughing again. "Do let's drop it!"

"No," he said, stiffly. "I don't like to look 'queer.'"

"Well, you don't, any more."

"Exactly how did I look 'different'?"

He had to know. He could not afford to look "queer," or "different." What Eva noticed other people might notice, too. "A queer change in Branscombe...."

"It was just that you looked—well—brooding," she said. Then it occurred to him that he could turn this incident to good account. He was surprised by the idea which came to him so easily.

"As far as that goes," he said, "I am worried. Very much worried."

"What about, you poor lamb?"

"You," he said.

"Me? But, Andy—!"

"You have confidence in me, haven't you, Eva?"

"Oh, tons, Andy!" she assured him.

"If you could just take my word for something, Eva, and not ask for an ex-planation—"

"I could, Andy!"

"I want to ask you not to see any more of that Evans fellow."

She said nothing. And that was unbearable. She sat there, across the table from him.... People talked about reading faces, but he could read nothing in this face, so familiar to him. She did not look angry, or startled; she was just silent, as if she had not heard.

"I asked you—" he began.

"Andy, I can't—do that," she said, unsteadily.

"Why can't you?"

"Because—I like him."

This was worse than he had feared. He needed her so much just now; she could not turn away from him to a stranger.

"Eva," he said, "I'm sorry. I'm very sorry. But I shouldn't have asked you to do this, if I hadn't had good reason."

"You see, Andy, I know him better than you do. I've talked to him—quite a lot, lately.... If you did know him, you'd like him. He's the kind of person you do like. He's intelligent and he's—nice—"

"You're mistaken," said Branscombe, filled with a great fear. "You're young and inexperienced. You don't know—"

"I know about him."

Her voice was gentle as always, but there was in it a quiet resolution he had never heard there before. There was danger, serious danger, that he would lose her.

"Eva," he said, "I hate to tell you this.... But I've found out something about Evans.... Please don't ask me to tell you.... Please take my word for it that—he's not fit for you to know."

"I couldn't—take your word about that, Andy," she said, winking away the tears that had risen in her eyes.

Again inspiration came to him.

"I hate to tell you this," he said. "But I've got to. When I saw that you were—getting friendly with Evans, I made some enqueries.... Only this morning I—saw this woman he's been living with."

"Andy, I can't—"

"It's true, Eva! She calls herself his wife. I found her in a second-rate boarding-house. An untidy, disgusting room, reeking with cheap perfume and tobacco smoke.... There she was, in some sort of dressing-gown—her hair not brushed.... She admitted that she called herself his wife.... She was in debt to the landlady; she didn't know when her—lover was coming back, and he'd left her without a penny. She cried.... It was nauseating! I suppose she's pretty—in a way—but slovenly—utterly lacking in character.... I paid her rent for her."

Eva had risen; she stood with one hand on the back of her chair, her eyes fastened on her brother's face. And in her eyes he saw not anger, not defiance or incredulity, but a shocked misery. He had never before lied to her, and she believed him now. Certainly he had spoken with conviction, seeing the image of Blanche before him.

"Had he—left her, Andy?"

"She was expecting him back. She hadn't the least resentment toward him for going off and leaving her penniless.... I suppose she takes that sort of treatment for granted. A slovenly, lazy hussy.... Her fingers were stained with nicotine.... There were a lot of cheap magazines about the place.... She was still in bed when I got there, at eleven in the morning...."

"I'm—glad you paid her rent," said Eva.

"One feels more or less sorry for such women," said Branscombe. "This one—Blanche, her name was—seems quite young...."

He had been inspired; there was no doubt of that. All these details gave it reality.

"Ordinarily," he went on, "I shouldn't particularly blame Evans. When I first met him, he impressed me as a—a sensual type. And as I said, the girl's rather pretty. Easy-going, I imagine, and amiable. I'm a man of the world. Such affairs don't shock, or even interest me. But when it concerns a man with whom you're friendly... I think you'll admit that I'm a pretty good judge of character. You remember how I was the first one to spot that card sharper on the ship? I'd already formed my opinion of Evans—but after talking to this girl Blanche, I saw—other characteristics in him.... Distinctly more unpleasant."

"Excuse me if I go upstairs, Andy."

He was sorry for her. But he meant to make up to her for all this.

"And she'll get over it," he thought. "It can't amount to anything much. The fellow's practically a stranger to her."

He rose, too.

"Of course, what I've just said is absolutely confidential, Eva. Technically speaking, I had no business prying into the man's private affairs. I'm glad I did so, though.... You see, don't you, that it mustn't be mentioned—to anyone?"

"Yes. I see..." she said.

When she had gone, he went into the library and stretched himself out comfortably in his chair. He was sorry for Eva, but beneath that superficial regret he was well content. Eva wouldn't leave him. As soon as he had thought of a way to manage Jerry and Blanche, he and Eva would go away, on a long cruise. He wasn't going to lose his one ally and friend.

CHAPTER XI

He would not have been surprised if Eva had remained in her room the next day; in fact, he was a little startled to see her appear at breakfast looking just as usual, cheerful, careless, and pretty.

"She doesn't really care for the fellow," he thought.

But then another thought came to him. He himself showed no outward sign of what he had endured, and was enduring. He had killed a man—and his hand was steady when he shaved; he ate a good breakfast. He and Eva sat here together, as they had sat a hundred, a thousand times; they knew each other better, perhaps, than they knew any other human beings. Yet she had no sus-picion of his horrible secret, and it might well be that he knew as little of what was in her heart. It gave him a feeling of chill and bitter isolation. This thing that burdened him could *never* be shared. All the rest of his life he would have this loneliness....

Very well, he could stand it.

"I'm driving in to New York—on business," he said. "Anything I can do for you, Eva?"

"Oh, just bring me back a diamond necklace!" she said

He went into an obscure little stationer's in the Bronx and bought a box of cheap writing-paper; he went to one of the large hotels downtown and in the lounge he copied the letter he had composed, addressed it to Hilda, and posted it. Then he went to another hotel and had a very nice little lunch and a half-bottle of Sauterne.

His brain was working well. That letter would keep Hilda from making a search for Patrell at present. Blanche would be resigned to waiting for a few days. Eva was safe now. There were only two people who worried him seri-ously; Colton and Jerry.

"Hilda can keep Colton quiet," he thought. "If he's uneasy about Patrell's absence the letter may satisfy him."

But he wasn't sure about that. He did not know whether Hilda was likely to show the letter to Colton, or to talk to him at all about her husband. He did not know how intimate Colton and Patrell might have been, how much Colton might know about Patrell's affairs and Patrell's character. Perhaps it was entirely out of keeping with Patrell's nature to go to Montreal with Blanche; perhaps he had had important engagements that would have made it impossible for him to have gone. Perhaps Patrell's absence at this moment would be astounding—to God knew how many people.

"If enquiries are made," thought Branscombe, "if our meeting is discovered, I'll simply have to tell my story and take the chance. I'll say he took the money I gave him and went away."

How was he to explain that he had been carrying with him a sum of money sufficient to satisfy Patrell? An investigation would disclose the fact that he had not drawn any considerable amount from the bank for days.

"I'll say I gave him a post-dated cheque. On condition that he left the country.... That's not a good explanation, though. He'd have trouble in cashing my personal cheque in some place where I wasn't known.... But it's the best I can do...."

He might, with luck and skill, keep Colton quiet. But Jerry would never be satisfied. He could not be bought off, for no matter what he was given he would come back for more.

"I'll have to make some temporary arrangement with him," he thought, "until I think of a plan, or until something happens. Plenty of things could happen to him. He's a criminal type. He might be sent to prison. He might be 'shot by one of his—associates. I wish to God he would be! If I'd lived four hundred years ago, in Cellini's day, the problem would have been simple— I'd have paid some bravo to get rid of him. I'd do that now, if I could. I'd have no scruples whatever about doing away with a rat like that."

It was odd, he thought, that a man of his position in the world should have such ideas.

"By temperament," he thought, "I belong to the Renaissance, not to the present."

A man of strong passions, of daring, of subtlety.... A man who combined within himself a love of the arts, scholarship, and a capacity for swift, ruthless action.... There was a mirror in the wall of the restaurant; he saw his own face there, and found in it something secret and dangerous, and he was reassured.

When he drove home after lunch he experimented a little. He drove faster than was his habit, much faster; he did not show his usual formal courtesy to other drivers. It exhilarated him. Reaching his own place, he turned sharply into the drive, swept past a man who was loitering there.

He knew who that man was, although he was so greatly changed. He wore a light grey suit, which made him look less slight; he was erect; he was no scarecrow now. There was a sort of swagger about him; with his olive skin, his sleek black hair, his narrow eyes, he was handsome in his own vicious fashion. He came toward the house, and Branscombe stood there waiting for him. These new clothes had been bought with Branscombe's money; the fellow's swagger was based upon Branscombe's helplessness....

"You can't hang around here!" he said. "Get out!" And in his anger forgot for a moment that he must be careful.

"Oke, I'll hang around somewhere else," said Jerry.

Again and again Jerry would come back. No end to this....

"Just came in my head I'd ask was there anything I could do for you," Jerry went on. "And I thought it would suit you better for me to hang around than if I was to go up to the house and ring the bell. Anyways, I forgot to bring my calling cards."

He laughed, and it was the same shrill hoot.

"Stop that!" commanded Branscombe.

"Stop what? Laughing? Can't a guy even laugh if something strikes him funny?"

"You've got a laugh like a hyena," said Branscombe. "Don't you realize that anyone who heard you or saw you with me would know there was something wrong? Would know that I couldn't possibly have any legitimate business with a cheap little cur like you?"

It was a horrible thing that Jerry showed no resentment; it was as if Branscombe's contempt and hatred were utterly negligible.

"That's all right about me being a hyena," he said, unruffled. "Maybe you got reasons for not being glad to see me. But let me tell you I met dames as high-hat as you—real society girls and all, and they didn't think I was no hyena. You'd be surprised! I got them hypnotized."

Branscombe stared at him, the shadow of an idea, still formless, rising in his mind.

"So the girls like you?" he said slowly.

"Do they like me!" said Jerry.

"If that's the case..." said Branscombe, "there may be a little job you can do for me...."

Jerry was silent; he asked no questions, only waited.

"I'll let you know later," said Branscombe. "Now clear out! I don't want the whole neighbourhood talking."

"Got a ten-spot to spare, mister?"

"No!" said Branscombe. He had to make some sort of stand against the fellow. He couldn't simply hand him whatever he wanted. "I gave you money yesterday."

"And you'll gimme more to-day. I got to have it."

"Has it occurred to you," asked Branscombe, "that if you drive me too far, you'll get nothing?"

"Why, I haven't even started yet," said Jerry. And suddenly his narrow face was so evil, so fierce that Branscombe recoiled. He gave him the money. He had to yield. He would never be able to refuse the fellow, would never be free from him and his demands. Never.

He turned away and entered the house. When the house-maid spoke to him he could have shouted at her. He wanted to be let alone....

"Well?" he said.

"Mrs. Patrell telephoned, sir. She asked would you come over to tea at four, sir. She said never mind about letting her know, sir, but if you'd just come...."

He looked at the girl with a frown that disconcerted her. He didn't want to go to Hilda's—and talk.

"But if I don't go," he thought, "I'll have to ring her up and explain. I'll have to go sooner or later, anyhow. It may as well be now."

He changed into another suit; he saw that he looked neat, correct, a little forbidding; and he thought that perhaps an aloof attitude would be as good as another. He had every right to be aloof, unhappy, honourably restrained. It would at least avert the possibility of an emotional scene, and that was what he dreaded most. For there was no sentiment in him now, no tenderness, nothing but a miserable preoccupation with his monstrous problems.

Her drawing-room had once been a haven of peace to him; he entered it this afternoon in a mood of fatigued annoyance. And Colton was there.

Branscombe had not expected this; he was greatly affronted; he greeted Hilda with stiff formality, and Colton only with a nod. There was, in the atmosphere, the same constraint that had marked their former meeting.

"Captain Colton has found such a nice little cottage..." said Hilda.

Neither of the men said anything, and Hilda seemed to find conversation very difficult. The house-maid brought in tea; she asked the necessary questions about lemon or cream and sugar; there were long pauses....

"What the devil did she ask me here for—with this fellow?" thought Branscombe. "If she can't even be civil...."

Then an idea came to him which turned him cold. Suppose she were angry at him?... She had said she was going to see Patrell this morning. Suppose she had gone to Mrs. Hawkes's, and had—found out something? He could imagine plenty of things she might have found out. That hussy might have gone back there; Hilda might have seen her, talked to her. If Hilda had got a description of "Mr. Brown," she might put two and two together. She might remember how Branscombe had asked for Patrell's address. She might be waiting for Colton to go, so that she could turn upon Branscombe, reproach him, accuse him....

"I won't stand it!" he thought. "I'll deny everything! She can't prove that I was Brown. She has no right to reproach me, anyhow—no claim on me—"

Colton rose.

"Well..." he said, with a sort of vague amiability. "I'll be getting along. Sorry I didn't see Coralie.... Better luck next time, I hope.... Good-bye!"

"Good-bye!" said Hilda and Branscombe in chorus.

The door closed after him and still Hilda did not smile or speak. It was intolerable.

"You asked me to come—?" said Branscombe.

"I didn't know Vincent was coming.... I thought it would be nice—to have a little chat with you."

"She doesn't know how to have a 'nice little chat,'" thought Branscombe,

annoyed. "She's altogether too naive for a woman her age.... She makes it obvious that something's upset her. No poise."

"I—went this morning to see Charles..." she said.

"Yes...."

"I told you why I was going," she went on. "To talk to him about Coralie....
To make—a definite arrangement.... But he's gone to Montreal."

"I see!" said Branscombe. But he couldn't "see" anything at all; he could not
tell from her face or her tone whether Mrs. Hawkes had mentioned Blanche
to her or not. Perhaps she knew, and pride kept her silent. He had to know
what she intended to do, though.

"So you'll wait, I suppose..." he said. "You'll take no steps until he comes
back?"

"I don't know," she answered. "There are circumstances that—I'd rather
not talk about, Andrew. But they've made me decide that there's no use in
trying to talk to Charles."

"I thought all the time that it was a mistake."

"I know.... I realize that now."

"What will you do, then?"

"Nothing, just now," she answered. "I don't want to make any plans, or
even to think about it for a little while. It was—very upsetting.... And then
for Vincent to come.... Of course, I know very well what's in his mind."

"What is?"

"He'd never change. He's still hoping to reconcile us, I'm sure. And when
I think that, being such a close friend of Charles's, he must know about
these—these circumstances, and still he wants me to overlook everything....
I can't help resenting it."

"Quite properly so."

"No," she said. "I shouldn't. Vincent is absolutely honourable. Only, his
behaviour seems so—*strange*. Coming here, all of a sudden, after all these
years.... And not saying anything, not even mentioning Charles's name...."

Strange...? So strange that it sent a chill along Branscombe's spine.

"I'm sorry I've been so stupid," she said. "Everything's been so upsetting...." She smiled; she wanted to atone now, to be friendly and cheerful with
him. But he pretended he had to hurry home, to take a telephone call that was
coming from Chicago; he invented a great many details about it.

What he really wanted was to be alone, and to think about the "strange-
ness" of Patrell's friend, Captain Colton.

CHAPTER XII

He was in a hurry to get home to lock himself into the library and think about Colton. And, to his surprise, he found that he was also in a hurry for a drink.

"I've never been a drinking man," he thought. "But then, I've never been so worried."

Directly upon entering the house he went to the dining-room and poured himself a whisky. It comforted him at once; he felt steadier. He was pouring himself another when the house-maid spoke to him from the doorway; he was startled, he was ashamed and angry that she should see him drinking in this hurried, stealthy way.

What is it?" he demanded, sharply.

"Excuse me, sir, but Mr. Evans is here to see you."

If it had been possible, Branscombe would have run away. It seemed to him that he *could not* face Evans. But he had to face him—and everyone and everything else.

"Show him into the library," he said, and when the girl had gone he swallowed his second drink.

"May be nothing but an ordinary call," he said to himself. But he did not believe it. And as soon as he saw the young man, he knew it was going to be bad. Evans stood in the centre of the room; his dark face was ominous; he did not smile; he gave no greeting.

"I'd like to speak to you, Branscombe."

"Very well, I'm here."

"It's about your sister. Something's happened. She won't explain—but something's happened to turn her against me. This morning on the beach she avoided me. I telephoned to her this afternoon to ask when I could see her. And she said—she expected to be very busy, and couldn't make any engagements."

"Yes?" said Branscombe. "Is that all?"

"She wasn't like that yesterday."

"That's too bad," said Branscombe coolly. "But I don't quite see what you expect me to do. Have you never heard of a girl changing her mind?"

"She's not that sort of girl."

"And—" Branscombe went on, more and more openly hostile, "it's never occurred to you that perhaps she simply doesn't like you?"

"Yes," said Evans. "That's occurred to me. But in that case she wouldn't behave like this. She wouldn't be friendly with me one day, and then drop me without any sort of explanation. She's—not like that."

"Perhaps you've been making rather a nuisance of yourself," said Branscombe.

It had come into his head that the way to handle this fellow was to provoke him, humiliate him, make him behave with a violence that would dismay Eva. But Evans had a remarkable—and alarming—self-control.

"No," he said, "I haven't. I wasn't—troublesome to her, and she didn't dislike me. Until to-day. Something's happened. And it's pretty obvious what it is. Someone's been lying to her about me."

"She couldn't have had much confidence in you, if she'd believe the first thing—"

"There's only one person she'd believe," said Evans.

Their eyes met. And Branscombe saw that he had made a mistake. In his supremely difficult position, he had made an enemy for himself, and a dangerous enemy. He decided to change his tactics, but not too obviously, too suddenly.

"Do you mean me, Evans?" he asked.

"Yes," said Evans.

"I suppose I ought to feel insulted," said Branscombe, lighting a cigarette. "And I can't say I'm not seriously annoyed at your implication. But I'm making allowances for you. A man in your emotional condition is never reasonable."

"I'm reasonable," said Evans. And, unfortunately, he was.

"No," said Branscombe. "Later, when you've come to your senses, you'll see how preposterous it was for you to come here and accuse me of God knows what, simply because a young girl has changed her mind. Or you imagine she's changed her mind. It's very likely that she never meant to encourage you."

"I think," said Evans, "that I'll say what I meant to say. Of course, as soon as I saw you, I knew you were a stuffed shirt—"

"Look here!"

"I'm looking," said Evans. "I saw, in the beginning, what you were doing to Eva. Ruining her life. Keeping her shut away from the world, no friends, no amusements—everything arranged to suit *you*. Everything *your* way. Naturally you don't want to lose her. You'll never find anyone else on earth who'd be so patient and so unexacting. But you're going to lose her."

"You're raving!" said Branscombe contemptuously. "Are you trying to pretend that Eva's a prisoner—that she's ill-used?"

"Her life's being wasted," said Evans. "And that's about the worst thing that can be done to anyone. She was beginning to like me, and that's not going to be stopped by you. You've said something to her that turned her against me. Either you'll unsay it, or I'll show you up to her some day, Branscombe. Take my word for that."

"What are you talking about?"

"You're more than just the ordinary stuffed shirt," said Evans. "More than a fool. You're dangerous."

"Dangerous, eh?"

"It's written in your face," said Evans.

It seemed to Branscombe that in the other's black eyes there was a strange and terrible knowledge; it was as if Evans looked into his spirit....

"What—are you going to accuse me of to my sister?" he asked.

"I don't know yet," said Evans. "But I'm going to find out."

"Get out!" said Branscombe.

Evans turned on his heel and walked off, without another word. And Branscombe stumbled into a chair behind his desk, sat there, staring at nothing.

He did not see how he could have handled Evans in any better fashion. All he could do was to get the fellow out of the house. Certainly he could not have argued with him. He had had to pretend that the charges against him were preposterous, and he must keep to that course, as long as he could.

As long as he could. But he had seen in Evans a passionate determination that was not to be deflected.

"He wants to take Eva away from me," he thought. "If he does.... That's one thing I couldn't stand."

He heard Eva's light, quick step in the hall, and he groaned to himself. No one would let him *alone*. He had no peace, no time for thinking, for the vitally necessary planning. He would have to face Eva now, without a moment's respite.

She stood in the doorway; as he raised his eyes to her face he was too dejected to attempt a smile.

"Andy—" she said. "Lew Evans came to see you...?"

He felt like an exhausted swimmer, trying again and again to reach the shore, and again and again flung back into the maelstrom. He couldn't answer. But she repeated her question and, with an immense effort, he selected an attitude.

"Yes," he said. "It was—very unpleasant. If you don't mind, Eva, I'd rather not talk about it."

"I'd like to know, Andy."

"He came here to accuse me of making trouble between you and him. He said that you had changed your manner toward him, and that he was certain I was responsible for this." He paused a moment. "Then, of course, I was obliged to tell him what I'd found out—about that woman. I'd—rather not go on, Eva."

"I'm afraid I'll have to know, Andy."

"He threatened to retaliate. He said he'd tell you something about me that would destroy any influence I may have with you. I didn't even ask him what the story was that he was going to tell you about me.... I tried to make allowances for him—but I did warn him that if he goes spreading scandal about me—"

"He's not like that."

"I wish you could have heard him this afternoon. You'd have got a new light on his disposition."

"Well..." she said, and tried to speak casually, but tears filled her eyes, and her lip trembled. "Well, anyhow, I'm sure he wouldn't really try to tell me any sort of lie about you."

"I hope he won't. I don't mind telling you that I lost my temper when he said that. I told him to go ahead, and be damned."

"He—probably didn't mean it. Dinner's ready, Andy."

She was taking the thing remarkably well, he thought; he admired her courage, and still more did he admire her loyalty to himself.

"Now if he tries to—talk against me," he thought, "she simply won't listen."

After dinner he and Eva sat on the veranda in the summer dark, smoking, talking very little. He thought of the extraordinary, the utterly unforeseen complications of this affair, and of the resourcefulness with which he had met them.

"There are elements in my nature which I never suspected..." he thought. "I might have done so much.... But I've wasted my life until now...."

A great hunger and thirst for life, vigorous, exciting life, filled him. He intended to waste no more time.

CHAPTER XIII

Having gone to bed early, Blanche waked early. She lay quiet for a time, looking about her at the neat, comfortable little room, then, with considerable hesitation, she lifted the telephone receiver.

"Well.... What time is breakfast, please?" she asked.

"Do you wish it served in your room, madam?" asked a polite voice.

That had not occurred to her, but she did wish it served in her room, and she enjoyed that meal very greatly. She felt so luxurious, sitting up in bed, with a little table beside her; she lit a cigarette when she had poured out her second cup of coffee, and she thought how different this was from Mrs. Hawkes's. She and Charlie had used to make their own coffee there, and Hawkes used to smell it and make a row, because cooking wasn't allowed in the rooms.

"Still, it was fun," she thought. "I miss Charlie a terrible lot.... I'd rather be back there with him than here without him."

She got up to fetch an ash-tray. Cigarette ashes made dish-washing harder.

"I hope Charlie'll come to-day," she thought. "I wish he'd of told me he was going away, so I could've said good-bye."

It made her unhappy to think that she had parted from him without any special word or caress, just a kiss and a careless, "I'll be seeing you."

"If I'd known he was in any kind of trouble," she thought, "I'd of said something—more loving...."

She did not know what to do with herself. She felt a profound gratitude to Charlie for sending her to this nice place, and she wanted to be a credit to him. She dressed hours earlier than usual and went down into the lounge, sat there, very neat, quiet, secretly uneasy. Two old ladies were there, and a young man reading a newspaper; she wondered if they thought she was "queer." She was afraid one of the old ladies might ask her questions....

By noon she was thoroughly bored and melancholy; she ate her solitary lunch and thought of her one recreation, the movies. She had enough money to go to a cheap one, but would it be all right?

"Maybe I'd ought to say something to the man at the desk," she thought, and in the end she did so. "I'm just going out to a show," she told the clerk. "In case anybody asks for me."

She saw a picture that made her cry; when she returned to the hotel she was thoroughly depressed, and even the good dinner she had could not console her.

"I feel like something's happened to Charlie," she thought. "I don't care what people say, I believe there's a lot in things like that. In feelings, and dreams.... If anything happened to Charlie, wouldn't it be natural for me to kind of feel it, when I care for him such a lot?"

She bought another magazine, but it did not hold her interest. She lay in bed and thought about Charlie.

"It must be true about his being in trouble," she thought. "I know he wouldn't take up with another girl, and I know he wouldn't just walk out on me. Anyways, look at all the money he must of left with Mr. Brown, for me to stay here."

She thought about Mr. Brown, but without interest.

"He's a funny kind of a fellow."

That was all. It was Charlie who filled her mind.

She breakfasted in bed again the next morning, and went downstairs early, to ask for letters. And when there were none, a sudden impulse came to her.

"How do I know that Mr. Brown was all right?" she thought. "I didn't like him.... Maybe it's all some kind of a plot, or something. I mean, maybe he just wanted to get me away from Charlie, and Charlie'd come back to Hawkes's and not find me."

The idea terrified her. She knew so well how slight a thing was the bond between them. She loved Patrell, she trusted him blindly, yet he was a stranger to her. She knew nothing about his family, his business, his past life; if he did not come back to her there was no possible way in which she could reach him. It was as if he had appeared from nowhere, had taken her hand, and led her off to Mrs. Hawkes's. If he vanished now, what could she do?

"It could be a plot!" she cried to herself in a panic.

For her it was not at all necessary to be logical. She did not even try to imagine why there should be a "plot" to separate her from Patrell. She loved him, and she was afraid, and she did what came into her head. She took the subway uptown and went to a tea-room where she had often lunched. There was a waitress there with whom she was friendly, an English girl named Queenie.

"Listen, Queenie!" she said. "When you go off to-night, will you stop at Mrs. Hawkes's, and ask is there any mail or any message or anything for me or Charlie? I've left there and I'm afraid things maybe have gone wrong.... Maybe Charlie'll be there himself. If he is, see him, will you, and tell him I'll be waiting in the corner drug-store."

"Rightie-oh!" said Queenie.

"I'll be waiting in the drug-store for you, anyways—to see if there's any letters. And maybe Charlie'll come with you."

She returned to the hotel, and now she was hopeful; now she felt certain that Queenie would find Charlie at Mrs. Hawkes's, and that in a few hours she would see him. How interested he would be in the strange story of Mr. Brown!

"It's funny, too, in a way," she thought. "Charlie's often been away longer than this, and I never felt so bad. I never felt worried, like this."

Queenie left the tea-room at seven; allow her fifteen minutes to get to Mrs. Hawkes's, ten minutes there, and ten to reach the drug-store.

"No use to get to the drug-store till around half-past seven," thought Blanche.

But she was there before seven.

"Waiting for Queenie," she told the soda-clerk.

He was a nice boy; she liked him. Whenever he was at leisure; he came and chatted with her, and she was glad, for with every passing moment she grew more and more nervous. If only, only she could see Charlie come walking in at the door....

But Queenie came alone, Queenie with her curly, coppery hair, her fair skin, her little knitted hat and silk coat that were at the same time saucy and completely lacking in style.

"There was just one letter for him, dearie," she said. "Nothing for you, and Hawkes said he hadn't been in. You'd better be looking out for another boy."

"Charlie's all right," said Blanche.

"All men are alike," said Queenie.

Blanche did not believe that Charlie was like other men. She took the letter that had come addressed to him and went back to the hotel, cruelly disappointed at not having seen him.

"Well, of course, maybe what that Mr. Brown said was true," she thought. "Maybe he really did have to go away, and he'll write to me when it's safe."

She examined the envelope. It was nice paper, she noticed, and nice, clear handwriting. It looked like a woman's writing.... There was a suburban post-mark on it....

"It could be his sister, or someone," she thought. "I don't know if he's got a sister.... Well, suppose it is from some other girl? He must of known plenty of other girls before he met me. That's nothing."

She wanted to know what was in the letter. Not because she was jealous, or suspicious, but because she was lonely and uneasy, and so greatly wanted some sort of contact with his life.

"I'll say I thought the envelope said 'missis,'" she decided.

She had no ethical scruples about opening the letter, no sense of disloyalty to Patrell. She thought that even if he were to know that she had read his letter, he wouldn't mind much, if she didn't make a row. She tore open the envelope, and the first words gave her a shock.

"Dear Daddy—"

"Oh, my Lord!" she cried to herself. "I didn't ever imagine—"

She went on reading.

DEAR DADDY:

I thought I would see you yesterday in the woods, but as I did not, I thought I would write you a few lines. I wish you would not mind if I told Mother about seeing you. I think if I could talk to her and explain things, she would see you herself and everything would be arranged. There are reasons which I can not explain but I think you ought to see her *right away*, or else it may be too late. If you will just drop me a line and say you do not mind if I tell her I have seen you, I think I can easily persuade her to have a talk with you and everything will then come out all right.

The weather is very pleasant and the garden looks lovely.

Hoping to hear from you soon,

Your loving daughter

CORALIE.

In dismay, in confusion, Blanche studied this letter from another world. Charlie had a wife and a child, and they wanted him back. She would never have dreamed of disputing their right to him; she never thought that she had any claim on him. Only, she loved him. And, in her vague, aimless life she had nothing else but him.

What she did was the classic thing for a girl in her situation to do. She did it on impulse, as usual. She wanted to see Charlie's home. She hoped she might catch a glimpse of Charlie's wife, to see if she was pretty.

She had no thought of making trouble for him; she was without malice. She copied out the address on Coralie's letter with a heart like lead.

CHAPTER XIV

Branscombe waked in the morning feeling wonderfully well and alert. He lay in bed for a time, thinking of the complications he must confront, but he was certain he could meet any situation that might develop.

"And that's the only way," he thought. "No use trying to take too long a view in a case like this. I'll deal with things—as they arise. I've managed pretty well so far. In the beginning, though— No, in the beginning I didn't do so well."

He thought how much better he could do now, with his new self-assurance and resourcefulness.

"My great mistake," he thought, "just about my only mistake, was in having anything to do with Jerry. If I'd simply knocked him down and driven on, he wouldn't have made serious trouble for me. In the first place, I don't think he'd have dared to go to the police. And if he had, I'd simply have denied his story that there was—anything in the car. Dam' dirty blackmailer! I wish to God I'd run the car over him and killed him the first time I ever set eyes on him!"

Death, he thought, was the only satisfactory solution for problems such as his. He wished Jerry dead, and Blanche, and Evans, and Colton. But, of course, they were not going to die, and he would have to go on managing them indefinitely. Very well! He could do it.

He found Eva in the dining-room, and she was agreeably matter-of-fact. The sun shone, the room was tranquil and gay; it was as if nothing had happened.

"What about a swim this morning?" Eva suggested. "The tide will be just right at ten."

It was more than likely that Evans would be on the beach, and Branscombe was by no means anxious to see him. "I'd like to, Eva," he said, "but I want to go over and see Mrs. Patrell this morning."

That was not strictly true. He felt curiously little desire to see Hilda Patrell, but he thought it would seem odd if he discontinued his usual visits, above all now, when she was troubled and unhappy.

"She'll get that letter this morning," he thought. "It will upset her."

He was very tired of her being upset. What had first drawn him to her had been her quietness, the feeling of friendly ease she had given him. And all that was gone now.

"If she talks about that letter," he thought, "and about Patrell—"

Well, if she did, he would have to listen, and to be sympathetic. He decided to walk the two miles, and taking his hat, he set off at a leisurely pace. He was in no hurry....

His house stood in a small private park, with other select summer residences; outside this park was a flat, dusty road that led to the village. He had no sooner stepped out of the park than he met Captain Colton coming toward him.

"Morning!" said Colton, without the faintest expression in his voice or in his sunburned face.

"Good-morning!" Branscombe answered, and would have gone on, only that Colton stood in his way.

"I was going to drop in and see you.... Bit early in the day—but—well..."

From the beginning Branscombe had distrusted this man; he felt a hostility toward him which he knew he must disguise.

"Anything particular you wanted to see me about?" he asked, as amiably as he could.

"Oh... just a chat..." said Colton. "If you're going to the village, I'll walk along with you. Nice place, here, isn't it?"

In spite of his limp, he was an excellent walker; he kept easily at Branscombe's side.

"Your people come from somewhere up the Hudson, don't they?" he asked.

"Yes," Branscombe answered.

"Know the Gedneys, in Poughkeepsie?"

"I know—of them," said Branscombe, more and more annoyed and uneasy.

"Bill Gedney was pretty hard hit when the market crashed," said Colton. "But who wasn't?"

This, thought Branscombe, was a most obvious and childish attempt to pump him.

"Patrell said he'd been making enquiries about me," he thought. "Was this fellow in it with him? A scheme to get money out of me, because I was—interested in Hilda? But in that case.... Does Colton know—what happened to Patrell? Is he playing a lone hand, or does he think that Patrell is—still in it?"

He glanced at Colton again, but he could read nothing in that face.

"I'm looking around for a little sailboat," Colton went on. "I told Coralie I'd teach her to sail. Extraordinary kid, don't you think?"

"Very nice..." said Branscombe.

"I mean," said Colton, "for a kid of that age.... Most trustworthy child I've ever seen."

"What do you mean by that?" thought Branscombe. And it came to him that, from now on, he must always be on his guard, always be wondering what people meant.... Had the trustworthy Coralie told this old friend of her father's about the meeting in the wood? If that were the case, Colton would have an excellent basis for blackmail....

"Hilda used to be fond of sailing," said Colton. "I'm sorry she's given it up. Sorry she lives as she does."

"I should think it was a pretty good way of living."

"Too retired," said Colton. "No—gaiety, y'know. Doesn't see enough people. Fact, as far as I can find out, *you're* about the only person she does see."

Branscombe was seriously uneasy. He was sure that Colton had not come
to see him without good reason; he was certain that Colton's words had a
meaning which eluded him.

"After all," he said, curtly, "Mrs. Patrell is entitled to live as it suits her."

"I don't like it," said Colton.

They went on in silence; they reached the village, and Branscombe hoped
that his unwelcome companion would leave him. But Colton kept at his side;
together they turned the corner of the street upon which Hilda's house stood.

"If I were sure about him—" thought Branscombe.

If he were sure that Colton were his enemy he would not keep up this difficult pretence of civility. But he was far from sure; he could not understand
the fellow at all, and he dared not antagonize him. Shoulder to shoulder they
went along the shady street; Branscombe opened the gate, and they went
through it.

Hilda came out at once; she was wearing a pale-blue linen dress that ad-
mirably set off her blonde beauty; she was cheerful this morning; there was
no sign of constraint in her manner toward Colton. That was another thing
he had to wonder about; he could not dismiss it as a feminine change of mood;
he could take nothing lightly any more.

"Has she seen him in the meantime?" he thought. "Has he talked to her...?"

Her manner was the same toward both of the men, and that angered
Branscombe; he turned away his head. And, standing in the street outside the
house, he saw Blanche. She saw him, too; they stared at each other, and he
realized she had recognized him.

At that moment something happened in his soul. For the past few days he
had been preparing for this; the seeds of it had been in him in his miserably
unhappy days at boarding-school. He did not recognize the thing for what it
was; he was aware only of an anger against the girl that was almost beyond
his control.

"She's come here—to tell Hilda..." he thought. "All right! Then I'll tell
Hilda what she is."

Horrible and astonishing words came into his head. He did not mind how
shocking they were; he felt that he would find an immense satisfaction in
shouting them aloud, in calling the girl what she was....

He turned away from her, but it was as if he could still see her. Now she
must be pushing open the gate; now she would be coming up the path, slender and slouching, in her dark dress and wide-brimmed hat. She would accuse
him, in the presence of Hilda and Colton....

Why didn't she come? Was she still standing there, staring at him? He was
forced to turn again, to see what she was doing—and she had gone. The street
was empty.

He looked at his watch and rose.

"If you'll excuse me—" he said. "There's—an errand I promised to do for Eva. I'd forgotten...."

He had interrupted Hilda in the middle of a sentence; he knew she was startled.

"I can't help it!" he thought. "Anyhow, I can set it right, later on. She'll believe anything."

He hurried down the street, and turned the corner. But there was no sign of Blanche. He could not retrace his steps, past Hilda's house again, to look for her in the other direction.

"If she goes to Hilda, I'll hear of it soon enough," he thought. "But perhaps the sight of me there frightened her off for a time."

She would return, though. She would identify him as "Mr. Brown." She would ruin everything—if she got a chance. He would not be ruined by her. He must think of some way to stop her.... He went to the station and got a taxi; he drove home in a rage that made him sick.

Jerry was waiting for him.

CHAPTER XV

He was not alarmed, or even especially disturbed, to see Jerry. He had been harried too much.

"What do you want?" he demanded.

"It's bad, this time," said Jerry, in a tone of profound regret. "I'm in a lot of trouble."

"You are?" said Branscombe. "I hate to think of you in any trouble—you damned gutter rat."

"Here! You quit that!" said Jerry, his eyes narrow and menacing.

But Branscombe was immeasurably more menacing. His handsome face, with the distinguished Branscombe nose, had the fierce insolence of Satan.

"I've had enough of this!" he said. "It's making people talk, to see a cheap little crook like you talking to me. Get out, and stay out, or by God, I'll knock you flat!"

Jerry was neither angry nor intimidated.

"After this I won't bother you so much," he said. "Only I got to have a thousand dollars to-day."

"Go to hell!"

"If that's the way you feel about it," said Jerry, patiently, "I got to get it from somebody else. I can collect from that dame. She'd sell her house or anything she's got before she'd see you burn. If you won't be reasonable—"

"I think—I shall be reasonable," said Branscombe. "Get the car out of the garage and drive me to some place where we can talk."

Jerry was very adroit in his handling of the car; he drove fast, his eyes on the road, and Branscombe's sombre eyes were on him. He was studying Jerry.

"I've got to get clear of this whole thing," he thought. "At any cost."

Jerry drove across a bridge and stopped the car in an enchanting spot on a quiet lane, beside a little brook that glittered like silver in the sun and vanished into a cool wood. There were no houses about, there was no traffic. Jerry lit a cigarette and looked at Branscombe, but Branscombe was in no hurry to begin. His idea was not yet wholly clear and definite to him, and such of it as was clear was—disquieting. He stood looking at the brook, and thinking, with a chilly aloofness. He missed the anger that had warmed him, that had made his actions impulsive, almost effortless. He was not angry now; he was regarding Jerry and Blanche as abstract problems.

"There's this," he said, at last. "You want me to be 'reasonable.' I'm prepared to be. I admit that you've got a hold over me. I admit that I've got to pay you for keeping your mouth shut. But I'm not going to keep on paying, as much as you want, whenever you choose to ask."

"Well, but how can you help it?" Jerry asked, with interest.

"I can always get away from you."

"No, you couldn't," said Jerry. "I got my eye on you all the time. I'd find you, all right."

Branscombe smiled.

"No," he said. "There's one way to be rid of you. If my life is to be made such a hell, I can always put a bullet through my head and get out."

"You wouldn't do that!" said Jerry, indignantly.

"I don't want to. But for a man like myself, death would be easier than a life like this. You want to bleed me white—"

"Say, listen! A thousand dollars isn't going to bankrupt you."

"You won't stop at that. I'll never have another day's peace. And life with this hanging over me isn't worth living."

"Listen! You give me this money to-day, and I'll clear out."

"You don't imagine I believe you, do you? No. I've been thinking this thing over. I very nearly decided last night to shoot myself."

"I got to hand it to you," said Jerry. "You couldn't of took a better line. Naturally I don't want you to shoot yourself. I'll be reasonable, too. We'll settle on a lump sum, and when I get it, I quit. See?"

"Why should I believe you?"

"Well, what *do* you want me to do? You talk about being 'reasonable.' Well, is it reasonable for me to pass up the chance of getting money in times like this?"

It seemed to Branscombe an amazing thing to hear the fellow talk like this, making no attempt to gloss over his criminal intentions, discussing them as another man might discuss his business. It had not occurred to him before that, to a criminal, crime was matter-of-fact. He was glad it was so; it made it easier for him to say what he wanted.

"I'll give you the thousand," he said, "if you'll do a job or me."

"Yeah?" said Jerry, thoughtfully. "Jobs like that are hard."

"What do you mean? Jobs like what?"

"Well," said Jerry, with a grin. "I don't guess you'd want me to rob a bank for you. I guess it's a job like—that other one."

"What other one?"

"Like that job you done for yourself."

"I suppose," said Branscombe, "that it's inevitable for you to think like that. You're not only a crook; you're a fool. You couldn't understand that a man in my position—"

"Your position don't look so hot to me," said Jerry, and that made Branscombe angry again.

"I have a certain standing in the community—" he said. "I'm not a criminal."

"You'd be surprised to hear what the cops would call what you done," said

Jerry.

Branscombe realized the necessity for controlling his temper.

"I'm not asking you to do anything—illegal for me," he said. "I simply want you to prevent a—certain person from annoying me."

"Yeah, and how do I do it?"

"That's your affair."

"That's out. You want to get me where I got you. If I do this little job, then you'll have something on me. It's a bright idea, only I don't like it."

"It's that, or nothing," said Branscombe. "You'll do what I want, and be paid for it. Or you'll get nothing. Ever."

"You wouldn't kill yourself," said Jerry. But he was obviously not at all sure about that. Branscombe had found the one threat that could disturb him.

"How do I do it?" he thought. "Where do my ideas come from? I've always led a more or less quiet life. I've never before come into contact with types like this. Yet I can manage him. I've managed Hilda, and Evans—"

But not Blanche. She, most docile of them all, had done this utterly unexpected thing, had come here, to Patrell's house. God knew what else she intended to do, what was in her mind.

"Who is it you want kep' quiet?" asked Jerry.

It was difficult to speak. When once he had spoken, it would be irrevocable.

"There's a certain person who's—molesting me," he said. "If you can induce this person to—leave the country, I'll pay you the money you want."

Jerry lit another cigarette.

"I'll indooce the bird, all right," he said.

Still Branscombe hesitated. He had to remind himself that if he were not bold and resolute now, he was lost. The girl could ruin him with a word.

"It's—a woman," he said.

"A woman?" Jerry repeated. "Well, that's harder. There's always more trouble, more in the papers and all, if it's a woman. You'll have to pay more if it's a woman."

Branscombe was not yet accustomed to the scale of prices in Jerry's line of business. A thousand dollars seemed to him little enough. But he knew better than to say so.

"I don't want to know how you manage the thing," he said. "If you can persuade this woman to let me alone.... Get her to go away...."

He glanced at Jerry; their eyes met. He knew what he was doing. He knew upon what journey he was sending Blanche. But he refused to admit the knowledge to himself. Whatever happened was Jerry's responsibility; not his. He asked only to be free from the menace of the girl's presence.

"And I got to have something in advance," said Jerry. "Five hundred now."

"I don't carry five hundred dollars in my pocket."

"You can get it. Five hundred now, and a thousand when the job is finished."

"Very well," said Branscombe.

"Now tell me where I'll find this dame," said Jerry.

Branscombe gave him Blanche's name and address.

CHAPTER XVI

Blanche cried on the train going back to the city. She cried because Charlie lived in that nice house, and because she had seen the woman who must be Charlie's wife.

"Real good-looking," she thought. "And such a lot of class...."

She had often enough wondered about Charlie; she knew he had come from some world different from her own, and she had sometimes imagined him in rather dazzling surroundings. But it was none the less a shock to see with her own eyes that tranquil old house in the shady garden, and that blonde woman on the veranda.

"He's *mean!*" she cried to herself. "Two-timing like that...."

But she could find so many excuses for Charlie. Maybe his wife wasn't nice to him. Maybe she was cold and haughty to him.

"I'm glad I didn't see the little girl," she thought. "I'd of felt worse, if I'd seen her. Somehow I never thought of him having children."

She was unhappy as she had never been in her life. She was struggling with an idea not yet clear to her.

"Did I ought to give him up?" she thought, and could not understand why she thought this. It was no great surprise to learn that he was married; she had suspected that before, and had not minded, or thought she was doing any harm.

"I guess it was *seeing* her," she thought. "It makes it kind of more real. Or maybe it was that letter from the little girl.... I won't be the one to come between him and his family. When I see him, I'll tell him so."

She meant to give him a chance to defend his conduct, though. She couldn't be really angry at Charlie.... She thought and thought about him, about his wife and his child. But she did not give any serious attention to Mr. Brown. He was a friend of Charlie's; it had seemed natural enough to see him there.

"I always felt there was something queer about him," she said to herself, and that was all.

She went to the desk and asked if there was a letter for her. Nothing.

"Well, has he just walked out on me?" she thought.

But it seemed to her cruel and wicked to think things like that about Charlie, when he had arranged all this to make her happy and comfortable.

"I'm not going to judge him till I know," she thought. "That Mr. Brown said he was in trouble. Well, people like Charlie can get in trouble as well as anyone else. Look at bankers, and all. If he'd of been going to walk out on me, he'd of just gone. He wouldn't of spent all this money to send me here."

When she was eating her lunch, she remembered that Charlie was paying for it, and a faithful tenderness filled her.

"I'm going to just wait till he explains," she decided.

It was very tedious, though. She wondered how the other women in the hotel filled their long, long days, what there could be to do. She sat in the lounge again and saw other people sitting there, apparently contented.

"Maybe you get used to it," she thought.

She saw a young man come in and approach the desk; she watched him, as she watched everyone, in her boredom. He spoke to the clerk; the clerk looked at her, and the stranger turned and approached her.

"Miss Brown?" he said. "Your brother sent me."

It took her a moment to remember that she was supposed to be Mr. Brown's sister.

"Oh...!" she said, non-committally.

"Your brother thought maybe you'd like to go out somewheres."

"With you?"

Her tone was uncompromising. No matter where she had met this fellow, she would have known better than to go out with him.

"Sure!" he said. "Why not? Mr. Brown knows about me. Moore, my name is, Jerry Moore. Ask him about me and see what he says."

"Mr. Brown is nothing in my life," said Blanche.

Jerry sat down on a chair beside her and looked at her covertly. If she knew him by intuition, he was also able to form a fairly accurate idea of her. One of those girls who give you a lot of trouble, he thought. He always avoided Blanche's type, but in this instance he couldn't; this time he had to discard his take-it-or-leave-it attitude. He resented the trouble he would have to take. He did not like Blanche. She was pretty, but her style of dressing was far too subdued; her manner was chilly and discouraging.

"Maybe she's mad at Branscombe for sending another fellow here," he thought. "You never can tell. Maybe it's not his money she's after. Maybe she likes him."

It was difficult to believe that any young and good-looking girl could care much for Branscombe, but things like that did happen.

"It's this way," he said. "I'm here in New York, and I got some money to spend, and I want a—nice young lady who will go out with me. I got a girl-friend in Chicago. Mr. Brown knows all about that. He knows I wouldn't—" He hesitated, not knowing the words to use for this girl who, he felt, would be so easily shocked and affronted. "He knows I wouldn't have any—serious ideas about you. If he hadn't of known that, he wouldn't have sent me here. He thinks such a lot of you.... Only, he knew I had this girl-friend, and he knew it was O.K. He thought we could maybe go to a movie—"

"It's not O.K. with me," said Blanche. "I don't care what Mr. Brown says. I've got a friend, and I don't care to go out with anybody else."

Stupid she might be, and irritating, but she said those words with a certain dignity that impressed Jerry. He was surprised, too. She implied that her "friend" was not Branscombe. Then was there another man involved?

"You never know where you're at, with that bird," he thought. "He didn't tell me the half of it. Just said she was staying here and calling herself his sister.... I don't see how I'll work this."

He was silent for a time, thinking. "Induce her to leave the country," Branscombe had said. But he could have managed that for himself, without calling Jerry in; he could have bribed the girl, or threatened her.

"That wasn't the idea," thought Jerry.

He had understood very well what Branscombe expected of him, and he had agreed, because he wanted the money and because he had to be careful with Branscombe. Very careful. He couldn't have Branscombe shooting himself.

"No," he had thought. "I got to make him feel confidence in me. If he thinks I'm liable to crack down on him any minute, he'll just die on me. The way he is now, if I'd of said I wouldn't do this, he wouldn't have given me a cent."

The money was not very much for a job of this sort, but Jerry had intended to take little risk. Branscombe was to be convinced that the girl had gone— permanently, but Jerry had not meant to do anything so dangerous. He had meant to introduce her to a friend of his who would "induce" her to join his theatrical touring company in Algiers. She wouldn't have been at all likely to come back from there. They never did.

"But that's out," he thought. "*She'd* never fall for Fred. I bet she don't even drink. She's dumb, all right, but it's a different kind of dumbness. I don't understand this thing.... She wouldn't ever have had the sense to shake down Branscombe. And she's not in love with him, or anything. Why would he be afraid of *her?*"

The whole thing was going to be far more difficult than he had expected.

"If I got to really bump her off," he thought, "he'll pay. He'll pay, by God! I don't like a job like this.... And lookit what he has the nerve to offer me!"

Still, it wouldn't do to go back to Branscombe and say that he had failed. Branscombe must, at all costs, believe him to be dangerous and competent.

"Of course, I *can* do it," he thought. "If I can get her out of here."

She can be found run over, on a lonely road. There would be no reason for thinking her death anything but an accident, and no way of connecting Jerry with it. If the desk clerk were able to give the police a recognizable description of him, Jerry would admit that he had come to the hotel to see the girl, and that they had walked to the corner together. No one could prove that they hadn't separated then. And for the later hours, he could provide himself with a watertight alibi. He had friends.

"But just the same, it's a risk," he thought.

He couldn't make up his mind. Sitting beside her, he thought of the problem from every point of view.

"I don't know..." he thought. "It don't look so good...."

He sighed to himself, and glanced sidelong at Blanche's profile.

"I'm disappointed," he said. "I'm lonesome, and I thought from what Mr. Brown said that you and me could go to a show or something."

"You can find somebody else, easy enough."

"It's you I want," he answered, with perfect sincerity.

"Why?" she asked, looking coldly at him.

"Well," he answered, "because you'd understand that I didn't have—serious ideas. We'd be just like a couple of friends. No monkey business. Because you got your friend, and I got that girl in Chicago. I want to see this picture—'The Passionate Princess,' and I don't want to go alone."

Blanche wanted to see that picture, too, very much. But it was too expensive. She frowned a little, thinking of the long, empty afternoon before her; she recalled Mr. Moore's words, and wondered.

"Is it true?" she thought. "Does he really want to go out just like friends? Or is it something Mr. Brown's got up, to make trouble between Charlie and me?"

She glanced at Jerry, and found him looking at her. He read the hesitation in her face, and knew he had found the right line. His personal charm would be of no avail here.

"I got to act like a gentleman," he thought. "Got to win her confidence." And aloud: "I don't want to bother you, or anything," he said. "If you don't want to come and see that picture, it's all right with me. But you wouldn't have any objections, would you, if I was to just sit here and talk to you a while?" And he added, a little anxiously: "Pardon my smoking."

She liked his saying that.

"I smoke, myself," she said, more amiably. "Only I didn't here, because the other ladies didn't seem to."

"Well, listen!" said Jerry. "I got my car here. We could take a ride round the Park, and you could have a couple of smokes before we went to the show."

She thought that over, and she could see no possible harm in it. It was broad daylight; there would be plenty of people about; if she had cause to be displeased with Mr. Moore she could get away from him at any moment. It would be nice to take a drive in the Park, to go to a show.

"Well.... All right..." she said. "I don't care if I do."

The magnificence of his roadster impressed her, as he had expected when he borrowed it from a friend who owned a garage. He drove very well, and he was courteous and always impersonal. They went to the show, and he did not try to hold her hand.

"He hasn't got Charlie's class," she thought. "You can see he hasn't got Charlie's education. But he seems to be all right."

She wasn't quite sure, though. No matter how well he behaved, she saw in Mr. Moore something that made her uneasy.

"Phony," she thought.

Still, it was better to be with him than alone in the hotel, and when he asked her to dine with him, she accepted in a tepid fashion, designed not to give him too much encouragement.

"I got to go to the hotel first," she said, "to see if there's a message for me."

"You can 'phone."

That didn't suit her. Suppose Charlie had come, she thought, suppose he was there, waiting for her?

"If it could *only* be like that!" she thought. "It seems so terrible long...."

But he was not there, and there was no message from him. She stood at the desk, staring blankly at the clerk. And suddenly she remembered that house in Westchester, that fair-haired woman she had seen on the veranda.

"Suppose I don't ever see him again?" she thought.

Her heart grew cold with desolation; she forgot the clerk, forgot Mr. Moore; her eyes filled with tears, and she turned away blindly.

"What's the matter?" asked Jerry.

"Nothing."

"Will we go out to dinner now?"

"I don't want to," she said. "I feel—sort of mis'rable."

He saw that he would have to begin all over again, and it wasn't worth it.

"Will you wait here for a minute?" he said. "I got to make a 'phone call."

He made up his mind that if Branscombe were not at home, he would postpone any further action. And that if Branscombe were not prepared to do considerably better by him, he would drop the thing altogether. He shut himself into a booth and called the number, and Branscombe was there.

"It's Jerry," he said, speaking out of the corner of his mouth. "This job you want me to do.... Well, it's a dam' sight harder than I thought. I can't do it for that money. I don't know if I can do it at all."

There was a moment's silence.

"Then you'll get nothing," said Branscombe.

"You'd be surprised!" said Jerry. "Don't you worry! You'll be seeing me soon."

"I told you how I intended to avoid—any unpleasantness," said Branscombe. "I definitely prefer that course to being continually molested."

His voice had a curt and contemptuous tone that filled Jerry with a sort of despair. He had never before met anyone like Branscombe and he could not understand him. For all he knew, his victim was quite capable of carrying out his threat, and killing himself.

"Listen!" he said. "I don't think you got cause to worry about that part, anyway."

"You don't know a dam' thing about it," said Branscombe. "Are you going to do the job, or aren't you? I want a definite answer."

"Listen! I got things lined up, only there's a lot more work than I thought. It ought to be worth three grand to you."

"No."

"I'll finish it for that. For three grand. Three thousand. That won't bankrupt you."

"In a few days you'll be asking for more."

"No. Pay me that and I go to Chicago right away. That's Gawd's truth!"

"You'll come back."

Jerry did not know how to make himself believed; he was altogether at a loss.

"Well, you got to have some confidence in me!" he cried.

Branscombe laughed.

"All right!" he said. "I'll agree to your terms. Telephone me to-morrow and I'll arrange about paying you. Don't come here again."

"You swear you'll pay me the three thousand?"

"Less the advance I've already made you," said Branscombe, and hung up the receiver.

Jerry returned to Blanche, and he had less trouble than he had expected. She was so unhappy, so entirely alone, that this stranger seemed almost like a friend. He had been patient and polite, and she had no one else. He took her to a good restaurant; he ordered lavishly. But not the way Charlie did; Charlie was always sure of himself, and Mr. Moore had a subdued sort of uneasiness about him. She couldn't stop thinking of Charlie....

"Want some champagne?" asked Mr. Moore.

"No, thanks."

"Want to take a little ride?"

"I don't care if I do," she answered.

He had not hoped for so ready an acceptance; he had thought it was going to be a long and difficult task to get her to come. But her vague fear of this man had left her now. She was used to him, able to take him for granted. And the thought of an evening alone in her hotel room was intolerable.

"It's a hot night," he said. "We could go out in the country a ways."

"All right!" she assented, listlessly.

He drove through the city as quickly as he could, and across the Queensborough Bridge he turned into dark, quiet roads.

"Now I got her where I want her," he thought. "But—now what? God! Now what...?"

CHAPTER XVII

For the first time in his twenty-three years Jerry was engaged in a moral struggle. He had, before this, been afraid, he had been doubtful, but he had never felt anything like this.

He had no liking for Blanche, nor did he feel any pity for her. He didn't care what happened to her. He knew that Branscombe would pay him if he got rid of her, and he wanted that money badly. He had no scruples about killing; he was not worried about the risk. Yet he could not do it.

"Getting soft?" he asked himself, in wonder and dismay.

If it had been a matter of robbing her, he would have killed her without a moment's hesitation. If he had been angry at her, if she had been in any way dangerous to him, it would have been easy. But he knew she had no money on her, and he could not work up any rage against her.

This was a good place, a very lonely road. She was entirely unsuspicious; all he had to do was to hold his big silk handkerchief tightly over her nose and mouth until she was quiet. Then he would put her out in the road and run the car over her.

He couldn't.

"Just doesn't seem any point to it," he thought. "Hell...!"

It occurred to him that if he were to try making love to her, and she repulsed him, he might get into a wholesome rage. But he couldn't do that, either; he was too indifferent toward her. He tried thinking of the money Branscombe would give him, but that seemed somehow remote and intangible. Jerry had peculiar ideas about money. When he could get his hands on any, he spent it at once, with swaggering lavishness, not so much because he was a fool as because he saw no use in providing for a very unlikely future. He lived like a roving man-at-arms in the Middle Ages; he would sell his services to anyone. He was not brave; he was reckless, for he had nothing to lose. When he had money he enjoyed himself; when he had none he was a mangy and starving wolf.

"We might as well be turning back," said Blanche, with a yawn.

That yawn, those commonplace words, made it worse. There was no excitement about this, no drama.

"Oh, hell!" he cried to himself. "You can't just turn around and kill someone that's sitting beside you."

But he wasn't going to lose all that money. He had had trouble enough to get her here, and he wouldn't be such a fool as to let her go.

"This is one time I got to have a few drinks," he decided. "I'll take her to Ben's. And that'd be a good thing in other ways, too."

He thought over this. As a rule, he was absolutely sober; it was dangerous not to be. But there were times when a shot of whisky helped a lot.

"I got to stop and leave a message for a friend," he said.

"Is it far? Because I want to get back."

"Coupla miles. It won't take a moment. Have a smoke?"

He felt a sort of friendliness toward her now. He stopped the car and held a match for her cigarette. When he had had some drinks, it would be all right.

"It's a nice night," he observed.

"Yes, I like the summer," said Blanche.

"The summer's all right in the country," said Jerry. "Hot in the city, though."

They were not very good at small talk; moreover, Jerry had never before tried to talk in this impersonal way to a girl. But she didn't mind long silences. She smoked in a sort of tranquility, solaced by the mild and quiet night.

He turned the car into a circular driveway before a roadhouse; Ben's Shore Dinners. The veranda was strung with coloured lights, an orchestra was playing inside; there was a forlorn sort of gaiety about the lights, the music, in this isolated place thickly set with trees. He drove the car up on the grass under the trees, at some distance from the roadhouse.

"If you'll just wait here..." he said. "I won't be a minute."

"Have you got a cigarette?"

"No. I'll bring you back some."

He had plenty in his pocket, but he did not want her to smoke just now. He didn't want anyone to notice the car at all. He went into Ben's alone; everyone would see him there, alone. He entered the main dining-room; the more people who saw him the better. Ben caught sight of him, and came across to his table.

"What are *you* doing here?" he asked.

"I just won a big pot off Louis and the boys. I feel good," said Jerry. "I'll buy me a couple of your bum whiskys."

"There's a game on, out back."

"Not for me!" said Jerry,

"Rosita's here."

"She can stay here," said Jerry. "I don't wanna see her."

He swallowed the whisky and ordered another. He was feeling better now.

"How much?" he asked Ben.

"You don't owe me nothing," said Ben. "It's on the house. Take another, Jerry."

Jerry accepted, and then rose.

"You're in a hurry," said Ben.

"I wanna get some sleep," said Jerry.

He felt all right now. He felt happy and swaggering. To-morrow he was going to have money in his pockets, and maybe he would have a party at Ben's.

Rosita wasn't so bad.

"Crazy about me, all right," he thought. "They all fall for me—except that one. Who does she think she is, anyways? I'm not good enough for her.... Is *that* so?"

He was working himself into a rage against Blanche now. When he reached the car he got in without speaking to her. "Did you bring me some cigarettes?" she asked.

"No."

"Well, can't we stop somewheres and get some?"

"I'll see if I can find one in my pocket," he said.

It was a good excuse for stopping. He drove to the spot he had in mind, a corner where two unfrequented roads met. He stopped the car and took off his coat; he pretended to look in the pockets. She sat beside him, waiting.

He flung his coat over her head. She gave a stifled scream and flung up her hands. She tore at the thing that blinded and smothered her. She clawed at Jerry's hands. She couldn't breathe.... He pressed the coat more tightly over her nose and mouth.... She gave an agonized gasp, and tried to pull away his hands.... She—couldn't breathe.... This must—be death.... All black— And no—air....

She became suddenly limp and quiet. He didn't want her to die. Death by suffocation produced very definite symptoms. She was to be found run over, and with no marks upon her of any previous violence. The police were smart about things like that, if anything aroused their suspicions. All he wanted was for her to be unconscious, or semi-conscious for a few moments. The moment he thought it safe he removed the coat.

He descended, and lifted her out. He laid her in the road—on the wrong side, so that an accident would look more natural. Her hat had fallen off, and he pulled it down on her head; he fetched her pocket book and laid it beside her. He drove along the road a little way, because he wanted to get up some speed. He had to calculate this thing carefully. You could run over a person in a way that didn't kill. And if she wasn't quite dead, she could talk.

He turned the car to go back and finish the job. And to his dismay and anger he saw that she had got up and was trying to run, staggering down the road.

"All right!" he said aloud, and drove the car after her.

She looked back over her shoulder and stumbled aside, just in time. He stopped the car and got out. He certainly had to finish this now, for his own sake. She screamed, but it was a feeble enough sound. She was among the trees by the road side. It was dark, but he could hear her panting. He would have to knock her unconscious now, and that would leave a mark. But he thought he could manage the rest of it so that an extra bruise wouldn't be noticed.

She was trying to run. She stumbled, and he was upon her.

"Charlie! *Charlie!*" she cried. "Charlie! Help me!"

Jerry stopped short. She struggled to her feet again, and grasped her arm.

"Who did you say?" he demanded.

"O God...!"

"Answer me, or I'll kill you, you—! Who's this Charlie?"

She was collapsing; he held her upright; he shook her.

"Charlie *who*?" he said.

"Charlie—Patrell..." she said. "I— Good-bye...."

He let her go, and she fell in a heap. He bent over her, felt her wrist, listened to her heart.

"Jeese...!" he said.

He lit a cigarette and went back to his car; he drove off. The glow of the whisky was all gone now; he felt cold as ice.

CHAPTER XVIII

Hilda Patrell waked very early, and lay looking out at the sky that was grey after a night of gentle rain. Her heart was heavy. She felt fatigued and listless.

"Am I doing right?" she asked herself.

All her life she had been asking herself that; even as a little girl, in this very house, she used to worry over her short-comings, used to examine her conscience; all her life she had suffered from the conflict between her ardent and impulsive heart and her stern sense of duty.

"I mustn't be over-righteous," she thought. "I mustn't deceive myself."

It was a sad thing that she and Charlie should be so irrevocably separated, the love between them so completely gone. She could not even be angry at this latest infidelity of his. She was only sorry that he should call another woman his wife, sorry that he had written that letter about Coralie, that he had proved himself so base. But her regret was almost impersonal; it was so long since she had seen him.

"If he wants a divorce, I'm willing now," she thought. "Perhaps he'll marry this poor woman. And then...? Shall I marry Andrew?"

Until he had declared himself, she had never thought of Branscombe as a lover.

"I suppose that was stupid of me. He came so often. But he was so—formal. It's hard to imagine him in love...."

She knew well enough that she was not at all in love with him, and never would be. But it was that very fact which made her consider marrying him. She had that fault of the over-conscientious; she was afraid of anything that she liked too well. Her reasons for considering Branscombe were impeccable. She respected him; he was firm and strong, she thought, a man she could trust.

"I think he's a little like Vincent," she thought.

There was no one in the world she trusted as she did Vincent Colton.

"I never can talk to him, though," she thought. "He's so obstinate and so irritating.... And I don't believe he likes me.... He's very sweet to Coralie— but Andrew is nice to her, too, in his rather stiff way. It would be the best possible thing for Coralie."

Coralie was beyond measure the most important thing in her life. If she could not honestly believe that it would benefit Coralie for her to marry Branscombe, she would let him go without a qualm.

"He could do so much for her," she thought. "I'm sure he'd be very generous."

More than once she had wanted to speak to Coralie about him, to find out, diplomatically, how the child felt. But she could not; her innate reserve checked her.

"Perhaps to-day—" she thought.

It would be a comfort to have Andrew at her side. She had been alone so long; she had been distrustful so long; it would be a balm to have a man she could trust utterly.

"Eva is a charming girl," she thought. "We'd get on well."

She sighed. There was a prospect of security and peace before her, but so much that was sorrowful and bitter for her to go through first. A divorce.... She hoped it could be arranged so that Coralie need know nothing about it. Not until she was old enough to understand a little.... She hoped that Charles would not behave badly about it, and make matters worse....

The door-bell rang, strangely loud in the sleeping house. She glanced at her watch; it was not yet six o'clock. Who could come at this hour? She got up and, putting on her dressing-gown and slippers, ran down the stairs. The lower hall was dark this rainy morning; she turned on the light before she opened the door.

A girl stood out there, and never in her life had Hilda seen so pitiable an object. Her face was white as paper and discoloured by a purple bruise on the cheekbone; she was soaked with rain, her hair clinging to her forehead under her sodden hat. And in her eyes there was some intolerable appeal.

"What's the matter?" cried Hilda.

"You're—Charlie's wife, aren't you?"

"Yes..." Hilda answered, with an effort. "Come in! You look ill."

But the girl did not stir.

"I didn't ought to of come to you..." she said.

"Come in!" Hilda repeated gently, and when the girl still did not stir, she took her cold hand and drew her inside. "You look so ill.... Will you tell me your name?"

"Blanche," said the other. She was looking about her at the drawing-room, that had an air of chilly stiffness in the grey light. A grand piano, shelves of books, flowers in vases....

"O God!" she cried, clasping her hands. "I didn't mean to ever do any harm to anyone.... But I must of done something awful—for this to happen to me!"

"Please sit down—"

"I can't. I'm sopping wet."

"It doesn't matter. Let me get you some brandy—hot coffee...."

Blanche sank into a chair.

"I didn't ought to of come here.... Only, where could I go? I don't know... I don't know.... Why would anyone want to *kill* me?"

"To kill you?"

"He came to the hotel. Moore, he said his name was.... He said Mr. Brown sent him.... He asked me to take a ride with him. I didn't like him very much, but I thought he was all right.... And all the time, when he was so polite, he must of had it in his mind—to kill me.... I can't—I can't understand it.... We didn't have any fight or anything—"

"Can't I do something for you? You're shivering."

"I'll *never* get over it! Not all my life! I went with him, to a kind of a hotel.... I waited outside.... There was music in there, and it sounded sort of sad and sweet.... He seemed all right.... If he was a lunatic, or anything, I could get over it. But he's not crazy! It gives you—such an awful feeling, to think there's anyone hates you that much."

Hilda listened, in a fog of confusion; she could make no sense of the story. But she could see how utterly unnerved and ill the girl was.

"I'm so sorry..." she said.

"First he tried to smother me.... Oh, that was—it was the way you must feel when you're dying.... When I sort of got my breath I was lying in the road, and he was in the car. He was driving—right at me.... You can't believe there's anyone really wants to kill you.... I tried to run away.... I got in some woods, but I fell down, and he caught me.... I guess he must of thought I was dead when he left me."

Tears were running down her face, slow tears, forlorn and bitter. Hilda was unbearably moved by this incomprehensible grief.

"Please come upstairs," she said. "You must get your wet clothes off. And a cup of hot coffee—"

"No, I can't! I can't! I—did you a wrong!"

"I'm afraid I don't quite understand..." said Hilda, with great effort. "Do you mean—Charles?"

"Yes."

"Are you—were you at that boarding-house?"

"Yes."

"You wrote me a note, didn't you?"

"No, I didn't! Never! I never would have made any trouble. Only this—this terrible thing happened to me—and Charlie was gone.... I didn't have *any-body*."

"Do you mean that—he left you?"

"I don't know. Only, Charlie wasn't ever mean to me, or anything. It worries me so, I'm nearly crazy. I had to come and ask you if he's all right. Because I can't help feeling it's all part of a plot.... I mean, it's all—been so queer—with Mr. Brown and Mr. Moore and all.... I wouldn't try to see him, or anything, if I can just know he's all right."

"I can't tell you... I'm so sorry... I haven't seen him or heard from him for some time."

"*You* don't know?" She gave a sound that was half sob, half gasp. "You see, this friend of Charlie's—Mr. Brown, you know—he said Charlie was in trouble. And I—" She began to weep, in a desperate, uncontrollable way. "Oh, I'm so worried!"

Most of what she said was unintelligible to Hilda. She had a confused idea that a murderous attack had been made upon the poor girl, by Heaven knew whom, and she had a very clear idea of the relation that had existed between her husband and Blanche. But taken as a whole, the thing did not make sense, and it alarmed her. She saw that the girl was on the verge of a collapse....

"Please come upstairs!" she entreated.

Blanche raised her miserable glance to Hilda's face.

"I wronged you!" she said.

Hilda was embarrassed and a little shocked; it seemed to her a dreadful thing that one human creature should show this humility toward another.

"I'm afraid you'll be ill—" she began.

"I pretended I was married to Charlie! I didn't know about you—but I did sort of guess.... I hadn't any right to come here— But I'm so worried— I'm just sick with worry about Charlie."

"You'd better worry about yourself a little. Please don't stay here like this, in your wet clothes."

"Well, don't you care? Aren't you—mad at me?"

"I'm only—so very sorry.... You've been through a horrible experience."

She tried to speak to Blanche as she would have spoken to any woman of her acquaintance, but it was not successful.

"Can't you do something about Charlie? The police would pay attention to you—"

"You haven't been to the police?"

"No, I don't want to. I don't want anyone to know about Charlie and me.... I must of lain in those woods a long time.... I finally got out to the road and some people came along in a car. They were real nice to me. I didn't tell them the truth. I just told them I'd been out with a man and he got impudent and I had a fight with him. I got them to drive me to the station, and I took a train to New York. I rang up the hotel to see if maybe there was a message from Charlie, but there wasn't. I was scared to go back to the hotel. I thought maybe Mr. Moore'd be there. And I didn't see how I could ever find Charlie again.... I went to the Grand Central and took a train out here.... I thought if I told you, you'd do something."

"I will!" Hilda assured her. "If you'll come upstairs and rest, I'll see what can be done."

Blanche rose docilely, and Hilda put her arm about her and helped her to the stairs.

"I didn't ought to bother you—only that Mr. Brown said Charlie was in trouble—"

"What sort of trouble?"

"He didn't say. I thought it was about a bank, or something."

"That doesn't seem—very likely."

"Well, you know, Charlie's got a wild streak in him."

How strange, how unbelievable, thought Hilda, that they should be talking to each other like this. How strange, and somehow how right, that this forlorn girl should have come to her.... It was as if she were in some measure responsible for her husband's misdeeds, and always would be.

"You're so weak," she said. "Do you think you can manage?"

"I'll try."

"Just a few more steps...."

"I'll try."

"That's the way! Now—!"

Blanche slid away from her supporting arm and collapsed on the floor of the landing.

CHAPTER XIX

On the floor above was Frank, the Portuguese gardener, and Rosa his wife, who was cook and house-maid; they had been with Hilda for years, and she was sure of their fidelity and affection. Yet she did not turn to them for help now; she went to Coralie.

"Coralie..." she said. "Something's happened. Can you help me?"

Coralie got up at once; her eyes were heavy with sleep, but she stood straight as an arrow in her severe white pyjamas; she was not startled; it took her only a moment to get awake. She was a child, but she was Hilda's own child; she had that quietness that Hilda valued above all things.

"A poor girl came here to see me about something. She's been in an accident. She's fainted, in the hall. I want to get her into the guest-room. Do you think we can manage it alone, Coralie?"

"Let's see," said Coralie.

She knelt beside Blanche. And to Hilda there was something pitiable in the contrast between Coralie's cool freshness and the utter weariness and exhaustion of the other. Blanche was young, too, yet she looked—finished.

"I'll get the room ready," she said.

She went into that room, that was orderly and fragrant, like every corner of her beloved house; she threw back the cover of the bed and spread a blanket over the lower sheet.

"You take her feet," said Coralie, and put her hands under Blanche's arms.

They had no difficulty in getting Blanche on to the bed; they had both the same easy and controlled strength.

"We must get her wet clothes off," said Hilda. "And then, if she hasn't come to, we'd better send for the doctor."

They were deft about the task; they got off the sodden shoes, the coat and skirt and blouse.

"Sort of cheap black underclothes with lots of lace..." said Coralie, and looked at her mother, as if asking what she should think of this girl. But in Hilda's grave eyes she could read nothing but concern for the other.

They made Blanche comfortable, in a clean nightdress, a hot-water bottle at her icy feet; Coralie was rubbing her damp hair with a towel when she opened her eyes.

"Are you feeling better?" asked Hilda.

"Yes..." Blanche answered, faintly.

"I'll bring you some hot coffee. Coralie will stay with you." Blanche sipped the coffee with a sort of weak eagerness; slow tears ran down her face.

"You're terrible good to me," she said. "You're— Would you mind if I had a cig'rette?"

"I'd be glad. Only I'm afraid there aren't any in the house."

"I got some in my bag."

Coralie got them for her out of the drenched velvet bag, and Blanche lay back on the pillows, exhausted, but quiet enough now. Hilda glanced at Coralie, who followed her out of the room.

"Coralie—I've telephoned to Mr. Branscombe."

"Why *him?*"

"But why not?" asked Hilda, surprised. "It seems to me that he's the best person—"

"Why don't you get Doctor Carew, Mother?"

"I wanted Mr. Branscombe's advice first. Perhaps she doesn't need a doctor. Only rest and care."

"He wouldn't know."

Hilda was somewhat at a loss.

"Perhaps she'd—rather not have a doctor, if it's not absolutely necessary."

"Is she a crook, or something, Mother?"

It was natural that the child should be curious. But, for all her blunt candour, she had her mother's sense of decorum, and her mother's capacity for decent reticence.

"I don't think so," said Hilda. "But it doesn't matter."

Coralie was silent for a moment.

"Wouldn't Uncle Vincent do?" she asked.

"I think Mr. Branscombe has more knowledge of the world."

"I don't," said Coralie. "And I—well, I wouldn't trust him about anything."

"But, Coralie!" cried Hilda, immeasurably startled. "I thought you liked him."

"No," said Coralie. "He's—" Her delicate brows knitted in an effort to find words for an idea not quite clear to her. "The way he drives," she said.

"I'm sure he's not reckless."

"Reckless!" Coralie repeated with scorn. "Gosh! Anything but! He's just thinking about himself and his own safety all the time. And he gets angry with people that get in his way. I don't think he'd care what happened, if it didn't hurt him. I bet you he wouldn't care if he ran over somebody, as long as it didn't get *him* in any trouble."

"I don't think it's fair to say things like that, Coralie. You can't possibly know—"

"Well, that's just the way I feel," said Coralie.

"You don't like him?"

"No. I don't like him a bit."

"I didn't know that," said Hilda.

She had grown a little pale. She knew that Coralie was looking at her, but she did not meet the child's glance.

"Don't you think that perhaps it's just—prejudice, Coralie?" she asked.

"I don't know. I *never* liked him. That first day we saw him at the beach I didn't like him. He was so sort of snobbish to the other people. And I *hated* his bathing-suit."

Now their eyes met, and in Hilda's was a sort of wonder. Coralie was a child, but Hilda had complete confidence in her integrity and loyalty. And now, for the first time, she realized that this child would soon be a woman, that even now she had something of a woman's way of thinking. She herself had not liked Branscombe's very conservative bathing-suit; it had seemed to her a little priggish for a man as young as he....

"Anyhow. I have telephoned to him," she said. "Will you stay with— Blanche, Coralie, while I dress?"

It had been instinctive to telephone to Branscombe, because of her trust in him. For Charles's sake she had not wished to send for a doctor unless it were imperative. The girl had said Charles was "in trouble," had talked incomprehensibly about a "plot." If Charles were in some serious difficulty, involved in something disgraceful, he must be shielded as well as possible, for Coralie's sake. That was obvious. But, after all, wouldn't Vincent have been the right one to summon? He was Charles's friend.

"Am I losing my judgment?" she thought. "Am I behaving like a fool?"

Her cheeks grew hot.

"I'm not a girl," she thought. "I'm a middle-aged woman. I—but have I been stupid about Andrew?"

It was hard to think that. His devotion had been so great a comfort to her, had somehow made her feel young again. She had taken it for granted that Coralie liked him.

"I know she's very intelligent, but she's only a child. I mustn't pay too much attention to what she says.... Perhaps he is a little snobbish.... But for her to say that she wouldn't trust him.... He's so honourable and straightforward...."

It occurred to her then that perhaps Coralie was jealous.

"She needn't be," thought Hilda. "No matter how much I like Andrew, he simply wouldn't count, compared to her. No one would. If it would make her unhappy for me to marry him, I'd never see him again. That's what used to make Charles so angry—my putting Coralie first. He said it wasn't natural. I never could see that.... And anyhow, whether it's 'natural' or not, that's the way I feel.... Of course, she's very young. Perhaps she'll change as she gets to know him better."

She thought again of Andrew's very conservative bathing-suit. She wanted not to think of it; it seemed unspeakably petty to let *that* matter.

"But it does!" she thought. "I really didn't like him, that first day."

She bathed and dressed, and went downstairs to wait for him on the veranda. It was a sweet summer morning; she sighed, because the world could not be happier.... The milk-wagon was going along the shady street, the trees stirred in the breeze, the sky was a pure blue. It was a scene familiar and dear to her; she could remember the long summer days of her childhood here; she could almost forget that Charles had ever been a part of her life, that she had been hurt and unhappy.

Branscombe's car was coming round the corner.

"He does drive rather slowly," she thought.

Surely that was nothing against him. Only, for a young man, he was remarkably cautious.... He got out and waved to her; his face looked anxious. But he stopped to lock the car.

"Why not?" she demanded of herself. "I'm being unreasonable to-day."

He came along the path toward her, and she looked at him with an absent smile. He was handsome, he was distinguished.... She had found him invariably sympathetic, chivalrous, admirable. And yet.... What was it about him that made his face seem like a mask? Why, in the morning sun, should he seem so unfamiliar, so strange?

"I must not let myself be affected by what Coralie said," she told herself.

Yet, looking at that tall, distinguished figure in grey, it seemed to her as if he walked in some chilly shadow, utterly alone.

CHAPTER XX

The telephone rang, and Branscombe waked with a violent start. For a moment he lay in a sweat of fear. He saw by his watch that it was not yet six. Who could ring him up at such an hour...? Jerry...? He would not listen to anything Jerry had to tell him....

The bell went on and on. It would wake Eva.... Suppose she spoke to Jerry...? He lifted the receiver and said "Hello!" in a curt, unsteady voice.

"Andrew...? I'm sorry if I've waked you. But something has happened..." said Hilda's voice.

These were words he could not ignore.

"Something's happened? What?"

"I'd rather not tell you over the telephone.... I know it's very early, but if you could come over, Andrew....?"

"At once," he said, and hung up the receiver.

He began to dress in haste, and with a nervousness that made him clumsy.

"No," he told himself. "This won't do. After all, it's probably only something about her damned child. She didn't sound much upset. It can't be anything serious. It's only the child, or Colton's done something...."

Had Colton found out about Patrell's disappearance, and told Hilda? If he had, very well. Branscombe had his explanation ready. No need to be so apprehensive. Above all, no need to feel this sickening dread of Colton. Colton was a fool, and he himself was clever. He went downstairs with the utmost caution; it would be unbearable if Eva should call out and ask him where he was going.... He was clever; he had managed to survive so many dangers. He could handle Jerry, and Evans, and Eva.... And Blanche...? No! That was Jerry's affair entirely....

"She's probably on board some ship now," he told himself. "I hope to God she is...."

If only he would never have to know.... But he would have to know; before he paid off Jerry, he would have to have some very definite proof that he would not be troubled again by Blanche.

"Those hussies always come to a bad end," he said. "And what does it *matter*...? If Jerry makes love to her, offers her money, she'll be off with him, and forget Patrell. She's utterly worthless...."

The freshness of the early morning almost startled him. It was a long time since he had been out so early; he had forgotten how beautiful and vivid the world was. He had got so wretchedly little out of life, had asked so little. He was young and vigorous; he had money; he could have everything. And he would. It was incredible to think that all he had wanted was to marry Hilda

Patrell and settle down to domestic monotony. He admired Hilda; in a way he was fond of her, but he could do better. Some exquisite and voluptuous woman, with dark, oval eyes and a ripe, subtle mouth... a Renaissance woman, loving him fiercely.... A woman capable of poisoning an enemy.... A woman who could understand the complexities of his soul....

An immense exultation filled him.... He could and he would escape from the bread-and-butter life. He would live magnificently. If he had purchased his freedom by crime, he would feel no remorse. Patrell's death had been, in a way, an accident; it had not been premeditated. But for whatever happened to Blanche he would be responsible. In his heart he did not believe she would leave the country. He believed that she was dead, and he was glad.

As he got out of the car Hilda opened the door of the house. She looked handsome, but completely unalluring. A nice woman, a good woman. But no mate for *him*. He put on a manner of grave and friendly concern.

"What is it, my dear?" he asked, holding out his hand.

She took it, but in an absent-minded way. He thought of a white, long-fingered, perfumed hand, adorned with jewels....

"It was kind of you to come," she said. "I do want your advice...."

"Something has happened?"

"Yes," she answered. "Very early this morning a girl came here. She was in the most pitiable condition—"

"A girl? A—a girl you know?"

"No. A stranger. She came because she's so desperately worried about Charles."

Branscombe looked at her, but he did not see her.

"This is the end," he said to himself.

The end of all his plans, all his intelligence, the end of his one brief moment of life. Despair was on him, and he was mortally stricken.

"She thinks Charles is in danger of some sort I can't quite understand—but evidently she's been through a horrible experience. She says someone tried to kill her.... The poor thing collapsed.... Andrew, you take it so very quietly.... You couldn't have heard about this before, could you?"

It was as if his cold and paralysed spirit groped and found, Heaven knows where, some vestige of fortitude and energy.

"No," he answered. "It's simply that the whole thing seems to me—too fantastic. This girl is probably imposing upon you."

"She hasn't asked me for anything at all, Andrew. Except to help her find Charles. She says he's disappeared. Apparently she's been living with him—"

"You can't believe anything a worthless hussy like *that* tells you...."

He saw a sort of grave wisdom in her eyes.

"I'm very sorry for her," she said. "I think she's honestly devoted to Charles. And certainly she's ill and exhausted...."

"You're so generous..." he said. "It would be only too easy to impose upon you."

"She's not imposing upon me," said Hilda briefly.

He saw that he had made a mistake, at the moment when any least mistake might destroy him; he saw that to Hilda he had appeared hard, or even bru- tal, when it was vitally necessary that she should have quite another im- pression of him.

"I suppose I'm prejudiced," he said. "But that's because of you. I don't like to think of your coming into contact with a woman of that sort."

"Somehow she doesn't seem like that," said Hilda. "She's so pathetic.... I can't quite understand her story, but it's plain that something dreadful has happened to her.... Perhaps I should have sent for the doctor at once, only.... On Coralie's account I'd hate there to be any public scandal."

"Naturally," said Branscombe. "Hilda, I think I'd better see the woman."

"She's only a girl," said Hilda, and he saw that again his tone had betrayed his savage hatred.

"I'd better see her," he went on. "Of course, if it's necessary, the police will have to be notified. But possibly you've misunderstood her."

"She's ill. It would be cruel to worry her."

"I shan't worry her. I'd simply like to learn the truth. If you'll let me see her, alone—"

"I don't think she'd like that. She's more or less used to me now."

"Let me see her alone," he urged. "This may be a very serious matter, Hilda; something that might affect Coralie's entire future. You can be sure that I'll use the utmost tact and discretion. But naturally, I'll be able to handle it bet- ter than you. A man's life brings him into contact with—with people you'd never meet."

She doubted that. She doubted if he could handle this matter better than she could. Looking at him, he seemed curiously old-fashioned and priggish, and she wished very much that she had sent for Vincent instead. But Andrew was here, and he already knew so much about her personal affairs.

"You'll be very gentle with her, won't you?" she said. "Coralie's sitting with her now."

"Coralie!" he exclaimed. "Hilda, the child's quite old enough to realize what this woman is."

"I think she does realize," said Hilda. "And I think she feels as I do. That the poor girl is very ill and very unhappy. I'll tell her to leave Blanche now."

He said no more. He stood in the hall, looking after Hilda as she mounted the stairs, and again he said to himself:

"This is the end. Blanche will talk. She'll tell about Jerry. And about me. There'll be a search made for Patrell. And the moment Jerry thinks it's to his own advantage, he'll tell the truth."

It was as if he stood within a ring of enemies, a ring that was narrowing. Blanche, Jerry—Evans, Colton, all enemies. And Hilda could become an enemy. The least suspicion of what he had done would turn her implacably against him. There was no one but Eva, no one in the whole world. Eva would never desert him.

Hilda was coming back now, and she did not smile.

"I asked her if she felt able to talk to a friend of mine, and she's more than willing.... She thinks of nothing but saving Charles from—I don't quite know what...." She was silent for a moment, her fair head bent. "Charles must have been very kind to her," she said. "I'm glad of that."

"You're 'glad' that your husband was unfaithful to you? You don't feel the least reluctance toward having a creature like that under your roof? Good God! You don't mind having your young daughter in the company of her father's mistress?"

He knew, from Hilda's face, that he ought to stop, ought to retract those words. But he could not. His fury against Blanche was uncontrollable.

"I'll be considerate toward her," he said. "I'll be diplomatic.... But women like that ought to be branded. They ought to be—"

Hilda turned away.

"It's the first door on the right," she said.

His knees were trembling, as he mounted the stairs. He had made a deplorable mistake.... He must not make another. He must keep his wits about him now. His life was at stake.

He realized that, and had to stop for a moment in a sweat of terror. His life depended upon his handling of this situation. He had been strong and resourceful before; he had met each danger as it came, and had triumphed. If he kept his head, perhaps he could triumph even now.... Only, he was growing so tired.... There was never a respite. He began to see what he could do now to save himself, but the idea formed more slowly; it was not one of those flashes of inspiration that had elated him.

The door of the room stood open; the sun was shining in; he stopped, looking at the cheerful colours, the wonderful quiet of that room.... Blanche lay back on the pillows; her hair was still damp, her face was white, with a livid bruise upon her cheek, her eyes looked hollow, dark, unspeakably weary.... And she was horrible to him. She was like the daughter of Jairus.... Dead and restored to life.... Impossible to imagine where she had been, or what things had happened to her....

He entered the room softly, closing the door behind him, and the click of the latch made her turn her listless head. She looked at him without interest.

"Are you the doctor?" she asked. "I got a fierce headache...."

"No," he said.

His voice made her frown; she stared at him with those sombre, hollow eyes.

"Are you able to talk?" he asked. "To understand me....?" She did not answer, only stared. And then she gave a hoarse outcry.

"Mrs. Patrell! O Gawd...?"

"Hush!" said Branscombe. "Do you want to ruin Charles Patrell utterly?"

"Him...?" she said.

"You've done enough harm already. I don't know if it will be possible to undo it."

"I came here to get someone to help him—"

"You couldn't have done anything worse. I've been talking to Mrs. Patrell. Apparently you've put it into her mind that there should be a search made for Patrell. Don't you realize what that will mean?"

"Aren't you...?" she began, but her voice was so unsteady that she paused a moment. "Aren't you—Mr. Brown?"

"Yes."

"Then it was *you* that sent Jerry..." she said, and began to tremble, as if in a mortal chill.

"Jerry?" he repeated. "I don't know what you mean. I didn't send anyone to you."

"He said so! He said Mr. Brown sent him."

He looked at her, shivering, exhausted, weeping, and he hated her as he had never hated before. That his life should be in danger from her....

"You're out of your mind," he said, contemptuously. "Who is this 'Jerry'?"

"No," she said. "No... I couldn't tell you.... Would you please ask Mrs. Patrell will she—come back.... I don't—feel good."

"See here!" he said. "Do you want to cause Patrell's death?"

"Death?" she repeated, in a whisper, staring at him.

"Exactly. He's in very great danger. He's hiding from the police."

"What did he do?"

"You'll have to ask him yourself. That is, if you ever see him again. He thought you'd stay in the hotel. I know that he hoped he would manage somehow to see you there. But now.... Now that you've come here, and started a search for him, you're not likely to see him again."

"Oh, what ever can I do! It was only because I was so worried and scared.... They tried to *kill* me!"

Her eyes were filled with a dreadful vision.

"They wanted to *kill* me.... And I can't understand.... I haven't any money. I haven't done any harm to anybody. I don't know why anybody'd want to kill me.... Unless it was a plot.... And with Charles gone, and me not knowing where he was.... It seemed so lonely and—awful...."

"Your reasoning isn't very clear, is it?" said Branscombe, with a faint smile. "As far as I'm able to understand, you got tired of waiting for Patrell, and you went off with some other man."

"He said *you* sent him."

"Life must be difficult," said Branscombe, "for such a trusting creature as you. Do you always believe everything that everyone tells you? Don't try to deceive me. You went out with some stranger. You had an unpleasant experience of some sort. And you've deliberately involved Patrell."

"I didn't! I didn't! I was so worried about him—"

"You may well be. Poor devil! I'm sorry for him. He was going to try to see you at that hotel, at great risk to himself. Very likely he went there last night and learned that you'd gone off with another man."

She sat up in bed. She was certainly too thin, but her neck and shoulders had lovely, delicate lines, her skin was white and soft.... His words wounded her, and he was glad.

"How can I tell Charles? Oh, please help me! How can I see Charles?"

"I don't know," he said. "I don't care. He'll communicate with me, of course, but I'm not going to add to his distress by telling him that you had the effrontery to come here—here to his wife's house. He'd rather see you dead than under the same roof with his wife and daughter."

"Well, I wish to Gawd I *was* dead!" she cried, in her anguish.

"You're not dead, though. You're alive, and making the trouble you can."

"How can I make it right again? What can I do?"

She was wringing her hands; she was trembling, ghastly pale. He was glad.

"I could help you," he said, "but I won't. You're not worth it. I'm going now. I'll warn Patrell that you've started the police on his trail."

"Let me see Charles, just once...."

As he moved toward the door she got out of bed and followed him, seized his arm.

"Give me a chance to see Charles..." she said. "I beg and *pray*...."

He looked at her.

"If I could trust you—" he said.

"You can! You can! I swear to Gawd—"

"You'll do exactly as I say?"

"I swear to Gawd I'll do exactly like you tell me."

"All right," said Branscombe, and wanted to laugh. Once again he had saved himself.

CHAPTER XXI

Hilda sat on the veranda railing, and Coralie stood beside her. They were both looking out over the lawn, with a curious similarity of expression. Branscombe, regarding them from the doorway, thought that they looked somehow as if they were on a ship, sailing for some unknown destination with matter-of-fact courage.

A dreadful grief seized him. Branscombe could never set off like that, free and calm. He was irrevocably entangled in a web; every move he made was potentially dangerous. And always would be. The crime he had committed had set in motion consequences he could not foresee, an endless chain of them. He wanted to get back, to return to his old world, where he had been free and safe. He thought if only he could undo what was done, could only get back, he would make his life a magnificent thing. He would enjoy every hour; he would be happier than any man had ever been.

But he never could. He would have to finish his days with this atrocious oppression for ever weighing upon him. And he felt a sick envy of Hilda, sitting there in the sun with her child.

"Hilda," he said, "may I have a word with you?"

They both turned, so much alike; in the child's brown eyes, in Hilda's sea-blue ones, so much the same steadfast appraisal. Hilda went with him into the drawing-room, and because danger, sharpened his senses, he was aware of a change in her. She was not hostile, but she was remote.

"I can't help it," he thought. "I have no time to worry about a woman's moods...." He hated women then, all women. "Hilda," he said, "I've been talking to that unfortunate girl. She—naturally, she talked more freely to me than she would to you."

"Why?"

"She's more accustomed to talking to men," he said, and again his secret venom coloured his tone. "She spoke very much more freely to me than she'd ever speak to you. She's ashamed of herself, and properly so, for coming here at all. And she mustn't stay here another hour."

"She's too ill to leave. And I don't feel as you do about this, Andrew. Charles and I have been separated for ten years. I never imagined he was living like a monk. I'm not shocked, I'm not distressed—except on her account."

"Obviously we have different standards," he said stiffly. "But that's not the point. On Coralie's account, you can't have a scandal."

"There needn't be a scandal if she stays quietly here until she's better."

"You don't understand the situation. The girl got into bad company last night. They'd all been drinking, and there was some sort of disgraceful brawl. The police will probably investigate. No matter how indifferent you are to public opinion, you can't want the police to find your husband's mistress here."

"I'm not going to turn her out while she's ill and wretched."

"I had no intention of suggesting your 'turning her out,'" he said, more and more stiff and frigid. "I propose to take her home with me until she's well enough to go back—to her old life."

"But, Andrew!" she exclaimed. "Think...! What about Eva?"

"Eva has a good deal of confidence in me. Eva is able to believe that I'm not only level-headed, but fairly humane."

"Andrew, I'm sorry. It's really very generous of you...." She was contrite now. Well, let her be. She had been suspicious, troublesome, hostile, and he did not forgive her. He looked at her; he saw that she was a handsome woman, but with no more charm for him. He looked at her—and he hated her.

"She's so worried about Charles, Andrew. Don't you think we'd better make enquiries?"

"Make enquiries?" he repeated. "Good God, Hilda, what are you thinking of? Can't you see what this girl is? A common—"

"Please don't!" she interrupted.

He controlled himself with an effort.

"You don't understand that type," he said. "Half of what she says is—" He wanted to say "a lie," but he dared not further antagonize Hilda. "She's hopelessly muddle-headed. Stupid and ignorant. I'll take her back with me now."

"She's terribly worried about Charles. And it is odd, Andrew. When I went to the address he'd given me, the landlady said he'd gone to Montreal—with his—'wife.'... Then I got a letter from some woman saying she'd gone away with Charles, but Blanche says she didn't write that letter."

"She did, though," said Branscombe. "She told me about that. Her brother came to tell her their mother was seriously ill. They started for the train, taking all the luggage along, but on the way they stopped at her brother's room, and then they got another message that the mother was very much better."

"But then what happened to Charles?"

"My dear girl," said Branscombe, "if I were you, I shouldn't enquire too closely into Patrell's affairs. He may simply be trying to shake off this girl. Or there may be other reasons.... After she's rested, I can talk to her. But in the meantime, there's nothing to worry about. I'll try to find out what muddle-headed ideas she has, and we'll see...." He paused a moment. "If you think that I'm likely to be brutal, at least you can have confidence, can't you, that Eva will behave with common decency?"

That finished it. With those words the nebulous relationship between himself and Hilda Patrell came to an end. They both knew it; they looked at each other, a long, clear look, without illusion.

She thanked him again for his offer, and went upstairs to find out if Blanche wanted to go with him. She found the girl sitting on the edge of the bed, pulling on her wet stockings, and at the sight of her, so frail and pretty, so strangely helpless, pity overwhelmed her.

"You mustn't do that!" she said. "I can lend you dry things—if you're *sure* you want to go with Mr. Branscombe."

"Mr. Branscombe?"

"He's just been speaking to you."

"Oh yes, thank you!" said Blanche. "I do want to go with him. But—I'll never, all my days, forget how nice and sweet you've been. I *wish* I knew how to tell you how I feel.... I wouldn't of done anything to worry you or the little girl for anything.... Only...." A sob stopped her. "Life is so kind of mixed up, isn't it?"

Hilda stood silent for a moment.

"It *is* hard to say what one wants to say.... Just please know that I'm not offended or hurt.... I'm only sorry.... If I can help you—ever...."

She went away hastily; she brought back stockings, underwear, a fresh white dress, and white shoes. She helped the girl to get ready.

"You'll let me hear from you to-morrow?" she asked. "Please ring me up...."

From the doorway she watched Blanche go along the path in the bright morning sunshine, holding Branscombe's arm. And she wanted to cry, because of her pity for the poor young creature, and because Andrew had gone, for ever. He had never really existed, that strong, quiet, upright man.

"He's petty," she thought. "He's narrow and petty—and cruel.... And I've been a fool—again."

She sat down to breakfast with Coralie, and she was beyond measure thankful for her child's quietness. No questions, no excitement.

"Uncle Vincent's coming early, Mother," she said. "He's going to take me to see a sailboat."

Hilda looked up.

"Do you like him, Coralie?"

"A *lot*," answered Coralie.

"Why?"

"Well..." said Coralie, "because he's—decent...."

It was an odd word to use, thought Hilda; it lingered in her mind. "Decent."

"Andrew isn't 'decent,'" she thought, "with that savage contempt he has for poor Blanche. And I'm afraid Charles isn't 'decent' either. But Vincent wouldn't be contemptuous, and he'd never be careless and selfish and—false.... He's irritating, but he's admirable."

Coralie was not quite ready when Colton stopped for her, and he lit a cigarette and sat on the veranda, with his air of illimitable patience. For ten years he had been patient, thought Hilda; for ten years he had kept steadfastly to his hope of reconciling Charles and herself. He must have come here now to make another attempt. It was stupid, yet it was somehow endearing. She glanced at his impassive face, and she spoke on impulse.

"Vincent... I wish you'd tell me candidly why you're here."

He was long in answering.

"I suppose—I've got to..." he said. "It's a bit hard.... You're angry at me already, and you'll be still more angry when you know.... I'm not going to stay here, Hilda. I promised Coralie I'd get her a boat and show her something about sailing it.... Doesn't do to disappoint a kid.... But old Ketcham says he'll look after her—and I'll clear out...."

"Why did you come?" she demanded. Her tone was a little imperious, but she could be imperious with him, if she chose.

"I had rather a row with Charles," he said. "He had an idea I couldn't stand... It's time I told you, but I don't enjoy the prospect.... Y'see, Hilda, Charles was—interested in a girl.... I never saw her, but from what he told me, I got the impression that she was—well, not a bad sort of girl. Pretty stupid, but faithful and affectionate.... In ordinary circumstances, I believe in minding my own business, but in this instance... I didn't like his—his ideas and I said so...."

"Vincent!" she protested. "I'm not a schoolgirl. Do please speak plainly."

"Always my difficulty," he said. "I'm not much good at talking. But—well—he said that if he were free, he'd marry this girl. I.... You may think it was disloyal of me, Hilda, but I give you my word it wasn't. It was you I was thinking of. In the beginning, as you know, I was always hoping to see you and Charles together again. But—not lately. Charles has changed. I mean to say—he has fine qualities. But—"

"I understand Charles," she said, a little sorrowfully. "You needn't defend him to me. But I wish you'd be more definite."

"Yes... I'm getting to it, Hilda, in a dam' clumsy way.... Charles said he wanted to marry this girl. Said that what he needed was a wife who'd never—well—never criticize him. I couldn't see anything against that. I couldn't believe that you'd ever be happy with Charles again. I advised him to tell you the truth. I told him I was sure you'd let him go—give him a divorce. But he had this idea.... He sent this fellow he knew out here, to pick up gossip. About you. So that's what I couldn't stand.... The fellow he sent came back with a tale—"

"What tale, Vincent?"

He looked up at her, with misery in his grey eyes.

"About you—and this Branscombe chap. Of course, I know there's nothing in it—but Charles... he.... Well, he's changed.... He... I don't believe he'd actually have done it, Hilda, not after he'd thought it over.... But he said he'd threaten you with divorce proceedings—and the loss of Coralie.... And that... that finished our friendship."

They were both silent for a time.

"I came out here.... My idea was to warn you. But I couldn't. Couldn't make up my mind even to mention this thing.... At first, I thought perhaps I'd say a word to Branscombe, if he was the right sort of man. But after I'd seen him—"

"You don't think him—the right sort of man, Vincent?"

"No," he answered simply. "Well, now I've told you, Hilda. I...." He rose. "I shan't come back," he said, "unless you need me."

"But I want you to come back, Vincent! You're an old friend.... I've always been fond of you. There's no need for you to be melodramatic."

"I feel a bit that way," he said.

"What do you *mean?*"

He looked straight at her.

"Whole thing's been a bit melodramatic," he said. "Charles was my friend. The first time he brought me to see you, it was bad enough. I mean—to feel the way I did about it. Girl my friend was going to marry.... Like a book.... I knew I simply had to stand it. I hoped I'd get over it. But I never have."

"Vincent!"

"I never shall."

"Vincent—you shan't—just go away...."

"I've got to."

"No," she said, and again she was imperious to him, as she had never been to any other man. "I'm worried and unhappy—and alone. I need you. I want you to come back to dinner."

"All right, Hilda," he said, with a sigh.

CHAPTER XXII

Branscombe made Blanche sit beside him in the front of the car, so that he could talk to her. He saw that, in her present condition of exhaustion and wretchedness, he would have to repeat all his reassurances and all his directions over and over, until things were indelibly stamped upon her mind.

"I don't know who this fellow Jerry was," he said. "Some enemy of Patrell's, I suppose. But anyhow, you're safe now. And if you do as I tell you, I'll try to arrange for you to meet Patrell. But you've got to be careful on his account. You'll meet my sister presently. Now, listen to me! You must not mention Patrell's name to her. D'you understand? You must not tell her anything about last night. You must not let her know about my calling myself 'Mr. Brown.' If you do, you'll be signing Patrell's death-warrant."

She believed him. She was too dazed to notice any discrepancies; moreover, she was impressed by his position in the world. He was a friend of Mrs. Patrell's, and Mrs. Patrell was to her a creature of supernatural goodness.

"All right," she said.

Branscombe smiled to himself at her stupidity, and his own astounding audacity. Only the utmost boldness could have saved him, and he had been bold.

"Wait here in the car until I speak to my sister," he said. "Naturally I shan't tell her what sort of woman you are. And try to behave with a little decency—if you can."

That made her cry again, but he didn't care how much she cried. He found Eva going over the household accounts for the week; she was a little flushed with the worry of this, and somewhat distrait at first.

"I've brought a—woman..." he said.

"That's nice...."

"It's very far from 'nice,'" he said. "I'm.... It's hard to tell you this, Eva...."

He had succeeded in alarming her now.

"What is it, Andy?"

"You remember that I told you about an unfortunate girl whose rent I paid?"

"You mean—?"

"Yes. That girl of Evans's.... I'm sorry, Eva... I'm very sorry even to speak of this thing again. But it was my mistake, ever showing her any sort of kindness. It doesn't pay, with people like that.... Last night she got herself into serious trouble. Some drunken party.... I won't go into details.... But she was assaulted and robbed, and she turned to *me*. She telephoned to me from the railway station.... And I couldn't see anything to do, at the moment, except to bring her here. After she's rested a little I'll give her some money, and she can go."

"Does Llewellyn know?"

"She doesn't want him to know. She says he'd be angry at her. Apparently she doesn't expect any help or sympathy from him." He glanced at Eva's face. "I gave her my word I'd say nothing to him. And of course you won't either. No use in making matters worse for her."

"I *can't* think he's like that—cruel and heartless!"

"My dear girl, you don't understand. I'm glad you don't. In an affair like that, there's no question of kindness, even of decency."

She turned away. "Shall we take her up to the guest-room?"

"Certainly not! She can lie on the sofa in the library. Tell the servants that she's a maid of some friend of yours who's been in an automobile accident."

He had to help Blanche into the house, and he hated to touch her. His fingers gripped her fragile arm so tightly that she winced. Eva stood in the doorway, and, as Branscombe helped his most wretched enemy up the steps, the two girls looked at each other. It was intolerable. He could not endure Eva's looking at this creature. He made Blanche hurry along the hall.

"Sit down on the couch," he said. "Try to pull yourself together, so that you'll be able to go and see Patrell."

He stopped with those words on his lips. For it had come into his head that that was just what she was going to do. She was going to join Patrell. He had known it for days, but he had not faced it. From the moment when he had seen her outside Hilda's house he had known what must happen to Blanche if he were to live. It was inevitable. Yet his present clear and definite realization was a shock to him.

He would have to do this thing himself, alone. And, though he had no pity for the girl, it was an awful thing....

"Could I have a cigarette, Mr. Brown?" she asked.

He took a packet out of his pocket and tossed it to her. It fell on the floor, and she had to pick it up herself.

"I'm not going to wait on that hussy," he thought.

She had taken off the hat Hilda had lent her; she was lying uncomfortably enough on the couch. But he would not fetch a pillow for her; he would not wait on her. He would not pretend to any compassion.

"I'll tell the house-maid to bring you some soup, milk, something of the sort," he said.

"No, thank you, Mr. Brown. I don't want—"

"You've got to," he said curtly. "You've got to get enough strength to leave here."

He went out of the room, closing the door behind him.

"O God...!" he said to himself. "*Why* does it have to be like this...?"

If only he could get away, be free again, even for an hour.... But he could not go, leaving her alive. He could not live if she lived. He went up to his own room and locked himself in; he was trembling.

"But—it's the law of life..." he thought. "Nature's law.... The strong and the clever are obliged to—destroy in order to exist. She's worth nothing, absolutely nothing, to anyone.... I've got Eva to look after. I'm a man of education and standing. Once this is over, I'll do some sort of useful work...."

He thought about that. He would never return to his writing; he could see now that that was futile.

"I can encourage artists, writers, musicians," he thought. "I'll put aside a certain percentage of my income for that purpose. I'm not creative myself, but I have taste, a genuine appreciation of the arts. I'll find young men who are struggling for recognition...."

The idea grew upon him. In the autumn he would take a house instead of an apartment; he would form a group of young artists; he would be their patron. Lorenzo the Magnificent.... It was a Renaissance conception.

"It suits my character," he thought.

He thought, too, that when he came to die, he would leave a written confession. It would be the most astounding document of the century; it would shake the modern world to its depths. This man, famous for his patronage, his profound understanding of the arts, had taken two human lives.... He had felt no compunction, because he was above the paltry modern morality. He had never even been suspected, because he had been unbelievably bold and subtle. The task before him was—unpleasant. But in a few hours it would be over. The others who worried him he could manage well enough: Jerry, Evans, Colton. If it seemed necessary, he would deal with Jerry as with Blanche....

Colton disturbed him. He could understand Jerry and Evans; he knew what they wanted. But he was entirely in the dark about Colton. He could not divine the man's character or his motives for coming here; he was aware only of a vague hostility between them.

"He's a fool, of course," he thought. "I wonder...." Something new was beginning to take shape in his mind; he had again that feeling of inspiration. He stood by the open window, and rapidly and lucidly his plan developed. It was so masterly that he felt a sort of awe. It would settle everything.

Eva knocked at his door.

"Lunch, Andy!" she said.

He opened his door at once. He had no desire, no need to hide himself.

"Andy.... Is she coming to lunch?"

"Certainly not! Send her a tray."

"I went in to see if she wanted anything. Andy, she seems—so miserable."

"Of course she's miserable," he said with a frown. "I wish you'd keep away from her, Eva."

"She won't do me any harm," said Eva, in a tone he had not heard before. He saw that he had better say no more. They sat down at the table together. And somehow it was all wrong, this isolation, this orderly, chilly life.

"I've got to give her more than this," he thought. "I can't expect her to be satisfied with this."

He began talking about a trip to Bali. She was polite, but she was not enthusiastic. It would take a little time, he thought, for her to get over her inconvenient infatuation for Evans and the shock of her disappointment. She was constrained and unhappy....

"Andy!" she said suddenly, and with an obvious effort.

"Yes?"

"Are you sure—absolutely sure that that poor girl has told you the truth?"

"No," he answered, instantly on his guard. "I shouldn't imagine she ever told the truth."

"But are you sure that—that Mr. Evans really is—involved?"

"Oh, I'm sure enough of *that*. Why do you ask?"

"You say she telephoned you from the station.... Did she say she'd just come from New York by train?"

"What's this?" he asked himself, in fear. And aloud: "That's what I understood. Did she tell you anything—?"

"No.... But I'm sure she's wearing a dress of Mrs. Patrell's. I recognized it at once."

His mouth was dry, his throat constricted.

"Impossible!" he said. "You know yourself that those dresses are turned out by the thousand."

"Mrs. Patrell has hers made by a dressmaker. And, I'm sure—"

A scream rang through the house—a scream of wild and uncontrolled terror.

CHAPTER XXIII

They both sprang to their feet. But instantly Branscombe's brain was alert to defend him. It was Blanche who cried out like that, and Blanche was a constant menace to him.

"Wait here!" he said, to Eva.

But she did not obey; as he hastened down the hall, she was with him. They found Blanche sitting up on the couch, staring out of the window, her dark eyes dilated.

"O Gawd!" she cried. "He's *right here!* The man that tried to kill me!"

It was Jerry, loitering in the road.

"Hush!" said Branscombe. "You're perfectly safe here...."

"Andy, who is that?" asked Eva in a low tone. "He's hanging around here so much...."

"I don't know," he answered, his own voice lowered.

"But I've seen you speaking to him."

It was intolerable that Eva should worry him like this, when he was so hard pressed. He drew her aside.

"If you must know," he whispered, "it's a detective."

"Andy...!"

"Don't bother me now!" he said, and turned again to Blanche. "Try to control yourself," he said. "There's no reason for behaving like this, and upsetting the whole house."

"But that's the man! That's—"

"I'll speak to him. Sit down and be quiet."

He spoke to her with the contempt he felt; he knew Eva was surprised, but he couldn't help it.

"Leave her alone, Eva!" he said. "She's hysterical!"

But again Eva didn't obey; she sat down on the couch beside Blanche; she took the girl's trembling hand in hers. Branscombe gave them a sidelong glance and went out to Jerry. In the few moments it took him to cross the sunny lawn he had come to an important decision.

Jerry would have to go, like Blanche. And he saw how to do it. Every detail fell neatly into place. He saw how he could save himself, and so great a relief filled him that he was joyous.

"Well!" he said.

"I thought you'd want me to come," said Jerry. "I thought you'd want to hear all what happened—all I done."

They faced each other with a serious wariness.

"Does he know that I know the truth?" thought Branscombe. "Or will he lie and try to collect the money?"

"I fell down on the job," said Jerry. "I didn't handle it right."

This candour was a little surprising.

"You mean you couldn't induce this person to leave the country?"

"Sure! That's what I mean," said Jerry. "I tried. I took a lot of time and trouble, but it went wrong on me."

"And now?"

"Now," said Jerry, "I'll have another try."

It seemed to Branscombe as if the stars fought for him. This was exactly what he wanted.

"Just what happened last night?"

"She nearly got run over," said Jerry. "But another car comes along, and she gets away."

"Where has she gone?"

"I wouldn't know. But I'll find out."

"How will you find out?"

"She'll go back to that hotel to get her things. I got a friend of mine there now, to let me know where she goes and to trail her."

"And what will you do when you find her?"

Jerry smiled.

"What will you do when you find her?" Branscombe repeated. He wanted to make Jerry commit himself, if it could be done.

"I'll wr-ring her n-eck..." said Jerry, between closed teeth.

"D'you mean that?"

"Try me!" said Jerry.

"I did try you once."

"This time I'll finish the job, all right. As soon as I find her."

"I can find her for you," said Branscombe. "If I were sure of you...."

"Listen, mister! Gimme five minutes alone with her, and I'll wring her neck."

There was for Branscombe an ineffable relief and satisfaction in this interview, in the fact that there was no need for disguise now. The masks were off; Jerry was frank in his savagery; there was no pretence about Blanche's fate.

"A bullet is better," he said.

"Unless you got a gun with a silencer, it's no good."

"There are places where no one could hear a shot."

"Yeah! Just try and get her any place like that! She's scared now."

"I can get her anywhere I want her," said Branscombe.

"Now? After what happened?"

"Yes."

Jerry stared at him.

"I got to hand it to you," he said slowly. "I never *seen* a guy like you."

His sincere admiration warmed Branscombe's soul. In all his life no one had ever really admired him before. Eva was fond of him, but she was fond of him for those qualities in which he had the least pride. What Jerry admired was his boldness, his ingenuity....

"If you'll do the job exactly as I tell you," he said, "you won't get three thousand."

"Say!" protested Jerry.

"You'll get five thousand—in cash. I'll bring it with me."

"Now you're talking. What's the idea, boss?"

"I'll bring her," said Branscombe, "to that barn where you went."

"*There?*" said Jerry, staring at him again. "I can find some other place."

"No. That place happens to suit me. I've got a revolver with me in my pocket. Here! Use this. I want you to go to that barn at nine o'clock exactly. Not five minutes before or after. She'll be in there, alone.... A few minutes after nine I'll come—with the money. And you'll get your five thousand if—you've earned it."

Branscombe spoke in an even, steady tone, but a light sweat broke out on his forehead. It seemed to him incredible that Jerry should not see through this... Jerry was experienced in every human baseness; surely he would at least see the possibility here for treachery, for double-crossing.

"Unless," thought Branscombe, "he's going to try to double-cross me himself. But I don't see how he can. Even if he had some witness of his own there, what could he point against me? But doesn't he suspect—anything...?"

"O.K.," said Jerry.

"You mean you're going to try—"

"Try? I'll do the job. What would stop me?"

"You'll be there at nine sharp?"

"On the dot. And if she's there—" He grinned again.

The incredible thing had happened.

"I can manage anyone," thought Branscombe, with a great wonder. "Everyone believes me. Everyone trusts me. I never imagined before that I was—this sort of man. I might have lived all my life and never known what was in me!"

He watched Jerry out of sight, and he thought that after to-night he would never be bothered by Jerry again. After to-night all his troubles would be over.

There must be absolutely no mistakes made now, though. Every detail would have to be arranged with the greatest care.

"Eva's first," he thought. Because, after all, Eva was the only human creature for whom he had an affection.

She was still in the library with Blanche; he frowned at the sight, and called her out of the room.

"This is damned awkward, Eva," he said. "I've been talking to that detective.... He's been following the girl for some time, and now he wants to arrest her."

"What for?"

"Shop-lifting. She recognized him, of course...."

"She said it was a man who tried to kill her—"

"My dear girl, you can't be so pitiably naive as to believe what she says! Please try to think straight for a moment. We don't want her around here, in my home."

"I don't want her around at all. She's ill, and she's.... Even if she really is a shop-lifter, I'm sure she's not—criminal. Can't we help her?"

"If she's around here, she's certain to tell her story about Evans. There'll be a disgraceful scandal altogether. It'll ruin him. Personally, I don't care. But if you're still interested in him..."

He waited, and after a moment she said:

"Yes.... Yes, I am."

Her words shocked him, and hurt him. But he had to endure it.

"I was afraid of that," he said. "I've acted against my better judgment— against my principles, Eva, on your account. I know it would be painful to you to see the fellow's wretchedness made public. I'm sorry—sorry beyond words that you're so blind about him—but I hope you'll get over it.... The detective had traced the girl here, and I lied to him. I swore she'd never come here. And because I'm not a liar, because I have a reputation for honesty, he believed me. He's gone. But he'll be back. If she's still here then—"

"Where can she go? How can she get away?"

"She'll know where to go. It's better for us not to know in case we're questioned. I'll give her some money."

"You'll give her—enough, won't you, Andy? She's so ill—"

He had never been so hurt in his life.

"You haven't a very high opinion of me, have you, Eva?" he asked unsteadily. "You think I'm petty and mean and hard...."

"It's not that, Andy. It's only that—you're so—so upright yourself that you're apt to expect too much of other people."

This was not the right tone to assuage his hurt. Eva was simply being kind. She didn't really admire him.

"I wish to God she knew what I really am," he thought.

Not petty, not mean, but magnificent! A man who could be ruthless when it was necessary, but who could be superbly generous. She must be made to see that.

"Eva," he said, "I realize how hard this situation is for you... I want to do what I can.... Wouldn't it divert you a little to spend some money? Buy some clothes, and so on...? I'll write you a cheque now, for a thousand dollars."

"What?" she cried. "Andy! A thousand...!"

"Do what you like with it," he said. "There's always more for you, Eva."

He wrote the cheque and handed it to her; he saw in her face more amazement than gratitude. But later, after he had done more things like this....

He went into the library and closed the door behind him, stood looking at Blanche, while she looked back at him, with her great, hollow dark eyes.

"I'm so dam' sick of her..." he thought.

"Did you speak to him...?" she asked.

"Yes. You've got yourself—and Patrell—into a nice mess. This fellow is Patrell's worst enemy—and you have no more sense than to go out with him—"

"But how would that hurt Charles?"

It wasn't necessary to take much trouble with her; she would believe anything.

"You'll have to wait for an explanation until you see Patrell," he said. "That is, if we can manage a meeting at all."

"But what's *happened* to Charles?" she cried. "If you'd only tell me—"

"I'm not going to," said Branscombe; "you're not to be trusted. On Patrell's account, I'll do what I can. If you make one single mistake, you'll never see him again."

She was confused and frightened and miserable, but it didn't matter. It would soon be finished.

"She'll really be better off dead," thought Branscombe.

Then he told her what to do. She was to go at once to the station and take a train to New York. But she was to get out at the next station down the line and go to a small hotel there, and get a room.

"And wait," he said. "Register as Miss Brown again. Stay in your room and hold your tongue until you hear from me."

"I don't know if I'm well enough," she said. "I do feel terrible weak."

"Snap out of it!" he said. "You've got to go. I'll get you a taxi to the station. Here's some money. Pull yourself together now. Get up!"

He felt a furious impatience with her. She was such a nuisance. He wished she were dead now. When she got up she was so unsteady, so white—people would notice her....

"I'll give you a drink of whisky," he said.

"I never drink."

"You'll drink this," he said. "Take this flask with you. I'll wrap it up. If you feel too weak, take another drink now and then. For God's sake, don't be so—spiritless!"

The taxi came and she went out of the house, alone. When she was told that she had to "pull herself together," she did. Branscombe watched her from the window, and he gave a sigh of relief. She had started on her last journey.

CHAPTER XXIV

He telephoned to Hilda.

"Hilda," he said, in a voice as blank, as expressionless as he could make it. "How can I get in touch with Colton?"

"But—with Vincent...? But why?"

He was sick and tired of these women with their questions. "I can't explain now," he said. "Only that it's a matter of importance. If you'll give me his address, please."

"I.... If it's anything you're doing for me, Andrew," she said, "please talk to me about it first. I've changed my point of view about a great many things lately...."

He disliked her so much that he could scarcely keep his tone civil.

"Self-righteous prude...!" he called her to himself. "What did I ever see in *her?*" And aloud: "It's not anything that concerns you personally," he said.

She gave him Colton's address, and he got out his car at once and drove out there. It was a little wooden shack, bleached by the sun, standing on a wide beach. A cheap little place, and Branscombe despised it. He despised Colton, too, and he was going to make a dupe of him.

It was an intolerable exasperation to find Coralie there, sitting on the steps with Colton. They both said good-morning to him, but obviously they were not glad to see him.

"Nice day..." Colton observed, looking out over the glistening water.

"Very..." said Branscombe. "I'd like a word with you, Colton...."

"Very well..." said Colton. "Coralie—mind waiting a while?"

She shook her head; her hair was shining in the sun; her eyes looked wonderfully clear in her sunburned face. She rose and strolled off; the two men looked after her in silence for a moment.

"A very awkward and distressing situation has developed," said Branscombe. "I came to you—" Because you're hostile to me, and I've got to destroy whatever suspicion you may have, you fool, he thought. He left the sentence unfinished, waiting for Colton to question him. But Colton said nothing.

"As you're a friend of Patrell's," said Branscombe, "I presume you know about this woman...?"

"Er—yes..." said Colton. "Yes."

"She's disposed to make trouble. You knew that she'd come here this morning?"

"Yes, Hilda told me."

"I took her to my house. It seemed to me necessary to get her away from

Hilda as soon as possible.... Hilda has no understanding whatever of the situation. Nothing but a sentimental pity for the girl."

"The girl had a pitiable sort of story—"

"Naturally. She's an experienced liar. I took her back to my house—with a good deal of reluctance. I didn't much like having her under the same roof with my sister.... I talked to her, and she was candid enough. She tried to extort money from me."

"How?"

"It's a damned unpleasant story.... Perhaps I've done wrong. I don't know.... My only object was to protect Hilda.... I've been paying blackmail to a man for some days."

"Explain it, will you?"

Colton sat down on the steps again and lit his pipe. Branscombe glanced at him, and with a sort of exultation he felt that he could read this man like an open book, could play upon his feelings, do as he pleased with him.

"You're probably aware," he said, "of my—interest in Hilda. I had no idea that she was still married. She never told me. I went to see her practically every day. I didn't see any reason for concealing what I felt.... Well, a few days ago a fellow came from God knows where. He told me he'd collected what he called 'evidence.' ... He knew the dates of the different drives we'd taken together. He knew of the times when Coralie and the servants were out, and Hilda and I spent the evenings alone in her house. Other things, too.... He told me he would be able to sell his information—elsewhere—unless I was ready to pay him to keep quiet. I paid him."

Colton's sunburned face flushed darkly.

"You paid him?" he said. "That's not the way to deal with a cur like that."

This was exactly the right way for him to speak, and to feel.

"Perhaps not," said Branscombe. "But I'm not a man of action.... I couldn't see any other way to protect Hilda from a scandal."

"Well, there is another way," said Colton. He rose, and walked up and down, with his slight limp. "Did this fellow say where he expected to sell his information?"

"To you."

"To me, by God! I wish he'd tried it!"

"You see," Branscombe went on. "I knew nothing about you, except that you were a friend of Patrell's. Even after I'd met you, I couldn't size you up. I don't mean any offence to you. It's simply that I can't make a snap judgment. I had to make up my mind about you."

He saw that Colton was impressed by his manly, straight-forward tone.

"The situation's got beyond me now," he continued. "The girl's taking a hand in it, too. She wants money, but she wants revenge still more. She's wild with jealousy. She came here with her cock-and-bull story, just to see what Hilda was like. And now she'd do anything she could to injure her.... Of course, you know Patrell, and I don't. It's possible that she has a grossly distorted view of him. But she thinks he'll be glad to get this information, and that he will use it to Hilda's detriment."

"You mean that she and this fellow are working together?"

"Yes. They've given me an ultimatum. I'm to meet the man to-night, and give him five thousand in cash.... I'd do that willingly if I thought it would end the matter. But I don't think so. He'll be back for more. Frankly I don't see what to do."

"Suppose you let me take a hand in this," said Colton.

Branscombe turned his head to conceal his triumph. Everyone did exactly as he wished; everyone believed what he chose they should believe.

"I shouldn't be sorry if you did," he said. "My idea was this. I'll meet this man, as I agreed. I'll have the money with me, in marked bills. I'll hand it over to him, and let him walk out of the place. Then, if you're waiting outside, you can be my witness that he's taken the money. We can threaten him then with the police—"

"I shan't bother with the police," said Colton. "Just a few moments alone—with your friend...."

"Typical soldier," thought Branscombe. "He didn't even notice all the holes in my story.... Blundering, pig-headed fool! I couldn't have a better witness."

It was possible that Colton would have a role more memorable than that of witness.... It was possible that Colton would die. But his death would be merely incidental. Branscombe did not mind if he lived; he was indifferent.

His plan was this: a little before nine he would bring Blanche to the barn, and he would shoot her. He was a good shot; he would not fail with one bullet at such close quarters. He would leave her there and go to fetch Colton. When he and Colton arrived, Jerry would be in there alone with Blanche. Branscombe would enter, would pretend to believe that Jerry had finished his job, would pay him.

He intended to be dramatic, then. He rehearsed the words he would speak.

"Here's your money.... You'd better get away—quick. The girl set the police after you. A detective was questioning me this afternoon.... I hope to God he didn't follow me to-night. If he did, you'll walk into his arms when you leave here."

Jerry would be armed. When he left, he would walk into Colton's arms. It was certain that he would shoot, with his life at stake. And at the first gesture toward drawing his gun, Branscombe would shoot Jerry. And kill him. Colton would be witness to that—if he lived. If he didn't live, it would be all right, too. Branscombe's story would be convincing to the police. Hilda would be able to identify Blanche. Eva would give evidence of Jerry's hanging about, and the money would be found upon Jerry.

"You'd better come around," said Branscombe. And he could have laughed aloud when Colton so readily agreed to that.

CHAPTER XXV

It was very hard to sit quietly at the table with Eva and eat his dinner. A violent excitement filled him; he had to repress his desire to be extraordinarily lively and talkative.

"I'm alive!" he thought. "God! Think of the years I've wasted...! I'm alive now.... I'm a man.... I've planned the most complicated and difficult crime imaginable, and I can carry it through without a hitch...."

There would be a little more explaining to do to Eva when the case came into court. He would have to tell her that Blanche had been Patrell's mistress as well as Evans's. But as long as she didn't talk to Evans, that would be all right.

"I've got to go out, Eva..." he said, and made his voice so solemn, so portentous, that she glanced up—as he had intended.

"Where to, Andy?"

"I can't tell you," he said. "But—don't worry...."

"Andy, please tell me!"

"I can't. Not now...."

He left her very much worried; it had to be like that. He went into the library and took out of the safe a revolver he kept in there. He put it behind a photograph on top of the bookcase. Then he rang for the house-maid.

"You know that revolver I always keep in my desk," he said. "I can't find it. Look around, will you?"

She looked, and she found it. She was afraid to touch it; she was afraid of Branscombe's distrait manner. All this would come out in the evidence. No one knew that he had two revolvers. He had bought one of them in Berlin, some time ago, and the other he had bought in New York from an ex-soldier. He had given the German one to Jerry, and it had had two chambers empty. The house-maid couldn't say that Mr. Branscombe had taken his own gun with him.

He got out his car and drove off. There was no need to bother about an alibi. He would simply say that the coming interview with his blackmailer had made him nervous, and he had gone for a drive.

He drove to the next town and telephoned to "Miss Brown" at her hotel.

"I've arranged for you to meet Patrell," he said. "Start at once. Your hotel is on Union Street. Turn the corner into Maple Avenue and walk straight ahead until you see me—"

"Is it far?" she asked. "Because I—don't feel good...."

"You can manage it," he said. "Start at once."

She would have a good half-mile to walk, but it really didn't matter much if it tired her. He drove about for a time, then he turned into Maple Avenue, where it was dark and quiet; he went slowly until he saw her approach. She was walking with an obvious effort; people would notice how ill she looked.

"Get in quick!" he said.

When she sat down beside him she was breathing fast; she leaned against his shoulder. It didn't matter if she had fainted; in fact, it would make things easier....

But whatever was wrong with her, she got over it. "I'm really going to see Charles?" she asked.

"You're going to join him. He's waiting for you," said Branscombe, smiling to himself.

He wished that he were not quite so excited. His heart beat too fast; his brain was working too rapidly. His thoughts were lucid enough, but he was aware that he was not controlling them. He wanted to concentrate upon the task in hand, and instead of that he had curious visions of the future. He saw himself on a tropic beach with a beautiful girl. He saw himself on a magnificent black horse, galloping through the narrow streets of some old town.... Suddenly these happy visions were dispelled by fear. Suppose Colton were late, and Jerry ran away from the barn in a panic....

No. Colton would observe a military punctuality, and Jerry would not leave until he had got his money.... Everything would go as he had planned, and he would be free.... He would forget all this. It would soon be over. Only, he wished he could quiet the violent beating of his heart, banish the strange sensation he had, as if his blood had grown as cold as ice, and tingled in his veins. "In cold blood...."

"I didn't *want* to do this!" he cried to himself. "It was forced upon me. I'm doing it to save my life. And certainly my life is of infinitely more value than hers, or Jerry's...."

There would be one bad moment.... Only a moment, though. Only the instant when the revolver must be aimed, when the shot rang out....

"I think I caught cold," said Blanche. "Getting so wet... it sort of hurts me to breathe."

He felt no sympathy, and there was no need now to pretend any. He did not answer. He fancied she was crying in a weak sort of way. Let her cry.... He turned into the lane where he had driven with Jerry that sunny morning. It seemed very long ago....

"Charles is *here*?" she said. "No! No! I don't want to get out here!"

"I told you he was in hiding...."

"Then ask him to come out.... I don't want to go in there.... I'm scared...."

A shot out here would be far more likely to be overheard. She had to go inside. He gave a sigh of exasperation.

"You're not worth bothering with," he said. "The poor devil is in there— ill. I won't ever ask him to come out. If you're too much of a coward to go in and see him, very well. I'll go in and tell him so, and you can sit here in the car."

"It's a terrible lonely place," she said, and her teeth were chattering. "There's no light.... Is he in there—all alone... in the dark...?"

"Is he...?" thought Branscombe. "What did Jerry do with him? Bury him...? Or is he—is he—*still there?*"

He had not thought of that before. He wished with all his soul that he had not thought of it now. It unnerved him; it made his knees turn to water. He could not—look at *that*....

"Why don't you answer me?" she cried, with a sudden vehemence that startled him. "You—you are so queer—and so mean to me.... What's Charles *doing* in that dark old barn...?"

With an immense effort Branscombe recovered himself.

"He's got a light in there. But naturally it's hidden from the road. Are you going in to see him, or not?"

"You go first," she said.

He had a powerful electric torch with him; he had a loaded revolver. But still he was afraid. His fear of seeing Patrell was monstrous, intolerable. He thought that if he were to see Patrell lying on the floor in there, his wildly beating heart would stop short.... If Patrell was lying there in the dark, with his eyes wide open....

The door was opened a crack; he slid it back. He let the light of his torch play over the cavernous blackness. He saw nothing there. Nothing. He entered, stood waiting a moment, and presently Blanche followed him. He turned the torch upon her. It seemed to him that her dark eyes were glaring at him. He was afraid of her. He could not shoot her if she looked at him.

He set the torch down on the floor, and it threw a circle of bright light upward to the high ceiling. He must make her turn her back.

"We'll have to go up that ladder..." he said. "There at the back...."

But she did not turn to look where he pointed. She kept on looking at him. Staring at him, with enormous black eyes in a white face. It was as if she read something in his face, and an atrocious knowledge were dawning upon her.... It would have to be done now.... She would have to stop—staring at him....

"Well...!" he said. He tried to speak in a reassuring, matter-of-fact tone; he tried to smile. And at the sight of his smile she screamed.

"Charles!"

He reached in his pocket for the revolver, staring at her as she stared at him. And he heard footsteps overhead.

He believed that her cry had raised Patrell from the dead. He believed that Patrell would come down that ladder. He felt such terror that he could not think. The footsteps ceased. He saw, dimly, a foot on the top rung of the ladder.

The girl did not see it. She could not take her eyes from his face. But he saw.

Someone was coming down, backward; a man.... Descending in silence—
slowly and shakily. A dead man. A corpse, with a bandage about his dark
hair.... When he reached the foot of the ladder, he would turn, and
Branscombe would see that awful face....

He had reached the floor, and he did turn. And once again Branscombe faced
Patrell.

CHAPTER XXVI

"Blanche..." said Patrell gently.

The girl turned, and tried to run to him. He came to her and put his arms about her.

"Steady, now, that's a good kid," he said.

The sound of his voice had broken the spell. He was no dead man.

"I never killed him," thought Branscombe. "All this has been—for nothing."

And now he was trapped. Now he was finished. He was here, in this lonely place with Patrell and with Blanche. In a few moments Jerry would come. The three people he had tried to destroy.... There was no escape.

Patrell's handsome face was bruised and scarred, but he was quite well enough....

"Anything to say in your defence?" he asked. "Before I rub you out?"

Branscombe was silent.

"I'm going to kill you—with my hands," said Patrell.

"I'm armed..." said Branscombe, in a queer, muffled voice.

"That doesn't matter. You can't hurt me. Anything to say—while you have the chance?"

He must find something to say, while he had the chance. "I admit that—I lost my temper..." he said. "I knocked you down—"

"You cur!" said Patrell. "'Lost your temper!' God! You were like a wild beast. You tried to kill, in just the way a cur would. When you got me down you went mad. You kicked me...."

"Charles...!" said Blanche.

"Don't say anything, poor kid. This is my turn. You tried to kill me. But you never even troubled to see if I was dead. You didn't care as long as I was out of the way. As soon as Jerry got me in here he knew I wasn't dead. God knows he's rotten enough—but he's a hero compared with you. He brought me some water. I'll never forget that. He brought me some water when I'd have died without it. Then he told me that you were paying him twenty-five dollars to dispose of me.... I told him he could do better than that.... We were going to get plenty of money out of you, Branscombe, before I finished.... Jerry's been bringing me food and whisky and smokes; he's been looking after me."

"Yes," said Branscombe. "I knew all that."

For in his extremity, inspiration had come to him once more.

"You damned liar!" said Patrell. "You thought I was dead. And you paid Jerry to kill this poor girl—"

"Charles! Was it him?"

He patted her shoulder and went on.

"Jerry was very fastidious. He didn't know who she was. Not until she called my name. When he knew she was my girl, he let her go, and he apologized to me very civilly.... I sent him back to you, Branscombe. He told me your new plans—that he was to kill her here, to-night, and be well paid for it. I didn't expect the pleasure of seeing you here. I planned to meet you—later—when you'd handed out the money to Jerry."

The last chance....

"You're rather gullible," said Branscombe. His brain was working well, but he could not steady his voice. He took out a cigarette and lit it with a shaking hand. "I've been surprised, all along, by your remarkable confidence in Jerry."

He inhaled deeply. He had only a few moments, so very few before Jerry came....

"I was panic-stricken, after I'd attacked you," he went on, and his voice was growing steadier and steadier. "I knew I hadn't killed you. I'm not a fool. I knew you'd recover and make trouble for me. For a man in my position, a scandal like this would be disastrous. I didn't pay him to dispose of you. I paid him to look after you, and try to persuade you to accept a cash settlement from me. Apparently he's been lying to you with more intelligence than I'd have expected of him."

"No use, Branscombe," said Patrell.

But there was a slight, almost imperceptible change in his tone that Branscombe, in his extremity, could notice.

"As for my paying him to kill this girl," he went on, "that's amazing. You might see for yourself that, apart from the senselessness of it, I'm not the sort of man for such melodrama. I went to your lodging. I posed as a friend of yours. I paid the girl's bill, and took her to a decent hotel. I told Jerry to let you know what I'd done. I'll admit that I did it in the hope of placating you. Because I wanted to avoid trouble. But she'll tell you herself that I did all I could to make her comfortable."

"Did he, Blanche?"

"Well, yes..." she admitted. "Only—he didn't like me.... And Jerry...."

"I don't know what Jerry's game was," said Branscombe. "But probably he thought I'd given the girl money, and he meant to rob her. I'm not in any way responsible for his attack upon her. When I found her at Hil—at your wife's house, I was shocked. I took her to my own house. I did what I could for her. And I promised her I'd bring her to see you this evening. I've done so."

"Did he promise you that, Blanche?"

"Well, yes.... He did," she said. "But he was looking at me in such a queer kind of way—"

"I was very reluctant to see you, Patrell. Naturally.... But I told Jerry to ask if you'd accept five thousand in cash to let the matter drop. He assured me that you had agreed, and that you'd be expecting me. I'm here—with the money."

There was a silence. Jerry might come at any moment....

"It's obvious that Jerry's been double-crossing us both," he said. "I don't suppose he's brought you any of the small sums of money I sent to you—fifty dollars once—"

"No," said Patrell, and straightened his slim shoulders. "I meant to make you pay.... But I don't now. I suppose you're telling the truth. I don't think you'd have the nerve or the brains to invent such a good lie. I suppose it's true that Jerry's been double-crossing me.... And that you've come here to-night with five thousand dollars to shut me up. Give it to me!"

"You'll let the matter drop?"

"I'll let the matter drop on condition that I never have to set eyes upon you again. Give me the money!"

Branscombe took out the neat packet of bills held together by an elastic band, and handed it to Patrell. But even now he wasn't sure.... It was almost too much of a miracle that Patrell should believe him. That now, in the very last moment, he should escape.

Patrell threw the packet in his face.

"Now get out!" he said. "While I'm able to keep my hands off you—"

A miracle. He stepped out into the cool summer night. He was free.... He walked toward his car, and he began to cry.... He was half-blinded with tears as he took the wheel. Another car was coming. That would be Jerry.

"I've got to get away damned quick," he thought.

Go home...? Now that Patrell was in the world again, Hilda would learn the truth.... Perhaps Jerry would be able to convince Patrell that it was Branscombe who lied, not he.... And Eva would surely hear something to make her suspicious....

"Colton...!" he thought. "Oh, God! What am I going to tell Colton...?"

He told himself that he could manage. He had managed before. He would think of plausible explanations for all these people.... For Hilda, for Colton, for Eva.... He would somehow get rid of Jerry.... He would have to explain—and explain—and explain.... Lie and lie....

He could not. Something had happened to him. He started the car and drove straight ahead. God knew where the lane led to.... He could not explain—so much to so many people.... He was hemmed in by enemies—by people de-termined to humiliate and disgrace him.... He was not the strong and subtle man of the Renaissance days. He was crying.... He was most horribly and des-olately alone. Eva loved that Evans fellow.... There was no one for him, and there never would be.

He saw himself. He saw the boy who had been ignored and despised in school because he had been a prig and a coward. He saw himself as he was now, a man of thirty who had been afraid to live, who had tried to shut himself away from the world. He looked haughty and distinguished, and he was so pitiably undistinguished, so abject.... Patrell would tell what had happened....

"He knocked me down and battered me while I was helpless. He kicked me...."

It was too much. He stopped the car and took out his revolver. His hand was shaking violently, and he held the muzzle to his temple.

Jerry found him. He heard the shot and drove up the lane, and discovered what was left of Andrew Branscombe. He was very much afraid of being blamed for this, so he drove away in haste. No one else had heard the shot. There was a violent thunderstorm in the night, but it didn't disturb Branscombe.

Eva notified the police when he failed to come home, and they discovered him. It was a good thing for him that he never heard what was said about him.

THE END

The Girl Who
Had to Die
by Elisabeth Sanxay Holding

CHAPTER ONE

"I'm going to be murdered," she said in her muffled, sad little voice.

Killian sat on the foot of his deck chair beside her, hands clasped between his knees, his neat, dark head bent, no expression at all on his face. He could not help hearing her; but he did not have to answer, and he did not have to look at her.

"Don't you *care*, Jocko?" she asked.

He hated that name she had invented for him, and maybe he hated her. He was not quite sure about that.

"Ever since I was fourteen," she said, "I've known I was going to be murdered—"

"Too bad!" he said, smiling and still not glancing at her. But he knew well enough how she looked: slight and delicate, in a pleated white chiffon dress with a silver belt, her pale, tawny hair brushed back from her brow, her young face wan, hollow temples, hollows beneath the high cheekbones, great forlorn eyes, wide mouth.

She leaned forward and laid her hand on his knee, a frail little hand with nails cut short in a careless, childish fashion. Typical of her. She didn't care about anything. More than once he had met her on deck in the early morning in faded blue cotton pajamas, her hair ruffled, last night's mascara smudged about her eyes.

"Jocko," she asked, "for God's sake, can't you say one kind word?"

He had to look at her then. "No," he said, with a tight-lipped smile that broke up his swarthy young face, made vertical lines in his cheeks, wrinkles at the corners of his eyes; he looked droll, and gay. "I'm not kind."

Her thin little fingers dug into his knee. "Oh, *please* be kind, Jocko! I'm only nineteen, Jocko. I don't want to die."

"How about a drink?" he asked.

She drooped forward and rested her cheek on her hand, so that her hair was directly beneath his downcast eyes; his breath stirred it. Misty hair, fine as gossamer, glittering, alive, fragrant. He turned aside his head.

"Let's have a drink, Jocelyn," he said.

"No," she answered, in a faint smothered voice.

"Well, sit up, anyhow," he said. "If someone comes along, they'll think—"

"I don't care what anyone thinks," she said. "Jocko, I'm cold. Jocko, I'm sick."

"Come on!" he said; taking her by the shoulders, he made her sit up. But her head drooped forward, the bright soft hair falling across her forehead; her eyes were closed. She looked dead, martyred. He pushed her back until she was

lying in her deck chair. "Shall I bring you a drink?" he asked, trying to keep
his fear out of his voice.

"Oh, God!" she cried. "Why do you want to keep pushing me down and
down? Making me go on drinking—when there's nothing but gin running
in my veins now. Little lights dancing in my head...."

"I don't want to push you down," he said. "Only what do you want?"

"I want you to be kind," she said. "I'm cold and sick and lonely."

A sort of rage came over him.

"If you wouldn't be such a damn fool—" he said. "It's nearly nine o'clock,
and you haven't had any dinner.... And you've kept me from having any either. Can't you pull yourself together now, and come down to the dining saloon?"

She did not stir, or answer, or open her eyes. He hated her all right. He had
had too many drinks with her; he was hungry, or tired—or something.... But
he couldn't walk off and leave her like this.

"If you're sick," he said, "I'll get the doctor."

"I'm going to die, Jocko," she said.

He rose, straight and square-shouldered and stiff in his white dinner jacket,
his dark face grim.

"Then you certainly need the doctor," he said.

"The doctor can't save me, Jocko. Not from murder."

There were tears running down her thin, wonderful face from her closed
eyes; her long lashes were wet.

"If you'll give me the name of the murderer," he said, "I'll speak to the Captain."

"Five of them, Jocko dear."

"Five of what?"

"Five men who want to kill me," she said, still weeping.

"You're crazy!"

"Maybe I am, Jocko," she said. "But I'm only nineteen. I don't want to die."

"Now look here, Jocelyn. Pull yourself together and come down to dinner."

"I've got the names all written down in a little book," she said. "I carry it
with me all the time. My Murderers. That's what I've written on the
cover."

"All five on board this ship?"

"One's enough," she said. "At a time."

"When you've had some hot coffee—" he said.

"You're such a damn little—*clerk*," she said in a monotone. "I've seen your
type everywhere—in Paris, London, in Vienna. The same face, like a fox—
ears pricked, ready to jump when someone gives you an order. Just a little
clerk. Why do I have to love *you*?"

"Maybe you'll be able to conquer it," he said. Hating her. She knew exactly
the words that goaded him most cruelly; she held up to him the image of him-

self he didn't want to see. The clerk, the subordinate who took orders, the obscure, hard-working young nobody.

"I'm going to get some dinner," he said. "Anything I can do for you before I go?"

"What's the matter with Starry Eyes?" asked a voice behind him.

It was Chauverney, the Purser, slender, olive-skinned, an Englishman queerly Latin. He spoke Spanish like a native, and with Latin gestures; seven years on this South American run had done something to him. All right! thought Killian. If he's such a man of the world—such a smooth caballero— let him look after her. "I'm going to get some dinner," he said aloud.

"How about Starry Eyes?" asked Chauverney, with a vivid smile; and she opened her eyes and looked at him. Starry Eyes.... Not blue, not grey. What colour? Violet? Misty with tears, the wet, dark lashes like rags, her mouth so sad and sweet. "Come along and have a bite with me, Starry Eyes?"

"Jocko asked me first, Purser," she said.

"Oh, never mind about me!" said Killian, and walked off. "In five days we'll be home," he told himself. "Then I'll never have to set eyes again on that hell-cat."

He went down to the dining saloon, and he was sorry that the other people had finished and gone. Dull enough people—two spinster schoolteachers and a prosy, middle-aged salesman of office fixtures—but he would have liked any or all of them now. They were cheerful and comprehensible. He didn't feel like sitting alone tonight.

She'll come and sit here if she feels like it, he thought. It was typical of her that she ignored her allotted seat in the saloon. She would wander in and sit where she chose; at his table, at the Purser's, at the doctor's, anywhere. Travels like a damn ghost, he thought. That last word startled him. A ghost? "I'm going to be murdered, Jocko." Was it because she was close to death that she was a ghost?

"The chicken is good, sir," said Angelo.

"Muy bien," said Killian.

Angelo was half Italian, half Brazilian. He looked like a gigolo, tall and willowy, with sideburns, long black lashes, a gentle elegance about him. He was a good steward, but Killian didn't like him.

"Soup first, sir?"

"No soup."

"Little salad, sir?"

"No salad. Chicken, and a pot of black coffee."

He lit a cigarette while he was waiting. Bad habit. Silly, neurotic habit. It's because I've been drinking too much, he thought. Every day since we left B. A. I'm going to quit. Not tomorrow, but now. I'm not going into the smoke-room after dinner. No nightcap. I'll take a walk and turn in early. I didn't know I had it in me to be like this.

A little clerk, she had called him. He had been a model clerk. Strictly sober and industrious. Ambitious. All ready and waiting when Opportunity knocked. We need someone who can speak Spanish, to substitute for Wilcox until he's well enough to go back to his work. Oh, I can speak Spanish, sir. I've been taking lessons in the evenings. *Good* little clerk. And where did it get me? Three months in B. A., and now home again to the same old job. Only now I'm ruined. I don't want to wander. I want to be rich, and important. On the inside of things.

Angelo hastened forward and pushed back a chair at the Purser's table. That was for Jocelyn; followed by Chauverney, she crossed the saloon with her light step, the pleated chiffon dress flattening back against her long legs. No one else had that grace of line and movement; no one like her.

"Jocko!" she called. "Come over here with us."

"Dinna fash yersel', laddie," said Chauverney, with his sudden vivid smile.

"I *want* you, Jocko!" she cried, as if in despair, or anguish.

But he wasn't going to take that seriously. "See you later," he said, and went on with his dinner.

Chauverney was able to talk to her. She was growing animated with him; she was leaning forward, looking into his face with a dazed, lost look in her eyes. She was interested, and suddenly she laughed. Killian couldn't stand that laugh of hers, low, almost hoarse. "Like one of those high-yaller wenches..." he thought.

"Coffee, Angelo, and cheese." Angelo did not answer, and did not hear him. He was staring at Jocelyn with his mouth open; giving him a forlorn and idiotic look. "Snap out of it, Angelo!" said Killian, sharply.

"Señor? Excuse. You want?"

"Nothing!" said Killian. He would have coffee in the smoke-room, or maybe he wouldn't have any coffee. He wanted to get away from Jocelyn. But he had to pass her table, and she reached out and caught his hand.

"Jocko, wait for me on deck. Jocko, I've *got* to see you!" she said.

"Well, we're on a ship," he said. "I can't escape." Certainly he smiled, and she could take it as a joke if she chose. He gave her shoulder a pat and went on out of the saloon. He walked up and down the promenade deck for a while, not a long while; then he went to his cabin and locked the door. "And she can't get me out," he said to himself. "No matter what she says or does, she can't get me out."

He was mistaken about that.

He put on a dressing gown and lay down on the bed with a Spanish book to read. The air flowed in at the open port like fresh water, warm and sweet; the sea was quiet to-night. Homeward bound, he thought. All right! I'll admit I don't want to go home. Back to the office, back to another room in somebody's apartment. In Buenos Aires he had lived in the house of a young German couple; a boy brought coffee to him every morning—coffee like

nectar—ran his bath for him, cleaned his shoes. When he came in after dinner, the bed would be turned down, the lamp lighted, pajamas laid out.

He lit a cigarette and read; after a time he turned out the light and lay in
the dark. I don't know what I want, he thought, filled with melancholy.
Nothing much. That's the trouble. I'm negative now.

A few months ago he had been positive, definite. Ambitious to get on in
the business. Now he didn't care. He felt cold, indifferent; he felt old. You
can't measure age in years, he thought. I'm old—at twenty-three.

He was asleep, or half asleep, when a strange, horrible sound shocked him:
a voice crying, "Oooooo...." He sat up straight, in a sweat, and it came again.
"Man ooo-verboard...." The ship quivered and jarred, checked; the engines
reversed.

He sprang up and ran across the cabin in the dark. When he opened the
door, he came face to face with a tall man with a grey beard, standing mo-
tionless, his eyes dilated.

"I fancied I heard—man overboard..." he said in a sort of bleat.

They stared at each other, and Killian ran past him along the alleyway and
out on deck. He saw four women starting up the ladder to the boat deck like
ducks. He went after them; the last one was stout and climbed slowly, bent
forward from the waist—so slowly that he pushed her a little. She looked back
over her shoulder.

"My! What a dreadful thing!" she said. "That poor girl!"

"What girl?" he asked.

"That bitch!" said another voice ahead of them.

The stout woman tried to cover that. "That Miss Frey," she said.

So it was Jocelyn.

The woman straightened up as she reached the boat deck, and Killian went
past her. An officer was superintending the lowering of a lifeboat in a strong
circle of light. "Oh, God...!" he said to himself. "Oh, God! Jocelyn in her white
dress.... She said that she was lonely." *Lonely?* Now she knew what that word
meant, all right. Still swimming, was she, in her white dress with the silver
girdle? That made you think of fishes with silver scales. Sharks. Swimming,
her long slender arms moving up and down, her slender legs wrapped in the
long white skirt.... Calling, screaming for help, all alone—until something
seized her and dragged her under.

"Got caught in the propellers," a man said. "Inevitable...."

That would be better, that would be quicker than swimming all alone.
Lonely? That was the absolute of loneliness, out there. There were stars in
the sky, and it's a fact that they twinkle. There were probably things in the
depths of the sea not yet discovered. Things worse than sharks. You look at
the ocean and call it empty, but that's a damned lie. It is teeming and crawl-
ing with life. Different layers of life. Jocelyn would not sink to the bottom.
She would drift down in her white dress. If the ocean was whisky, and I was

a duck, I'd dive to the bottom, and I'd never come up.

"I want a drink," Killian said aloud. There were a lot of people on the boat deck, but he was not talking to them. The ship had stopped, and that made him seasick. Very sick. He went below to the smoke-room and the bar was closed.

I'm glad! he thought suddenly. He did *not* want a drink, or anything to blunt his sick horror. If *she* had to go through this, let him bear his part of it, every moment of it. He sat down on a table, barefoot in his dressing gown. "Oh, God!" he said to himself. "God, what a way to die! She said she was lonely...."

Some people were coming into the smoke-room, and he left it and went to his cabin. It was dark in there, and hot; the breeze was gone. Because we're lying to, he thought. He could hear, or thought he could hear, the motor in the lifeboat. Only a gesture, to lower a boat into this vast, dark sea, to look for a girl in a white dress.

"I hope it's all over now," he said to her. "I hope you're dead. Starry Eyes... I hope to God you're dead now." Not still swimming; he had seen her in the pool in a black knitted suit. Slight and tall, elegant. Elegance in the set of her head, in her wrists and ankles. Only nineteen....

"So things like this *do* happen?" he said to himself. Life and death were real, were they? Merrily, merrily, merrily, merrily, life is but a dream.... Don't kid yourself, you fool. It's no dream.

Sitting on the edge of the bed, he lit a cigarette. They say there's no use smoking in the dark. That's another lie. The end of the cigarette burned red. Port light is red. She would have seen the lights of the ship rushing away from her. Did she call me? Did she call "Jocko"? She asked me, she begged me to wait for her. I didn't. My fault? My fault?

The ship shook in a preposterous way, making his teeth chatter; everything in the cabin rattled. Then the breeze came back. We're under way again. We've left her. Adios, Starry Eyes! Quede con Dios.... Remain with God. With the sharks, with the little fish and the great fish.... He lay flat on his back on the bed, so very sick....

He wanted another cigarette and he could find no matches; he felt in the pockets of his dressing gown, sat up and groped among the things on the table, rose and moved around in the dark cabin. Impossible to turn on the light. He rang the bell, and stood by the door waiting. Very promptly someone came, knocking.

"Can you get some matches for me?" he asked.

"Yes, sir," said the voice of the watchman. A decent old fellow with a grey moustache. What does he do all night? Every night.... He knocked again. "Here you are, sir." Killian opened the door and held out his hand, and the watchman filled it with matchbooks. "Nobody's getting much sleep to-night, sir."

"No, I suppose not," said Killian.

"It's a funny thing, sir.... Young lady like that.... You'd say she had everything to live for. Yet she wants to kill herself."

"Kill herself?"

"That's what they're saying, sir. It's a funny thing. I'm sixty-six years of
age, sir, but I can enjoy life. And there's a young lady like that, rich, everything to live for, you'd say; and she tries to kill herself."

"Tries...?"

"Didn't you hear, sir? They picked her up and brought her back. They're
working over her now."

"Thanks," said Killian, and closed the door.

CHAPTER TWO

The surf came raining down like hot silver that sizzled when it touched the deep blue sea; the sky was a bright burning blue. The steward came knocking at the door with Killian's coffee.

"Great excitement last night, sir," he said. "Wasn't it?"

"Just put the tray down, will you?" said Killian.

The moment he was alone, he began to drink the coffee, black and strong. "I wanted that," he said to himself. "In a way, I know what's the matter with me. In a way. The reason I'm so damn miserable is because I'm a fake. I've made myself into this. This good little clerk. Underneath it I'm—what? A crazy Irishman. I had to choose. I knew that when I was a kid. I knew that I could be either a crazy little fool or a good boy. I chose to be a good boy. Hardworking. I save money. I make plans and I stick to them. But if I let go for one minute, I'd be—the other one. It's there all right. I can't kill it. I can just kick it into a corner, and keep on kicking it...."

He lit a cigarette and looked out at the burning blue day. It's never like that at home. Home was never like this. When we stopped at Trinidad... Hibiscus and bougainvillaea, and there was a barracuda in the harbour.... She was nice that day. Nice when we first went ashore. She was gentle; sat in the car, holding my hand, and she was quiet. Until we stopped at that place and she started drinking rum.... Drunkard.... Little tramp.... She didn't die.

He got up and took a bath and dressed, all very slowly. I'll have to see her, he thought. Four days more. If we dock in the morning, I'll go straight to the office.... Sunburnt. He looked at himself in the mirror, his narrow skull, his deep-set eyes, his long upper lip. Monkey face, he thought. Ears pricked up ready to take orders.... What'll I say to her? I hear you fell overboard. Quite an experience.

He went into the dining saloon at eight, as usual, and he was surprised not to see the schoolteachers there. They were cheerful; he had a great wish to see their faces, their eyes smiling behind their glasses.

"The ladies are late," he observed to Angelo.

"They sit there, sir," said Angelo, with a discreet gesture; and Killian saw them sitting at a table across the saloon.

"What's the idea?" he asked.

"They asked the Purser to put them away, sir."

"But what's the idea?" he asked.

"I don't know, sir," said Angelo.

A queer thing to do. Rude. They had made rather a pet of him; they had laughed at his jokes; they had consulted him as an authority upon the whole continent of South America. He wanted them back. But if they didn't want to be here, let them go. He ate his breakfast alone and went up on deck. The passengers were not given to early rising; he found no one there except the man with the grey beard whom he had confronted last night. "Good morning!" Killian said. And the man didn't answer him; deliberately glared at him, and didn't answer.

Killian walked off into a sort of nightmare. It was peculiarly lonely on deck; it had never been like this before. The schoolteachers had moved away from his table, and the old fellow with the beard wouldn't answer him. "What's the idea?" he asked himself, and told himself that probably there wasn't any idea. It didn't mean anything.

But when other people came on deck, he avoided them. If anyone wants to talk to me, they can come after me, he thought. He regretted this course as soon as he had started it; pacing up and down the enclosed deck with his hands behind his back, he felt like a pariah, a melodramatic one. Nobody did come after him.

It's something to do with Jocelyn, he thought. It has to be. She's said something....

The ship's doctor was coming along the deck, stopping before a chair here and there, bending his lank body like a courtier; a blanched man with a lantern-jawed, white face, and white hair, dressed in a white suit. "He looks like a candle that's just been blown out," Jocelyn had said. I suppose she's clever, thought Killian. Only you never think of her that way. She can always find the right phrase for anyone. She speaks French, and Spanish, and German. Maybe she's clever. And maybe she's the most ghastly fool.

The doctor was approaching him, and Killian moved forward. And with a poor effort at absentmindedness, the doctor turned back. Killian went after him.

"Look here!" he said. "How is Miss Frey?"

"She's in a bad condition," said the doctor, with his eyes lowered. He had a face that expressed nothing at all but a faint peevishness; a flat voice.

"What's the trouble with her?" asked Killian.

"Bad condition," the doctor repeated, and moved aside to pass Killian.

But Killian was not satisfied. "Shock?" he asked.

The peevish expression on the white face deepened into a fretful frown. "The trouble is that she doesn't want to recover."

"You mean that she's depressed?"

"I mean she doesn't want to live," the doctor answered irritably.

"Well," said Killian. "As she gets stronger, I suppose that'll pass."

"You ought to know better," said the doctor. He tried again to pass Killian, but he found himself against the rail.

"I...?" said Killian.

"You ought to know better," the doctor said. "It's deplorable."

Killian let him go, and almost at once regretted this. "I should have had it out with him," he told himself. "I ought to have made him put it into words. I'm responsible, am I? My fault if that neurotic little drunkard is in a 'bad condition'? What's she told him, I wonder?"

Had she gone around spreading that tale?

He thought of the two schoolteachers and the man with the beard. Doctors never tell. Maybe. And maybe the tale was running all over the ship. She doesn't want to live because she loves Killian. Dying of love. It's deplorable.

What's the way to handle it? he thought. I'd better behave just as usual—pay no attention to anything hostile.

But he wouldn't naturally go out of his way to invite rebuffs. He wouldn't approach anyone. Simply when anyone approached him, he would be normal. Nobody did approach him. He went to his cabin and put on his bathing trunks; went up to the pool on the boat deck. The usual people were there lying in the sun, some in dark glasses, some with their eyes closed; all of them silent, intent upon the even toasting of their bodies. The pool was empty at the moment; the sun shone in making the water a limpid green. Killian dived in and swam up and down fast. But he did not escape his preoccupation.

I'm bound to see her before long, he thought. That's going to be awkward. I'll have to speak to her. What's the tactful thing to say to someone who's tried to commit suicide? I hope this will be a lesson to you.

"Hello!" said a voice; and looking over his shoulder, he saw Mrs. L'O standing halfway down the ladder, dark and slim, ineffably stylish in a pale blue bathing suit with a flared skirt and a high collar in front, and at the back nothing above the waist but a little bow at the nape of her neck. A blue bandanna was tied in front in a coquettish bow; unsmiling, a little haggard, she presented a picture of detailed perfection. "W.O.W.," Jocelyn had called her. "And that doesn't mean Wow, Jocko. It stands for Woman of the World. Poise and Taste, and Savoir Faire—all laid on so thick."

"How are you?" he asked, civilly, but with no disposition to go on talking to her.

She slid into the water and swam toward him. She swam very well; she did everything very well. "I want a chance to speak to you alone," she said, stopping beside him. "I don't suppose you know—"

"Know what?"

"It's a beastly story," she said. "And it's spreading like wildfire." She grasped the rail with both hands, standing upright in the deep water, bending her head. With her neck arched, with her straight little nose, she looked, he thought, like a little sea-horse. Spirited, and pleasing. "I hate to tell you," she said.

"Kind of you to bother, Mrs. L'O."

"Elly," she said.

"Elly," he repeated, suddenly liking her.

"You know that Piggott girl?" she asked. "She was on the boat deck last night when—the thing happened, and she's running around telling everyone she heard Jocelyn call out your name when she went overboard."

Killian felt as if he had got a violent blow in the midriff. He was silent for a moment, trying to get over it. "Not so good," he remarked, presently.

"There's more," she said. "The Piggott girl says she saw you and Jocelyn sitting on the rail together, a little while before it happened."

"She didn't," said Killian.

"There's still more," she said. "And worse. Mr. Bracey says—"

"Who's Mr. Bracey?"

"The man with the grey beard. He says that, just after the sailor called out, 'Man overboard,' you came rushing down to your cabin, all white and shaking."

"The damned old liar!" said Killian, astounded. "He saw me open my cabin door and look out, after the sailor had shouted a couple of times. He was standing there in the alleyway."

"Well; that's his story," she said.

Killian still had the feeling of having got a violent blow; it made him confused.

"But what's the *idea* of his telling such a lie?" he asked, staring at Elly L'O.

"He doesn't think it a lie any more," she said. "Both he and the Piggott girl believe the stories now. It makes them very, very happy."

Killian began filling his cupped hand with water and splashing it on his head. He had to do something.

"Hard to believe that people can be like that," he said. "To lie that way out of sheer malice—"

"I don't think it's exactly malice," said Elly L'O. "They're delighted with anything sensational. Everybody's running after them now, and naturally they like that."

"Well," said Killian after a moment, "let them go ahead. I'm not going to bother."

"You'll have to bother, John," she said. "It's too ugly, and too serious to ignore."

"I'm not going to bother with it."

"You were sitting on the rail with Jocelyn," said Elly L'O. "You had a quarrel with her. You were so cruel to her that she jumped overboard. And you ran to your cabin—without giving an alarm. That's the story."

He was stricken; and that was the only word for it. This attack on him was so senseless, so insane, he could not feel any anger, any impulse to protect himself. The tribe had turned upon him; he could only face them in stoic silence.

"All right!" he said. "If anyone can believe that tale—"

He swam away. Elly L'O stayed where she was, holding to the rail, and he came back to her. She was the only friendly creature left in the world.

"I didn't tell you the story just to make you miserable," she said. "I've thought of a way to stop it. When the Piggott girl told it to me, I said I knew for a fact that there wasn't a word of truth in it, and I just walked off. I needed time to think up something, and now I have. It's beautifully simple. You spent all the evening in the Purser's cabin with him and me."

"Chauverney wouldn't agree to that."

"I know he will."

"He can't do it. He's an officer. If there's any sort of enquiry—"

"Really, he will," she answered him. "He'll say that you and I were in his cabin having a quiet little chat, and we didn't hear anything, or notice any-thing, until the engines began to go astern. Of course, that sent us all flying out to see what was the matter."

"No," said Killian, "you couldn't get Chauverney to agree to that."

"I can," she said.

He looked at her sidelong, but she was looking down into the clear green water.

"Yes," she went on. "We'll all three stick to that story, and it will stop the other ones."

"You're taking a lot of trouble," Killian said. "You're very kind."

"Aren't I?" she said, and smiled. "I'm like that, you know. A heart of gold."

Killian caught sight of three other people coming down the ladder into the water; he turned his head away from them. "I think I'll be going," he said.

"I'll speak to Chauverney," she said, "and I'll let you know. But I promise you in advance that he'll agree. You can start telling our version to anyone you like."

"You're very kind," he said again.

He did not see who had come into the pool; he climbed out, put on his dress-ing gown, and went dripping down to his cabin without looking at anyone. He dressed, and then he sat down in the wicker armchair and took up a book. He lit a cigarette; he turned pages; he wanted to improve his Spanish. He was perfectly cool, composed, sensible. The steward knocked and came in to fill his thermos jug with ice water; he slipped in and out with a downcast, almost a demure air.

"All right!" Killian said to himself. "I'll admit it. I'm afraid to go out of here. Miller knows that. He never saw me sitting in my cabin in the morning be-fore. He knows I'm afraid. I can't face the music. Sweet music. This is some-thing I didn't know. I didn't know how you'd feel when you were slandered. What the hell is the matter with me? Why don't I defend myself?"

There was no impulse in him to defend himself. He was stricken and he wanted only to abide. He was stunned, appalled. Two of his fellow creatures were willing to lie about him, for no reason at all, and others accepted the lie without question. They were not surprised to hear that he had done a mon-strous thing, that he was guilty of the most brutal cowardice. Perhaps everyone believed it; Miller, too.

The Captain would have to investigate such a rumor. Mr. Killian, I've been informed that when Miss Frey jumped overboard you went to your cabin without giving an alarm. Mr. Killian, I've been informed that you ran away and left Miss Frey to drown. Swimming in the sea in a white dress with a silver girdle. With the sharks. With all the monsters of the deep. Well, no, I didn't, Captain Portman. Oh, you didn't, didn't you? Miss Piggott says you did. Mr. Bracey says you did. You look like that. You look like a mean, cowardly, little clerk who'd do exactly that. There's something in your face that makes everyone believe that about you.

Maybe you are like that.

I've never been tested, he thought. How do I know what I'd do in an emergency?

He made up his mind that he would not try to defend himself. He wouldn't say anything. If the Captain asked him questions he would simply say, "No, I wasn't with her. I didn't know anything about it." And his statement would be completely unconvincing. He did not expect anyone to believe him. He would sit alone in the dining saloon; he would walk alone on deck.

Elly means well, he thought. But her idea won't work.

Exactly as if he had had a violent blow in the midriff. He just wanted to be left alone. But someone came knocking at the door.

"What d'you want?" he called.

"It's Doctor Coyle," said the toneless voice.

"Come in!" said Killian, not stirring.

The doctor entered, closing the door behind him; he stood with his hand on the knob, and Killian pretended to go on reading.

"Miss Frey has made a statement," said the doctor.

A dying statement, thought Killian. In a statement made shortly before her death, Miss Frey accused Mr. John Killian of—everything.

"A statement to the Captain—in my presence," the doctor went on, the peevish frown on his white face again. "The Captain—naturally—has to enter the matter in his log."

"All right! Let him!" said Killian.

"Miss Frey wants to see you."

"Is she dying?" asked Killian.

"No, she's not!" said the doctor, irritably. "She wants to see you."

"What about?"

"That girl's in a very bad condition," said the doctor. "As a matter of common decency, if she wants to see you—"

"What does she say in her statement?" Killian asked.

"That's confidential," said the doctor. "Are you coming, or not?"

"No," said Killian. But that was his mind speaking. His blood, his muscles, his nerves, his soul, perhaps, brought him to his feet. "Where is she?" he asked.

"In her cabin, of course."

This amazed Killian. Her cabin was on the promenade deck; he knew that well enough. She had got him in there once to drink a cocktail with her, and she had tried to get him there other times. But when he had been walking up and down the deck, it had never occurred to him that she might be lying in there, a few feet from him. He had thought vaguely of a sick bay, the ship's hospital; he had thought of her as shut away somewhere.

The doctor went before him, walking in a nervous, fussy way; he knocked at the door.

Her low, mournful voice drifted out to them. "All right." The doctor opened the door, and they went in. She was alone. That was queer, thought Killian. Someone ought to be with her—a stewardess, someone. But there she lay, alone, in her unearthly beauty.

I didn't know her hair was so long, Killian thought. It was spread out over the pillow in a soft mist about her pale, worn face. Her eyes were heavy with sorrow; her bare arms lay at her sides above the top of the neatly folded sheet. He saw a band of delicate ecru lace against her white breast.

"Monty, go away, will you?" she said.

The doctor raised her limp wrist, lifting his eyebrows; and she looked up into his face, with her lips parted in a smile.

"Monty, you're such a phony," she said.

He smiled back at her as if complimented. "Five minutes!" he said. "No more. See that she doesn't excite herself, Mr. Killian."

They were alone together.

"Give me a cigarette, Jocko," she said.

"Better not."

"Give me a cigarette," she repeated. "I've been smoking on and off, from four o'clock this morning."

"It can't be good for you."

"No," she said. "You're right. It can't. And I've got to look after my health, haven't I, Jocko? So that this can happen again."

"I don't know what you're talking about," he said flatly.

"I died," she said. "It was just the same as dying. Try it, sometime, and see. Try swimming alone in the ocean in the middle of the night. Then you'll know exactly what it's like to die. But they fished me out, so that I'll have to die all over again sometime. That's what I call hard luck. Jocko, give me a cigarette, my precious one! I need one."

He gave her one, and bent over to light it. And he thought that a bitter smell of salt water came from her hair.

"The Captain came in," she went on. "He explained how he had to write a report about this 'occurrence.' He called it an 'occurrence' a hundred thousand times. He was so shocked, Jocko. He asked me if I was strong enough to give him an account of the 'occurrence'; and I did."

She moved her head on the pillow and gave a tiny sigh.

"You won't ask any questions, will you, Jocko? Why don't you fold your arms? It would look more suitable. Don't you want to hear what I told the Captain?"

"Yes."

"I told him I was drunk, Jocko. I told him I was so drunk I didn't know what I was doing. I told him. I went staggering out on deck, and sat on the rail all alone, and fell overboard."

"Did he believe it?"

"Why shouldn't he? It's much easier to believe than the truth."

He lit a cigarette for himself, standing by the bed. "Well," he said. "I'll buy it. What is the truth?"

"You must have talked to people about it," she said. "What explanation have you given?"

"Nobody's asked me for an explanation."

"If you do get asked?"

"Nothing to say. I don't know whether you fell overboard or jumped overboard."

"Yes," she said slowly. "I thought you were the one who started all that suicide talk."

"I didn't."

"The Captain had heard it," she said. "He was terribly shocked. I had to make up my mind on the spot which tale I'd give him, and I liked the accident one better than the suicide one."

"It was one or the other."

"Like hell it was!" she said. "What's the idea of this, Jocko? I'm not drunk now. Do you think I don't remember? Or did you think I didn't know?"

"Didn't know what?"

"It was murder, Jocko."

"That's just what I'd expect from you," he said; and his voice shook with anger, with a sort of fury.

"You mean, to be murdered?"

"I mean, to say a thing like this."

"Don't worry," she said. "I haven't told anyone else. I've protected you."

"Protected *me?*" he almost shouted.

"Take it easy!" she said.

"This is one time in your life when you have to be rational," he said. "What are you talking about?"

"I'm talking about how you murdered me," she said.

CHAPTER THREE

"Take it easy," he said to himself. "Don't yell. This needs a bit of thinking over. I've got to get away from her, and think it over."

"Where are you going, Jocko?"

"Just out on deck," he answered, in a nice persuasive way. "Just to take a walk."

"Jocko! Even after *this*, can't you say one kind thing?"

"Listen, Jocelyn," he said, still in that persuasive way. "What you said startled me. It's—I can't talk to you now."

"If *I* can talk after what happened to *me*, you can listen."

He stood still, with his hand on the doorknob.

"I was sitting on the rail," she said. "I was tight. As usual. All those little sparks twinkling inside my head. When I get to that stage, I'm happy. I forget all my troubles. Only it's growing harder to reach that stage. I *am* a little tramp, aren't I, Jocko?"

"I haven't known you long enough to answer that, Jocelyn," he said. Trying to be ironic, to be cool and detached, maybe amused.

"I was sitting there looking at the moon. There wasn't any moon, but I didn't know that. Suddenly somebody took me by the throat in a queer way. Not squeezing my throat, just pressing it at the sides, and I went out like a light. Until I struck the water. I went over backwards, headfirst. I went down— oh, God knows how far. Down to the bottom of the sea, down to hell. When I came up, the ship was rushing away. You don't know how fast. I screamed— when I could—but the ship was far away then. I swam after it, and the lights were getting littler and littler. I was left alone in the dark to struggle as long as I could. That's dying, Jocko. I went on swimming like a mouse in a pail of water. Only there weren't any sides to my pail. I didn't squeak any more. I kept on swimming the way you keep on breathing, because you don't know how to stop. But all I thought was: Let this be over. Let this finish, quick. I kicked off my slippers. My skirt got wound around my legs, and I tore most of it away from the waist. The ship was a million miles away then. I thought: When it's out of sight.... Give me your hand to hold!"

He sat down on the bed beside her and took her hand. "Don't talk about it any more," he said.

Her thin little fingers clung to his hand frantically, as if she were drowning now this minute, with her pale hair floating out from her pale face.

"I didn't know when the ship stopped. It was too far away. I didn't know when the boat came after me. I didn't hear it coming. The waves make a noise, or something does. Something roars in your ears."

"Take it easy," he said. He had known it was like that.

"Then I thought of the fishes," she said. "I knew they were all around me, and underneath me."

"Take it easy. Smoke your cigarette."

She threw it, alight, on the floor, and he set his foot on it.

"Then I saw the light from the boat, whatever it was. A torch, was it, Jocko? That was the worst. I turned back and tried to swim faster, away from it. I thought it was something horrible, coming after me. Something worse than the fishes."

He could not get his hand away from her desperately clinging fingers. Clumsily, with one hand, he got out another cigarette and put it between her lips. "Let go, Jocelyn, just a moment, and I'll give you a light."

"All right," she said. Her fingers relaxed; her lashes went down, brushing her pale cheeks. "They say you see your whole past when you're drowning. But I wasn't drowning. I was just dying of loneliness, and I didn't see anything but you."

He struck a match and held it for her. I'm sorry for her, he thought. I'm so sorry for her. She's not responsible. Maybe she's crazy. Maybe she really believes what she said. Maybe if I talk to her.... Don't say you can't talk, because you've damned well got to talk. You've got to end this thing. Take the right tone. That's important. What is the right one?

She put her hand around his neck and tried to pull down his head, but he kept it rigid.

"We're a lot alike, Jocko," she said. "We could go places, you and I. If I had you, I could pull myself together. That's because you know why I've gone all to pieces. It's something that could have happened to you, but you didn't let it. You know how it is when everyone throws stones at you. When you hate everything, even the sun. That's why I have to turn to you. You're the only one."

"I couldn't help you," he said, with a sort of gentleness.

"Kiss me," she said.

"I could do that," he said.

She pulled his head down on the pillow beside her, so that her cheek was against his. He thought that there was that smell of salt water in her hair, and with it the perfume she used, musky and subtle.

"I don't care if you murdered me, Jocko," she said.

"You exaggerate things, darling. You don't feel dead."

"I've been told, Jocko, that you didn't wait on deck to see the lifeboat come back. Other people thought that was strange, but I didn't."

"Didn't you?" he said.

"The nice people," she said, "the kind, tolerant people are saying that all you did was to lead me on and make me so desperate I tried to kill myself. That's the kindest thing that's being said about you."

"We-ell," he said. "No. No, I don't think so. You don't impress people like a girl who is easily led on."

"Would you like to hear what some other people are saying, Jocko?"

"I have heard."

"About how you pushed me overboard, and then rushed down to your cabin? How you came up on the boat deck for a few minutes, looking like a ghost, and couldn't stand it, couldn't wait, until the boat came back. Mr. Bracey saw you going into your cabin, looking like a ghost. And your steward says you looked like a ghost when he told you I'd been saved."

"Why not? Maybe I felt like a ghost."

"One word from me, Jocko, and you're sunk."

He moistened his lips. "I'm sorry about that, Jocelyn. I—it's hard to explain."

"You don't have to explain things to me. I know how you felt. I know why you did that."

"Jocelyn, let's get things straight. If you can get anything straight. I did not choke you and throw you overboard."

"Skip it!" she said. Her lashes fluttered against his cheek. "You did it, and somebody saw you, Jocko; but I don't care."

"Who saw me?"

"Skip that, too, Jocko; when we land, I'm going to visit the Bells out on Long Island. Come with me."

"No. Who saw me committing this little murder?"

"That's my trump card. I don't play it yet, Jocko. Come with me just for the weekend."

"No."

"If you're going to resist, Jocko, I'll turn on the heat."

He pushed away her head and sat up, looking down at her.

"Do whatever you please, Jocelyn," he said. "I won't try to stop you. You could make a lot of gossip on the ship, that's all. But I'm getting off the ship—"

"You just don't get the point," she said, interrupting him. "If I say you pushed me overboard, you'll go to jail."

Yes, he thought, she might be able to do that. There's plenty of suspicion against me already. God knows why. If she felt like it, she could make it serious. Let her! I'm sick and tired of this. Of her.

"Will you come with me to the Bells', Jocko?"

"I will not, Jocelyn."

"You'd rather go to prison?"

"Much rather."

"Think it over," she said. "You'd hate it. But I shouldn't. I like things to be dramatic and sensational. I'd like to see you in the dock charged with assault and intent to kill, and the whole thing in the headlines. You'd probably get off in the end, but you'd be ruined. I'm ruined already, so I don't care.

I'd a damn sight rather see you in prison than lose you."

"You could see both, you know. I suppose you could make trouble for me with a trumped-up charge."

"Why trumped-up?" she said. "Somebody else saw you, too. There was a witness to that little job of yours."

"I'm going," he said. "I don't want to talk any more."

"You *can't* go!" she cried. "Good God! What more do you want! You *murder* me, and I forgive you. I keep on loving you."

"Jocelyn..." he said unsteadily. "Please—"

He was shaking, and that worried him; he wanted to give all his attention to stopping that. His hands shook, his knees; his heart was doing something.

"I only ask you to give me that weekend. Just a chance to make you love me. You've *got* to do it!"

"Can't!" he said.

"You *murdered* me!" she cried. "I'll never forget the look on your face."

"Please don't talk so loud," he said.

"Look at me!"

He turned his head. She was sitting up straight; her mouth was open in a queer way; tears were raining from her wide-open eyes. That's anguish, he thought. That's what they call anguish. How can I make her shut up? What can I say? What's the matter with me?

"Jocko!" she screamed. "You look the same way *now!* You're ready to kill me *again!*"

He strode across the room, opened the door, and went out. He ran full tilt into the doctor; it knocked the breath out of him for a moment.

"I was coming to turn you out," said the doctor. "She's been talking too much."

There was nothing to see in his face but that look of peevish fretfulness. That's the only way he can look, Killian thought. He'd look just the same if he'd heard her. I don't know what to do. I'll have to think this out. Very serious, this is. Or isn't it?

He went to his cabin and locked the door. Then he hastily unlocked it. If the steward came, it would look.... How would it look? Everything he did, or could do, would look wrong. Time for lunch. Go down and sit at that table like a pariah? I must say he has a wonderful appetite. Not much upset about the poor girl, is he? Or, he can't eat a thing. Naturally.

Elly means well, he thought. And maybe Chauverney would have agreed to that story about my being in his cabin. Would have, when it was just a matter of shutting up a lot of gossips. But not if Jocelyn's going to accuse me of murdering her. That is very silly. You can't talk about murdering someone who's alive. But if she says I tried to kill her, Chauverney won't stand by that story. Not if Jocelyn makes a charge against me. Chauverney wouldn't commit a perjury for me. Nor for Elly, either.

He lit another cigarette. Smoking too much, he thought. He stood in the middle of his cabin because he didn't know what to do. Whether to go down to lunch or not.

You look the same way *now!* You're ready to kill me *again!*

It worried him that his hands shook so. Of course, I didn't try to kill her. I never even thought of it. But when she started screaming like that, you felt... You felt that you wanted to stop her—at any cost. Want to make her be quiet. At any cost. You felt.... You felt....

Let it alone. Never mind how you felt. There are those things below the surface immemorially old and hideous, like black, prowling beasts. Leave them alone. You've got them chained. They can't get out. As a man thinketh in his heart.... Not at all! You've thought some damn queer things about that girl, on and off. And it doesn't matter. As long as you don't *do* anything. You can shake like a leaf, shut up in your own cabin, and whose business is that?

"This is a curious experience," he said aloud.

There was a knock on the door. "Purser's compliments, sir," said a cheerful little boy, "and will you please join him in his cabin for cocktails in ten minutes, sir?"

"Tell him, yes, thanks," said Killian.

Chauverney moved about in his cabin; the word for it was 'flitting,' thought Killian. He was impressed with the extraordinary frivolity of the Purser as he talked—talked nonsense, smiling his very vivid smile. His boy brought in cocktails and left them on the table; three glasses, Killian noticed. "The stock market..." Chauverney was saying. On and on. "Reminds me of the story of the stockbroker and the parson's daughter." On and on.

There was a light knock at the door, and Elly came in. She had her black hair done in a pompadour, and she wore a dark green silk dress with tiny glittering buttons up the front of it; she looked, thought Killian, like a heroine from a novel of the Nineties, stylish and self-possessed.

"Not so hot," she said.

"Who isn't?" Chauverney demanded.

"Oh, I mean the *weather!*" she said, and they all laughed.

Chauverney sat down, but the effect of flitting remained. His mind was flitting, obviously reluctant to settle.

"There's been some shifting about in the dining saloon," he said suddenly. "I'd be very pleased if you'd sit at my table, Mr. Killian."

"Thanks," said Killian, and waited for more. But Chauverney and Elly were both silent. Killian was silent, too, trying to think, but his mind was doing something else; it was not possible to think until he got free from this smothering cloud that oppressed him. He thought that if he could talk.... "Well, why?" he asked.

"Oh, glad to have your company," said Chauverney.

"No," said Killian. "The women who were sitting at my table...." He raised his hand and checked it in mid-air. He realized with some surprise that he had been going to make a very theatric gesture; he had been going to draw the back of his hand across his forehead. "All this...."

"Oh, least said, soonest mended," said Chauverney briskly.

Least said? thought Killian. I've just been listening to Jocelyn. You wouldn't call that the least. All about my murdering her. Love—murder.

"I think Mr. Killian would rather have things more definite," said Elly.

"But there's nothing definite about the situation, Mrs. L'O," said Chauverney. "Nothing but gossip—ship's gossip. When you've been at sea as long as I have.... I assure you it's better to ignore the whole thing. If Mr. Killian will sit at my table.... We'll simply carry on, eh?"

Mr. Killian, Mr. Chauverney, and Mrs. L'O—all sitting here. The Gay Nineties. Let's behave like ladies and gentlemen. Jocelyn is impossible. Let us ignore her, and then she will disappear.

"Another cocktail, Mr. Killian?"

"No, thanks."

Elly took another, and so did Chauverney.

"This idea of Miss Frey's is very sound," said Chauverney. "This idea of our going to the Bells' for the weekend."

"Our going?" said Killian.

"Yes. You and I. Miss Frey spoke to me about it as a practical way to put a stop to—everything. I mean to say the passengers will certainly go on talking after they go ashore. But if we both go off with Miss Frey.... That's the best thing. The Captain will make his report, of course. The newspapers may get hold of something; but if we accept Miss Frey's idea.... Very sound. The whole thing will blow over then."

"You'll have to go with her," said Elly without emphasis. "She's a damned dangerous, sadistic liar. It's a great pity she was ever fished out of the sea. I wish she had been drowned."

"My God!" murmured Chauverney.

Elly rose and took up her white purse, very smart.

"Let's go down to lunch," she said.

CHAPTER FOUR

The people at the Purser's table were superior. There was a doctor, a heart specialist taking a holiday; and a young couple, very rich and very unostentatious—both of them tall, good-looking, serious about social problems, and conscientious about taking part in things. They signed up for everything, bridge tournaments, ping-pong tournaments; they were superlatively good at games—they would have won everything if they had ever played as partners. They talked about the entertainment they were getting up; they wanted to consult with Chauverney, but their good breeding and their social conscience made them include the doctor and Elly and Killian in everything.

If they've heard that talk about me, thought Killian, they wouldn't believe it. They're like that. But I'm not. I can believe in evil without any trouble.

The lunch was immeasurably soothing to him; and when the young couple asked him to play quoits with them, he accepted gladly. He had stepped into another world, polite and normal, in which Jocelyn was impossible. He could forget her. The young couple introduced him to some other people he had not spoken to before, and everybody liked him. He felt popular, quite blithe. Later he went into the pool again; before dinner he had cocktails with a little group in the smoke-room. And that evening he danced.

He had not danced since he came on board, nor wanted to; several times he had sat with Jocelyn watching the others, both of them in that mist of loneliness that she evoked. "I hate dancing," she had told him. "Being guided around. I get in a sort of panic." It was a defiance of Jocelyn to be dancing with the tall, superior girl from the Purser's table; the music and the little coloured lights were a defiance of the ocean. None of these pleasant, nice people had mentioned Jocelyn, and that put her in her place. She was something that had happened on a voyage, that's all.

Elly spoiled everything. "John," she said, when he was dancing with her, "you're going to the Bells' aren't you?"

"Let's not talk about that now," he said.

"Let's *never* talk about it," said Elly. "Just go, and that will be the end of it."

"Sorry," he said, "but it's the end of it for me when I put my foot on shore."

"It won't be the end, if you thwart our little friend," she said.

"She might just as well be thwarted now as later," he said.

She gripped his hand and frowned, with a look of exasperation. "Don't be pig-headed! I've tried to help you," she said.

"I know that," Killian said. "I appreciate it. But—"

She still held his hand, still frowning. "Then do this for me," she said. "One weekend out of your life can't hurt you, and it will really help me."

"How do you mean, help *you?*" he asked.

"Oh, it's complicated," she said. "It's crazy and horrible. But Jocelyn's got it in her head that I can persuade you to come, and if you won't come she'll blame me."

"Does that matter?" he asked, frowning himself. "Do you mind being blamed by her?"

"We all have our horrible little secrets," she said with a sigh. "I do mind. She could make things *very* unpleasant for me."

So she's got something on you, has she? thought Killian. And this weekend is the cure for everything? I can't see it. It's easy to believe that Jocelyn would make all the trouble she could for anyone. I like Elly. She helped me, and I'd be glad to help her. But this weekend idea won't do any good. Couldn't. I'm not going to visit these Bells. I'm going to get away from Starry Eyes. Maybe it's because I hate her, or maybe I'm afraid of her; but I'm going to get away from her.

He went to bed, and he was nearly asleep when someone knocked at the door.

"Radio message for you, sir," said the calm and melancholy voice of the watchman.

He put on the light, and took the message. "Delighted to welcome you. Will meet ship. Luther Bell."

He tore the message into pieces and threw them out of the port. He saw them spin and flutter in the light, and then float away into darkness. He put out the light and lay down and went to sleep at once, feeling that he had accomplished something important.

He went down to breakfast in the morning with a feeling of confidence, of vigour, that made him happy. Across the room he saw the two spinsters who had abandoned him; one of them gave a bleak little smile, but he did not return it. He was now, thank God, in another world, and they were left behind with Jocelyn and Mr. Bracey and the doctor and other shadows. Chauverney was alone at his table, smoking a cigarette.

"Oh, good morning!" he said eagerly, and pushed back his chair as if he were about to rise respectfully.

Angelo came forward, anxious and gentle, and Killian gave him his unvarying order.

"Did you get a wireless from Bell?" asked Chauverney, and laughed. "I never quite get used to American hospitality. It's overwhelming. Still, I hear that the Bells do you very well. We ought to have a good weekend."

"I'm not going," said Killian.

Chauverney's dark face was too mobile; his expression of surprise was exaggerated. "Oh," he said, "I understood that when we talked the thing over yesterday with Mrs. L'O... I thought the thing was settled."

"I never considered it for a moment," said Killian. "I have my own arrangements. I'm not going to visit these people I never heard of before."

"Look here, Killian!" Chauverney began, and was unable to go on for a while. "Killian," he said at last, "that girl can do you a great deal of harm."

"Not too much."

"Killian," he began again, "it's a matter of—" He stopped and made an odd grimace. "I'll be frank," he said, getting out another cigarette. "The situation is dangerous, Killian."

"For me?"

"Yes."

Killian waited.

"The doctor..." said Chauverney. "He told me he heard the girl say—a very peculiar thing."

"Oh, yes! She said I murdered her. But I don't think that needs to be taken very seriously. In the first place, y'see, she's not dead. And, in the second place, she's already given the Captain one account of the thing. If she suddenly came out with another version, he wouldn't be entirely convinced, would he?"

"If she makes a charge against you, he's got to take it seriously."

"*I* don't have to," said Killian. "When a girl tells me I've murdered her, I take it with a grain of salt."

"There's a bit more to it than that," murmured Chauverney. "The doctor says he heard her say—says he couldn't help hearing her say—that you were going to try it again."

"She did say that."

"In the ordinary course of things, I'd have reported it to the Captain. But in the circumstances, I advised the doctor to let it drop. I told him it was obviously"—he paused—"a love affair."

"Very tropical love," said Killian.

"And if you and she leave the ship together—go off for a weekend together—he'll be convinced. He's very fond of talking, y'know, Killian."

"Everybody seems to be," said Killian.

"For God's sake!" said Chauverney in a sudden rage. "*Can't* you behave decently? If you don't care anything for your own reputation, can't you consider other people?" He jerked back his chair. "Take my word for it," he said. "If you won't do this very trifling thing, all hell will break loose."

He walked off, slender and elegant in his white uniform; and Killian drank his coffee. I won't go to the Bells', he thought. I won't behave decently. I won't consider other people. How many other people? I wouldn't know.

All morning he was waiting for a summons from Jocelyn; at noon he went to look for the doctor. "How's Miss Frey getting on?" he asked.

"She's exhausted," the doctor answered fretfully. "I've forbidden any visitors."

And it went on that way.

Everything was so pleasant. The weather was pleasant, calm and warm; the young couple and the heart specialist were pleasant, and they introduced Killian to two or three other pleasant people. This little group stayed together all the time; they never broke up without arranging to meet again. "Then I'll see you up at the swimming pool at four?... Then we'll meet in the smoke-room at half-past six?"

Nobody mentioned Jocelyn; she was not to be seen. Killian was able to forget her. He lived in this pleasantness for three days as if it were Heaven—no past, no future; and he made no plans. Then on the last night the weather changed.

The rain came down hissing into the rumbling sea; a rough wind blew; the ship rolled heavily. Killian started his packing before dinner, and it was difficult and irritating. Things fell down; the little wicker chair balanced on its hind legs, creaking; everything creaked and strained; his cabin was damp and chilly and blue with smoke. It was sad.

He shut and locked his trunk and got ready for dinner. They had had the Captain's dinner last night. Paper cups, noisemakers, champagne at the Purser's table. Elly had been given a little Scotch bonnet of plaid paper, and she put it on with the style that was natural to her. To-night everyone looked strange. No more white suits. Everyone in dark clothes; all looking strange and a little common. Peasants going to town. I look like a gun-man, he thought. Dark and sinister. *What's happened to me, anyhow?*

The pleasantness had evaporated; no one had anything to say. All of them preoccupied, thinking ahead.

"There's Miss Frey," said the heart specialist in his quiet voice. "At the doctor's table."

Killian had his back to that table. If he didn't look at her, maybe she wouldn't really be there. The orchestra was playing Gems from Gilbert and Sullivan. Gems from Victor Herbert. The ship wallowed slowly, and the stewards came slanting across the saloon. Angelo leaned back a little, carrying his great ceremonious tray loaded with silver dishes.

Well, she's there, thought Killian. The more you don't look at her, the worse it is. He turned in his chair and saw her. He saw her face in profile, pale, sweetly delicate against her bright, misty hair. She wore a white silk blouse, and it took the gentle lines of her slight shoulder and bosom. "That is beauty," he said to himself. Oh, I could look at you forever. Anyone could write a poem, looking at you. Your throat is beautiful, my beloved, and your little narrow feet are swift. Your waist is like a wand, and your legs are slim and nervous as a gazelle's. Beauty is only skin deep. Beauty is a delusion and a snare. Get thee to a nunnery.

He rose and went to her. "Glad to see you down again," he said earnestly. "Feeling better?"

She raised her tired lids, and her eyes were violet, not starry. Dark; fath-
omless and dark. She didn't answer at all, and he went back to his place.

The pleasant people all went up to the smoke-room together. They had to
do that. They sat there and had liqueur brandy. Only Elly had a Kümmel. The
steward was nimble and composed. He had already presented his chits; he had
already got his tips. Was he disappointed, or did he have some infallible sys-
tem by which he could figure out in advance what he would get? They broke
up early; they all had packing to do. Killian went to his cabin, and Jocelyn
was there.

She was sitting in the little wicker armchair, her long legs stretched out, her
arms hanging limply.

"Close the door," she said, and he did so. She held up her arms to him, and
he drew her to her feet. She clung to him wildly, trembling. There was a
dreadful sense of urgency and haste upon them, as if in a moment the world
was going to end.

"*Forgive* me!" she cried. "I don't know any better."

"Dear," he said. "Don't, dear."

He stroked her hair back from her forehead; he had wanted to do that for
a long time. She was sobbing, but with no tears; she clung to him; she
turned to him for comfort, for help. But he felt no triumph, only a tenderness
that was almost anguish, an overwhelming gentleness.

"Don't, dear," he said.

"I love you so," she said. "I don't care about anything else."

She was right. Nothing else mattered. He sat down on the chair and took
her on his knees; she laid her head on his shoulder, one arm around his neck.
"It's only for a little while," she said. "Let's be happy while we can. Let's
not care."

He didn't care.

CHAPTER FIVE

At breakfast he gave Angelo a good tip—not lavish, but good. A degrading custom, the heart specialist thought, but Killian didn't agree. "It must make life a damn sight more interesting than a fixed salary," he said. "And it's an incentive to work, too. I wish I got tips myself."

"It's a matter of self-respect," the specialist said.

"Well," said Killian, "I have to get my money from somebody else. I can't demand anything. I have to take what's given to me, and I'd be glad of a little extra now and then. I could call it a bonus, of course."

He went on deck. They had run out of the bad weather; it was a fresh and glittering May morning, very exhilarating. He was not able to think and could see no necessity for trying. He lit a cigarette and stood by the rail; two or three people stopped to talk to him, and they were all happy. We're like convalescents, he thought, getting back into life. Where's my girl?

If people wanted to talk to him, he would talk. If they let him alone, it was just as good. He saw the gentle hills of Staten Island, and that made him remember taking a ride on the ferry last summer with a girl. A fat man in a grey cap with a camera slung over his shoulder sat down in Jocelyn's deck chair, and that upset Killian. He wanted to tell the fellow to get out. Get off the earth.

It was her earth. She came out on deck in a black suit with a collar of silver fox that brushed her pale face, a black hat with a veil across her eyes. She was a princess, shrinking a little from contact with other people, aloof, almost frightened.

"Jocko?"

"All packed, dear?" he asked. "Everything under control?"

"I haven't any money for tips," she said. "All my money was in my little silver evening bag; and that went overboard."

"Sit down, and I'll get you some money." He went to the Purser's office and got a couple of traveler's checks cashed.

"You pay them, Jocko," she said. "I never know how much to give."

"Steward, stewardess, table steward—anyone else, dear?"

"I don't know, Jocko. The deck steward? He's done things."

Nobody came to talk to her. When he returned after distributing largesse, she still sat there alone. "How about your passport, Jocelyn? And your landing card?"

"I don't know," she said.

"You can't land without your card."

"Chauverney will do something about it," she said.

He got her to look in her purse, and then in her pockets, and she found the card. "Do you feel all right?" he asked, troubled.

"I hate to go ashore," she said. "I'm frightened."

He sat down on the foot-rest of her chair; he lit a cigarette for her and tried to make her talk. Nothing she did, or said, was irritating to him. He had never before been patient with anyone, but for her he had a patience without limit. "Nothing to be afraid of," he told her.

"I don't want to go to the Bells'," she said.

"Don't then."

"I have to," she said. "Please, Jocko, don't ask me about it. I have to go, Jocko. I wish I'd never told you anything about myself."

"What you told me doesn't matter."

She gave him a veiled, furtive glance. "I haven't had a drink for five days," she said. "I hope I'll never take another."

You wouldn't, he thought, if you had someone to look after you. A crazy kid, drifting around, lost and lonely. Wasting her life, throwing away her youth, her beauty, all the bewildered gentleness of her heart. If there were someone to help her....

The people at the rail were beginning to wave at friends they saw, or thought they saw, on the pier.

"Any of your family coming to meet you, Jocelyn?" he asked.

"No," she answered. "They don't know I'm on this ship. If they knew, they'd meet me, all right. With their hard-luck stories. They'd want money."

"Have you any money?"

"Enough," she said, and took his hand. "Jocko, don't go away! Not yet! Wait till I get back on earth."

"I'm going along with you."

They waited until the first eager crowd had gone ashore; then they rose, without speaking, without looking at each other. She went down the gang-plank first. A woman came up to her and drew her aside, and Killian went to wait for his luggage. He did not look in Jocelyn's direction. I don't want to see the Bells, he thought. They're rich. Probably Jocelyn's rich. And I'm feeling very poor, just now. My dear Jocelyn, who is this impossible young man? A mere clerk. A fortune hunter. I have nothing to declare. That's symbolic. C'est la vie. La vida. Vida es sueño. Well, if life is a dream, it's not a peaceful one.

"Mr. Killian?" said a voice. "I'm Harriet Lamb."

That's nice, thought Killian. Only who is Harriet Lamb? A darn cross-looking lamb you are, if you ask me. A tall girl, sunburnt to a biscuit colour, with sandy brows straight across her face, and half-closed eyes, and a straight, wide mouth; sandy hair, curly and short, with two points at the temples like little horns. No hat, no coat, no gloves—just standing there in a blue cotton dress.

"We're ready," she said. "If you'll come along."

"I'm sorry," Killian explained, "but I'll have to clear my baggage."

"The chauffeur will do that. Give me your keys and that thing—that slip—whatever you call it."

"Do you belong to the Bells?" he asked.

"Yes. Of course," she said, and held out her hand.

You want the keys, he thought. You're a bully. A rich vixen. He took her outstretched hand and shook it. "Very nice to see you, Miss Lamb," he said, earnestly.

Her eyes got a little narrower. "If you'll hand over your keys," she said, "we needn't waste any more time. The others are waiting."

He gave her his key ring, and she handed it to the chauffeur in uniform who hovered near her. "This way," she said, and set off, walking fast, toward the little group waiting for her: Jocelyn, and Elly, and Chauverney. "Ready?" she asked.

"I'll see you later," said Chauverney, smiling at everyone.

"This way!" said Harriet Lamb again. She herded them into an elevator and down to the street, where a very superior open car waited. "Mr. Killian, will you sit in front with me?" she said.

She set off, driving adroitly through the traffic, and Killian looked sidelong at her. She's handsome, he thought. In her way. Her features were a little sharp, and her underlip a little outthrust; and that, combined with her narrowed eyes, gave her a dogged and even menacing look. But, just the same, she was handsome, and finely put together—nice spaces, strong lines, good wrists. And who may you be, Miss Lamb? What's a Lamb doing among Bells?

What am I doing among Bells? I don't even know where I'm going. Long Island, Chauverney said. I'm just going along with Jocelyn. As if I couldn't help myself. And maybe I can't. That's love, isn't it? To get caught in a current, and dragged along. And drowned?

Very likely. I don't know what I'm going to do with Jocelyn. Marry her and put her into a cute little apartment in Brooklyn? She may have a lot of money. She said she had "enough," but God knows what that means. If she has a lot of money, that will be a problem. And if she hasn't, that will be another problem. And it is my job to solve all problems, forever more. The great handicap is that I don't seem to have any brains.

"Did you have a nice trip?" asked Harriet, suddenly.

"Fine, thanks!" he said.

She waited a moment. "Do you live in New York?" she asked, with the same suddenness.

"Yes, I do," he answered.

"Do you work in New York?" she asked.

She wants to know about me, he thought. Why not? "I'm a clerk," he said.

"A clerk?" she repeated. "What's that?"

"I work in an office," he said.

"Oh, that? 'Clerk's' a funny word to use." She waited again for a moment. "Have you got any judges or generals and so on in your family?" she asked.

"I had an uncle who was killed by the Black and Tans in Ireland," he said.

"Well," she said in a pompous way. "That's very interesting."

"I don't think so," said Killian.

"Rebel, are you?" she said, looking at him sidelong.

"No," he said. "I'm resigned."

"My mother likes to get a line on people," she said.

"Mrs. Lamb has the right idea," said Killian.

"My mother is Mrs. Bell," she said.

They were out of the city now, and Killian looked about him dispassionately, at a landscape like a nightmare, filling stations of crude, fantastic designs and bright colours, hot-dog stands, fields of broken-down old cars.

"This is how the world is going to look after the next war," said Killian.

"Nope," said Harriet. "This is nothing but a transition stage."

"It could be a transition into something even worse."

"No," she said in her curt fashion. "We've got enough brains and enough good will to make it better."

"Who's we?" asked Killian.

"If you're psychologically healthy," said Harriet, "you'll always think We. Not Me—and the rest of the world."

"What do you call it if you just think about Me, and not about the rest of the world at all?" he asked.

"That's insanity," said she.

Now they were driving through a town, old houses with wide lawns and fine trees delicately green.

"We had a letter from Jocelyn," said Harriet. "She sent it air mail from Trinidad."

"Oh, did she?" said Killian.

"It was a pretty queer letter," Harriet said. "About her being murdered."

"Well, well!" said Killian affably.

"She wrote that if anything happened—anything that looked like an accident—it would really be murder."

They drove on and on.

"Did she say who was going to murder her?" Killian asked.

"I didn't see all of the letter," Harriet answered. "It was to Mr. Bell. But I think she did say."

"Dramatic," said Killian.

"Well," said Harriet, "nothing did happen to her—no accident. So we needn't bother."

With nonchalance, with style, Harriet turned the car into a driveway. This is an Estate, thought Killian. You couldn't see the house at all until you turned a curve in the road. This is a Mansion, he thought. A long façade of yellow brick, faced with white, a brick terrace with a blue and white striped awning over it.

I'm going to meet Mr. Bell, he thought. I'd like to know…. But it's what you'd call a delicate subject. Oh, Mr. Bell, by the way, I wonder if you got a letter from a—er—mutual friend, mentioning me as a possible murderer? If you did, I assure you, my dear Mr. Bell, that the thing is very much exaggerated. In the first place, the party is still alive; and, in the second place, she's engaged to me. If that's what you call it.

A man-servant came running down the broad stone steps and opened the doors of the car; and they got out: the lean and sandy Harriet, chic little Elly, and Jocelyn, like a lost princess, pale and strange.

He went up the steps with her, and a man came out of the house. He had to be Mr. Bell, Killian thought, a big man with a big chest pushed out nobly, a square, handsome, noble face, and white hair. The Stuffed Shirt Supreme, he thought. You could never talk to him, and he avoided talk. He has records inside that head.

"Mr. Killian? I'm glad to welcome you to Christmas House…. There's a little story connected with that name. Some years ago a nephew of mine came here, as a small boy. It had been snowing, and he was much impressed by the various evergreens we have here. 'Are those Christmas trees?' he asked his mother. 'Yes,' she answered. 'Yes.' 'Then,' cried the little fellow, 'this must be where Santa Claus lives!'"

Killian laughed and laughed, and Bell was pleased. "Harriet," he said, "we might foregather, don't you think?"

"They'll want to wash first," she answered.

"Then shall we say in fifteen minutes?" asked Bell.

"In half an hour," said Harriet.

She herded the guests into the house. She gave Jocelyn to a housemaid; she gave Killian to the man-servant; and she herself took Elly. It was all done quietly and with an air of inexorable coolness.

"This is your room, sir," said the butler, opening a door. A fine, large room furnished in chilly grey and blue; with the Chesterfield upholstered armchair, the thick carpet, the framed pictures, it looked wrong to see a stark little bed there. "This is the telephone, sir, connected with my quarters. If you wish anything…. This is the bathroom, sir." He opened a door, and there was the bathroom with a man in it, a huge fellow wearing no more than a pair of white trunks. He stared at them from under his knitted brows, his head lowered like a bull's, his big, brawny body easily balanced, his fingers curled. The white-tiled room glittered with light; he looked as if he were being exhibited in a box, or something too menacing to be let loose.

"Pardon me, sir!" said the butler, and shut him in again. "The bathroom is also used by Doctor Ponievsky, sir," he explained, and went out, closing the door behind him.

"Now I've got to think," Killian said to himself. He lit a cigarette and began to smoke, standing in the middle of the room, where he could watch the door into the bathroom and the door into the hall. That was how he felt. Threatened.

"That's damned nonsense," he told himself. But, just the same, that was how he felt. I've got to think. Suppose the worst has happened. The worst being that Jocelyn wrote about me to Bell. About me murdering her. But, my God, she's not dead! That ought to count for something in my favour. What they call extenuating circumstances. Every time she accuses me of murdering her, that's going to be my defense. But, Your Honor, she's not dead. That's a good point.

This is a nice room. This is a nice house. It's a nice day. See it? Blue sky, sun shining. But I am frightened. I don't know what I'm afraid of, but I'm frightened all right. It must be the devil. No use watching the doors. Dat ole Debbil, he come whar he want. It's not funny. It's like a fog. Like a damn cold sea fog. You can't see ahead. What's happened to my life? What's happened to me?

There was a knock at the door. He moistened his lips and said, "Come in!" very politely. It was the chauffeur with his three bags.

"Will you want your trunk up, sir?"

"No thanks. I'm leaving to-morrow," he answered.

When the man had gone, he rapped on the bathroom door and, getting no answer, went in there and washed. He took his comb and stood before the mirror, and his face was like a mask. A mask of a man in torment, black hollows under his cheekbones; his deep-set eyes were hollow; his mouth looked stretched.

"What's the matter with me?" he cried in his heart.

It was the light over the mirror. It was nothing else. When he looked at himself in the bedroom mirror, he was all right. A neat, sober young man in a dark suit. I don't know whether it's ten minutes or half an hour, or an hour and a half, he thought, but I'm going down now. To foregather. This must be where Santa Claus lives.

They were all out on the terrace, having drinks. As Killian appeared, a woman came toward him, a thin and long-waisted blonde, with a horse-like face, hollow cheeks, big, square teeth revealed by a dazzling smile. "Mr. Killian, I'm Sibyl Bell," she said. "This is Doctor Ponievsky. Eric, Mr. Killian."

"I think we have met before," said the doctor, with a wonderfully foxy look. He burst into a great laugh, and held out his hand. "I did not know, in that moment, that I had a neighbour yet," he said. "From now, we shall live very harmoniously, eh?"

"Help yourself, Mr. Killian," said Sibyl, with a gesture of her hand toward a table; and he went there and poured himself a modest drink of whisky. "There's soda and ginger ale," said Mrs. Bell.

"No, thanks," said Killian. He drank the whisky straight; then he looked round with a smile. A genial smile. Hello, boys and girls. Harriet was sitting on the stone balustrade; and Ponievsky stood beside her, looking down at her with bland delight. And she looked up at him with a frown.

He turned his head to find Jocelyn. She was sitting in a wicker chair at the end of the terrace all alone, no one talking to her, no one standing near her. She was still wearing her hat with a veil, and that gave her a fugitive air; she didn't belong here, or anywhere else.

"Where do you live, anyhow?" he asked.

"I told you I had a family," she said. "They've got a floor in a house."

"Is that your home?"

"Sure," she said, with a faint smile.

"You're too mysterious," he said, curtly.

"It's a good line."

"Only it's not a line," he said.

"I'll tell you anything you want," she said. "Just ask me."

"All right! Why are we all here?"

"I come here a lot. And I wanted you with me, Jocko."

"All right! But why the others?"

She looked affrighted, and almost humble. "It came into my head, Jocko...."

"All right! We'll let it go. But there's another thing?"

"Yes?" she said, with her sorrowful dark eyes fixed upon his face.

Maybe I won't go on, he thought. Maybe I'll keep clear of the murder motif. It gets on your nerves. He finished his drink and stared into the empty glass. No, let's be frank and manly. Square your shoulders and look the wench in the eye. Humph, humph. "You wrote to Mr. Bell," he said. "Air mail from Trinidad. All about how you were going to get yourself murdered?"

"I didn't know then," she said.

"Didn't know what?"

"I didn't know I was going to love you," she said, faintly.

"I'm sorry," he said, "but I'm dumb. Brutish. No finesse. I'm afraid we've got to have an understanding."

"We have an understanding," she said. "We love each other."

"Yes," he said. "That's nice. That's cute. But still I want to know. Did you write Mr. Bell, air mail, that I was going to murder you?"

"I didn't mention any names."

"But you thought I *was* going to?"

She still looked down, and not at him. "I knew how you felt," she said in a low, unsteady voice. "But I didn't know how I felt. I didn't know that even that wouldn't kill my love."

"Either you're crazy," he said, "or you're a damned liar. Or both."

She looked up then, straight into his eyes. They looked and looked at each other.

"I wasn't the one who brought this up," she said. "If you'd let me alone, I'd never have spoken of it again. I don't care. If I'd died, I'd have gone on loving you until the end."

Fury rose in his throat, choking him; his head pounded. "As long as you think that," he said, "I quit."

"Wait!" she said as he turned away.

"Nope! All is over."

"It will be," she said. "I'll kill myself."

"That'll be a nice little change from murder," he said.

He had turned his back on her. He could walk away now. This was the time to go; this was the only time, the last chance. If she had called him, he could have left her; but the blank silence was unbearable. He had to see what she was doing.

She was sitting there in her hat, with the veil over her eyes, completely alone, abandoned, and in despair. Yet it was not pity that made him stop, and it was not love. We belong together, he thought.

It was like that. Not pity and not love. When he had sat beside her, the day after she had been fished out of the sea, she had clung to him. She couldn't help it; she had nobody else. And he couldn't help it, either. They belonged together. He went back to her with a business-like smile. "Have a cigarette?" he said. "Pull yourself together. Don't be so morbid. It's boring."

"I'm tired!" she cried, and her eyes filled with tears.

"All right! Go upstairs and go to sleep."

"Come with me?" she asked.

"No," he said. "We'll meet at dinner."

She got up; stood with her hand on the back of her chair, swaying a little. As if she were drunk, or as if she were faint, ill—very ill. Her eyes were wide and blank in her pale face. She was incredibly slight and frail. She turned and started to walk away.

"Whither now?" he asked.

"Just going to take a walk, Jocko."

"I'll be seeing you," he said, in a hearty way, and went back to the others.

Ponievsky was now sitting on the balustrade beside Harriet; his twinkling, smallish eyes were fixed upon her steadily; he looked amused, pleased, charmed. His very obvious interest didn't embarrass her; she was talking to him in her own fashion, composed, curt, with long pauses. When she had nothing to say, she was silent, making no effort.

He went over to Elly, who sat beside Sibyl; Luther Bell was standing before them, nobly benevolent. They all talked very nicely. The country at this time of the year.... Lovely, but we do need rain. Now—er—in Buenos Aires, the climate? Nice climate. Is that so? Luther Bell had a fine voice, flexible and deeply sincere. Did he, or did he not, receive a letter containing a statement to the effect that the defendant did wantonly, and with malice aforethought, murder the said Jocelyn Frey?

If she did write that to him, thought Killian, he's the wonder of the world. Doesn't show any curiosity about me. Maybe she mentioned another murderer. She said there were five, didn't she? It's a mistake; it's a big mistake to have drinks at half-past three in the afternoon. You don't want to go on drinking until dinner time, but what else can you do?

Sibyl took charge of that. "We'll have time to go and look at the sea wall and the pier," she said. "The storm made a perfect holocaust of them."

"Holocaust is a burnt sacrifice," said Ponievsky. "It cannot be that a storm should make it." He was not rude, he just knew everything, that was all.

"I'll take your word for it," said Sibyl.

She herded them all into the car, with Killian beside her, and she drove them off along a road lined with estates, down to the shore. They got out, and walked on a wide, empty beach; they inspected a stone wall battered down by the sea, and a wooden pier broken in two. The sea was calm enough today, pallid, no colour at all beneath the sky that was filled with mother-of-pearl light from the westering sun.

"The sea is a great hypocrite," said Ponievsky. "You see how she is purring now, when she has done all this bad work." He was pleased with this. "She is purring, but she is not asleep. She will strike again." He glanced at Harriet to see if she appreciated this. But her face was not to be read; she was looking out over the sea. She moved away and he went with her.

"Don't go there!" Sibyl screamed, suddenly.

Ponievsky and Harriet were on the pier; they were standing at the very edge of the break, both so tall, outlined against the pearly sky.

"They know what they're doing, my dear," said Bell.

"Come back!" screamed Sibyl, in a voice as harsh as a seagull's; and they heard her, and they did come back.

It was growing chilly now. The tide was running out; the light was running out of the sky; a raw little salt wind blew up against their faces. They stood on the damp sand and waited until Sibyl gave the order to retreat; then two by two they went up the steps to the road and got into the car.

All very sad, thought Killian. But tranquil. Like the end of something. I got away from Jocelyn for two hours, and I didn't think about her. I forgot her. That shows character. I'm not the type to be dominated by a woman. Oh, no, indeed! Not me.

Sibyl turned the car into the drive, and stopped before the house. A little army of men hurried toward them, coming out from behind the trees, like an ambush. It was astonishing.

"What's this?" Sibyl demanded.

"We represent the press, madam," said a bald little fellow with a cynical and tired face. "We'd like to get a couple of pictures."

"Of what?" asked Sibyl.

"Of the victim," said he.

Now it's starting again, thought Killian, with a sort of despair.

CHAPTER SIX

Sibyl had superb aplomb. She looked the invaders over with a hardy and calculating eye. "What victim?" she asked.

"We want a couple of pictures of the girl who went overboard," another
man said. "You Miss Frey?" That was addressed to Harriet.

"Miss Frey isn't here," said Harriet.

A camera clicked, and another one. This will be a funny picture, thought
Killian. A carload of us, sitting here like dummies. The victim—

"Miss Frey is resting," said Sibyl. "Come back tomorrow."

"Too late," said the little bald man. "Give us something now, will you? How
did she happen to fall overboard?"

"She's too tired to talk now," said Sibyl.

"You her mother? Any relation?"

"I was on the ship when it happened," said Elly. "I'll be glad to tell you
what I can." She got out of the car and faced the army, polite and smiling.

"Find Jocelyn!" said Sibyl in Killian's ear.

She and her husband joined Elly, it was their duty to stand by her. And it's
my duty, is it, to find Jocelyn? He went into the house; and there was a par-
lourmaid standing in the hall with an eager air, which she quickly banished.
"D'you know where Miss Frey is?" he asked.

"Yes, sir. Miss Frey's in her room, sir, resting."

"Show me which room is hers, please," he said; and the girl went briskly
and neatly up the stairs, and along the carpeted corridor.

"This is Miss Frey's room, sir," she said; trained not to say "her" or "she";
trained not to ask any questions, and not to show any curiosity. Only she lingered.

"Thank you," said Killian, and she went away.

He knocked on the door, and there was no answer. Quite natural, he
thought. She wouldn't be in any room where you'd expect her; and if she
was, she wouldn't answer. He knocked again. "Jocelyn?" he said. Then he
tried the knob, and the door opened. It was dusk in there, and a chilly breeze
blew in at the open window. He felt for the switch and two lights came on:
one over a dressing-table; and a little lamp on a desk. In that mild, rosy light
he saw Jocelyn lying on the bed in her blouse and skirt, her shoes and her hat
on the floor. Her eyes were closed, and she did not stir.

He went over to her; when he saw that she was breathing, he gave a profound sigh. So you're not dead, he thought. You're a nuisance and a pest, but
God knows I don't want you to be dead. You're lovely, and gentle, and
young—when you're asleep. You look nice now when you're peaceful.

No use waking her up just to tell her to keep quiet. Maybe she'll wake up in a minute, he thought: and he lit a cigarette and sat down in a chair where he could look at her. I'll watch over your slumbers, lady. Maybe we can be different, Starry Eyes. Maybe we can be a Young Couple. A nice, pleasant young couple. I wouldn't know.

She stirred, and opened her eyes. "Jocko?"

He went over to her and sat on the bed beside her; he took her hand.

"I'm tired," she said.

"Then take it easy," he said.

"D'you care if I don't come down to dinner?" she asked.

"No," he said, "I don't care."

"Jocko," she said, after a moment, "you couldn't stop loving me now. No matter what happened."

"Yes, I could," he said.

"No!" she said, gripping his hand. "Tell me you couldn't stop!"

"I won't tell you that," he said. "I'm not that type. Not the knightly type that suffers gladly."

"You can't get away from me," she said. "No matter what happens."

He rose, still holding her hand. "Take it easy!" he said. "I'll stop in to see you after dinner." He let her hand go, and she turned on her side again and closed her eyes.

I'm not that type, he thought. I would not love thee, whatever thou didst. I could get away. He went to his room; he took a cold shower, and dressed in his dinner jacket. Six o'clock, and time for a cocktail, he thought. I'm timid about going down. Sibyl and Mr. Bell and Harriet all know now about Jocelyn being murdered. Elly wouldn't tell them that I was the murderer, but it might come into their heads. Maybe I look like that. It's going to be in the news-papers now. The victim, that guy called her.

As he descended the stairs, he heard a pleasant sound of voices from below; and he heard Sibyl laugh, a loud and hearty laugh that didn't go with her man-ner. She wasn't born Mrs. Luther Bell, he thought. She's been around. She's a little battered. And her child's a tough little guy. He followed the sound of voices to the library. The real McCoy, he thought, shelves of books on three sides, thousands of books, an air of dignity and rather shabby com-fort. Not Luther's doing. He must have had ancestors.

He was surprised to see Chauverney's neat, slender back, in a grey suit. I'd forgotten Chauverney, he thought. Here we all are, boys and girls.

"Martini or a Manhattan?" asked Sibyl, and Chauverney turned at the sound of her voice; he gave Killian his quick, vivid smile, only it turned into a grimace.

He looks shot to pieces, thought Killian. He looks ill.

"Oh, Martini, thanks," Killian answered. He felt unreasonably concerned about Chauverney. I never saw anyone look like that before, he thought. He looks like a ham actor registering mental anguish. Overdone.

Harriet was sitting in a chair, and Ponievsky on the arm of it. Elly was standing beside Luther Bell, talking to him, looking up at him with that artificial
but very effectual charm of hers. So I talk to Sibyl, thought Killian.

She looked him up and down, smiling, as if to cover her secret calculations.
"We're beginning to think about the Flower Show," she said, instantly. "In
July. You must try to come. We got two prizes last year." She went on, talking about flowers, and she doesn't, thought Killian, give a damn about flowers. She was wearing a black dinner dress with floating sleeves that now and
then fell away from her muscular arms; her black hair was done high on her
head in glossy curls. "We're hoping for great things from this Angelo," she
said.

The name checked Killian's wandering thoughts. "Angelo?" he repeated.

"Jocelyn found him somewhere," said Sibyl. "She asked us to give him a job.
Apparently he can do anything—gardening, cooking, anything."

"That's nice," said Killian.

"Isn't it?" said she.

There was Jocelyn, in a room upstairs, sleeping because she had taken something. Yet she ruled everything, as the moon rules the tides of the sea. She had
brought them all here; she drew some people together, and others apart. Does
she know what she's doing? he thought. Why Angelo? It's mysterious; I
don't like it. Tough luck to be in love with the moon.

The butler announced dinner, and they went into the dining room. It was
a good dinner, a very good dinner, with superb service. Sibyl knows her job,
he thought. The talk, too, was well handled; they all knew the right things
to say. They talked about the theater, about books—best sellers—about how
nice Maine was in the summer.

They had coffee in the library, and Bell suggested bridge. Killian didn't
know how to play, and Sibyl took charge; she put him on a sofa with
Ponievsky, and she showed them rare books. She knew all the points, like a
dealer, but she wasn't interested; neither were they. It was a long evening,
very long.

At the end of the first rubber, Chauverney excused himself. "I brought
along some work," he said. "We're sailing again on Wednesday."

Ponievsky took his place, and the game went on.

Sibyl brought another book for Killian to examine. Yawns rose in his throat;
he could choke them down, but his eyes filled with tears.

"Why don't you go to bed?" she said.

"But I—" he began.

"Luther will keep on playing until somebody faints from exhaustion," she
said. "Come into the dining room, and I'll give you a nightcap." He pretended
no more; he rose gladly and went with her, and she poured him a drink from
a decanter on the sideboard. "I'll join you," she said, and sat on the edge of

the table. With the floating sleeves thrown back, she looked, Killian thought, like a big, solid bird, a formidable bird.

"That's a queer story about Jocelyn, isn't it?" she said.

"Isn't it?" he said.

"She fainted, and fell overboard," Sibyl went on. "She didn't mention it. Nobody mentioned it to anyone. The reporters picked up the story from the other passengers."

"Well," said Killian, "you know how it is. You don't feel like talking about a thing of that sort." His reasonable and confidential tone did not seem effective. Her pale eyes were fixed upon him steadily.

"It's a queer story," she said again.

"A distressing experience for Jocelyn," he said. "But why queer?"

"Damn queer," said Sibyl.

A furious impatience rose in him. He resented her calculating glance, her tone of mysterious significance. "And after that letter Mr. Bell got?" he said. "That makes it all very sinister, doesn't it?"

She sipped her drink, which was a big one. "There's only one thing on earth I'm really afraid of," she said, "and that's newspapers. I don't give a hoot what happened on the ship—"

"I do, though," he interrupted. "I'd like very much to know what you're thinking about that accident."

"I don't think about it," she said. "I don't care what happened. I don't care what's going to happen, either, as long as it doesn't happen here."

The butler had come to the doorway; and there he stood, a heavy-shouldered man, with arms that hung in a helpless-looking way and dry black hair, parted in the middle. It's dyed, Killian thought, or it's a wig.

"What is it, Moffatt?" asked Sibyl.

"Drinks are required in the library, madam."

She got up from the table. "Good night, John!" she said. "Sleep well."

There's one comfort, thought Killian, as he went up the stairs. I'm having a nightmare now. Maybe when I'm asleep, it will be nicer. The hall upstairs was perfectly quiet; he stopped and listened, and then went hastily to Jocelyn's room. He knocked lightly; no answer. He tried the knob, and the door opened into windy darkness. He closed it and went to his own room. This is a nightmare, he thought, and I have no one to talk to about it.

No importa. What d'you want to talk for? Go to bed and go to sleep. It's now eleven P.M., courtesy of my own watch. To-morrow we will resume the adventures of our persecuted hero, John Killian, falsely accused of murder by practically everyone on earth. In the end the truth will triumph.

The bed was turned down; pajamas, dressing gown, and slippers laid out; there were two brand-new books on the bedside table, a thermos jug of ice water, an ash tray, a cedarwood box of cigarettes. Sibyl knew her job, all right. A comfortable bed; a fresh wind blowing in at the open window. To-morrow will be another day.

He waked with a jerk; he sat up with his heart thudding. The curtains were streaming out into the room; there was a curious sort of stir in the dark; something flapped. And something was breathing. There was a pale rectangle before him. That's the door, he thought. The door is open. And there's something in here. If I move, it will move.

Face it. He reached out and turned on the lamp. And he saw Chauverney standing just inside the door, leaning against the wall, and staring at him with enormous dark eyes.

"What's wrong?" he asked. Chauverney didn't answer. He looked amazed. "What are you doing here?" asked Killian. "What d'you want?"

Chauverney raised his left arm a little, and his hand was red with blood. "A burglar," he said. Killian got up and went toward him. "A burglar," Chauverney said again. "I thought Ponievsky.... Get Ponievsky. Don't tell."

He slipped down on the floor and lay there, graceful and limp in his light grey suit, his eyes closed. Killian shut the door into the room, and went through the bathroom to Ponievsky's room. "Ponievsky!" he said, not loudly.

He got an answer at once. "Yes?" The light came on, and the big man sat up in bed.

"Come and take a look at Chauverney," said Killian, in a low, disagreeable voice. The great thing was for everyone to be quiet. He had a feeling that someone might suddenly yell, and that would be horrible.

Ponievsky got up and came along, barefoot, in red and white striped pajamas. He knelt beside Chauverney, he lifted that bloody hand; he rose with effortless ease, went back to his room, and returned with a little black bag and a wooden shoe tree. "I will raise him, and you will take off the jacket," he said.

He took Chauverney under the arms and held him up, and his head lolled forward on his chest, his face as white as paper and very tranquil. Killian got the jacket off, and the shirt sleeve beneath was soaked in blood. Ponievsky laid him down again, rolled up the sodden sleeve, and made a tourniquet with the shoe tree just above the wrist.

"We will take him on the bed," he said, and together they lifted Chauverney and carried him across the room.

"Is he dead?" asked Killian.

"He must go at once to the hospital," said Ponievsky. "A transfusion is necessary. Will you telephone for an ambulance?" He was getting things out of his bag, a hypodermic of some sort.

Killian took up the French telephone from the table, but nothing happened. "The wire's dead," he said.

"That telephone's only for the house," said Ponievsky. "You must go down to the library for an outside wire. Dial the operator and say you want an ambulance."

"No!" said Chauverney unexpectedly. "No, thank you."

"Take it easy," said Ponievsky with great gentleness.

"No hospital," said Chauverney. "No—talk...." He was crying out of a ghastly weakness; his eyes were a little open. "An accident," he said. "My ra-zor—" Ponievsky wiped away the tears that ran down his face. "Razor slipped," said Chauverney. "Accident."

Ponievsky raised him again and looked over his shoulder at Killian, raising his brows and forming the word "telephone" with his lips. Chauverney's eyes were closed now; his head rested against Ponievsky's broad chest as if in supreme trust. Killian crossed the room, opened the door, and came face to face with Sibyl in a scarlet chiffon negligee.

"What's going on here?" she asked in a low, furious voice.

"A little accident," said Killian. "I want to telephone."

"What's going on?" she repeated. She tried to push past him; and when he barred her way, she rose on tiptoe like a big, angry bird. She tried to look over his shoulder, but she was not tall enough. "I insist!" she said, raising her voice.

Killian went into the hall, and closed the door, and stood against it. "Chauverney's had an accident," he said. "I want to get an ambulance."

"No, you don't!" she said. "I'll see for myself first, before you do anything of the sort. Let me in!"

"No!" said Killian, growing angry himself. "There's no time to lose."

She stood facing him, her pale eyes blinking; you might expect her to flap her wings and peck at him. "Now, see here!" she said. "Before you make all this trouble and scandal, I'm going to see if it's necessary. You let me in."

"Ponievsky's there. He says it's necessary—"

"Eric!" she said with a laugh. "If you leave Chauverney alone with Eric, he won't need any ambulance. He'll need a coffin."

The door opened and Ponievsky looked out. "You telephoned?" he asked.

"I'll telephone," said Sibyl. "For my own doctor."

"For an ambulance," said Ponievsky. "It must be quick, too."

"All right!" she said curtly, and turned away.

Ponievsky withdrew, closing the door. Killian stood where he was for a moment, and then an idea came into his head. He went after Sibyl. She was halfway down the stairs when she heard him; she glanced back and began to run. He ran, too; but she had a good start. She went into the library and locked the door. He could hear the little clicking of the telephone dial; he heard her voice. "Doctor Jacobs? This is Sibyl Bell. Can you come at once, please?... Yes. Yes, an accident. Yes...."

She came out; she had the key in her hand, and—she locked the library door. She went by Killian with a glare, and up the stairs again. Again he went after her, and into the bedroom. Ponievsky was smoking a cigarette, standing at the bedside; there was an odd look on his face. A noble look, was it?

"She didn't send for an ambulance," said Killian. "Only for a doctor, and she locked the library."

"Give me the key, madam!" said Ponievsky.

"No!" said she.

With no appearance of effort he opened her fingers and took the key. "Please wait here, Killian," he said, and he and Sibyl disappeared.

There was a dark patch on the brown rug where Chauverney had lain. Dark, not red, a very large patch. Everything was perfectly quiet. Here I stand, thought Killian, with my two hands as long as each other, and the man on the bed dying; or maybe it's dead he is already. What's the idea of talking to myself like a stage Irishman? Well, because it's like a play. A high-brow play, done with masterly restraint. A burglar, Chauverney said at first. And then said an accident. What if it's murder?

CHAPTER SEVEN

I've got murder on the brain, he thought. Murders aren't like this. They're done in the dark, with a scream, chairs and tables upset. People start running around. Not quiet, like this. Chauverney looked astonished when he came in. Surprised to find himself murdered? Well, who wouldn't be? Jocelyn wouldn't. She expected it. Maybe she wants to be. Perhaps there's a name for that. Desire-to-get-murdered neurosis. Ponievsky was smoking. I could smoke.

He looked at Chauverney to see if he would object to smoking. He looked very comfortable now, very graceful. He also looked dead. I'm sorry, old man. I'm damn sorry. This is sad. This is the saddest thing I ever saw.

"No need for you to stay here," said Ponievsky.

"Is he dead?"

"No. An ambulance is coming."

"A knife wound?" said Killian.

"Exactly," said Ponievsky, and paused. "The wound had been bleeding for quite some time before you called me."

"So what?" asked Killian.

Ponievsky shrugged his big shoulders. "Another doctor is coming. He will give his opinion."

"I suppose we'll be asked questions."

"Then we shall answer them," said Ponievsky.

He sat down near the bed, and Killian wandered out of the room. It was dim and quiet in the hall, all the doors closed. That wasn't right. People ought to be running around, up and down the stairs, bringing up hot water, being agitated.

The library door was unlocked now, the lights were on; it looked bright and comfortable in there. He lay flat on the divan, with no pillow, his knees drawn up, hands clasped above his head. I want to think this out. It's important....

Sibyl was shaking him in a rough way that made him furious. "Stop that!" he said. He wanted to kill her.

"You must get to bed," she said. "You can't stay here."

"Yes, I can!" he said.

"My dear," she said, using the society voice. "I've got a nice comfy room ready for you, and all your things moved into it. You must get to bed."

"I'm very comfy here."

They looked squarely at each other.

"Has Chauverney.... Is Chauverney..." he asked.

"He's fine!" she said, a little shrill. "Doctor Jacobs is upstairs now. He's a marvellous doctor."

He lay flat on his back, and she stood over him like a big, angry bird.

"For God's sake, get up and go to bed," she said.

"Why?"

"I don't want the servants to find you lying here. It's getting on for five o'clock."

"I don't want to go to bed at five o'clock."

"I ask you as a favour to get out of here—go upstairs where you belong."

"I'll get out of here," he said.

"And go upstairs."

"No," he said. "No, thanks."

She sat down on the divan near his feet. "You're plenty hard, my lad," she said.

His eyes narrowed; he lay still, thinking about that, in wonder and some-thing like fear. What makes her say that? I've never been quarrelsome. I'm quiet. Orderly. Excellent sense of discipline. They wrote that to my father when I was in boarding school. Sure. All right. But *you* know about that other one. That crazy Irishman you *could* be. You haven't been like that yet, but you could be. Maybe you will be. Maybe it's coming on you now. Jocelyn said I tried to kill her. She said I had "that look" on my face. "Well, I haven't any grudge against you," he said.

"Then couldn't you cooperate a little?" she asked.

"Just by going upstairs?"

She gave a one-sided smile, curiously tough. A tough baby, she was. That soft, red chiffon negligee didn't suit her. The whole house was full of emo-tion, grief, pity, fear. The great motif—Love and Death—kept coming up now and again. Like a Wagner opera. Liebestod. And the only one who seemed undisturbed by love or pity was this Sibyl.

"All right!" he said. "I'll cooperate."

As he sat up straight, he saw her stiffen; she sprang up and went toward the door with a slightly rolling gait. A little bow-legged, he thought.

"Well, doctor?" she said in a brisk tone. "How's the patient?"

"There's no immediate danger," said a deep, deep grave Voice. "But I should advise a nurse."

"Oh, of course! If it's *necessary*," said Sibyl. "But you know how a nurse upsets a household. Harriet and I are both good at looking after sick people. Don't you think we might manage, doctor?"

"Possibly," said the deep, deep voice. "Possibly. I'd like to know where she got that stuff."

"*She?*" Killian said to himself.

"I know she's in the habit of taking some sort of sleeping medicine," said Sibyl. "I've always thought it was dangerous to keep that stuff beside you.

You might take a dose, and then forget you'd taken it and take another. That must happen sometimes."

There was a pause.

"I have an operation at the hospital at eight," the deep voice resumed. "I'll come back here as soon after that as I can. And possibly Miss Frey will be able to answer a few questions then."

"Oh, I'm sure she will," said Sibyl.

"I trust so," said the deep voice. "In the meantime, your daughter has full instructions."

"Harriet is wonderful with sick people," said Sibyl.

"She seems level-headed," said the deep voice. "Well, I'll be back, Mrs. Bell."

The front door closed, and Killian came out into the hall. "New developments," he observed.

"Yes," she said. "Jocelyn was sleeping too soundly. We couldn't rouse her, and sent for the doctor."

"What about the other patient?"

"There isn't any other patient," said she.

"I thought Chauverney was a little indisposed?"

"He rallied," she said, with a one-sided smile. "He's gone."

"What d'you mean by 'gone'?"

"He's left the house," she said. "He was in a temper, and he left."

"Well, no," said Killian, "I don't think it was like that."

"You think too much," said Sibyl, and turned away and went up the stairs. Killian went after her.

"I want to see Jocelyn," he said.

"Come right along!" said Sibyl, and opened the door of Jocelyn's room.

In the little circle of lamplight Harriet had turned into a blonde, fair-haired, fair-skinned, in a white terry robe over white pajamas. She sat in an armchair facing the bed, her knees crossed, hands clasped behind her head, in an attitude of quiet, unshakable patience. She looked at Killian out of the corners of her long, narrowed eyes and didn't stir.

He went to look down at Jocelyn. There was a change in her. She looked flat, sunken into the mattress, as if crushed. Her breathing was shallow; she was white as paper, with dark rings under her eyes and a reddish stain about her mouth. "What's that?" he asked, in a whisper. "What's happened to her mouth?"

"Doctor Jacobs gave her an emetic," said Harriet, in an ordinary tone. "And then a stimulant."

"Has she been like this—been unconscious long?" he asked, and he would keep on whispering. Harriet would keep on using a normal tone.

"She was conscious while the doctor was working on her," said Harriet. "Very much so. Now she's supposed to be resting."

"How would you know if she got worse?"

"By her pulse," said Harriet.

"I'd like a nurse for her," said Killian.

"My dear," said Sibyl, "don't be a fool. *You* ought to be just as anxious as we are to keep this quiet."

He meditated upon that for a moment.

"Doctor Jacobs will be coming back before long," said Harriet. "He'd be almost sure to notice if we murdered Jocelyn."

"And we hate publicity," said Sibyl.

There was an unholy humor in these two women, and a complete understanding. I probably am a joke, thought Killian. Doctor Jacobs said she wasn't in any immediate danger. He was willing to leave her in their charge. Of course, he doesn't know all I know. I'm a sort of expert on murders that aren't murders. But even at that.... "I'll stop in later," he said.

Harriet smiled a drowsy, tigerish smile. It irritated him and he wanted to say something about it, but that was not practical. He went away, with a curious sense of defeat. It was unbelievably quiet on the upper floor. All the doors were closed except one. He went to that one, found a neat, well-lighted room, bed turned down, his pajamas laid out for him. He surveyed this for a moment and then went to that other room. It was in darkness, and the window wide open; he turned on the switch, and there was the dark patch on the rug. They can't get away with this, he thought. This is too much.

Chauverney had been dying. Maybe he was dead now. They couldn't hide him permanently, dead or alive. Who's "they?" Who wants to do this? What did they *do* with the poor devil? Throw him out the window? Well, questions will be asked. If not by anyone else, then by me.

The sky outside the windows was pale, a strange filmy grey; he stared at it, disturbed. Ha! It's the dawn! I've got to make enquiries. I must be kind-hearted because I care. I care a hell of a lot about what's happened to Chauverney. I didn't like to see him lying there, dying. Ponievsky seemed to be kind. But he's a dark horse. Sibyl said if you leave Chauverney alone with Eric, he'll need a coffin. What did she mean by *that?* She's a dark horse, too. Veneer of grande dame on top of something very different.

The air had a piercing chill in it. The dawn wind, he thought, if there is such a thing. So Jocelyn had taken a drug, had she? Took it herself, or did someone give it to her? Trying to murder her? She's so fond of murder. This thing is certainly developing. Drugs and knife wounds. Steps ought to be taken. By me? Certainly. By you. Do something. Find out what's happened to that poor devil. Find Ponievsky. I am a good citizen. Law-abiding. I will not countenance murders.

The dawn wind was very cold. That, or something else, made him shiver. He went through the bathroom and knocked on Ponievsky's door. No answer, and it was locked on the other side. He went back and then into the room got ready for him, and Sibyl came in there after him.

"For God's sake, what a pest you are!" she said. "Why don't you go to bed?"

"I want to find Chauverney," he said.

"My dear, I told you he went away. He packed his bag, and telephoned for a taxi."

"Well, no. He couldn't pack a bag. He couldn't telephone."

"You don't *want* to make trouble, do you?" she asked.

"I don't care much about that," he said. This room faced east, and from the window he saw rosy clouds coming up softly above the horizon, beautiful and amazing. The moon is beautiful, but it is not amazing. You wait for it calmly. But the sunrise takes your breath away.

"Come back to earth!" said Sibyl.

You bird of ill omen, he thought. "I'm going to find Chauverney," he said. "If I have to tear everything wide open."

"He's probably gone back to his ship. You can call him up on Monday."

"Let's not be funny. The man was dying."

"My dear, be sensible. You wouldn't know if a man was dying or not. I tell you he went away in a taxi."

"Alone?"

"With a driver."

"I'll get hold of the driver then. What's the name of the garage he got the taxi from?"

She didn't answer.

"I'm going through with this," said Killian.

She looked ugly, with deep lines from her nostrils to the corners of her mouth; she looked weary and miserable. "Be sensible," she said in a half-hearted way.

"I will be," said Killian. "I just want a few words with the driver who took Chauverney—somewhere."

The sun was sliding up, bright gold; the rosy clouds were vanishing in the flood of light; everything was growing clear in outline but still without colour. A man was walking over the lawn, far away, looking all black and grey, like a figure on the screen; he was slender and straight, and slanting backward a little. "That's Angelo," Killian said to himself. "I'd think it was queer, seeing him here, if I had any standards of queerness left."

"Charlie Chauverney didn't go in a taxi," said Sibyl. "And didn't pack a bag."

"Elly packed a bag for him. She and Eric Ponievsky took him in one of our cars."

"Took him where?"

"To a hospital, a good long way off."

"Like a rat," said Killian thoughtfully. "Will not, *must* not, die in the house."

"He'll be lucky if he dies," she said. "He tried to die."

"Suicide?"

"What do you think?" she asked. "Do you believe in the burglar—cutting his wrist with a knife? Or do you think it was an accident?"

"Well, how about murder?"

"Be sensible," she said. "Would he just stand still and let somebody cut his wrist? And not even complain about it?"

"I've got more imagination than you," said Killian. "How do you like this? Someone creeps up on him with a knife. There's a struggle, in which Chauverney gets hurt. He dies without mentioning the name of his assailant, because it's someone he loves."

"Elly?" said she. "Do you see Elly creeping up on anyone with a knife?"

"Doesn't have to be Elly."

"Well, he didn't love *me*," she said. "So I'm out of it. And Jocelyn was sleeping off a dose of something. There's nobody else in the house he would have loved—except Harriet, and he didn't love Harriet. No, you'd better keep out of this."

"The hospital's going to make enquiries. The steamship company, too."

"I know that," she said. "There's going to be plenty of trouble. You needn't make it worse."

"D'you think it's making things better, to do this?" asked Killian. "To hustle a dying man out of your house? By the way, what happened to the ambulance?"

"Eric sent for it, and I countermanded it the moment he was out of the way. I'll do more than that," she said. "You'd be surprised how much I'd do to avoid a scandal."

"I don't think much of your technic."

"I took a chance," she said. "I've taken a lot of chances in my lifetime."

"Are you lucky?" asked Killian.

She looked very ugly and very tired now. "Yes," she said, "I'm a damn sight luckier than I deserve." She gave a sigh. "Be sensible, will you?" she said once more, and left him.

Maybe I will be sensible, he thought. Ponievsky I don't know about. But I'd bet on Elly. If she's had a hand in this, it can't be what it looks like. Perhaps it's not complicated. Just a plain honest suicide. He slashed a vein, like a Roman. But when the end comes, you want someone else around.

Why was it me, I wonder? No reason, maybe. He just opened the first door that was handy. Motive? That's outside my field. I don't know enough about him.

The suit he had worn ashore was hanging up in the closet; he changed into that; taking plenty of time about dressing. "This is Sunday morning," he said to himself. "I'll have to go back to New York to-night, so that I can be at the office bright and early Monday morning." But I'm not going until I've talked to Jocelyn, he thought. Not until I know she's all right. Maybe I could take her with me. And what would I do with her? Put her in a pumpkin shell. And there he kept her very well. Ancient wisdom in that nursery rhyme. Poor guy who had a wife and couldn't keep her. Even in those days that happened.

There was a knock at the door. "*Come* in!" he called; and in came Harriet, in a neat, clean, rust-coloured linen dress. This time her hair was red.

"Would you like to come and have breakfast on the boat?" she asked.

"No, thanks," Killian answered. "I'm waiting until the doctor comes back."

"I'd like to tell you something before the doctor comes back," said Harriet. "We can be back here when he comes. It's something you'd better hear."

"Something I'll like to hear?" he asked, warily.

"No," she said. "Something pretty bad for you to hear."

"Then suppose we skip it?"

"And just let it come down on you like a ton of bricks?" asked Harriet.

"All right!" said Killian, after a moment. "Let's go."

CHAPTER EIGHT

There was a car waiting outside the house, and they got into it.

"Give!" said Killian.

"Wait till we get on the boat," said Harriet.

"That's a good technic," he said, approvingly. "That's the way to make bad news worse."

"Oh, don't be such a clown!" she said. "This isn't any fun for me."

"Then why are you doing it?"

"I've got to."

"I know why you're *going* to tell me this bad news," Killian said. "Because it's *right*. It's the Decent Thing to do. It's playing the game. It's—"

"Oh, shut up!" she said, and that made him laugh.

He liked her to say that. She narrowed her eyes so that her ginger-coloured lashes were meshed; she looked like a cross little yellow cat, and he liked that. He liked her to be cross and vigorous and young.

"How old are you?" he asked.

"Twenty-two," she answered.

Three years older than Jocelyn, are you? he thought. Only Jocelyn hasn't any age. She's like the Lorelei, or one of those things. This Harriet is young. "Do you go to college?" he asked.

"No," she said, "I'm a teacher."

"What kind of teacher?"

"I teach art," she said. "Want to make something of it?"

"Well, are you an artist?"

"Very talented," she said.

He was delighted; that was the only word. He was pleased by everything she said, pleased by her looks and by her voice that was a little rough. He admired the way she handled the car.

"Do you like me?" he asked.

"Yes," she said.

She turned into a lane, with high rocky banks; they came out of this on to the shore road and, abruptly, upon a miserable little settlement of tumble-down houses, wired chicken yards, a clothesline strung between two pine trees, and then a strange blank space, with a shack, a pier, and a signboard. Boats for Hire. A motorboat was tied up to the pier, very smart, white and yellow paint, and a dark blue awning. As Harriet was locking the car, a man came out of the cabin, stepped on to the pier, and came toward them. A big, gaunt man, burnt brick red, with fair hair rather long and parted on the side, a string of fair moustache. He was in shirt sleeves and braces, with a white covered yachting cap on the back of his head.

"Well, good morning, Captain," said Harriet.

He touched the visor of his cap. "'Morning," he said. "Where's Miss Jocelyn?"

"Sound asleep," said Harriet. "I've brought Mr. Killian."

He touched his cap again, and turned back to the boat. There were wicker armchairs on the afterdeck, and a table. Harriet and Killian sat here, and the Captain brought them an excellent breakfast: coffee, toast, bacon and eggs, melon. Nobody said a word. When he had set everything before them, he went inside and started the engine, and off they went. There was a good breeze, the awning slatted, the white tablecloth fluttered.

"Swede?" Killian asked.

"Scandinavian of some sort," she answered. "Anderson, or Peterson, or Larsen—I've forgotten, because he's always called Captain. He was a ship's captain once, but something happened to him."

"What happened to him?"

"It's a mystery," said Harriet.

"Do you know it?"

"Yes," she said. "It's pretty ghastly. Poor devil...! Jocelyn found him, you know. She brought him here, and Mr. Bell gave him a job—sort of caretaker and so on."

She poured him another cup of coffee, in a nice domestic way. "Light a cigarette," she said, "and take it easy."

"Because now you're going to tell me the worst?"

She lit a cigarette for herself and leaned back, looking out over the water with her narrowed eyes. "It's about Eric Ponievsky," she said. "And it's not nice."

"And it's about Jocelyn too," he said.

"You're right," said Harriet. "Pretty nearly every damn thing is about Jocelyn."

"Maybe you don't like her."

"I don't dislike her," said Harriet. "I'm sorry for her. But I wish she was dead."

"Out of sheer kindness?" asked Killian.

"I want to tell you about Eric," she said. "I'm going to marry him."

"Is that bad news?"

"You needn't be so flip," said Harriet. "You won't be when I've finished. Eric was on the way to being a famous surgeon. And Jocelyn ruined him."

"I knew that was coming," said Killian.

"This happened two years ago—"

"She started ruining people at seventeen?"

"God knows when she started," said Harriet. "This was two years ago. Eric had offices in New York then, and a fine practice. Somebody sent Jocelyn to him—I don't know why. She said she suffered a lot of pain; but he couldn't find anything wrong with her, and he told her so."

"Because he's like that," said Killian. "Honest. Sterling. Noble."

"He's a professional man with decent standards," said Harriet. "Does that seem so extraordinary to you?"

"All right! I'll take Ponievsky's high standards for granted," said Killian.

Harriet gave him a steely look, which he met without wilting. They were enemies now, and perfectly frank about it.

"She kept at him to give her something for this mysterious pain," Harriet said. "When he refused, she went back to the waiting room and sat there, crying."

"Is that what ruined him?" Killian asked.

"It didn't help him any. One of his patients tried to console Jocelyn, and she told Eric he was heartless about the poor child."

"Yes," said Killian.

"She came back the next day, and Eric thought it would be better to see her. He tried to talk honestly to her. He advised her to see a neurologist. But she said she'd taken a fancy to him."

"Girls of seventeen don't talk like that."

"She probably didn't talk like that," said Harriet. "I'm just giving you the gist of it."

"And he repulsed her."

"He did. The next evening she came to the hotel where he lived and called his room from the lobby, where everyone could hear her. She said the pain was unbearable, and would he please give her something for it. That put him in a spot."

"Why?"

"Doctors can't afford that sort of thing. He came downstairs to see her; and he gave her a prescription for some harmless little pills, to keep her quiet. Then he tried to find out who was responsible for her, and the next day he got in touch with her father. After that he had the whole crew on his neck. They tried to blackmail him; and when he wouldn't pay, they put on the screws. They came to his office and to his hotel. They accused him of giving her habit-forming drugs. They drove away his patients, and it finished up with a scene in his hotel that got into the newspapers. He had to quit."

"That's Eric's story."

"Yep," she said, "that's Eric's story. He came out here, to start over again. Mother introduced him to people, and he was just getting on his feet again. You can imagine how he felt when she turned up yesterday."

"No, I can't imagine Doctor Eric Ponievsky's feelings."

"He knew he was likely to meet her some day at the house. He was ready for that. But she started right in again with the old game. Begging him to give her something for her nerves."

"And he still wouldn't."

"Naturally not."

"Does he expect to be ruined all over again?"

The Captain appeared and began clearing the table. "I lash de wheel," he said. "I know dese waters like a book. Like a book."

"You certainly do," said Harriet.

"Maybe Miss Jocelyn come out dis afternoon?"

"Maybe she will," said Harriet.

"My! Such a lovely young lady," he said.

He took off the cloth and shook it out over the rail. Seagulls came swooping down for the crumbs. "Dose birds are wise," he said, and vanished again.

Harriet was trying to light another cigarette, but the wind blew out one match after another.

"Allow me!" said Killian, rising. He shielded a match in his hands, and their eyes met. She drew on her cigarette, and leaned back again.

"Eric's gone," she said. "He waked me up last night and told me. He said Jocelyn had taken some sort of drug. And he said she'd be sure to say he gave it to her."

Killian remained standing. "I wonder how he knew she'd taken this subtle drug?" he said.

"He went to her room," said Harriet. "He wanted to talk to her. And he found her in a stupor."

"Then what did he do?"

"He waked me. He told me he was going to get out and stay out until Jocelyn had gone."

"Then I suppose you sent for Doctor Jacobs?"

"No. Eric said there wasn't any danger."

"I think Eric understated the case."

"Think whatever you please," said Harriet. "Now I've told you."

"Was it just to warn me?"

"No," she said, "I want to make a plea. I want to *beg* you to take Jocelyn away."

Killian stood with his hands in his pockets, looking out at the water. "Let's go home," he said.

Harriet got up and called inside to the Captain. "Let's go home!'"

The boat made a fine sweeping curve, and headed back. "You don't believe me?" Harriet asked.

"It's not your story," he said. "It's Ponievsky's."

They didn't say another word. A kid of seventeen, Killian thought, crying in a doctor's waiting room. A blackmailing family. What sort of life has she led? What sort of breaks has she had? And if there could be anyone to give her a break, anyone to stand by her, who knows if she wouldn't turn out to be quite a decent little guy? She's stopped drinking. Maybe she'll stop all the rest of it. Maybe it's worth trying.

The boat was heading toward the pier, straight as an arrow.

"Anyhow, I've told you," said Harriet. "You know what to expect. Jocelyn's going to accuse Eric of giving her something. Poison; she'll probably say."

"And what's her motive for that?" Killian asked. "Just for the sheer fun of ruining Eric?"

"She's afraid of Eric. She's afraid he'll tell you the truth about her."

"A subtle revenge," said Killian. "She poisons herself so that Eric can be accused of poisoning her."

"All right!" said Harriet. "I quit."

The boat glided along into the pier, and Harriet jumped ashore, quick as a cat. "Thanks, Captain!" she said.

"Come again! Come again!" he said.

They moved toward the car, side by side.

"There's this," said Killian. "Jocelyn won't stay in your house forever—"

"Not *my* house," said Harriet.

"She won't stay in Mr. Bell's house forever. She'll leave, and this Eric can come out of hiding, and all will be well."

She said nothing to that; she started the car and they drove off.

"Eric isn't hiding," she said presently. "He's just staying at a sort of little hotel until Jocelyn gets out. We'll stop and see him."

"I don't want to see him."

"I do," said Harriet.

"In fact, I won't see him," said Killian. "I want to get back to see Doctor Jacobs."

"You'll get back in plenty of time," said Harriet. "I'm just going to stop by and see Eric."

"I suppose I can get a taxi," Killian said.

She drove down the lane that was like a miniature canyon again, and this time she turned right, along a smooth, empty road lined by fields, up a hill, through a stone gateway with a sign: The Maples. Private Board.

What's private board, anyhow? Killian thought. What would public board be? Before them was a big, old-fashioned house with a veranda. Rocking chairs, he thought. Stewed apricots and baker's cake, Sunday night.

"I'll only be a minute," said Harriet. "I want to tell Eric that *you* know the truth." She stood in the road, looking down at the ground. "Look here!" she said, glancing at him. "If I bring Eric out here, could you say something?"

"No," he said. "I'm sorry, Harriet."

"You wouldn't have to say anything direct. You could just have an attitude. Just let him see that you don't think he's a—a criminal."

"I'm sorry," he said again, "but I haven't got any attitude yet."

"You've seen Eric," she said. "You know perfectly well he's not a poisoner."

"I don't know anything," said Killian.

"You don't believe what I told you?"

"I believe you believe it," he said. "But everything has two sides, or more. Don't bring him out, Harriet."

"I'm going to," she said. "If you can look at him, and still think he's poisoned anybody, all right."

"Let's skip it, Harriet. Give me time to think about this."

"Time to hear Jocelyn's version," she said. "No! You've got to see Eric, even if it's just to say good morning, before you listen to Jocelyn."

She went off along the drive, and Killian lit a cigarette. I don't think Ponievsky tried to poison Jocelyn, he thought. I don't believe in murder. It's unnatural—very poor taste. I won't countenance it. It's quite possible that Jocelyn *will* accuse Ponievsky. She did it to me. She said I murdered her. But I lived through that, and I wasn't ruined. Ponievsky can bear it. Harriet takes the whole thing too seriously. That's love.

The Maples was very quiet, very, very quiet. Why wouldn't it be, on a Sunday morning? I must be nervous. I'm having presentiments. Behind this Sunday-morning quiet lies Tragedy. Battle, murder, and sudden death. Harriet didn't seem to be coming out and bringing Eric. I'll smoke one more cigarette, and then I'll take steps. I want to get back and see Doctor Jacobs.

The screen door gave a muffled bang behind Harriet. Coming out alone. She walked jerkily, coming down hard on her heels. He opened the door of the car, and she got in beside him.

"Well!" she said in a loud, harsh voice. "Well, he's gone."

Killian waited until they had turned into the highway, leaving The Maples behind them.

"Gone?" he repeated.

"He's run away," said Harriet.

CHAPTER NINE

D'you realize what this means, you poor little devil? thought Killian. He glanced sidelong at Harriet. Yes, he thought. You realize, all right.

"Harriet," he said. "I'm sorry. I mean it."

"Well," she said, "you ought to be glad. It's a big help for Jocelyn's version."

"Jocelyn hasn't given any version yet."

"Please don't be mild and wise!" she cried. "I'm not going to be hypocritical about this. I— Here! Do you want to drive?"

"Yes," he said. She was crying. She stopped the car, and they changed places. "Next left turn," she said. "I know what this means. Eric wouldn't run away for nothing. It's possible that he made some pretty awful mistake. Gave her the wrong medicine—something like that."

"Yes," Killian said, in a thoughtful way. "That's possible."

"Well!" she said. "I don't believe that, and neither do you."

"We'll have to wait and hear what Jocelyn says."

"Oh, no, we won't! Eric left a note for me. He said he had to sail for Poland on the next ship. He said it's to see about an estate over there. All of a sudden, on a Sunday morning. No. He's running away."

"If he's made a mistake," Killian said, carefully, "that's probably the best thing he can do."

"It *isn't!*" she said, flatly. "It's never the best thing, to run away."

"You're wrong, sister," said Killian.

"Well," said Harriet, "maybe it's a good thing for him. But it's a damn bad thing for me. I had a lot of respect for him. I honestly looked forward to marrying him."

"That's a funny way to put it. How about love?"

"Phooey," she said, briefly.

"Love is a lot of things," said Killian, "but it's not phooey."

She was silent for a while, blinking her ginger lashes. "I want a life with some *sense* to it," she said. "Eric was doing a good job. Doctors are useful when they're intelligent, like Eric. He'd have done his work, and I'd have done mine. But—well, it's finished."

"Maybe he'll come back," said Killian.

"Not to me," she said. "The landlady at The Maples said Eric telephoned to someone this morning. She heard him ask, 'How is Jocelyn?' She was all agog; she knew there was something queer. He said, 'Oh! She's better? Jacobs has seen her?' Then he went upstairs and began to pack, and he told the landlady he was called away on business."

A mistake? thought Killian. It doesn't look like that. It looks— My God!

Jocelyn said five men wanted to murder her. Is it true? Ponievsky was one of them? *Is* this true?

He stopped the car before the house, and Harriet got out. "Thanks!" she said. She ran up the steps and into the house, and Killian went slowly after her. Elly was sitting on the terrace, and he sat down in a chair beside her.

"Hello!" she said gaily.

Her face shocked him. She had too much rouge on her cheekbones; her mouth was too red, and it was tight and stretched, like a poor little clown's.

"Hello!" he answered. "Elly, how is Chauverney?"

"He's *fine!*" she said.

"Good!" said Killian, heartily. "That's good."

"Have you seen the newspapers?" Elly asked, and picked up a section from the floor beside her; she opened it and folded it over and handed it to Killian.

It was an inconspicuous item. Passenger Rescued at Sea. New York Girl Falls Overboard in Mid-Ocean. Miss Jocelyn Frey, nineteen, residing at the Hotel St. Pol, had an attack of vertigo while sitting on the rail of the Williams Line M. S. *Las Pampas* on the evening of May 12th, and fell overboard. Prompt action on the part of Captain K. E. Portman resulted in her immediate rescue by the crew of a lifeboat. Miss Frey is resting at the home of friends on Long Island.

"Not much, is there?" said Elly.

"No, there isn't," said Killian. There was a little silence. "Well," he said, "I'll see you later, Elly."

He went into the house, with a sort of timidity. I'm nothing but a guest, after all, he thought. And Jocelyn's a guest. What you might call an inconsiderate guest. Always getting murdered.

He looked into the drawing room, with some idea of asking somebody, politely, if he might go up and see Miss Frey. But there wasn't anybody there, or in the library, and he went up, and knocked at her door. "Come in!" she called.

She was sitting up in bed in a little blue silk jacket, her soft hair loose; there was a breakfast tray across her knees, white cloth, pink and white china, a pink rose in a little vase. The sun was shining into the room, there was a glitter of silver from the dressing table; the whole effect was luxurious and charming. And sweet. A delicate and beautiful young girl, having her breakfast on a spring morning.

"Hello, Jocko, dear!" she said, with a little anxious smile.

"Hello, Jocelyn!" he answered, and closed the door. "How are you feeling?"

"Tired," she said.

"But happy?" he asked.

She took up the cup of coffee in both her thin little hands, and bent her head to drink it. Then she lay back on the pillow looking at him. "Take away the tray, will you?" she said.

As he took it, he saw that she had eaten nothing at all, and that made him angry. "Here!" he said, with a frown. He sat down on the bed beside her, and cut two slices of toast into neat strips. "Here!" he said. She took a bite; she went on eating. He held the glass of orange juice to her lips, and she drank it. When the toast was all eaten, he took away the tray.

"Give me a smoke, Jocko?" she said.

"I don't know if it's good for you," he said.

"I don't care," she said. He gave her a cigarette and lit it for her; she leaned back, and took his hand. "I'm tired," she said.

"Tell me about this drug business," he said.

"Last night I asked Eric to give me something to make me sleep, and he did."

"It looks that way."

"Maybe it was something new, that he didn't understand very well," she said. "Or maybe I was especially susceptible to it."

"You're taking a very reasonable tone. Admirable."

"I'm saying what you'd say. There's no use telling you the truth."

"The truth being that you've been murdered again?"

"What's the use of talking about it?" she said.

"I'd like to hear," he said. "I'd like to hear the whole story about you and Eric."

"That means you've heard somebody else's version already," she said. "You can hear mine, if you like."

"I won't like."

"I don't remember when it was," she said. "About two years ago, I guess. I was just about crazy with pain from a sinus infection, and somebody sent me to Eric. He gave me something that helped a lot. It was cocaine, but I didn't know that. I didn't care, anyhow. It stopped the pain, and it made me feel glorious. Some people react that way to cocaine. I was wildly excited and happy. But that night the pain came back. I wanted that stopped, and I wanted to feel glorious again. I wasn't reasonable. I don't stand pain very heroically. Eric took a lofty tone. I *think* he told me the pain in my head wasn't bad. I just didn't agree with him. I tried everything. I drank God knows how much whisky. I went to Eric's hotel. I didn't know what it was he had given me, but I wanted more of it quick. Do you want the rest of it?"

"I think so."

"He went all Continental," she said. "Maybe it was just to keep me quiet. We went into a little sort of sitting room. I led him on. I wanted to get my pain-killer, and I thought it was worth a little love-making. But he went too far. The pain in my head was awful. I made him a scene, a good one. When I went out into the lobby, I was crying; and suddenly I had a terrific nosebleed. That made things worse. People thought Eric had hit me, or something. It cured me, though, and I went home. I didn't know until later what all that had done to Eric. I didn't care when I did know."

"Your family took an interest in it, didn't they?"

"My family's always taken a wonderful interest in my career," she said. "Do you want to hear that, too?"

"If you feel like talking."

"I was fifteen, Jocko, when I met a man on a Fifth Avenue bus."

"That was the first man you'd ever seen," said Killian.

"I wasn't a very nice kid," she said. "I thought I was going to be the world's greatest actress—without doing any work, of course. But I *was* a kid. He was old, and I thought he was being fatherly. He was sitting behind me, and he began to talk. I told him about my ambition, and he seemed to be impressed. He said I was a remarkable girl, and that I ought to have everything— clothes, education, and so on. That was just what I thought myself. He came that evening to see my mother and father. They thought he was the chance of a lifetime, and he began to ease things up for them and my brother."

"And you?"

"And me. He bought me a fur coat. It was a lousy little coat, but I didn't know much then. I wore it to school, and I thought I was a lucky girl. He talked about my taking dancing lessons and singing lessons and going to a private school, but that never happened. He took me around to restaurants and shows. He took me out in his car, and my great ambition sort of vanished."

"All this time you thought he was just your rich uncle."

"Oh, no!" she said. "I found out what he was like. But my mother and father knew, too, and they didn't care. I made up my mind then that I'd look out for myself, and get all I could. For nothing. That didn't help my disposition any. And it gave me a champagne appetite, Jocko. Well, he passed on, and he left me my little income, and I drifted around. That's my story."

"Dictated, but not read."

"Do you believe it, Jocko?"

"Yes. It doesn't matter. I wasn't going to ask you any questions about your past, ever."

"I've never loved anybody but you. That sounds like old stuff, doesn't it? Only it's true. Nobody else ever made me eat toast. Maybe I can be nice now, Jocko."

"Maybe you can," he said. Her cold little fingers hurt, he thought. A pain runs up my arm to my heart, and squeezes it. "Let's skip the past," he said. "How's about the present?"

"Well, what?"

"Why did you get us all here?"

"I wanted you here."

"Yes. But why Chauverney? And Elly? And Angelo?"

"Chauverney wanted to meet Luther. He loves rich people. And I asked Elly because she's in love with Chauvie."

"All right. Now Angelo."

"I didn't ask him. He came. He'd signed off, and he didn't want to go back to sea. He begged me to get him a job on shore."

"Luther Bell seems to be very obliging."

"He's no mystery," she said. "He's just a damned old fool. You can see that for yourself. He was married to one of these Ladies with a big bust and grey hair and pearls, very social. She kept him in order. But when she died, he went off the rails and married Sibyl, the artiste. She was in vaudeville a million years ago. A real old-timer in tights, winking at the boys."

"You're a gentle little thing."

"I don't like anybody but you," she said.

He was silent for a while. "All right!" he said. "Where do we go from here?"

"Anywhere you want," she said.

"The thing is, you're rather exotic for my income," he said. "I make all of thirty-seven fifty a week."

"I've got that income. Two hundred a month."

"You're a clever little manager," he said. "Traveling to Rio, so de luxe, on fifty dollars a week."

"I'll tell you about that, if you want," she said.

"Never mind."

"Plenty of things I'd hate to tell you," she said. "It's a nasty little story. I'm a nasty little tramp. But maybe I could be nice, with you."

"I'm old-fashioned," he said. "I want to get married."

"You want to marry me?"

"Yes," he said. "I think I do. Only I don't like your little income."

"I've been poor," she said. "Mother had a sort of boarding house once, and I cooked for ten people."

He stroked her hair back from her temples. "Thirty-seven fifty a week?" he said.

"Do you think I care about that?" she said. "All the other men I've known have hated me. They called it loving me, but it was hating. Nobody's ever been kind but you. Go on feeding me little scraps of toast. That's all I want."

"We could try," he said.

"Yes," she said. "We could try."

He unclasped her fingers, and laid her hand neatly at her side. "Get well," he said. "I'm going to do some thinking."

But it wasn't thinking. He went into his own room and stood by the window. "It's so damn sad," he said to himself. "It's so sad. Not only Jocelyn and me, either. There's Ponievsky, and Harriet. And Chauverney and Elly. The whole house is so damn sad, it chokes me. I'm going downstairs to see what's going on."

He went down the stairs; and in the lower hall he stopped, listening for voices. Nothing to be heard, and he went out on the terrace. Luther Bell was sitting there in white flannels and a grey coat with a belt; he looked very handsome and very noble.

"Oh, good morning, Killian!" he said, seriously. "Good morning!"

"Good morning!" Killian answered.

Bell put down the newspaper he had been reading. "I'd like to have a talk with you, Killian," he said. "We seem to be alone for the moment."

"Yes, we do," said Killian.

"It's a little matter of business," said Luther Bell. "You probably know something about Bell, Fiske and Waters."

Killian sat down opposite him, and met Bell's earnest glance with one just as grave.

"There's one thing a man learns in business," said Bell. "And that is to size up people. I find that I do that almost subsconsciously."

"I see!" said Killian.

There was a brief pause. "I'm always willing to back my own judgment," said Luther Bell. "I've studied you, Killian, and I believe I know you."

"I see!" said Killian again.

"I believe you're intuitive, forceful—and loyal," said Luther Bell. "Excellent executive material. We'd like you in our organization, Killian."

"I scarcely know what to say, sir," said Killian, looking modestly at his shoes.

"We can start you at seventy-five a week," said Luther Bell. "And your future is whatever you choose to make it, Killian."

"Well, I swan!" said Killian to himself. "This is so sudden, Mr. Bell. This smells, Mr. Bell."

"I propose," Luther Bell went on, "that you stop over until morning, Killian. Then you can come into town with me, and I'll introduce you to my partner, Harvey Fiske." He waited, and a faintly uneasy look came into his blue eyes. "I'm a great believer in intuition," he said.

"I see!" said Killian.

"Then we'll take it as settled."

"If you don't mind..." said Killian. "I appreciate this, sir, but I'm afraid I can't go so fast. You see, I've got a job already."

"It's possible that we may be able to do somewhat better in the way of salary," said Luther Bell. "I'll take it up with Harvey Fiske to-morrow, after he's met you."

"I'm sorry," Killian said, "but I'm afraid I'll have to take a little time to think, sir. That's the sort of mind I have. Judicial."

He's baffled, Killian thought. Judicial is a word he can't help respecting, even if he doesn't like to hear it used against him. I certainly need time to consider this offer. Seventy-five a week is bribery. But bribing me to do what? To keep still about something? What important secret do I know?

Mr. Bell coughed—hem, hem. "If I'm going to think over this bribery, it's only decent to go away and think privately," Killian said to himself. And to Mr. Bell he said, "May I reopen this matter later, sir?"

"Yes," said Mr. Bell indulgently. "This evening, no doubt."

Killian moved away, with a serious and purposeful face. He had no idea where he was going. He walked deliberately to the end of the terrace and turned the corner. All very sad, he thought, but in a way I'm happy. Happy, because Jocelyn really was murdered. It wasn't a lie. She sat in Ponievsky's office, and she cried, and she was seventeen years old. A nice family, she must have. She's been well brought up. She ate because I fed her. That's symbolic, of something. It might mean that she needs me. Maybe that stimulates and inspires me, and maybe it paralyzes me with fright. I fed her, and she held my hand.

From this side of the house he saw a little plantation of pines and, through the trees, the roof of the garage. A chauffeur in uniform was coming through that little wood, very slowly, in a wandering way. He stopped, looking at Killian, and Killian looked at him. Everything here was peaceful, in the morning sun, and everything had been quiet at The Maples. After a while this sunny peace gets on your nerves. You think it's the quiet before the tempest, or something like that.

The chauffeur came out of the little wood, and stopped again; a stolid, thickset young man with blue eyes. He stared and stared at Killian.

"What's the idea?" Killian asked.

"Could I speak to you for a moment, sir?" he said.

Killian went down the steps. "There's a man out in the road, sir," the chauffeur said, very low. "It looks to me like he's dead."

"Where?" asked Killian, brisk and business-like.

"If you'll get in the car, I'll take you, sir," said the chauffeur.

"I'll come," he said to the chauffeur, and went with him, through the wood, to a clearing in front of the garage.

They got into the car that stood there, and off they went down the drive. It's Chauverney, thought Killian. Someone had to be dead. For days and days everything's been working up to that. Up to murder. A good old-fashioned murder, with a body.

They went out on the highway. Very quiet there at this hour of a Sunday morning; no cars passed. The trees stirred in the light breeze, there were little clouds, white as milk, in the blue sky. The car stopped just where the wall of Bell's place ended. There was a man lying face down on the side of the road. Not Chauverney. It was Angelo.

He's dead, all right, thought Killian, standing in the grass and looking down at him. Jocelyn was murdered, and she's still alive. But Angelo is dead, all right.

"Looks like he's been run over," said the chauffeur.

"Yes, very much so," said Killian, and suddenly felt sick.

CHAPTER TEN

"I guess I ought to tell Mr. Bell," said the chauffeur.

"You'd better tell the police," said Killian.

"Well, I'd better tell Mr. Bell first," said the chauffeur.

"Why? What's this got to do with Mr. Bell?"

"Well, he hired this man yesterday."

"Even at that, it's a matter for the police."

"Well, I better tell Mr. Bell first," said the chauffeur. "See what he wants done about it."

"Afraid he won't like this?" asked Killian.

"He's funny about things," said the chauffeur.

"Funny about people getting killed?"

"About anything getting in the papers," the chauffeur explained.

"This will get in the papers," said Killian. He lit a cigarette and drew on it, not looking at Angelo.

"Hit-and-run driver," said the chauffeur. "Only there's elements in it."

"Elements?" Killian repeated.

"Yes, sir, I'd say so. Look how far on the side of the road he's lying. Straight road, too."

"As if someone had moved him, after he was run over?"

"He was some kind of an Eyetalian," said the chauffeur. "That's another element you got to consider."

"Undoubtedly!" said Killian.

"They're great ones for that, the Eyetalians are," said the chauffeur.

"For getting run over?"

"Well, for revenge," said the chauffeur.

Killian threw away his cigarette; it had a bitter taste. "Where's the police station?" he asked.

"I'll have to tell Mr. Bell first, sir. I'd lose my job if I didn't."

"Why did you bring me here?" asked Killian.

"Well, like a witness, sir," said the chauffeur. "The cops ask you how the body was lying and all."

They got into the car and drove away, leaving Angelo lying in the sun. It's happened, thought Killian. It had to happen. After all this talk about murder, somebody had to be dead. In a way, it's a relief. Everything's been working up to a crisis, and this is it.

"Maybe he was chased," the chauffeur proferred.

"What d'you mean?"

"Well, for revenge," said the chauffeur.

Chased? thought Killian. I'm sorry you said that. It gives you images. After all, a murder isn't a relief. It causes a lot of unpleasantness. It causeth the cops to come. It casteth a shadow upon the dwelling, and all those within. *All* those. Let's call it an accident. Let's forget it. Let's skip it. Let's *not* think who was driving around this morning.

He was glad to find the terrace deserted. "I'll tell Mr. Bell," he said. "Or Mrs. Bell."

"Thank you, sir!" said the chauffeur. He sprang down to open the door, and stood as if frozen. Another car was coming. It was a sedan, driven by a cop, with two men sitting side by side in the back seat. It drew up beside them, and the two men in the back seat got out.

"Mr. Bell around?" said one of them, a severe, youngish man in spectacles. "Tell him that Captain Warren would like to see him."

"Well, if you'll ring the door-bell, sir..." said the chauffeur.

Captain Warren and his companion, burly and red-faced, went up the steps shoulder to shoulder. The Captain rang the bell; they stood there very straight until the butler opened the door, then they marched in.

"They must of received information," said the chauffeur.

"Yes," answered Killian.

"Had I ought to wait here, sir?"

"Don't ask me," said Killian. "I don't know anything—about anything."

He sat down in a deck chair and stretched himself out comfortably, clasped his hands behind his head, and stared up at the sky. This is an interval, he thought. Sensible, to relax, while I can. Things are going to happen. Things I won't like. Because this is the real McCoy. This is the kind of murder people get arrested for, and put into jail for. And get hanged for. The police won't overlook the "Elements." They'll ask questions. Who was driving around this morning? Harriet and I were driving around. Maybe we'll get arrested. But we haven't any motive. At least, *I* haven't. Harriet might have one.

All clear as daylight. Harriet gets up early and takes out the car. She chases Angelo and runs over him. Then she returns to the house, to get me. She takes me out on the boat and then to The Maples, for an alibi. The flaw in that theory is, that Harriet is not a murderess. How do I know that? By instinct. By intuition. I never knew anything so well.

I could suspect Sibyl. I could suspect Luther Bell—if he even knows how to drive a car. I could suspect Ponievsky. Elly? Not Elly. My girl friend? She was in bed, recovering from her latest murder. Personally, I prefer Ponievsky. For excellent reasons. He's already committed one murder; and that will count heavily against you, Doctor Ponievsky. And then he's run away. That's as good as a confession. All these murders have been committed by this fiend in human form. This man, masquerading as a healer of human bodies is at heart, gentlemen of the jury, a ruthless murderer. He has run away—to Poland. Give a verdict of guilty, gentlemen, and let's drop it. Let's forget it. It makes me nervous.

"What are *you* doing?" asked Sibyl.

"Thinking," Killian answered.

"Let's take a stroll before lunch," she said.

"Lunch?" Killian repeated.

"Come on!" she said, and led him across the lawn, where they slackened their pace, out of hearing but in full view of the house.

"My dear," she said, "if you're going to take Jocelyn, take that job Luther offered you, too."

"I'm high-minded," he said. "I don't want a job I can't fill worthily."

"You'll be worthy, all right," she said. "I've worked hard to fix this up for you."

"You?"

"Me," she said. "Take it, John. You'll be worth anything they give you. You're a smart boy. I gave you a wonderful build-up to Luther."

"That was certainly friendly."

"Well, I am friendly," she said.

They strolled on in silence. Used to wear tights, thought Killian, and wink at the boys. A million years ago. Not quite a million. In your forties, now, I'd say. And a good sport. Fighting for a place in the sun. "What happened to the police?" he asked.

"They've gone," she said.

"Coming back, aren't they?"

"Why should they?"

"I thought maybe they'd want to ask me questions."

"My dear, they don't know you exist," she said. "A truck driver saw this man in the road, and he reported it to the police. They came here because it was the nearest house. They wanted to see if anyone could identify him, and, of course, Luther could. The poor man had been run over, and left there. They'll try to check on cars that might have done it, but it's practically impossible. Luther's going to get in touch with the steamship company to-morrow, and try to find out if the poor man had any relations."

"Chauverney might know about that."

"My dear, a Purser really doesn't know much about the private lives of the stewards."

"He might," said Killian.

"Well, we'll ask him," said she. "Luther's going to pay for the poor man's funeral," she added.

"There'll be a post-mortem, won't there?"

"Oh, everything necessary will be done, of course," she said. "There'll be an inquest, and so on. But the cause of death is pretty obvious." She paused. "And the police don't want to cause Luther any more trouble than can be helped."

That would be nice, thought Killian. Just to drop this. When you come to think of it, a lot has been happening this last week. A strain, for a sensitive, high-strung lad like me. Less than a week since Jocelyn went overboard. That did something to me. Changed me—permanently. It's as if I were the one who fell overboard. And was drowned. The good ambitious John Killian died, and there's this left.

Everything passes, and this, too, will pass. A few weeks. A nice, quiet weekend in the country. Chauverney coming into my room bleeding to death. Angelo lying in the road. Elly crying, and Harriet crying. Ponievsky's gone, and my youth has gone. That's poetic. Gone, alas, like my youth too soon.

He began to sing to himself. "Oh, the sound of the Kerry dancers. Ah, the ring of the piper's tune." He couldn't remember all the words, and it bothered him. "When the boys began to gather, in the glen of a summer night...."

That's what my ancestors did, I suppose. Gathered in a glen on a summer night. The pipers played and they danced. With their girls. You can't fit Jocelyn into that. She'd be sitting on a rock with a flask of whisky and a pack of cigarettes. Very morbid girl. Extremely morbid thing for a girl to swim around in the sea in a white dress. And I did it? She'll have to get that idea out of her head. I don't like it.

He felt sick of smoking. Everything was quiet in the afternoon sun. A Sunday in May. Chauvemey won't be ruined. And Elly won't be ruined. Harriet isn't ruined. She's too young and strong for that. Only Angelo is ruined, very definitely. And maybe me. Yes. Maybe that's what's the matter with me. I'm ruined. It makes you feel pretty flat, to be ruined.

"Well?" said Sibyl.

They looked at each other. Both sat down.

"I thought," she said, "that it would be nice for you and Jocelyn to have dinner on the boat."

"Just Jocelyn and me?" he asked. "I've never tried to run a cabin cruiser."

"The Captain will do that," she said. "I rang him up, and he'll be ready for you any time this afternoon."

"Will Jocelyn like that?"

"Tell her it's what you want," said Sibyl. "For God's sake, John, get her out of this house."

"Does she bore you?"

"Oh, I could take it," she said. "But she gets on Luther's nerves pretty badly. He's upset, anyhow. He'll have to identify that man—what was the name?"

"Angelo."

"He'll have to identify Angelo, and that bothers him. He objects to anybody dying. And Captain Warren wants to come back, and ask more questions about Angelo. He said he was not 'altogether satisfied.'" She sighed. "John," she said, "for a thousand dollars, will you take Jocelyn away, now, and keep her away?"

"Is this a joke?" he asked.

"No," she said. "I've got a check all written out."

"If it's not a joke," he said, "then probably it's an insult."

"I suppose I could have been more tactful," she said. "But I'm tired, John. I've suffered from your girl friend for four years. The first time she went to South America, I hoped she'd marry a somebody there and be very, very happy. The second time she went, I hoped she'd break her neck. For four years she's been blackmailing Luther."

"Them's fighting words," said Killian.

"Yes. I've tried to fight her. But I'm licked, John. For the last year Luther has been trying to settle with her. But she won't make any promises; she won't sign anything."

"Do you mean she's got something on Luther?"

"He picked her up on a bus, four years ago," said Sibyl. "She said she was eighteen, and he believed her. She said she was an actress, and he believed that, too. Luther has lots of good points, but he's not very bright. It was quite a while before he found out that she was a schoolgirl of fifteen. Then, naturally, her family cracked down on him. He had to pay them to keep quiet. And he's gone on paying and paying. It's a story he wouldn't like to see in the newspapers."

"Is that where she gets her little income? From your husband?"

"I was pretty sure you didn't know," she said. "At first I thought I'd just let you go ahead. But I've changed my mind."

"Why?"

"Kindness to you."

"I don't think it's that," said Killian.

"Maybe not," she said. "The motive doesn't matter, does it? You're getting the truth. Your fiancée is living on blackmail, and she means to go on. The job Luther offered you is blackmail, my dear."

"I haven't accepted it," said Killian.

"You can't get away from her," said Sibyl. "I'll tell you what she did to Eric."

"I've heard that tale."

"She'll do worse than that to you, my dear. She loves you. She'll *never* let you go."

Killian said nothing.

"Wherever you go, whatever you do, she'll follow you. Even if you leave the country, she'll get money from Luther and go after you. She'll make scenes such as you've never imagined. If you have any family, any friends, they'll be dragged into it."

He looked up and met her pale blue eyes.

"You're inciting to riot," he said.

"No, only trying to persuade you to take her away."

"To take her where?" he asked.

They kept on looking at each other steadily.

"That's not my business," she said after a moment. "I've got a check for you—"

"Very kind of you, but I don't want that check."

"The job in Luther's business is still good," she said. "No matter what happens."

"Nothing's going to happen," he said. "And I resign, here and now, from Bell, Fiske and Waters."

Her pale blue eyes flashed over his face as he looked away over the lawn.

"I suppose," she said, "that I married for money. That's what everyone said. I certainly wanted money. But there's more in it than that. I'm fond of Luther. I've been in love in my time, but this is something else again. As I told you, and you've probably noticed it yourself, Luther's not very bright. But he's different. I've never known anyone else like Luther. He has a code. It's dumb. It's—maybe it's a thousand years out of date. But I like it. I like his ways. I like the way he treats the servants. He feels responsible for them."

She paused for a time. "He trusts me," she went on. "He trusts me with everything he has. His money, and his reputation. I've been a good wife to him. I've learned a lot. I can hold my own now, even with his damn snooty friends. He knows he can count on me. He depends on me. And I'll never let him down."

"You could forgive him when he strayed?"

"When Jocelyn got hold of him," she said, "he was sixty-three, poor devil! He told me about it. He told me he was sorry; and he was sorry, even before she put on the screws. I'd do a lot, John, to save Luther from any more of this."

"I believe you," said Killian.

"Will you take her away to-night?"

He thought for a while. "Not to-night," he said. "I'll go back to town myself."

"And leave her here?"

"While I make arrangements. I've got to do that."

"What arrangements? What are you going to do with her? Have you any money?"

"Enough," he said.

"Do you imagine she'll be satisfied with what you've got?" asked Sibyl. "For four years she's had everything she wants. If she wanted a mink coat, she got it; and I wore my old coat. She's been to South America, to Paris, to London." She paused again. "It's not only that Luther's afraid of the story getting known," she said. "That's bad enough. But he believes he's ruined her life. And her character. He's like that, you know. He says things like that. 'I feel a great and crushing moral responsibility.' Poor devil! She was fifteen, and he was sixty-three and he was a poor, silly little rich boy, and she was—well, I won't go on with that."

"Let's not talk," said Killian.

"All right!" she said. "Take her away for dinner, though. I'd— God! I'd choke to death if I saw her at the table tonight. I'll order the car, and the chauffeur will drive you down to the wharf. You and Jocelyn can have dinner on board, and a nice, quiet talk."

"About what?"

She turned her head away a little, and her face in profile looked old, and heavy, and sad. "If you'll persuade Jocelyn to go away," she said, "I'll make the check for five thousand."

"I don't seem to make myself very clear," said Killian. "I don't want any of Mr. Luther Bell's money. Jocelyn doesn't want any more of it, either."

"Suppose she does want more of it?" Sibyl asked, and waited; but he didn't answer. "There's one thing to remember," she said. "If anything goes wrong, don't worry. Luther's like a king out here. Practically unlimited influence."

They looked and looked at each other.

"Nothing will go wrong," said Killian.

The butler was coming toward them, not looking at them.

Is there a rule about that? thought Killian. A butler must be three feet two and one-half inches from his betters before he addresses them.

"Lunch is served, madam."

CHAPTER ELEVEN

"Lunch is an interlude," Killian said to himself. "It's a welcome interlude. I can pull myself together. After lunch, I'll have to see Jocelyn. I didn't know that anything could ever hurt me this much."

She told me she was a little tramp, he thought. She told me about the bad old man. All right, then. Why does it hurt so much to find out that the villain is Luther Bell? I've eaten Mr. Luther Bell's food and drunk his liquor; I am now mounting the steps to Mr. Luther Bell's home, to break bread with him again. And it is hell. I'm being unreasonable. She told me this story. The past is past. But just the same, this is hell. I feel—how can you put it? My honour is tarnished.

"Want a drink, John?" asked Sibyl.

"No, thanks," he said.

No more of Mr. Bell's drinks. I'll have to sit at his table. I can't make a scene. But this is the finish. She asked me to take her away, and that's what I'll do. After lunch. Back to New York. Not out on Mr. Bell's boat. I think Sibyl was hinting that I'd better murder the girl. Jocelyn doesn't seem very popular. I'm afraid we won't have much of a social life, after we're married.

After we're married. I'm going to marry her. I've got to. I'm elected, because I fed her with toast. Because, as far as I can see, I'm the only living soul who doesn't hate her. I'm the only one who doesn't feel injured by her. Or ruined by her. If I'm ruined, I did it myself. I let that crazy Irishman come out of his cave and take charge. I don't like myself any more, but that's not her fault.

Harriet was there at the lunch table, looking clean and alert and cross, in green linen. Elly was there, in a thin black dress with little pink bows up the front, very dainty. Still with that face like a piteous little clown. Mr. Luther Bell sat at the head of his table.

I won't look at him, Killian thought. After lunch, Jocelyn and I will go away. Somewhere. Five men, she said. Five names written in a little book. Ponievsky is one. And Luther Bell is another? He could want to murder her. Easily. He's not very bright, and he wouldn't know how; but he could want to. He might ask Sibyl to look after it for him. And Sibyl passes the buck to me.

There was something magnificent about Sibyl. She made a conversation. John, what was the *food* like in Buenos Aires? How *interesting!* Luther, do you remember the Brazilian woman with all the little dogs? Do tell that story. Mrs. L'O, *what* sort of hats will we have to wear in the autumn?

"I think that what I feel is called grief," Killian said to himself. "She's so beautiful, and she's nineteen, and there's all this. She told me about this. I don't think she's a liar. I think she's a victim. I do think that. Victim of what? Her family. Mr. Bell. Something born in her. I wouldn't know. And it doesn't matter. I'm elected. Maybe I can help her. Maybe yes, and maybe no."

It was a good lunch. But Mr. Bell's food doesn't agree with me, he thought. I do not like thee, Mr. Bell. I won't look at you, because if I did I'd look at your neck and think about choking you. Like a king, are you?

The lunch was coming to an end, and Sibyl was arranging their moves. Like an automatic chessplayer, Killian thought.

"Luther, I suppose you *will* go on with your writing?"

"Yes," he said. "Yes."

"His book, you know," Sibyl explained. "It's about progress."

"Progress in relation to industry," said Luther Bell.

"All his holidays given up to that," said Sibyl. "Harriet wants to show you some of our lovely countryside, Mrs. L'O. She'll drive you out to the Country Club for tea, and, of course, we'll see you here in time for dinner. I'm going to keep John, and make him look at my flowers."

Pushing me around, are you? thought Killian. I'm not going to look at your flowers. I'm going to take Jocelyn away. I'll have to show her to my father, in the course of time. My bride. He won't be pleased. An upright man. A C.P.A., and they send him all over, even to China, and what he says is so. He minds his own business; he doesn't talk much. But he'll look at Jocelyn. What sort of marriage is this? What are you thinking of? Father, this is love. Phooey on love.

Sibyl rose; they all rose.

"Come up to my room," Elly murmured. "The first moment you can. I'll be waiting."

Sibyl and Luther went out onto the terrace, and Killian with them. He tried to think of an excuse for leaving them; and in the end he just walked off, into the house. He liked Elly; if she wanted to see him, he complied automatically. But as he was going up the stairs, an idea came into his head that stopped him.

Chauverney's dead, he thought. That's what she wants to tell me. He felt sure of that. That's why she looked like that. He's dead. Well, why *talk* about it? It's too bad. But there's nothing to be done.

It seemed to him impossible to go on up the stairs and face Elly. And talk. I'm sorry Chauverney's dead. But when a person's dead, he's dead. Nothing to talk about. Elly'd better go home and carry on as well as she can. There's no sense in my going up to her room, just to hear that Chauverney's dead.

The sound of footsteps in the hall below started him up in a hurry. You have to hear things. You have to listen, and be decent, even when you're completely indifferent. He knocked at Elly's door, and she opened it, and let him in, and closed it. She looks terrible, he thought.

He saw two suitcases, very smart, the lids open, showing some admirable packing. She does everything nicely, he thought. She was kind to me on the ship.

"I've got to tell you something," she said, standing with her hand on the back of a chair.

"I'm sorry," he said.

"But do you know...?" she asked.

"Well... Chauverney, isn't it?"

"Do you know?" she asked, again. "Did she tell you?"

"You mean he's worse," said Killian.

"No," said Elly. "He's better. But he told me last night.... He and Jocelyn are married."

"Really?" said Killian, raising his eyebrows.

"If he'd only told me," she said, "I'd have understood."

"Sit down, Elly," said Killian. "And look here, Elly! Don't cry."

"I won't," she said. "At least, I don't think I will. Only, it's so...."

She did sit down in the chair; and he sat on the edge of the bed, facing her. "Take it easy," he said.

"They were married nearly a year ago," said Elly. "But they never got on. How could they? She went to Mexico and got a divorce."

"Then they're not married now," said Killian.

"Yes, they are. Charlie thought he was divorced. He—we planned to be married in the autumn. But *she* came on board, in B. A., and she told him. Her lawyer had told her, months ago, that the divorce wasn't valid, but she had-n't bothered to tell Charlie. She told him then, on the ship."

"I see!" said Killian.

"She was going to start divorce proceedings when she got back to New York. You know what that means, in this state. All that sordid, nasty busi-ness. And it suddenly came into her head that she'd name me as correspon-dent. Charlie told her there were no grounds, but she didn't care. He was al-most frantic. He felt he couldn't let it go undefended, on my account. And if he did defend it, it would be in the newspapers and ruin him. The company wouldn't keep a Purser who'd got mixed up in a scandal with a passenger."

"I see!" said Killian again. He couldn't say anything else.

"He tried to argue with her. But he couldn't stop her."

Did he try to stop her?

"That's why he came here," Elly went on. "He hoped Mr. Bell could per-suade her. He really shouldn't have left the ship yesterday; but he got twelve hours' leave, and came here. And Mr. Bell was odious. He said he wouldn't be hurried. He said he wouldn't discuss the matter at night, because it kept him awake. So Charlie did *that*."

"Tried to kill himself."

"No! He only meant it to be an injury that would be an excuse to stay here a day or two, until he'd talked to Mr. Bell. He was going to say he'd cut himself while he was shaving."

"Cut his wrist?"

"The razor could slip. Anyhow, that was the only thing he could think of. But the cut began to bleed dreadfully. He held it under cold water; he tried to tie it up. He said he got so curiously lightheaded. He said he felt sure he was dying, but that he wasn't at all frightened or unhappy about it—only surprised."

"That's how he looked," said Killian.

"Sibyl Bell's one idea was to get him away, so that he wouldn't die here."

Like a rat, thought Killian. Positively will not die in the house. "Yes," he said.

"I was shocked, furious at her. And Doctor Ponievsky agreed with me that he must be moved. But then he came to, and he said he wanted to go. He told me—about this. He thought he was dying. We took him to a little private hospital, and they gave him a blood transfusion. He's going to live. But he's ruined."

"Well, not necessarily," said Killian.

"He is—unless you stop her from going on with this divorce."

"Well, she might change her mind," said Killian. "She often does."

"She won't. She's doing this, in a hurry, so that she can get free—to marry you."

"Well," said Killian, "the chances are she'll drop it."

"John, won't you see to it that she doesn't go on?"

He did not answer.

"Won't you *stop* her?" cried Elly.

"Well..." he said, with a vague smile.

Elly rose. "I suppose," she said, unsteadily, "that you don't care what happens to Charlie. You don't care about anything but marrying Jocelyn."

It was very hard for Killian not to burst out laughing. He could not control a wide grin.

"What are you grinning at?" Elly demanded.

"I'm sorry," he said, hastily. "Just a reaction."

"Will you stop her? Get her to go to Reno."

"I'll see what can be done," Killian assured her.

But she was not satisfied. "Please try to realize what this means to Charlie," she said. "His whole career is wrecked."

"He hasn't managed very well," Killian said.

"He was desperate," said Elly.

How desperate? thought Killian. Desperate enough to tip her overboard? Was he with you all the time that evening, Elly? Every minute? Or did he leave you for a little while? A thing like that wouldn't take long to do.

"I thought you'd help me," said Elly.

"Well, I'll see," he said.

Her stretched lip quivered; her dark eyes fixed on his face, filled with tears. She was hurt, astounded, bewildered by his vagueness.

"All right!" she cried. "If you don't care...."

"I don't care about anything but marrying Jocelyn," he said to himself, and laughter came rushing up again, and he had to gulp it down. Jocelyn's so ab- sent-minded, he thought. She forgot to mention that she was married. Not that it matters, of course. Only, when she was talking about marrying me, she might just have mentioned it. Casually. Darling, I will marry you, as soon as I get rid of Chauverney.

He sat on the edge of the bed, staring at the floor. "You've made a fool of me, Jocelyn," he said to himself. "Something more than a fool. You've done something to me. I don't quite know what, but maybe you've ruined me, too. Among others. I think I feel ruined. You lied to me. You've been false to me. False, in every way. And now I quit."

He got up. "I'll see what I can do, Elly," he said. "I'm sorry, very sorry." She didn't believe that. She didn't understand, and he could not explain. "See you later," he said, and left her.

He went into his own room, and locked the door. "I quit," he said to him- self. "I'm sorry about Elly; but I can't help it. I quit. It's finished. I can't see Jocelyn again. I couldn't speak to her. I don't hate her. I just want to get away from her, that's all. No explanation, no note. I'm going, that's all."

She's poison, he thought. She can't help that, any more than a rattlesnake can help it. But you have to get away from her. My father would be upset. He's an upright man. He'd be very much upset if he knew I'd been making love to another man's wife. Worse than that. Getting all set to marry another man's wife.

He could laugh now. I fed her with toast. I knew she was a little tramp— but I did not know she was a rattlesnake. Married to Chauverney, and liv- ing on Mr. Bell. On blackmail. Chauverney's got away, to a hospital; and Doc- tor Eric Ponievsky is going to get away, to Poland. And where am I going?

Back to New York. To look for room with refined couple, mid-town section, references exchanged. I'll walk into the office to-morrow morning. Hello, Kil- lian! How was the trip? Fine, fine! How about the beautiful señoritas down there in South America? Oh, boy! Oh, boy! Come out and have a drink and let's hear about the beautiful señoritas. Sorry, but I'm poisoned. By Cupid's darts.

Someone knocked at the door, but he thought he wouldn't answer. The someone rattled the knob.

"What do you want?" he called.

"It's Harriet."

What of it? he thought. "I'm dressing," he said.

"Put something on and open the door," she said. Not imperiously, just in a young way.

He opened the door, and in she came.

"I've been talking to mother," she said. "She says she's told you about—the situation. Of course, you had to know it; but it must have been hard to bear."

"Not so good," he said, embarrassed.

"I'm sorry," she said. "I think you're a darn nice boy."

He stared at her. A nice boy?

"Well, no," he said presently.

"I think so," she said. "I wanted to tell you that before I go."

"Going away?"

"Yep. Going home. I have a nice little apartment in New York."

You're a girl, he thought. You have a nice little apartment. You have a job, and you have friends. You go to the movies. You're an honest-to-God girl. He felt as if he had known her a long time ago, and lost her, and now he wanted her back. He wanted all of that back. This is Sunday, he thought. You could go to the zoo, with everybody else. You could go to a little French table d'hôte for dinner, and take a ride on top of a bus. With everybody else. I used to have all that. I used to work and live along with everybody else—until somehow this happened, and I got cut off.

I am cut off now. Like a ghost.

Harriet came over to him, and put her arm around his shoulders; she tried to draw him close to her, but he was too bony and unyielding. Oh, God! he thought. I feel like going all to pieces. I feel like resting my head on your shoulder and closing my eyes. And letting go.

"I'm sorry about all this, Johnny," she said.

"I'm sorry about what happened to *you*," he said, politely.

"About Eric?" she asked. "That's different. It was a jolt, but it's different. I'm different from you. Tougher, I guess."

"Maybe you are," he said.

"Mother said you're taking Jocelyn out on the boat."

"I'm not!"

"Do!" she said. "Get it over with."

"It is over with."

"But you'll have to hear what she's got to say for herself."

"No," he said.

"You'll hate yourself, if you don't." She took away her arm. "Johnny, ring me up soon, and I'll ask you to dinner. I'm in the telephone book."

"She thinks this is going to end," he said to himself when she was gone. "That was a very strange idea. She thinks I can have an honest, manly talk with Jocelyn; and then we shake hands and say good-by. 'Tis better thus. Oh, God! A nice boy."

Get it over with. You'll hate yourself if you don't. And you'll hate yourself if you do.

CHAPTER TWELVE

He stayed in his room, sitting on the edge of the bed, smoking. He was on guard, very alert; he was all ready—for something. For a knock at the door. He was ready for it, tense and resolute. Waiting for something.

It came, as sudden and breath-taking as a pistol shot; a knock. He got up. "Well?" he said evenly.

"Miss Frey says she's ready, sir," said a soft little voice.

"Oh! Oh, thanks," he said.

"Miss Frey says she'll meet you on the terrace, sir."

"Thanks," he said.

I'll have to see Mr. Bell, Killian thought. And Elly. And Sibyl, and Harriet. Now, let's see. What face shall I wear? The nice-boy face? I've lost it. He looked in the mirror while he combed his hair and straightened his tie. I don't know what face to wear. Jocelyn's made a fool of me, only I don't feel like a fool. I feel like a ghost. All right! Be a ghost. Walk down the stairs and out on the terrace, like a zombie. Don't speak, and don't look at anyone.

He walked down the stairs and out on to the terrace, and there wasn't anybody there. Nobody there. That made you feel pretty flat, my boy. Nobody here. Just look at the nice quiet Sunday afternoon. The sun is shining, and that lawn is like green velvet, and there are those fine old trees against a blue sky. You came ready to be melodramatic, and here's what you find. I'm smoking up all the Bahia cigarettes I bought to give my friends.

Jocelyn came out of the house. She came in her drifting way, light as a leaf. Her hair was tied at the temples with little black bows, and she wore a thin, long-sleeved white blouse and a white flannel skirt, and she carried a white coat over her arm.

"Isn't the car here?" she asked.

"I don't see it," he answered.

She sat down in a chair and leaned back, with her ankles crossed. *She* looks like a girl, he thought. She looks gentle and tired, and she's beautiful, and she's nineteen.

"What's the matter?" she asked, in her slow, muffled voice.

"Nothing at all, Mrs. Chauverney," he answered.

You thought that was going to be dramatic, did you? Wrong, m'boy! She never turned a hair.

"Do you want to talk about that?" she asked.

"Not here."

"Nobody to interrupt," she said. "Sibyl and Harriet are shut up together, and Elly's gone, and Luther's taking a nap. He doesn't like that mentioned.

He's sixty-five years young. He does exercises in the morning. He has a sort of bicycle machine to sit on—all the windows open. He sits there pedalling away, with his chin up, and then he eats vitamins."

"Sure. He's a fool. Everybody's a fool. Isn't that so?"

"Maybe. But that's not the way people look to me."

"And how do people look to you, Mrs. Chauverney?"

She looked at him. "Cruel," she said. "Like you."

"Am I cruel to you?" he asked. "When you're so kind to me? So kind, and faithful?"

"I've been kind to you," she said, still looking at him steadily. "And faithful."

"My feelings are hurt," he said, "because you haven't confided in me. I know it's only a trifle, but I'm hurt that you didn't mention you were married. I'd have felt very much embarrassed if I'd found that out after I'd married you."

"I'd have told you before that," she said. "But Chauvie's begged me to keep quiet about it."

"That's a very worthy reason. But still and all, I do think a girl ought to tell her fiancée when she's married to somebody else. It's only etiquette."

"This isn't important," she said. "I never pretended you were the first man in my life. Our marriage was just wretched. It didn't last six weeks. It was finished months ago."

"It seems not to be finished."

"There won't be any trouble with the legal part of it."

"Mere man-made laws," said Killian.

"I don't understand you," she said. "Does it really mean such a lot to you that I've been married?"

"Are married."

"All right. Call it being married, if you like. Is it so important?"

"You've lied to me," he said. "You've made a fool of me."

"I've never lied to you," she said. "Never once, about anything."

"This is what's called quibbling," said Killian. "When I asked you to marry me and you said you would, and you didn't tell me you had a husband, that's what I call a lie."

"All right," she said.

He waited. But she didn't go on.

"Now we just drop the subject?" he asked.

"Well, what more is there to say? Chauvie asked me to get a divorce, and I did. I went to Mexico and got one. I did it on his account. I didn't care. I wasn't thinking about marrying again, ever."

"Your next plan was different, wasn't it?" Killian asked. "This next divorce was going to ruin him."

"He wanted to get rid of me, and I tried to do it his way. It didn't work. Do you think I ought to go on, trying to spare Chauvie's feelings? He's nearly twenty years older than me."

"Even at that age, he won't like being ruined."

"I'm not vindictive," she said. "*You* ought to know that. But I won't pre-tend I care too much what happens to Chauvie. I want to get free, that's all."

"I like Elly," Killian said. "I don't like to see her squashed."

She clasped her hands behind her head, and then let them fall, as if she were too tired.

"You don't want Elly to be hurt," she said. "Or Chauvie, or anyone. Only me. I could tell you a little about that marriage. I suppose I could put up a case for myself. But I won't. What's the use? You've made up your mind in ad-vance that I'm in the wrong, about everything. Let it go."

Made up my mind in advance? Killian thought. Before I heard you? Maybe. But let it go. I don't want Elly hurt, or Chauverney, or anyone, except you? Let that go, too. I'm a zombie, a ghost. I don't feel at all any more. I hope I never do any more.

"Is this a trial?" she asked, in a low, even tone. "I love you. I tried to show you that. But you're standing before me like a judge. What is it you want to know? I've never told you a lie. I'll tell you the truth now, about anything you want. Only tell me what I'm accused of. What is it I've done to make you hate me?"

"I don't hate you," he said.

"What have I done?" she asked again. "I came here to clear up everything. I wanted to get out of that wretched marriage. Was it my fault that Chau-verney nearly killed himself in his panic? I was finished with Eric. I wasn't even interested in him. Was it my fault that he tried to kill me in his panic? Am I supposed to be so wicked and so dangerous that I've got to be killed?"

"I'm not your judge," Killian said.

"You've judged me, and you've condemned me," she said. "All right. I'm not going to beg for mercy."

"What about Bell?" Killian asked, with a painful effort.

"Well? What about him? I told you that story, all of it, except his name."

"And except that you were living—you're living now, on his money."

"Why *shouldn't* I?" she demanded, sitting up straight. "I was a child when I met him. I might have grown into something decent. I wasn't a drunken little tramp *then*. Doesn't he owe me something?"

"This isn't any good," Killian said. "We don't see things the same way, that's all."

"I don't see things any way," she said. "I don't care about anyone or any-thing but you. I don't care about a divorce. I don't care about Luther's money. I'll walk out of this house with you now if you want. Just as I am. Without a nickel. Without even a hat."

"What the hell d'you think I could do with you?" he shouted.

Her eyes were wide, and he thought they were purple. The colour of sorrow? It made him sick to hear himself shout at her. It made him afraid. "I'm sorry," he said. "But—but that's not practical."

A car came gliding up, a great, long, sleek black car. She kept on looking at him, waiting to see what he would do, to hear what he would say. Only he didn't know what to do, or what to say.

I can't go now, like this, he thought. I can't turn my back on her, and go. The chauffeur was waiting, and she was waiting. For him. And how did he know what to do?

"Well," he said, with a nervous, silly smile. "Well, shall we go and get something to eat on the boat?"

She got up and went down the steps. She left her white coat behind, and Killian went back after it.

"You never know," he said. "It may turn chilly. This time of the year...." I'm talking like Luther Bell. They got into the back of the car, and they were all enclosed in glass; the chauffeur was shut off by a sheet of glass. Snow-white in a glass coffin, Killian thought. He glanced at Jocelyn; she was leaning back with her eyes closed, and her mouth had a line of sorrowful patience. As if she were horribly resigned to any blow.

You've ruined people? he thought. Or have they ruined you? Are you bad, corrupt, beyond any helping? Or are you a victim? I don't know. Would I be a brute to leave you, or the fool of the world to stand by you? I don't know.

He opened a window, and the sweet air streamed in and blew her hair across her pale cheek. The sky was a clear, faint blue; they were driving past a red barn and a stone wall, and then they turned into that lane again. It's like a dream, he thought. I've seen all this before. It's as if everything that's going to happen has happened before. Jocelyn and I drove in a big black car—when?

They came to the squalid little settlement with the chicken yards; they came to the open space where the wooden pier was. The boat was there, too, just as it had been this morning, and the Captain. Only now he wore a white drill jacket, much too small for him, so that his sunburnt wrists showed, and his shoulder blades were pulled forward. "Miss!" he said, and gave her a smile that made a network of wrinkles in his face.

"What time shall I come back, sir?" asked the chauffeur.

"Oh, nine o'clock," said Killian at random.

The Captain was standing on the deck, holding out both hands to Jocelyn; she took them and stepped on board. He hurried ahead of her and moved one of the wicker chairs a little. She sat down, and he stood beside her, stooping with that broad smile of delight.

"Now we go to the Nort' Pole?" he said.

"Not to-night, Captain," she said, gently, and seriously.

"You vant to see something fine, you come to the Nort' Pole," he said. "My, dat's fine! All snow and ice, all glittering. The vater, she's blue and green. Deep. Vat do you say, ye go to the Nort' Pole, hey?"

"I haven't got my fur coat along, Captain," she said. "I'll need that, you know."

"That's right! That's right!" he said. "Ve got to vait, hey?"

"I'm afraid we will, Captain."

She did not smile. She looked into the man's smiling face with a clear, steady gentleness. He wrinkled his nose and frowned, anxious and faintly confused.

"Some day you see dose Northern Lights," he said. "My dat's fine! I tell you one time I see a polar bear? She's sitting on a berg, floating, floating along, far, far away from shore. She puts up her head, and she cries. She can't get back home."

"But that's all over now, Captain. It's nice here."

"No," he said.

"It's nice when you play your radio."

"Yes," he said reluctantly. "Dat's nice."

"And your cat gets up in your lap."

"Yes. Dat's a good pussy," he said. He was silent for a moment. "All right!" he said. "Now ye take a little ride, hey? Den I cook something?"

He disappeared into the cabin; the engine started, and the little craft shook. He came out again and cast off, and they started smoothly through the smooth water.

"He's crazy," Killian said, half to himself.

"No," Jocelyn said. "Not really. He's had a bad time, that's all."

"Who hasn't?"

"He was in a shipwreck," she said. "He was in a small boat with four or five other men, for days and days in the tropics. And in that horrible sun he used to think about the North Pole."

"And he still thinks about the North Pole."

"That's what everybody does," she said. "When we're perishing of thirst and anguish, we think about a cold, empty, white world."

How can you talk like that? he thought. How can you look like that? So kind, and so patient.

"Why do you pick him out to be sorry for?" he asked.

"He's had a bad time," she said again.

I've judged you, thought Killian, looking at her. I've decided that you're not capable of any pity, or any kindness, or anything good. I've decided that you're poison. My decision is final. I stand before you, like a judge.

Her hands lying in her lap, looked helpless. The breeze blew her hair and fluttered the sleeves of her blouse. What have I done? he thought. Look at her! Nineteen. Look at her lovely face, so quiet and sad. Look at her lovely throat and her little hands.

"May I have a cigarette, please?" she asked.

He felt in his pockets, but he had none.

"I've got some, I think, in my coat," she said.

The white coat lay over a chair behind her. He felt in the pocket and brought out a crumpled pack, and an envelope. It was addressed "Angelo," and very dirty.

Killian took out the note that was in the envelope.

Meet me Sunday morning at six-thirty where the wall begins. I'll bring what you want. Burn this.

                                        JOCELYN.

He read it over again. When he glanced up, Jocelyn sat half-turned in her chair, looking at him through a veil of loose hair.

He first thought he could not speak a word. But he had to. "Did you—do that?" he asked.

"Yes," she said.

"I mean," he said, "did you run him over?"

"Yes," she said again.

"It was an accident, I suppose."

"No, it wasn't," she said. "He was the one who saw you throw me over-board. I had to keep him quiet. For your sake."

CHAPTER THIRTEEN

He threw the pack of cigarettes overboard.

"Why did you do that?" she asked.

"I don't know," he said. "Keep quiet. Let me alone."

She got up and wandered away, into the cabin, and he stood by the rail. The sun was very low, standing on the horizon in a lake of fiery gold.

I'm alone, he thought. Let me stay alone, that's all I want. I'm free now.

He was as free as an unborn soul. He felt no love and no hate, no regret and no hope. He remembered nothing; he wanted nothing but just this—the salt wind and the swift motion, and the solitude. They were passing a low spit of land, and he saw little sandpipers moving on it; the quiet water lapped the shore; a shaft of sun made the reeds a pale, translucent green.

They're alive, he thought, watching the sandpipers.

You talk about the sun going down, but that's not what happens at all. The earth runs past it. You could almost think that the earth runs over it and crushes it out. Angelo had the life crushed out of him. When the sun came up this morning, he was alive. Now he's dead. She did that. Then she went home and had her breakfast. I fed her with toast. She could do that. She could eat and drink, and look so sweet.

I'm free now. I'm alone.

When you are not thinking about anything and not feeling anything, the time slips by very easily. The earth has run over the sun now; nothing left but a few little light clouds. They fade, and there is nothing but a vast grey calm. Rather a nuisance for those lights to spring out on the shore, twinkling. Why twinkling? Why not steady? A long string of them, twinkling sadly in the dusk. That must be a road.

The harbor of Rio is one of the most beautiful in the world. When I first saw Rio.... A horrible pain seized him. He remembered exactly how he had felt when he had first seen Rio. Before sunrise, it had been, and he had stood on deck, thinking how he would describe this when he got home. He had been violently happy, as if he had accomplished something admirable. This was the first foreign port he had seen. So the world is like this, he had thought. It's better than anything they told you. I'm young and strong; I can see all the rest of it. I got myself here; I can do anything.

Youth was gone now. All those strong, clear feelings were gone. Can I go back? Can I be like that again?

Lights came on in the roof of the deck. He resented them; he wanted to get away from them. The boat stopped; the anchor went overboard. What's the idea of this, he thought? What are we stopping here for?

"Come in and make a cocktail, Jocko?" said Jocelyn from the door of the cabin.

"I don't want a cocktail," he said in a queer voice. That was because his throat was stiff.

She came out to him. The overhead lights made her face look wan. "Cigarette, Jocko?" she said, holding out a pack.

"No, thank you. Where did you get those?"

"From the Captain," she said.

"Why have we stopped?"

"Oh, just while he cooks," she said, and sat down on the rail.

Don't sit on the rail! But he didn't say that aloud. "The Captain's an interesting character," was what he said aloud.

He was only talking to stave off something that was pressing in on him. She was sitting on the rail in a white dress.

"I saw a lot of sandpipers a while ago," he said.

"Jocko, are you thinking about Angelo?"

"Don't talk," he said. "Keep quiet and let me alone."

"Nobody will ever know about it," she said. "I got my note out of his pocket. Nobody will ever know what you did, either."

"I didn't do that," he said.

"Angelo saw you. I gave him some money to shut him up, but he wanted more. He'd have kept on wanting more."

Don't ask any questions. "Did you chase him with the car?" he asked. Had to ask that one.

"No. I dropped my purse and he went to pick it up."

"Then you ran over him. You squashed him. Then you got the note out of his pocket and you went home and had breakfast."

"I did that," she said, "because *you* made me."

"No," he said in a flat, unconvincing way. "No, I didn't."

"I'm glad I killed Angelo," she said, very low. "I'm glad I've done what you did. It's a bond between us, stronger than anything else could ever be."

Two sinners. Two damned souls. Paolo and Francesca, flying through Hell in each other's arms, forever and ever. Only it's not like that. Sibyl sent you here to get murdered. By me. But I will not. There is no bond between us. I won't look at you, sitting on the rail in a white dress.

"Jocko, let's go away," she said, in that same low voice, a little unsteady. "Let's start again. Let's forget all this, and start again. I'll be different, Jocko. I'll try—"

"Please don't talk!" he said.

I've got to get away, he thought. There's a dinghy tied astern. If I could get rid of her for a few minutes, I could get into the dinghy and row ashore.

"Jocko, let's get out of this," she said. "I've got things I can sell for enough money to get us away."

She rose. He moved backward, but she followed him. "Don't!" he said. "Please don't, Jocelyn. Please let me alone."

"Oh, Jocko!" she cried. "What's happened? I haven't anyone but you. Have *you* turned against me?"

Thou, too, Brutus? You, the trusted one, you, too? Yes. I've gone, too.

"I'm sorry," he said anxiously, and put out his hand to keep her away. She caught it in both of hers. She was clinging to him again. "Dear..." he said, with the most ludicrous falseness. "Sit down, dear."

She let his hand go, and he was off guard for a moment. She put her arm round his neck and laid her cheek against his. Her face was wet with tears.

"You *couldn't* not love me, now, Jocko. Not after this."

Not after murder? He caught her in an embrace so fierce that she gasped. She yielded completely, limp, crushed against him, breathing with difficulty. Murderess. You've been talking too much about murder, my dear girl. You love me, do you? And I love you, do I? *Do I?*

You're wrong! This is not love—murderess. This is something else. You're hanging round my neck, murderess, and I've got to get rid of you. Somehow. *Anyhow.*

"No!" he cried, and pushed her away so suddenly that she staggered back against the rail.

"Jocko, what—"

"I have a chill," he said. Maybe that was true. He was shaking. "I want some whisky. See if there's any whisky."

She went into the cabin, and he ran aft and lowered himself into the dinghy. He was trying to untie the painter when a door opened just above him, and there she was again.

"Jocko!"

"I'm just going to row ashore," he said. "I'm just going to get some aspirin. I'm just going to get some cigarettes."

"Take me with you," she said, and she jumped down into the dinghy, and it rolled over and nearly capsized. The oars went overboard.

"I'll have to get the oars," Killian explained, and began to take off his shoes.

"Hurry!" she said. "The current's taking them away."

"Yes. I certainly will," he said.

He took off his coat and went into the water. It was very cold. He started to swim; the idea was to get out of the path of light from the boat. To get into the dark. He heard a clank on board. It didn't matter what happened there. What *he* had to do was to get away. He knew very well what he had to get away from.

"Jocko, are you all right?"

"Fine, thanks," he answered, from the cold black water. Getting farther and farther away from her.

The engine started. "Jocko!" she screamed.

He stopped and turned, astonished. The boat was under way, pulling the dinghy after her. He saw Jocelyn stand up, swaying from side to side. She fell down on the seat. "*Jocko!*"

The boat was going faster than anything you ever saw in your life, heading out for the open sea. Red light, green light, shooting forward like an arrow.

He knew about *this*. He knew what it was like to be swimming alone in the sea at night. Now the lights of the boat were gone, and there was nothing. Except whatever might be living in the water. "No," he said to himself, "it's not the same. The shore can't be far. Stop swimming out to sea. The shore isn't far. Take it easy. Stop swimming out to sea. You're a fool."

He turned his head until he saw that row of little twinkling lights. Not far? It was as far as Heaven.

"You can't expect me to swim there," he said indignantly. The water was like ice. He swam and swam, and made no progress at all. The little twinkling lights were fainter, he thought. I'm swimming like a mouse in a pail.

This was perfectly right. This was what had to happen, and what ought to happen. Everything was very clear in his mind now. It was Angelo himself who pushed her overboard. Must have been. Not me. I didn't kill her.

Dying? There's nothing to it. His arms were moving, trying to drag a tremendously heavy log through the water. All he had to do was to stop this struggle. It's too damn cold to swim. But the sandpipers. He remembered them, running among the green translucent reeds, alive. Maybe they were somewhere near here, asleep. But alive. I'd like to see them again, he thought.

Cold, isn't it? Yes, *isn't* it, though! That was the way Sibyl talked. Here's five thousand dollars, and take her away. And kill her. I must be swimming upside down, it's so hard. If it wasn't for those damned little sandpipers, I'd quit. Too hard, this is. I'm not getting anywhere. The lights....

The lights had gone.

CHAPTER FOURTEEN

The lights had gone, and there was nothing at all. He turned on his back and floated, surging up and down on the gentle swell. "I'm sorry," he said. "I'm very sorry. I've done very badly. I took the wrong turn, and I knew it. I was a stubborn sinner. Well...."

He was no more than an immensely heavy log floating gently up and down. It wouldn't last much longer. But the sandpipers, he thought. You don't quit. I'm sorry, but I have to quit. Too cold, and too tired. You don't quit. Even one light would be enough. Even a star would be enough.

Well, if you haven't got a light or a star, then you go on in the dark. A mouse in a pail goes on. He turned over, and his face went under the water. He lifted his arms and his head; he pushed that tremendous weight through the water. A great black shadow loomed over him. What's that? he thought. That was The End.

It's all right to die, as long as you don't quit. Swim into that black shadow. His frozen numb feet touched something. He tried to stand, but that was not possible. He kept on moving his arms, and the water got shallow so that he could kneel. He went forward on his knees, and after a while he could see over the top of a bank. The lights were there, still twinkling.

Between him and the lights was an illimitable empty desert. He had to walk like a bear, like a gorilla, all bent forward, and he kept falling down. The wind was like a knife. An Arctic wind, he thought. His feet were certainly dead; but when they struck things, a pain came in his shoulders. If you could call it a pain. He kept on falling down, and it was impossible to get up, and sometimes he crawled for a little way.

A dog was barking. I've got to stand up, if there's a dog. If there's an animal, you can't crawl like an animal. Only this time it was hard to get up. The dog jumped up at him, and knocked him down.

"What's wrong with you, brother?" said somebody.

Brother. He did what he could about getting up. A little tremor went through the log lying on the grass. "Mr. and Mrs. Luther Bell," he said....

"You're certainly tough," said Sibyl.

He knew she wasn't really there. The thing for him to do now was to keep his eyes closed and not breathe.

"Swallow this, dear," she said.

And a glass came bumping against his mouth. He opened his lips, and whisky came flooding in. Only he had forgotten how to swallow; he kept it in his mouth until it burned his gums, and then he let it run down his gullet.

"More, please," he said.

He swallowed as much as she would give him. Unfortunately he had forgotten how to open his eyes. If I could find my hands, I could pull up my lids,
he thought. Then the whisky began to run through his veins like hot sunlight.
He could breathe now, and he could open his eyes.

And he saw the sun, up in a blue sky.

"Where?" he said.

"What, dear?" said Sibyl.

"When—is this?"

"It's Monday, dear. Are you better?"

Monday? Monday, Tuesday, Wednesday.... No. Sunday. Monday. Tuesday...
Sunday....

"Jocelyn?" he said.

"Oh, she's fine," said Sibyl.

He was lying in bed. He was warm now, but much too heavy to stir.

"Who's the other one—breathing?" he asked.

"Doctor Jacobs, dear."

"I see," he said.

He was all right now, except for being so heavy. He knew where his hands
and feet *were*, anyhow.

"Where's Jocelyn?" he asked.

"She's *fine!*" Sibyl said, again.

"No," he said, "I'm all right now. I want to know. Come on, sister. Give!"

She and Doctor Jacobs murmured together. The doctor came from somewhere and took his wrist.

"Give!" said Killian.

"My dear," said Sibyl. "We don't quite understand what's happened."

"Has the boat come back?"

She took a long time before she said, "No."

"Anything heard of it?"

"No," she said. "Not yet."

"Wait!" he said, and dragged a great flapping hand across the blanket.
"Time?" he said, with a lot of trouble.

"In a moment," Sibyl said. She didn't understand.

He pulled himself together, and it hurt. It was pulling hundreds of little
strings and making them tight. "*Time!*" he said, again.

"Just a little while," she said. He gave up. She didn't understand.

He had to wait until the machinery was running better. My heart is pick-
ing up, he thought. Accelerating nicely. When the engine stops jumping like
this, I'll be all right. So when he was all right, he said, "What time is it,
please?"

"Just about noon," said Harriet.

"I see!" he said. "Wait, please."

"I won't go," she said.

He looked at the sun in the blue sky for a while. "Harriet," he said, "I want to know."

"Yes," she said.

She's young, he thought. She's young enough to understand. She's cross. That's a good thing to be. Young and cross, and she tells the truth.

"The Captain?" he said. "Is he crazy?"

"I never thought so," she said. "He used to seem a little queer sometimes when he talked about the shipwreck, that's all."

He was quiet for a while, getting better.

"Are they looking for the boat?" he asked.

"Of course."

"Is there any news of her?"

"Do you want it?" Harriet asked.

"Yes," he said. "I do."

She was young enough to tell the truth in the right way. "The Coast Guard station got a report from somebody," she said. "Somebody saw the boat heading straight into a squall last night."

"Nothing else?"

"Not yet," she said.

Never, he thought. Jocelyn's gone to the North Pole with a crazy skipper. Exaggerated. Very poor taste. Now she's dead. She's drowned. I did that. She said I would murder her, and I did.

"Well," he said, "that's that."

I'm certainly being reasonable, he thought. I'm certainly taking this very well. Wonderfully well. I'm certainly a tough guy.

He turned over and buried his face in the pillow. Oh, God! Starry Eyes, I'm so sorry.... So sorry, Starry Eyes....

THE END